I0653648

SHAMI STOVALL

24-HOUR
WARLOCK

Published by
CS BOOKS, LLC

This is a work of fiction. Names, characters, places, and incidents either are the product of author imagination or are used fictitiously, and any resemblance to actual persons, living or dead, business establishments, events, or locales, is entirely fictional.

24-Hour Warlock
Copyright © 2025 Capital Station Books
All rights reserved.
https://sastovallauthor.com/

This book is licensed to the original purchaser only. Duplication or distribution via any means is illegal and a violation of international copyright law, subject to criminal prosecution and upon conviction, fines, and/or imprisonment. No part of this book may be reproduced in any form or by any electronic or mechanical means, including information storage and retrieval system, without written permission from the author, except for the use of brief quotations in a book review, and where permitted by law.

Cover Design: Chris McGrath
Editors: Nia Quinn, Celestian Rince

IF YOU WANT TO BE NOTIFIED WHEN SHAMI STOVALL'S NEXT BOOK RELEASES, PLEASE VISIT HER WEBSITE OR CONTACT HER DIRECTLY AT
s.adelle.s@gmail.com

To John, my soulmate.
To my patrons over on Patreon, because they're amazing.
To Drew, for being a great agent.
To my Facebook group, for all the memes.
And finally, to everyone unnamed, thank you for everything.

BOOK 2 RECAP

Adair Finch—the only warlock in the world bonded to Chronos, the Titan of Time—had made a deal, as warlocks tend to do. This time, it was with Kullthantarrick the Sneak, a mischief spirit with a penchant for chaos and an eye for opportunity. In exchange for her trickster magic, Finch agreed to find her a human body.

Which is how he ended up in a morgue, casually perusing corpses like a man shopping for produce.

But corpse-hunting was put on hold when Finch received a call from Jay-W, a particularly shady landlord out of Oakland, CA. Word on the street was that Finch was back in business, and Jay-W desperately needed help. Against his better judgment, Finch agreed to hear him out.

On the drive to Oakland, Finch and Kull stumbled upon a fresh corpse—none other than Fox-Pistol, a famous social media star. Kull then seized the chance and inhabited Fox-Pistol's body, claiming it as her own.

But becoming human again came with consequences. No longer just a spirit of mischief, Kull was suddenly flooded with emotions—real, raw, and overwhelming. She no longer felt an insatiable need for chaos, and that frightened her. She asked Finch to help her become human, and perhaps even help her find out what it means to truly love someone.

So now, on top of dealing with a brand-new case, Finch had to play mentor to a former spirit with all the romantic curiosity and impulse control of a caffeinated raccoon.

When Finch finally arrived at Jay-W's, the man got straight to the point: "Find out where my wife, Charlie, goes every weekend. She's cheating on me. I know it."

Finch was about to tell him to deal with his own marital problems, but then Jay-W slapped $100,000 onto the table. With a sigh, Finch agreed to take the case.

While investigating Jay-W's wife, Finch stopped by Level 22, a club notorious for serving the supernatural. A werewolf bartender—prone to mood swings and casual violence—took issue with Finch's face and threw a claw. The fight turned into an ugly brawl, but Finch had the upper hand with his fire magic. He won, and the werewolf reverted to his human form.

Turns out, the werewolf was Elijah Harris, a former Oakland detective and Finch's old friend. Only, he wasn't Elijah anymore. Now, he went by "Enzo," because after getting infected with lycanthropy, the Oakland PD had faked his death and told his wife and daughter he was gone.

Without a family or purpose, Enzo was spiraling. So Finch made him an offer: Join his newly formed PI firm.

Enzo, desperate to feel useful again, agreed.

With their team assembled—Finch, Enzo, and Kull— they tracked down Charlie, only to discover she wasn't cheating at all. Instead, she was deep in debt, gambling away everything she had at the redwood elf casinos in town.

And Finch, a man who had the ability to rewind time and loved to use it, knew exactly how to solve this mess. By cheating.

Using his magic to rewind time, Finch memorized the outcome of a high-stakes poker game and played it like a master. Of course, this also meant dodging angry elves who were out to kill him, bar fights, and keeping Kull from getting lured into bad decisions.

Somewhere in the middle of it, a woman lurking in the

background watched them closely—desperate, searching, obsessed with finding a man.

Once Charlie's debts were cleared, Finch turned his attention back to Fox-Pistol's killer. With a little help from a pack of werewolves, he was led to an abandoned hoarder's house.

Inside?

Bodies.

Stacked, stuffed, and rotting under layers of garbage and dust.

And the killer? A draugr. A sentient zombie who had been murdering men who wouldn't date her. Because why deal with rejection when you can just kill and collect?

Finch, not exactly thrilled with this development, subdued the draugr and handed her over to the authorities. Case closed.

After everything, Kull decided she wanted to experience life—all of it. And she couldn't do that under Finch's protection. She had to make her own mistakes.

She told Finch she was heading to LA to chase her dream of being a social media star, where she could become her own human. Finch, having grown somewhat fond of her, didn't argue.

But before she left, he made a choice. He gave his entire $100,000 payment to Enzo.

And what did Enzo do?

He left it on the doorstep of his wife and daughter's house.

No note. No explanation. Just one final act of love for the family that thought he was dead.

And Kull, watching from the sidelines, finally understood what love truly looked like.

Now on to "24-Hour Warlock," the third book in the series...

CHAPTER
ONE

Adair Finch sat at his desk in his private office, looking at ridiculous articles about "demons" on the internet.

Magicless mortals had little knowledge about demons—that was made extremely clear from the many articles he found about Beelzebub. Finch clicked through them, trying to remember which sites were hosted by a trustworthy coven of witches. A few websites, specifically meant for wizards, warlocks, witches, and cursed humans, provided basic information, though most of it was cryptic.

What was the most popular one called?

Something stupid, was all Finch could remember.

Then it struck him.

Magipedia.

"Quite possibly the dumbest name they could've picked," Finch muttered to himself as he typed out the address.

His new PI firm, *24-Hour Investigations*, had just opened, but had no cases yet, so Finch used his free time to catch up on research he had been meaning to do for a while.

He knew there were certain demons who often sought out full moon witches, and he needed to make a comprehensive list.

A whole coven of full moon witches had murdered his brother, after all. And he knew they had demon allies.

Finch wanted a counter to any trick the witches and their demons might pull.

A *crash* echoed out in the front room. Finch drew a deep breath and then exhaled all his irritation. He stood from his chair and reminded himself to stay composed and not barge out of his office in a fit of rage.

"It's probably something ridiculous," he said to himself.

Finch took a moment to relax, taking in the barren walls of his personal office. The aroma of fresh McDonald's wafted in under the door.

The City of Stockton only had three settings—smell like fast food, smell like hot garbage, or smell like car oil. Finch considered himself lucky it was a *McDonald's Day*.

Then the phone at the front reception desk rang, much to his surprise. His little PI firm didn't get many calls.

Finch circled his large wooden desk, and headed for the door. The concrete floor was stylish, he supposed, but his feet were already hurting.

When Finch exited his office, he found himself in the middle of a circus.

Four little creatures scurried around the giant front room, sliding across the smooth floors. They appeared to be tiny people, no more than ten inches tall, shaped like humans, except their heads were fatter. They wore doll-sized clothes, though in the fashion of 1800s Germany, except for their hats, which were quite bizarre.

One wore a hat that resembled a toad's head. One wore a hat that appeared to be a kitten's head. And the other two had squirrel heads.

Finch knew these creatures—they were brownies. Not the edible little dessert, but the European fae-folk who often dwelled in old homes. Brownies were an offshoot of a hobgoblin, and Finch rarely enjoyed interacting with them.

"This way," one of the brownies squeaked. "I see more paper clips!"

The other three replied in German as they all ran by Finch's feet.

And indeed, there were many paper clips on the floor—as well as paperwork, a shattered coffee mug, and hundreds of pens. When Finch glanced around, he spotted a bookshelf on the far wall that was missing a shelf, and he pieced together the whole mystery.

That was the crash he had heard.

The brownies gathered up the paper clips, even going out of their way to push the papers around and kick the shards of mug to the corners of the room.

Normally, brownies wouldn't be out in the open, nor would they be roaming around at 11:04 a.m., but Finch's PI firm was anything but normal.

Thankfully, the curtains on their floor-to-ceiling windows had been drawn and the front door locked. The lights overhead kept everything well lit, even though natural light would've saved them a high electric bill.

"What's going on?" Finch shouted over the chaos.

His voice echoed throughout the massive office. It was an open work environment for fifteen people, complete with a high-end kitchenette and a large reception desk. Finch's personal office was the only one not located out in the open with the main office space.

Most of the office wasn't in use, but there were two desks with computers—for the only other two people who worked with Finch. The first desk was occupied by Liam Blackstone, and the other belonged to Enzo, the resident werewolf, but he wasn't in. Enzo was off picking out a printer.

The phone continued to ring.

Liam scrambled out of his chair and around his desk. He held a small woodworking knife in one hand, and a piece of cherrywood in the other.

"Oh, Adair?" Liam asked, turning his attention to Finch. "Is something the matter?"

Finch sarcastically swept his arm out, motioning to the whole damn office.

Liam nervously chuckled.

He was the sort of man who resembled an upturned mop, his complexion pale, his hair a bristle-brown. Liam's button-up shirt and slacks hung loose on his body, evidence he had lost weight he probably couldn't afford to lose. Liam also wore thick-rimmed glasses that sat on the bridge of his crooked nose, the only part of him that seemed larger than average.

The phone rang incessantly.

The brownies snickered as they quickly piled their new paperclips into the corner of the office.

"Well?" Finch demanded. "What *is* happening here?"

"I needed help," Liam stated. He forced a smile. "And this family of brownies has helped my family for generations, so I thought I could introduce them to the office, and—"

"You didn't ask me first?" Finch snapped.

Liam swallowed the last of his words.

Then someone answered the phone.

"Hello? This is *24-Hour Investigations*, how can I help you?"

Finch whirled on his heel to face the receptionist's desk.

Standing next to the desk, with the phone in hand, was none other than Bree Blackstone, Liam's twelve-year-old daughter. She had long brown hair, a shade similar to her father's, and a bright smile that could illuminate any dark corner. She wore a pair of jeans and a black hoodie with a cat picture on the front.

"Yes, we have a certified private detective," Bree said to whoever was on the other line. "He's the best in the biz!"

The brownies snickered. "*Best in the biz*," one repeated, like it was a hilarious saying.

Bree clutched the phone close to her ear as she smiled. "He would love to do that!"

"What?" Finch asked.

"Okay, I'll let him know! Please use our website to message us all the details. Thank you so much for calling and requesting our services. You won't be disappointed."

Bree hung up the phone, her expression a mix of smug and elated.

"Who was that, sweetheart?" Liam asked.

"That was the public defender!" Bree flew over to Finch, practically skipping over the scattered paperwork and loose pens. "He needs a private investigator to, uh, what did he say?" She stopped and frowned. "He said we have to *serve someone*." Bree lifted an eyebrow as she spoke the last two words.

"That means he wants a PI to hand someone else paperwork," Finch said with a groan. "And you told him *yes?*"

Bree nodded. "Yup. He's going to pay us *two hundred dollars* to do that. And it sounds so easy! Is this what PIs do all the time?"

"Two hundred dollars isn't going to cover the six thousand dollars rent on this place," Finch mumbled. Then he pinched the bridge of his nose as he held back a tirade. "Bree —we're not a normal PI firm."

"I know." She placed her hands on her hips. "So what?"

"So we don't take normal assignments. We're here to

help witches, wizards, warlocks, and anyone else who has a supernatural problem. I don't want to physically serve a man his court paperwork. It's not worth the two hundred dollars."

"But you weren't doing anything anyway," Bree said.

Which was a blow to Finch's ego.

He *hadn't* been doing anything for the past two weeks, ever since they set up the office. Few people knew he was back in business, and Finch hadn't wanted to advertise the fact. Obviously, they were going to need to change that.

The team of four brownies scurried past Finch's feet again, each carrying an armful of office supplies. They made their way to Liam's desk and dropped everything off. Then they ran back and gathered more materials, even scooping up the scattered paperwork.

Finch supposed they would *eventually* clean up the office.

In a few hours.

"Why is there a mess?" Finch asked.

Bree pointed to the bookshelf. "I placed a coffee mug on the shelf, and it broke. I promise I didn't do anything weird. I think the bookshelf is just... old."

It was ancient. Finch had used the decrepit bookshelf when Carter was alive over ten years ago, and even then, they had gotten it from some sort of hand-me-down store.

Bree shook her head. "And when the shelf broke, everything fell, and the papers and supplies got all mixed up."

"The warlock asked us to help around the office," one of the brownies interjected, his voice squeaky like a chipmunk. "We told him we could do that. We'll get it done."

The other three sang something in German.

Finch wanted nothing to do with this. "Liam, did you really employ brownies to houseclean for us?"

"No, not to clean." Liam shuffled over and then stared

at the little hobgoblins. "I hired them because I need certain materials from time to time. I can't craft magical objects without specific supplies, and sometimes looking for them is time consuming. Brownies are famous for their searching skills."

All four of the pint-sized men stood a little taller—perhaps all the way to eleven inches.

"Why don't you send them out for materials?" Finch asked. "This mess doesn't require their attention."

Liam nodded once. He walked over to the front door and unlocked it. "Do you four think you could acquire me some sundew petals? And perhaps some chains, for necklaces?"

"Sundew and chains," the lead brownie with the toad hat repeated. "Understood."

Then the brownie pulled the hat down over his face. In front of everyone, the humanoid brownie transformed into a hideous toad, his skin lumpy, his eyes bulging and wet. With a croak, the creature leapt for the door.

The second brownie pulled down its kitten hat, and *poof*. The tiny man practically pranced forward in the form of a black-and-white kitten. The last two brownies became squirrels at the same time, yanking down their hats and transforming mid-run toward the door.

Brownie magic was simple. It gave clothing mild magical properties to hide and change shape. Finch had once made a pact with a brownie to better blend into certain crowds, but that had been for a short period of time, and many years ago.

Liam opened the door, and all four brownies rushed outside. If anyone had been standing on the sidewalk, Finch was certain they would think his PI firm was a front for trafficking wacky pets.

Just as Finch was about to explain that this was a professional business that required professionalism, his cellphone rang. He withdrew the device from his pocket and stared at the screen, shocked to see it was a call from *Jessica Finch*.

"I need to take this," he muttered, holding up a finger.

Finch quickly retreated to his office. Once the door was closed, he answered the call, his voice quiet.

"Hello?"

For a prolonged moment, there was no response. Finally, a voice on the other end reached his ear. "Adair?"

"Yeah," he said. Then he coughed and straightened his posture. "It's me. This is... Jessie, right?"

"That's right."

It had been a long time since Finch had a conversation with his sister-in-law. Well, his ex-sister-in-law. Ever since Carter's death, Finch's relationship with Jessie had been awkward at best. She had moved, and Finch never bothered to stay in touch.

Years had passed.

Ten years.

Recently, however, Jessie had been trying to get a hold of him. Texting. Calling. Yet whenever he attempted to engage with her, Jessica shied away, like a nervous dog that wanted food, but didn't trust the hand feeding it.

"What's up?" Finch asked, trying to sound casual but failing. He cleared his throat and tried again. "How are you?"

"Adair..."

"It's been a while." Finch paced the length of his office, turning on his heel whenever he reached a wall. "Too long. It's my fault, really."

"It's not," she whispered.

Finch took a deep breath. Then exhaled. "Look, Jessie, I've been doing some work lately. I've got a new office, and—"

"I know. A friend told me."

"Oh? You know already? Good. That's good. Really good."

Why did he sound so nervous? And how many times could a person say *good* in a single reply?

Jessie's voice quavered a bit. "Adair, I need your help."

"Anything," he replied, perhaps a bit too quickly. "Whatever you need."

"Can I swing by later this afternoon? I want to speak to you face-to-face. If you don't mind."

Finch shook his head, even though she couldn't see it over the phone. "I don't mind at all. I'll be working all day, so come on by whenever you want."

Ever since Carter's death, Finch had ignored the world. He didn't want to do that anymore. That was why he restarted his PI business. He was ready. He wanted to help Carter's widow, and hopefully set things right. If Jessie needed help, he would be there—no matter what.

"Thank you, Adair," Jessie whispered. "I'll be there in a few hours."

CHAPTER
TWO

Finch paced his office for a full hour. Once his feet hurt too much to continue, he headed back out into the main room.

Liam sat at his desk, scrolling through Etsy listings of rocks and crystals, while Bree watched YouTube videos on Enzo's computer. The moment she spotted Finch, her eyes went wide, and her smile wider.

"Adair!" She leapt from her chair and jogged over. "What was that phone call about? Was it about the paperwork you have to serve?"

Finch had completely forgotten about that. After a short sigh, he replied, "No. My sister-in-law will be stopping by the office." He turned his attention to the broken bookshelf. Everything had already been tidied up, much to his surprise. "If you two could look, uh... busy... that would be appreciated."

Bree responded with a salute. "Understood."

"I *am* busy," Liam muttered, his brow furrowed.

"Busy with something a little more *important* or *impressive*." Finch rubbed his temple. "Carter and I were always swamped... back in the day. I just want Jessie to think nothing has changed."

Liam closed Etsy and brought up a blank spreadsheet. Then he typed in random numbers.

"*More* impressive, Papa," Bree scolded.

Liam sighed as he sarcastically added a couple zeros to the end of all the numbers.

The front door to the office opened, and in strode a man with purpose. He was tall, his skin dark, and his polo shirt even darker. He wore white slacks, though, and due to his muscular physique, appeared like a weightlifter cosplaying as a golfer.

Enzo—real name Elijah Harris—was once a police detective, and when he entered the office, he scanned it with the same kind of suspicious tic Finch was used to seeing in men like him.

Enzo held a box under one arm, which contained the greatest personal printer anyone could buy at their local computer store. He had a box of paper under the other arm, carrying them both with little effort.

"Oh, you're back!" Bree bounded over to Enzo. "Can this print pictures, too? I was thinking we could make posters and flyers and handouts. That way I can hand them to people to let them know we're in business."

Enzo smiled as he strode over to the reception desk and set everything down. "Yeah, I'm sure it can print pictures. The ink cartridges require you to take out a mortgage to pay for them, though, so maybe not too many of them at one time."

With his hands free, Enzo reached into his pocket and withdrew a bag of Skittles.

"I grabbed these for you," he said, handing them to Bree.

She lit up as she took them. "Oh, nice! I love the tropical

flavors. Thank you so much!" Bree walked over to her father's desk, opened one of his drawers, and dropped the Skittles inside.

The whole drawer was packed with candies, all of them a fruity variety, because those were Bree's favorites. Enzo always brought her candies whenever he went out, almost without fail. He had purchased so many candies that Bree couldn't keep up with eating them all.

"Jessie will be showing up soon," Finch said, turning to Enzo. "She's in trouble."

"What kind of trouble?" Enzo wore *serious* like most people wore clothing. It was his default expression and tone. "Are we gonna have to crack some skulls?"

"I don't know yet. She hasn't told me."

"And where's Kull? Is she going to help out on this or what?"

"She's off filming YouTubes or whatever social media stars do." Finch shrugged. "She said she wanted time to herself to *figure out how to be a human*, so I'm not going to interfere until she says she's done."

"I love watching her prank videos," Bree interjected. "Kull is the best version of Fox-Pistol."

Enzo ran a hand over his perfectly bald head. "Well, since we're down a person, and nothing with you has ever been simple, I'm going to change into something more suitable to wolfing out."

As he headed for the office's restroom, Finch noted of the white tattoo behind Enzo's left ear. It was likely a marking to let other magical individuals know Enzo was actually a werewolf, but Finch had never asked the man about it.

He wanted to ask the man at some point, but it always slipped his mind.

"Am I going to help you with whatever problem Jessie

has?" Bree clasped her hands together. "Please? You still have to train me to be the best warlock ever, and we've barely done anything."

"It really depends on what Jessie tells me," Finch said.

"But you're still going to train me, right?"

"I said I would, so I will."

Bree held back a giggle. "Yes! Perfect. Because I'm off school right now, so I have lots of free time."

"Oh, that's why you've been here all day," Finch muttered to himself. Then he coughed and said aloud, "Don't worry. I'll make sure you're well versed in the ways of the warlock."

Liam stopped making up arbitrary numbers and just stared at his screen. When Finch headed for his office again, Liam got up from his chair and followed. Finch gave the man a glare, but it didn't deter Liam.

"Can I speak with you for a moment?" Liam motioned to Finch's office door.

They went inside together, though Finch wasn't entirely certain why they couldn't speak out in the main room.

As soon as the door shut, Liam smoothed his ironed shirt as he turned to face Finch.

"Adair, I meant to speak with you about this sooner, but... I think you should, perhaps, encourage Bree to become a full witch instead of a warlock." He spoke the last half of the sentence in a whisper, as if his confidence was failing him.

"I tried," Finch snapped. "I told her being a witch was better—because she'd get her own innate magical abilities—but the kid is stubborn."

"Yes. Well. She takes after her mother."

Finch shrugged. "So? What do you want me to do about it? You want me to tell her I can't train her as a warlock?"

"No. No, no." Liam waved his hands and shook his

head. "She would be devastated. I don't want that. However, she, uh... Well, it's *shark week*, her first one, so you know what that means."

Finch honestly stared at Liam for a solid thirty seconds, the silence stretching between them.

"What?" Finch finally barked. "What the hell is *shark week?*"

Liam's face reddened. "Her period."

"Why would you—"

"*That's how she said it to me,*" Liam interjected, his volume rising. "I didn't pick that term! It was a very awkward moment, and I wanted her to describe it in the manner she felt comfortable, so *shark week* it is."

Finch pinched the bridge of his nose, hating every second of this conversation. However, he now knew why Liam was so excited to speak to him about Bree becoming a witch.

It was because someone couldn't become both a witch *and* a warlock. Every human being had five cores of magic— the crown, the eyes, the heart, the soul, and the loins. Warlocks made pacts with creatures to fill the cores with borrowed magic. But witches...

Witches had one year from the start of their first "shark week" to complete their training and then drink moonlight. Once they did, they filled all five of their cores with their own unique magic, fully becoming a witch.

But that meant they couldn't make pacts with creatures, because there weren't any empty cores for the creature to pour their magic in to.

Not everyone could become a witch. Someone had to be born into it—they had to have the blood of the first witch somewhere in their ancestry. But any magicless boob could become a warlock, so long as they knew about magical creatures.

Technically, *witches* could make pacts in reverse, where they poured their magic into a human, becoming a patron of a warlock. It was because witches were magical beings all on their own.

And witches could forcibly bind demons and other powerful beings to their cores, but that was permanent, and often without the other creature's consent—entirely different from warlocks.

"If Bree doesn't fulfill her ritual, she'll lose out on the opportunity to become a witch," Finch whispered.

Liam nodded. "She doesn't have much time..."

Witches did some sort of ritual to drink moonlight.

Finch didn't know the exact details; he just knew the basic process.

Witches came in five varieties—full moon, half moon, waxing crescent, waning crescent, and new moon. A witch's designation came from the time she reached her full magical potential. If a witch finished her ritual during a full moon, she was a full moon witch, and if during a waxing crescent, she was a waxing crescent witch, and so on.

"Vera was a waning crescent witch, right?" Finch asked absentmindedly.

"That's right. And I've been trying to convince Bree to begin the process, but she adamantly refuses at every step. She says she knows she wants to be a warlock more than anything."

"You should be proud."

With a glower, Liam said, "She never cared that I was a warlock until she met *you*." After another round of silence, Liam finally relaxed a bit. "Please try to convince her. We both know being a warlock is more difficult. She could get hurt—or worse. The pacts warlocks make are complicated. Sometimes costly."

His words were filled with concern, and Finch found himself holding his breath.

Liam was correct. Warlocks had it rougher than most. All their magic came at a cost, and sometimes that cost took a warlock's life. Finch never wanted to talk about the pacts he had made with Chronos or Ke-Koh. They were both extreme.

If Bree became a witch, it would be safer. Her magic would be innate. She wouldn't owe anyone anything.

Liam continued. "Vera... her mother... would've wanted Bree to become a witch."

"I'll think about it," Finch said.

"I also think you should convince her to become a waning crescent witch. It'll give her the most freedom."

Waning crescent witches didn't have covens. In old fairy tales, any witches who were living in the woods all alone, or old crones, were waning crescent witches. They drew power from individual sources, and often made their homes their sanctuary.

Finch likened them to spiders with their webs. They always knew what happened in their personal domain.

"I'll have a chat with Bree." Finch shrugged. "But she'll need a witch to show her the ropes. I don't know what they do to call forth the moonbeams or whatever."

"I can look for someone, but her mother also left her a book with intructions."

"Hmm... Jessie is technically a witch."

Liam lifted a brow. "*Technically*?"

From what Finch remembered, Jessie was a witch, but had barely used her magic. What kind of witch was she? Finch couldn't remember. It hadn't mattered to him much —all that mattered was that Jessie and Carter had been so in love. So happy.

"I'll speak to Jessie," Finch muttered.

"I'll also find others." Then Liam forced half a smile. "Thank you. I appreciate you helping me with this."

Out in the front room, Finch heard a door open. His heart practically stopped when Bree's muffled voice filtered into his office.

"Good afternoon!" Bree shouted. "Are you Jessie? Adair's sister-in-law? It's, uh, so nice to meet you!"

CHAPTER
THREE

F inch glanced at his phone.

10:56 a.m.

He marked the time and then took a deep breath. Whatever Jessie needed, he would be there for her.

Liam eyed the door and waited. Finch exited his office first, his expression set into something neutral. But when he laid eyes on Jessie, he locked up.

When Finch knew Jessie—ten years ago—she had been shy and kind. Jessie had been raised with her elf father in the realm of fairies for most of her childhood, and had only later been cared for by her human mother when she needed to start middle school. That led to her being rather socially awkward, and quite fond of rules, which human children didn't empathize with.

At least not American ones.

When Jessie met Carter, she had opened up and found her happy place in life.

Today, the Jessie who walked into Finch's PI business was a stranger. She entered as a whirlwind of leather and attitude, the smell of gasoline trailing in her wake. Her boots, scuffed from miles of open road, thudded against the worn concrete floor with a deliberate confidence.

Her black hair had once hung long, but now it was cut pixie-short. Her bronze skin, from Finch's memory, had been flawless—now it was scarred on her chin and knuckles.

Jessie was just as lean and athletic as ever, though. Her black leather jacket hugged her like a second skin, and so did her jeans. Patches adorned the jacket sleeves, each one telling a story of a place she'd been. Some patches were from London, others Tokyo, a few from Madrid. It seemed Jessie had been globetrotting for quite some time.

Her helmet, tucked under one arm, bore the scars of the road.

Her eyes, hidden behind tinted sunglasses, scanned the room with a practiced wariness, almost identical to Enzo's police tic. Jessie took her time, absorbing every detail with the precision of someone who knew to expect the worst but still hoped for the best.

"J-Jessie?" Finch asked, stuttering on the word. "It's good to see you again."

Jessie turned to him, her lip curling upward.

No.

Finch wanted this to be perfect. He activated his magic.

Chronos, the Titan of Time, had given Finch control over twenty-four hours from whenever he made his mark. Time froze—the room, the people, the wind outside. Everything was perfectly still. A moment later, the colors drained away. The office's brown and gray, the vibrant colors of everyone's clothes... they all faded until there was nothing left but black and white.

And finally, the objects in the room collapsed like a candle under too much flame.

Finch stood in a void of white until he blinked his eyes. And then he was back in his office.

10:56 a.m.

That had to be the shortest amount of time Finch had gone before resetting everything. He smoothed his jacket, and then with a purposeful gait, he strode out of the office.

There she was. Jessie stood in the middle of the front room, her helmet under one arm, her stance lax.

"Jessie," Finch said, clear and confident this time. "It's been a while."

Yes. This was better. This was the demeanor Finch wanted to project.

With a casual gesture, Jessie removed her glasses and tucked them into a front pocket on her jacket. Her brown eyes, flecked with emerald, were the only real indicator she was half elf, as her ears were rounded, just like a human's.

"Adair, it's good to see you." Jessie stepped closer and gave him the once over. "You've definitely grown older."

"Says the woman clearly going through a midlife crisis," Finch quipped.

That was the problem with wearing confidence—sometimes sarcastic comments slid out his mouth before his brain could filter them.

Jessie tensed, her eyes narrowing. "At least I've been doing *something* all these years." She always spoke in a softer tone, but now there was an edge to it. Which was strange.

Ultimately, this wasn't how he wanted the conversation to go, either.

Finch hadn't been prepared. On the phone, Jessie had been skittish and distant. Now she seemed angry. What had changed?

Whatever the reason—Finch had to try again.

He activated his magic.

The world froze. Then the color drained, leaving everything a void of black and white, like a cheap coloring book. And finally, the shapes melted away.

Finch blinked his eyes, and he was once again in his office, Liam standing by his side.

10:56 a.m.

With confidence, but not too much bravado, Finch stepped out and found himself face-to-face with Jessie for a third time.

"Jessie, it's been a while." Finch went straight to her side, and offered to take her helmet.

With a hesitant look of consideration, she handed it over. Finch placed it on the receptionist's desk and then nodded to her.

"You look good," Finch said.

Jessie gave him the once-over, like she had before. "Adair... You've definitely grown older."

He ignored the comment. "How can I help you?"

"How can we *all* help you?" Bree chimed in.

Finch had forgotten there were other people in the office. Bree and Enzo stood by the desks, watching the conversation unfold. Finch had been so preoccupied with Jessie that everything else had been background noise.

Bree bounded over, smiling wide. "Finch said you were in danger. What can we do for you here at *24-Hour Investigations*?"

With a calculating glance, Jessie took note of Bree. Then she frowned. "Is this your daughter, Adair?"

"We're not related by blood," Bree quickly replied, "but we're super close. Definitely family."

"She's *my* daughter," Liam muttered from behind Finch, almost like he was too afraid to speak up. He was still half in Finch's office, not fully in the room with everyone else.

Jessie crossed her arms. "So, you and another man adopted? I never would've guessed."

"That's not—" Finch exhaled and rolled his eyes.

"Never mind. I just helped the girl and her father solve a murder a little while back. They work here now."

He motioned to the office.

It was nice. Almost too nice. It was the height of modern and fancy, and it shone with perhaps too much polish for what Finch was trying to convey.

"You've just been working?" Jessie's words were now icy. Still calm, but filled with hate so cold it could cause frostbite. "You haven't gone after Carter's killers? You've been putzing around Stockton?"

When she shot him a glare, the stink of brimstone briefly wafted through the air. Her eyes were red—only for a second—and Finch knew something was wrong. This wasn't the Jessie he remembered. What sort of demonic magic was clinging to her?

"Are you okay?" he asked.

"Do I look okay, *Sherlock*?" Jessie snapped.

That was fine with Finch. Jessie wanted to bark? He could do that. He had a whole tirade about the event he could offload at a moment's notice. Where had *she* been for ten years? Why had she *taken off* after Carter's death?

But Finch heard Carter's voice in the back of his mind, reminding Finch that Jessie didn't deserve that. His chest hurt from bottling his own anger.

"I'm disappointed in you," Jessie whispered. "You weren't the type to just be a lump. What would Carter think?"

"*Hey*, don't speak to Adair that way!" Bree's face brightened to a tomato red within seconds. "He's amazing. He saved me and my papa, and you can't—"

Liam stepped around Finch and reached for his daughter. "It's okay, Bree! Let's just leave them to their talk."

"But did you hear her?" Bree half-heartedly fought against her father as he actively tried to pull her back toward the desks. "She doesn't get to call him names! *She's* the one who's a lump!"

Jessie snatched her helmet from the desk and shook her head, the flash of red sparking in her eyes all over again. "You're clearly having too much fun with all this to bother with your brother. This was a mistake. I'm leaving." She slammed her way out of the office, her strength much more than a human's. She shattered some of the glass on the door as she went.

After a long sigh, Finch muttered. "Goddammit."

Then he activated his magic.

Stillness. Black and white. Objects melted away.

Finch blinked his eyes, and he was back in his office, everything undone.

10:56 a.m.

After a long exhale, Finch slapped himself on the cheek. "Get a hold of yourself, Adair."

Liam just watched as Finch headed out of the office.

Finch was fully prepared for the conversation this time. He knew more. Jessie was angry. Even if she didn't look like it at first. She resented him. That was fine—he could deal with that.

Jessie scanned her surroundings, just like before. When she removed her reflective sunglasses, Finch was ready.

"Jessie," he said as he strode over. He took her helmet and placed it on the desk. "I'm glad you came."

She gave him the same once over she had done in all the previous time loops. "Adair, it's good to see you. You've definitely grown older."

"The last few years have been rough," Finch replied with a weary smile. "What can I do for you?"

Bree bounded over to them. "What can *we* do for you? Because we're all members of *24-Hour Investigations*!" She placed a hand on her chest. "I'm a warlock-in-training."

After Jessie looked Bree up and down, she frowned—identical to last time. "Is this your child—"

"*Nope*," Finch said, cutting her off. "She's Liam's daughter." With a sweep of his arm, Finch motioned to his office. "Why don't we discuss whatever problems you have in private?"

Bree held up a hand, like she wanted to join them, but Finch had to give her a sideways glance. She lowered her arm and nodded once, clearly understanding that Finch needed to handle this on his own for the moment.

Finch and Jessie walked around Liam and then shut the door so it was just the two of them. Facing his sister-in-law, Finch steeled himself. She stood in the middle of his office, not even giving the chairs a single glance. The woman didn't want to sit.

"What's going on, Jessie?"

She was back to being her quiet self. Jessie folded her arms across her chest and stared, unseeing, at the wall ahead. For a long while, it was dead silent between them, with only the hum of Finch's computer to keep them company.

When Jessie finally looked over, Finch straightened his posture.

"What have you been doing the last few years?" she demanded.

"Recovering." Finch didn't want to dwell on the topic, but he knew he owed her an apology. "Jessie, look—I'm so sorry I wasn't there for you. Truly, I am. I just wasn't myself." Finch's gaze fell to the floor as he pictured his life after the loss of Carter. "It was hard to... feel things. Everything seemed pointless. It was like being underwater, drowning, but the death just never came, ya know."

Finch hadn't really tried to put into words his experience after Carter's death, but that was the closest he could describe it.

"I want to help you," he said, lifting his eyes back up to meet hers. "What can I do for you?"

Jessie bit her lip, nervousness visibly setting in. She inhaled, and then exhaled before she said, "We haven't been in touch much, but... I got tangled up with a wizard."

"Which wizard?" Finch asked.

Jessie hardened her expression and maintained a stiff posture. "Actually, it's not *tangled up*. The word is more like *hunted*. I had some dealings with this man a few years back, and it's coming back to bite me on the ass."

"Which. Wizard." Finch attempted to hold back his impatience, but the whole problem hinged on this one question.

Some wizards were quite friendly and reasonable.

But some of them weren't. Finch would even say some of them were sociopathic lunatics.

"Alonso Maldonado," Jessie finally whispered.

Finch ran a hand down his face. That was a name on the *sociopathic lunatic* list.

Maldonado's full name was *Alonso del Maldonado XIV the River Coatl*—it was so on-the-nose evil he might as well have been named *Adolf Mal-Bad*. He was a wizard who claimed territory in central Mexico, and largely gained fame by turning magical creatures into goo that people could ingest for temporarily superhuman speed and strength.

He also dealt with a metric fuck ton of demons, and traded them off to anyone who was willing to pay his outrageous prices.

Maldonado was not a good wizard. He wasn't a good man. He was a downright *vile* man who drew much of his inspiration from the Aztecs.

Additionally, wizards—who were men born with the ability to absorb and cultivate magic—siphoned magic from the world when they reached puberty. That was why

Maldonado took the title "river coatl." When he was young, he had siphoned the magic from a coatl, killing it, and then cultivated that magic within himself.

"Why did you go to him?" Finch finally asked. "Why Maldonado, of all people?"

"He sold demons to the witches who killed Carter." Jessie's tone once again turned icy. "I paid him for their locations—and anything else he knew about them."

"You could afford his prices?"

But that was when Jessie went quiet once again. She looked away, and Finch already knew the answer.

"Well, how much do you owe him?" Finch asked.

"It's not money he wants," she whispered. "And it doesn't matter. The thing I promised him... It's gone. So now he wants my life." Jessie shook her head. "I'm sorry, Adair. He sent people after me. They're already in Stockton. They probably know I was going to meet with you. I just... I've run out of people to turn to."

CHAPTER
FOUR

"W hy didn't you come to me sooner?" Finch asked.

Jessie stiffened and shot him a glare, the slight red to her eyes returning. "I've been calling you for months! I honestly thought you had died because no one had seen or heard from you in so long."

"You knew I wasn't dead."

With a sharp turn, Jessie glanced away. "*Still.*" She spoke the word through gritted teeth.

"So why didn't you come to see me before you bargained with Maldonado? You had my address. I could've prevented this!"

"I..." Jessie gulped down whatever tirade she had. With a shaky exhale, she shook her head. "I didn't know if I wanted to get you involved..."

"Listen, I'm sorry," Finch quickly stated. "I'm sorry, all right? I should've gotten my shit together sooner. I can't change what I did for the last few years, but I'm here now."

The words didn't help Jessie relax. Finch wasn't entirely sure what to do. What could he say to make up for not being there? He didn't know. He didn't even know what Carter would do in this situation.

His only option was to fix things.

Finch was determined to make it right—but first he needed more answers.

"What's going on with you?" Finch motioned to her whole body. "You smell like a demon vomited on your clothes and you never got around to cleaning them. Did you take one of Maldonado's creatures?" When she didn't answer, Finch gritted his teeth. "Tell me you didn't."

Jessie pulled her leather jacket tighter around her body. "Never mind that. I can't... undo what I did. Let's just focus on the immediate issue. I need a place to hide. Somewhere Maldonado can't reach me."

A safe house? From a wizard? That was a tall order. The only good news was that Maldonado's seat of power was far from California. How many mooks could he realistically send to the Central Valley? Not many, Finch assumed, but he didn't want to take any chances.

"You and Carter... always knew everything," Jessie whispered. She visibly relaxed as she turned to meet Finch's gaze. "No matter what happened, the two of you always seemed to *know*. Why aren't you like that now?"

Jessie wasn't aware of Finch's pact with Chronos. She hadn't known about Carter's, either.

Back when they worked as a team, Carter and Finch had only told a handful of people about their agreement with Chronos to prevent the knowledge from falling into the wrong hands. Jessie hadn't wanted to join their PI business —she had wanted to start her own business venture opening gates to the fae world for a price.

That was why they hadn't told her. Some fae could read minds...

But now Finch had told everyone in his office, including

the young Bree. Why should he hide it now? Life was different.

11:09 a.m.

"Jessie," Finch began.

Then Bree screamed.

With ice instantly dumping into his veins, Finch flew for his office door. He slammed it open and immediately snapped his attention to the problem. A thin creature made of shadows was in the main office. It had long arms and long legs, with the vague torso and head of a human, but it was completely made of void. No eyes. No mouth. Its spindly fingers ended in claws; its feet were twisted to resemble hooves.

The monster would be ten feet tall if it stood straight, but instead, it was crouching in the middle of the room, one of its freakishly long hands gripped around Liam's chest, its claws piercing the fabric and drawing blood.

A shadow imp—a lesser demon known to serve more powerful entities. They were cunning, often invisible to the naked eye, and had no odor to speak of. If you wanted intel, or to spy on someone, shadow imps were the way to go.

Bree, shaken, balled her fists. "Let him go!"

"Get back!" Liam shouted.

The imp had no mouth, so it didn't say anything, but its actions conveyed its intent. The monster squeezed Liam harder, drawing more blood.

Liam grunted, losing the last of his breath and unable to shout.

The next couple seconds were so chaotic that Finch acted on instinct.

Enzo ripped out of his human flesh and exploded into his werewolf form mid-lunge at the imp. With enough power to send everyone sailing, Enzo slammed into the imp and then carried it right through the glass windows that made up the front of their office. They crashed through—Enzo, Liam, and the imp—and hit the sidewalk with a *slam* and *crash* that could wake all of Stockton.

When Bree attempted to follow, Finch grabbed her by the arm and pulled her back.

Shadow imps weren't beasts you could hold down.

And sure enough, the imp slipped through Enzo's claws and slid across the ground like only a shadow could. As liquid darkness, the imp darted back into the office and then rose up like ink given solid form. It stepped from the shadows and was back to hunching in the office, looming over Finch, and Bree, claws extended.

Finch's hand burst with fire, and he stepped forward, ready to destroy the entity.

"*Don't!*" Bree screamed. "You might hurt Papa!"

In that split second, Finch held back.

And that was enough time for Jessie to step around him. When the shadow imp slashed with its hand, she reached out and grabbed the beast's wrist.

Demonic energy flared through the office. The smell of brimstone so overpowering, Finch almost gagged.

Holes opened in the floor, revealing a deep pit of inky void. Chains shot upward, seemingly from some black hole of a pit underneath the building, and lashed onto the creature, shackling the imp.

"You're just trash," Jessie stated.

The chains tightened, and the imp was slammed down into the pit, gone within a second, no noise was uttered as it was banished from the mortal world and pulled into some demonic prison.

Then the holes in the ground closed like they had never been there. The brimstone stink lingered.

Enzo leapt back into the office, his black fur on end, his fangs bared. He turned his attention to Jessie, his eyes wild.

"Oh, goddammit," was all Finch could mutter before Enzo lunged again, this time at his sister-in-law.

Werewolves were not known for their self-control. Once transformed, they were basically ravenous beasts cursed to seek flesh and destroy anything that stood in their way. Their rage fueled them—any emotion did, really—and they were quite powerful and damage resistant.

Enzo crashed into Jessie, slamming through Finch's office door and tearing it from its hinges. He was nearly eight feet tall in his werewolf form, and his arms were so muscular that it almost appeared as though he was hiding bowling balls beneath his fur.

"Ah!" Bree shrieked, shaking. "Adair!"

Since Chronos's magic was bound to Finch's crown core, he needed to concentrate in order to use it. If Finch was too distracted, or emotional, the magic wouldn't function properly.

Thankfully—or perhaps sadly—Finch was used to this kind of wanton chaos in his life. He focused, activated his magic, and thanked whatever good stars were watching over him that Enzo froze mid-swing with his claws aimed straight at Jessie's face.

The two were locked in a fierce struggle, with Jessie's eyes burning bright red, her demonic magic creating a mild circle on the floor around her. She had been planning to fight Enzo, that much was certain.

Bree just watched on in horror.

Liam was frozen outside on the pavement, glass shards puncturing half his body.

What a mess.

Then the colors drained away. Then all the shapes.

Finch enjoyed his half second in the white void of nothing—it was peaceful here.

When he blinked, he was back in his personal office. An

office that wasn't yet destroyed. Liam stood next to him, a concerned look on his face.

10:56 a.m.

Finch strode out of his office. Jessie was in the main room, her helmet under one arm. With a sigh of irritation, Finch walked over, took the helmet, and offered her a forced smile. "Jessie. You brought company." Then he turned his attention to the darkest corner of the room.

Sure enough, the edges of the darkness flickered with movement, betraying the imp's hiding spot. The devilish creatures were known for being able to hide in plain sight.

Finch snapped his fingers, sparking a light in the palm of his hand. With a nonchalant gesture of his hand, he blasted the corner of the room with flames like he had lit the stream from a hairspray container.

His fire magic was tied to his heart core, and was only as powerful as his strongest emotion at the time of use. Since his most potent emotion was currently *irritation*, his flames weren't as strong as they usually were.

But that didn't matter. Shadow imps were as flammable as paper dipped in gasoline.

Whoosh!

The shadow imp caught fire, the embers outlining its spindly body.

"*What is that?*" Bree shouted.

Her father flew out of Finch's office and wrapped his arms around her. With a dramatic twist, he flung her around so his back was to the fire, shielding Bree from any dramatic burst of flames or explosions.

Jessie's face was twisted in irritation and panic.

She hadn't known the creature was here, obviously.

The fire consumed the shadow imp in a matter of seconds. It *poofed* up in ash and left the mortal world without a noise.

Bree poked her head around her father. "*Was that a Slender Man?* Or a cool nightmare given flesh or something?" She sounded way too enthusiastic for the situation.

"Let's stay away from that corner of the room," Liam muttered, almost inaudible.

Enzo stomped over, his werewolf form threatening to take control. Black fur was starting to sprout across his arms and shoulders. Thankfully, his black skin tone hid it well.

"What's going on, Adair?" Enzo snapped.

"My sister-in-law made a deal with Maldonado." Finch slowly turned, placed Jessie's helmet on the receptionist's desk, and sighed. "Which means we have a big problem."

"You already know?" Jessie pulled off her sunglasses and stared. "You and Carter... You always somehow knew..."

Enzo glared at the ashes and then offered Finch a frown. "You can't possibly mean Alonso del Maldonado XIV the River Coatl. Not *that* Maldonado, right? That fuck-face is always trouble."

"*Language,*" Liam chided, speaking much louder than before and gesturing to Bree.

"Papa, I've used the internet." Bree crossed her arms. "I'm not a baby."

Enzo relaxed a bit, his werewolf form disappearing. He shivered and shook himself off before frowning. "Please, Adair—tell me you mean a different Maldonado."

A long silence stretched between them. Then Enzo leaned his head back and exhaled, venting his frustrations at the ceiling.

"First thing we need to do is find a safe house," Finch said. "So let's roll out."

CHAPTER
FIVE

inch, Enzo, Bree, Liam, and Jessie all squeezed into Finch's Toyota Celica. Finch drove, Enzo rode shotgun, while the other three filled the back. It wasn't comfortable. It was the opposite of comfortable. To make matters worse, the whole vehicle smelled of brimstone and wet dog.

Three blocks into the trip, Bree leaned forward, poking her head between the two front seats. "You need to buy a van," she said.

"I'm renting the single most expensive office space in all of Stockton because you wanted a fancy and cool location," Finch said, emotionless. "And now you want me to get a *van*? The most fuddy-duddy vehicle of all time?"

"*What*? Vans are super awesome!"

Finch glanced over his shoulder to sarcastically stare at the girl. He said nothing. The look conveyed everything.

Bree huffed. "It's cool for *detectives*. Like Scooby-Doo."

"Yes, we should model ourselves after a cartoon dog and his crew," Enzo sardonically interjected. "Name one other detective. Any detective you know who has a van."

"Uh." Bree half shrugged and narrowed her eyes. "The A-Team?"

Enzo snapped his attention to Bree, a deep frown on his face. "How do you know about the A-Team? That damn show aired forty years ago. It's three times your age."

"Nothing dies on the internet," Bree said, rolling her eyes. She sat back in her seat and crossed her arms. "I know all the memes. But that's not answering my complaint. We *need* a van. For more space. And maybe some cool neon lights inside. I've seen vans like that on Instagram."

Finch ignored the inane conversation. He already knew he was going to eventually break down and buy a damn van, so he didn't want to think about it anymore. All he really needed to figure out was how he was going to make it a company asset and business expense.

The sweltering afternoon heat blanketed Stockton and made every reflective window a chore to even glance at. Years ago, Finch had had friends and associates he would go to if he needed a safe house, but those days were long gone. He was fairly certain most of his best contacts had moved out of California, or at the very least, out of crime-filled Stockton.

So, Finch went to the one place he considered so off the beaten path that it might as well be a safe house—*Nico's Brew*.

He parked his Toyota in front of the sad hole-in-the-wall joint. The neon 'open' sign blinked in the window, clearly on its last legs and struggling to find the energy to keep going. The exterior was painted black, and thick blinds hung over the windows. There was no sign indicating what kind of store this was; only the aroma of coffee beans hinted at its purpose.

Finch and the others entered *Nico's Brew* to find it mostly empty. Only the owner, Nico, was inside. Thankfully, the man had the AC at full blast. A refreshing arctic breeze rushed over Finch as he went to take a seat in the far booth.

Nico stood behind the counter. Piles of coffee bean bags were on display behind him, each with a label from the country it had been grown in. Apparently, coffee grown in different regions of the world had unique flavors and different acidic grades. Nico cared about that, but Finch didn't.

A flatscreen TV hung in the top corner of the coffee shop. A volleyball game played, and Nico only half watched as the strange group of people took a seat.

Jessie panned her gaze around before leaning onto the table and lowering her voice. "Is this some sort of witch-protected hideout?"

Finch shook his head. "It's just a coffee shop."

"Is it owned by another warlock?"

"It's just a coffee shop."

"Then... have you safeguarded it against demons or curses or—"

The TV flickered, and a loud noise buzzed throughout the place. Nico grunted out a profanity before picking up a broom and then unceremoniously whacking the side of the TV a couple times. The image returned, showing the last of the volleyball game, and Nico retook his seat at the counter.

"I think Adair means it's just *barely* a coffee shop," Enzo quipped. "And nothing more."

Jessie ran a hand through her short hair, taking in a deep breath as she did so. "Adair. This is serious. Maldonado has been chasing me for years, but it's gotten personal. His goons are all over the city."

"Don't worry, this is part of the process," Finch said.

Jessie eyed the coffee bags, the old table, and the quiet shop. "*This*?"

"I need more information." He sat forward. "Why don't

you start from the top? Tell me how you got mixed up with a wizard, and we'll go from there."

Before she could begin, Nico ambled over with a small notebook in hand. He was a large man with an even larger gut. His mustache was puffy, and he tamed it with a few strokes before he approached the table.

"What can I get you all?" Nico asked, looking at each of the odd diners in the booth.

Liam, who was seated in the deepest part of the booth, lifted a hand, one finger raised. "Can I please get a venti mocha?"

Nico frowned as he wrote in his notebook. "One... medium... girl coffee."

"Do you serve beer?" Enzo asked.

For whatever reason, this caused Nico to frown deeper than the Starbucks order. He gave Enzo an icy glare. "My brother, I am an artist, and my canvas is coffee. I have *real* coffee, from the Blue Mountains of Jamaica, and you came here asking for *beer*? Did I hear that correctly?"

"Yeah," Enzo said, unfazed. "Coffee makes me jittery. I don't like it."

Nico sighed. "Fine. I'll go next door to the sports bar and buy you a bottle of something. It'll be an extra twenty dollars."

"Fair."

Nico finished writing that and turned to Adair. "The usual?"

Finch nodded once.

He liked Nico. The man was his kind of speed.

"I'll have the same thing but with cream and sugar please," Bree said, smiling.

When Nico turned to Jessie, she didn't even meet his gaze. She shook her head. "Water."

With everyone's order taken, Nico walked off. He

started some brews, and then slipped out the front door, likely heading to that sports bar for the most expensive bottle of beer anyone had ever ordered outside Disneyland.

Finch was about to remind Jessie to spill the details, but she didn't need prompting. As soon as the door to *Nico's Brew* slammed shut behind him, she took a deep breath and started speaking.

"I went to Maldonado for information." Jessie's tone was serious, and her words quick, as though she wanted this part over with as fast as possible. "Carter was killed by that coven of full moon witches, and I knew Maldonado had supplied them with demons. He knows where they live, where they hide, where they do their magic—and he was willing to sell it to me for a price."

Finch didn't say anything. He hadn't thought to track down Carter's killers by approaching someone like Maldonado. Instead, Finch had gone way out of his way to make a pact with Ke-Koh the Ifrit of Rebellion—a creature with devastating flames.

That was because the coven of witches just happened to be mostly vampires as well, and nothing short of gasoline burned brighter than a witch-vampire.

"Maldonado said he would give me all the information I needed if I killed a few people for him." Jessie stared a hole in the booth table, her gaze never wavering. "They were... members of SHADOW."

"The *Supernatural Hazard Analysis and Defense Operations Wing*," Enzo quickly replied. "Those SHADOW boys are like CIA agents. They stop magical criminals in other countries trying to do bad things in the States."

"That means they're not part of the FBOI?" Bree asked. "Because Adair said they handled magical criminals."

"The FBOI handles criminals *inside* the US. Like the FBI."

"Oh. Right. That makes sense."

Again, Finch remained quiet. If Jessie had killed SHADOW agents, he would have a lot more trouble than just with Maldonado.

"I told Maldonado I couldn't do it," Jessie added. "I told him I'm just a half moon witch, and most of my magics aren't offensive in nature. I'm not an assassin. I've dedicated myself to finding and detecting the fae."

"You're a witch?" Bree whispered, her eyes growing wider.

"That was when Maldonado told me that I was the only one who could do this. One of the SHADOW agents was a fae himself, and a master of invisibility. I was one of the few witches who could possibly see through it."

Liam cleaned his glasses on his button-up shirt. He had been nodding along with the story, and finally interjected. "You've mastered the ability to overcome fae trickery? Their glamors and illusions are some of the most complicated—"

"I'm half elf," Jessie stated, cutting him off. "And I studied magic in the fae courts. So, yes, it's complicated, but I can do it."

"That's really cool," Bree whispered.

Jessie continued. "Maldonado gave me one of his demons. It was... Let's just say it was very powerful. He wanted me to trick the SHADOW agents, kill them, and then return with his demon intact. Once I gave him the teeth of the agents, he'd give me all the info I wanted."

She paused for a moment, and the whole shop was silent except for the coffee machine buzzing as it continued its work.

No one wanted to ask the obvious question. Thankfully, Jessie didn't force the issue.

"I went to kill the agents, but..." She sighed. "I couldn't. Mentally, I mean. I remembered Carter, and figured I'd just be taking someone else's husband away." Jessie closed her eyes and placed a hand on her face. "But that realization only came when I was already deep within the SHADOW offices."

Bree leaned forward on the table. "What happened?"

"There was an incident. I ran, but I didn't get away unscathed. Since I didn't want to fight them, I... I bound myself fully to Maldonado's demon to gain greater access to its power. Then I got away—but now Maldonado wants his demon back."

"So give it back to him," Bree said.

There was another long and awkward pause in the conversation. Full moon witches typically had the ability to steal magics from other creatures, including demons and oni. Half moon witches, on the other hand, usually had the ability to integrate magics into their own—merging themselves with other things, for lack of a better description.

And while full moon witches could return magics once stolen, half moon witches never released their magic. It was one with them forever.

If Jessie had fused this demon with her cores, she couldn't *give it back to Maldonado*. If she was killed, however, the demon would be released, and able to be contracted, captured, or somehow dealt with again.

Which was probably what Maldonado wanted now.

He wanted Jessie to die so he could get his powerful demon minion returned to him.

CHAPTER
SIX

ico returned with a beer, dropped it off at the table, and then prepared everyone else's coffee before serving it. Liam took a sip of his drink first, his eyebrows shooting to his hairline.

"This is some amazing mocha," he said.

"Should be," Nico replied. "It's from Yemen, the land where mocha was born."

"Wow. Incredible."

Nico grunted something and then made his way behind the bar. The volleyball game was only halfway through, and he gave it his undivided attention.

"How long has Maldonado been after you?" Finch asked.

"Two years," Jessie replied. Then she sighed. "He didn't know what I had done at first. I told him I needed time to go after the agents, and I tried to find a hiding place, but none of the fae will take me now that I've bound myself to a demon. Most of the gates won't even work for me."

Liam slowly sipped his coffee. After a moment of

silence, he put his mug down. "Has Maldonado discovered what you've done?"

Jessie nodded. "That was when he started sending his men to kill me. He knows he'll never get his demon back unless I'm dead. I don't know what to do."

"Don't worry, we'll solve this," Bree interjected, smiling. "You came to the right warlock, because Adair Finch can do anything!"

"*Shh*," Finch hissed. He gestured to Nico and glowered. "He's not in the know, and I'd rather you didn't scream at the top of your lungs about warlocks."

Bree quieted her tone as she continued, "We'll solve this whole problem. Don't worry, Jessie."

"We?" she asked.

Bree placed a hand on her chest. "I'm Adair's apprentice, and Enzo is Adair's assistant."

"Since when was my title *assistant*?" Enzo sardonically asked. He took a swig of his beer and then glanced around the table.

"Be thankful she fast-tracked you," Finch quipped. "You got to skip the *junior assistant* phase entirely."

"I used to be a cop, goddammit. I can handle the title of *Private Investigator* just fine."

Bree smiled wider. "That's good! That means we have two, so we're going to solve all our problems twice as fast."

"If only it worked that way," Liam murmured.

"Oh!" Bree touched her father's shoulder. "And Papa is our researcher, so we're a complete team. You really have nothing to worry about, Jessie."

That didn't seem to reassure Jessie. She held her cup of water, staring at the smooth surface of the liquid, unblinking.

Her situation was worse than Finch had previously imagined. If Maldonado needed whatever demon she was bound to, there would be a never-ending stream of goons coming for her life. Even if he only sent low-level demons, like the shadow imp, sooner or later they would get lucky and do real harm.

If Maldonado sent one of his talented goons after Jessie, the situation would turn dire.

"Do you know who he's sent after you so far?" Finch asked. "Did Maldonado send witches or warlocks or maybe some manner of demon or fae? The more I know, the better."

Jessie slowly spun her glass around. "I'm not sure. They've just gotten more aggressive. I'm surprised something hasn't already come into this coffee shop to deal with me, that's how closely they've been dogging my steps."

After a long sip of his coffee, Finch slid out of the booth. He already had the information he needed to start this investigation, so the next step would be to gather intel on Maldonado's forces in the area. Perhaps, if Finch beat enough goons, he would force some valuable info out of them.

"Enzo, I'm gonna need your nose." Finch motioned to the door.

"Junior assistant reporting for duty," Enzo sarcastically said as he stood.

"Wait!" Bree quickly hopped out of the booth and stood next to Finch. "I'm going, too, right? I'm your apprentice."

Finch shook his head. "You stay here while I roam around town. Keep watch over Jessie for me, all right?"

"But I can't learn all your warlock ways if I'm here. You're at least going to draw the mark on me, right?"

"The mark?" Jessie asked. She turned away from her drink to glower at Finch.

Not wanting to explain himself, Finch pushed Bree toward the door. "All right, all right, you can come." He glanced over at Liam. "*You* watch Jessie. Just stay here, and call me if anything happens, got it? I won't be far."

Liam almost spilled his mocha in his attempt to hastily put the mug down. "Me? You want *me* to watch her? But—"

"You can handle it, Papa." Bree waved as she headed for the door, smiling the entire way.

Nico increased the volume on the TV, passive-aggressively telling everyone what he thought of this conversation.

Once Finch, Enzo, and Bree were outside, Finch breathed a sigh of relief. He wasn't entirely certain when he wanted to tell Jessie about his pact with Chronos, the Titan of Time, but he knew he didn't want to do it now.

He glanced at his phone.

11:28 a.m.

Finch hated re-marking the time. Whatever mark he made, he couldn't go backward beyond it. His current time marked was 10:56 a.m., but he had learned so much, and found a good spot to lie low, that he didn't want to have to go through that again.

Finch marked the time, resetting his "save point" to 11:28 a.m.

He hoped he wouldn't regret his decision.

Then Finch got into his vehicle, and the other two followed suit, with Bree sitting shotgun. She immediately opened the glove compartment and pulled out a permanent marker.

"Okay, draw the mark," she said, handing the pen to Finch.

He took it and complied with her demands. First, he drew the Mark of Chronos on Bree. It was just four lines— three down, one across, making them look like three little T's—but as soon as he was finished, his time magic was woven into the twelve-year-old girl.

Now, when he next rewound time, Bree would remember everything.

Finch motioned for Enzo's arm. The man was African American, and had dark skin, but that didn't matter for the mark's magic. As soon as Finch finished drawing the mark, Enzo had the same magic woven in him as Bree.

They would both remember.

Unfortunately, Finch would have to redraw this mark every time he rewound time—at least, if he wanted them to continually remember. If he forgot to draw the mark, and then he rewound, everything they remembered would be lost.

Bree sat back in her seat. "Why don't you draw this on Papa and Jessie, too?"

Finch threw the pen back into the glove compartment. "I don't think they need to know just yet."

"Where are we going to go?"

"Wherever Enzo tells us." Finch pulled out of his parking spot and got onto the road. He tapped the side of his nose. "Werewolves have a great sense of smell, and Jessie has a very distinct scent. I'm hoping we can follow it backward and run into whoever is following her."

Bree turned around in her seat to stare back at Enzo. "Do you really think you can follow Jessie's scent?"

"Oh, yeah." Enzo leaned back in his seat. He was large, and muscled, and the Toyota Celica seemed like a car made for children when he was inside—yet another reason to get a van. "Jessie reeked of demonic magic. I'll be smelling it for weeks."

"Cool."

Enzo motioned to her seat. "Can you please buckle your seat belt? You're making me nervous."

Bree did as he requested, but not without rolling her eyes.

"We're going to head back to the office and go from there," Finch stated.

———

Standing outside *24-Hour Investigations*, Finch waited as Enzo sniffed around the area. It didn't take him long to motion to the sidewalk.

"Jessie rode her motorcycle," Enzo said. "And her scent is all over the streets. Let's walk for a few blocks—I get the feeling she stopped somewhere before driving over to our office."

Finch nodded. "Lead the way."

Werewolves had incredibly heightened senses and physical capabilities, even in their human form. If Enzo transformed, he'd be ten times more effective, but they couldn't have a wolf-man walking the streets of Stockton, so they'd have to make do.

Enzo strode forward, his eyes on a distant target like a tracking hound.

Finch, Enzo, and Bree headed into downtown Stockton. The theater, courthouse, and tall buildings had their own smells, each more powerful than the last. Finch could only focus on the buttery popcorn, and he had no idea how Enzo continued to steer them beyond the Indian restaurant.

They rounded a corner with a Walgreens Pharmacy, and Bree grabbed Finch's sleeve.

"Uh, can we stop here?" she asked.

Finch shook his head. "We're in the middle of following Jessie's trail. It can wait."

"*Please*," Bree said, not really a question, but a demand.

Enzo stopped walking. His nostrils flared as he turned on his heel. "We should stop."

"Really?" Finch let out a sigh. "Fine. Whatever. But let's make this quick."

Bree smiled as she ran into the pharmacy. The inside wasn't anything special—a normal store with normal things for sale. Finch wandered in only because he knew he had to pay for anything Bree might want.

She went straight for the aisle labeled *feminine hygiene*. When she emerged, she was carrying a small box under her arm, like she was trying to hide it from view. But Finch had seen—it was just tampons.

"I need this," Bree said when she returned to Finch's side.

Finch pointed to the register. "If you're done, let's get out of here."

In a quiet voice, Bree asked, "Y-You're not embarrassed, right? This isn't... gross?"

"I'm not embarrassed. It's not gross. But you know what this conversation is?"

"What?"

"A complete waste of my time," Finch quipped. "So, let's walk over, buy our lavender-scented wings, or whatever you call them, and never step in this place ever again."

His flippant attitude seemed to break down all Bree's nervousness. She half-giggled at the statement, held the box like a normal person, and went to the register.

Finch pulled out his credit card, but when he went to pay, the machine prompted him to put in a tip for the worker—the worker who had done nothing but sit at the register; the worker who hadn't even bothered to say *hello* when they entered; the worker who avoided all eye contact by playing on his phone through the transaction.

When had this become the norm?

Finch didn't care if everyone else did it, he refused to tip someone who contributed less effort than his microwave.

"Oh! We should get Enzo a water." Bree grabbed one from a nearby glass-doored fridge. "Since he's doing all that hard work leading us around."

Finch paid for that, too, and then they headed outside. Bree, with a paper bag dangling from her arm to hold her supplies, happily made her way to Enzo. She handed him the bottle, and then pointed forward.

"Mush," she playfully said.

"Really?" Enzo gulped down some water. "A dog joke?"

"O-Oh. I thought you'd think it was funny. I'm sorry."

Enzo flashed her a bright white smile. "I'm pullin' your leg, kid. Thanks for the water." He literally downed the rest of the bottle and then tossed it into a nearby trash can. "Let's go. That parking lot right over there is where Jessie was parked for a while, I can tell."

It was a large parking lot next to the waterfront. The signs around the outside indicated parking was expensive, but only during certain times of the year. Festival season. Currently, it was too damn hot for any of that, so there was no cost for parking.

Oak trees were planted around the asphalt square, covering everything with acorns.

A black car was parked under the shade of a tree—and that was it. Otherwise, the parking lot was empty.

"See those two guys?" Enzo asked, gesturing to the car. "They stink of demons. Jessie was here for a bit, so these might be the ones following her."

"We already found them?" Bree softly clapped her hands together. "Awesome. Having a werewolf on the team is so useful. We're going to have this all solved in no time."

Finch began his trek across the parking lot, heading straight for the vehicle. "Let me do the talking. Maybe we can handle this without cracking some skulls."

"Aww," Enzo whined. "Fine, ya spoilsport."

CHAPTER
SEVEN

F inch approached the driver's side of the car.

12:35 p.m.

Enzo hung back with Bree, watching from a good twenty feet away.

The two men in the car could've been cosplaying as yin and yang, that was how opposite, yet still the same, they were. The man in the driver's seat wore a vibrant white shirt and baggy jeans. Tattoos littered his arms, most of which were ill-defined and likely done in prison. His pale skin made every terrible mistake stand out.

The other man in the passenger's seat wore a black shirt and dark gray sweats. His tanned skin was free of all *prison tats*, but he wore enough gold jewelry that it bordered on gaudy.

They both wore sunglasses, and their music—Finch hated to call it that since it was just screaming—was so loud, they apparently didn't notice Finch's approach.

After a moment of standing next to the vehicle, Finch tapped on the glass.

The tattooed thug muted his stereo and then rolled the window down a crack.

"*What the fuck do you want?*" he asked, all aggression, no calm.

Unfazed, Finch just asked, "Are you fine young gentlemen searching for Jessica Finch?"

The mere mention of her name got both the yin-yang brothers excited. They exchanged quick glances before opening the vehicle doors at the exact same time and stepping out into the parking lot.

Both were packing heat, something Finch hadn't noticed until they stood. They had the guns tucked into the waistbands of their pants, the grips just visible.

They both sported Colt Emiliano Zapatas—handguns that were needlessly fancy, .38 Super caliber, and royal blue polished. The slides of the guns were silver-etched with Mexican flowers, and the grips were made of pearlite, sparkling something fierce.

Finch had seen *many* Zapatas throughout his lifetime. Maldonado's goons used them, but so did several gangs all throughout California. They were flashy enough to be cool, but still small enough to be easily concealed.

"Do you know Jessica?" the white-shirted goon asked.

"We got some cash if you take us straight to her," the black-shirted one added. He reached into his sweatpants pocket and pulled out a tightly coiled roll of bills.

Both the armed men ignored Bree, but gave Enzo a sideways glance before returning their attention to Finch. They tensed, but said nothing else.

"I assume you two aren't the ones calling the shots, right?" Finch asked. "Who do you answer to? A warlock? Maldonado himself? Because I have some questions that need answering."

The white-shirted man huffed out a laugh. He smacked the other guy on the shoulder and then shook his head. "Who do you think you are?"

"I'm Adair Finch."

"Who?"

The black-shirted man frowned. "Are we supposed to know that name?"

How old were these two? Eighteen? Twenty? They would've been children when Finch and his brother were world-famous warlocks for hire. Of course they didn't recognize his name—they probably weren't even old enough to legally drink.

Finch sighed. "How about you call up your direct superior and tell them I need to speak to them."

"What're you? A warlock Karen?" The black-shirted goon chuckled.

The other one shoved the guy's arm. "He wants to speak to our manager."

"He doesn't know who he's messin' with."

"How about you—" The white-shirted man pulled his Zapata, held it sideways, and jabbed it into Finch's chest, "—tell us where Jes—"

Finch grabbed the gun and wrenched it to the side, both pointing the barrel away from him and twisting the man's wrist in an unnatural way. The thug yelled, and Finch stepped closer, hooked his ankle with his foot, and then slammed the man with his shoulder. The white-shirted idiot fell back, his head clipping the hood of his own vehicle before he tumbled to the ground.

Finch maintained his hold on the handgun, easily slipping it from the man's broken grasp.

In the next second, the black-shirted moron reached for his own Zapata, but he was too slow on the draw. Finch flipped his new handgun around and aimed it at the man, keeping at least a couple feet between them so he couldn't have his own firearm taken from him in the same disarming technique.

The thug stopped mid-draw, his eyes narrowed, his arm twitchy.

He was going to attempt to quick-draw and fire. Finch saw it in his desperate expression.

Fortunately, that never happened. Instead, a black-furred werewolf came flying in at the edge of Finch's peripheral vision. Enzo, fully wolfed out, was a massive eight-foot-tall humanoid—pure muscle and rage.

With pointed ears, fangs as long as fingers, and claws that could rip through metal, anyone who saw him would immediately understand why werewolves were dangerous.

Enzo crashed into the thug and slammed him to the pavement. The goon somehow managed to get his gun up and fired four rounds straight into Enzo's stomach. Unfortunately for him, that wasn't enough to stop a werewolf.

With his own blood soaking his tank top, Enzo crunched his fangs down on the man's neck, crushing the windpipe—and everything else in the man's neck—in one fell swoop.

Finch didn't have long. Once that thug was dead, Enzo would be a loose cannon, attacking anyone and everything until the cursed magic was used up.

"Adair!" Bree shouted. She had her hands up over her face, her eyes scrunched closed. "M-Make this stop!"

Finch activated his magic.

Everything stopped. The wind, the blood gushing onto the pavement—everything. Then the colors drained, leaving the world black and white.

Finally, all the shapes melted away, along with Finch's adrenaline.

When he blinked, he found himself outside *Nico's Brew*, along with Bree and Enzo. The first thing Finch did was whirl on his heel and stare through the window.

11:28 a.m.

Liam and Jessie were inside, casually sipping their drinks.

Sighing in relief, Finch turned back around. "I forgot how much I hate thugs with guns."

Bree ran her hands down the sides of her face. "*Ohmygosh*," she said, the words spilling out without pause. "Those were crazy gangsters! We have to do something about them, Adair."

Enzo ambled into the parking lot, putting distance between himself and everyone else. He wasn't a werewolf, but he was clearly still shaken from the event. His muscles rippled, and he had to flex his hands to keep the claws from coming out.

The lycanthropy curse was primarily tethered to the heart core—meaning that, in order to transform, they had to feel a deep emotion. Enzo *could* transform on command, and stay in his werewolf form while retaining his self-control, but if he was *forced* to transform due to anger, depression, or shock, he would become a raging beast incapable of speech or control.

It was the reason werewolves tended to stick to themselves. They didn't have friends or family once they were cursed—they joined little supernatural leper colonies, basically.

Losing control and killing everyone nearby was the fear of every wolf.

Especially Enzo.

And why wouldn't it be? Finch completely understood. That was why he had been working with Enzo to get control of his anger. With his time-rewinding powers, Finch figured they would eventually get Enzo to control himself no matter the situation.

"Don't dwell on it," Finch said, motioning to his friend. "Listen, we're going to take deep breaths and remember to stay calm."

"Should we go back inside the coffee shop and let Papa and Jessie know what happened?" Bree asked.

Finch shook his head. "No. We haven't figured out enough information. First, we need to figure out a way to deal with *handguns*."

There were plenty of magical creatures, both human and animal, who could grant him abilities to overcome standard firearms. Either by increased toughness, or the ability to shield himself—he just needed *something*. If Maldonado had a whole army of pistol-packing goons wandering the city, looking for Jessie, Finch didn't want to constantly worry about taking a bullet to the head.

"Are you going to make a new pact with something?" Bree clasped her hands as though trying to hide her overwhelming excitement. "*Are you*? If you do, can I make a pact with it, too? Can you show me how to be a better warlock and—"

"*Shh.*" Finch held up his hand.

Bree immediately stopped talking, but Finch knew it was a temporary condition.

He needed to think. He had made pacts with many creatures in the past to overcome human-made problems. Dealing with firearms was a constant problem he and Carter had had to deal with.

"Are you going to summon something to us?" Bree whispered. She inched closer to Finch until she was right next to him. "Like when you summoned Kull? Can I help?"

Finch sighed. It was impossible to think when Bree's blue eyes were staring into his soul.

"Listen," he said, holding back his irritation. "I'm trying to remember what kind of creatures I made pacts with in the past. I remember I once made a pact with a dragon to get skin that basically couldn't be pierced."

That was one of the advantages of being a warlock. Finch could make pacts with all sorts of creatures, and temporarily gain access to their magic. Once he completed the pact, he could release the magic and get something else —and he could have something tied to each one of his cores.

His crown core was tethered to Chronos, the Titan of Time. Through concentration, he could use the time god's magic.

His heart core was tethered to Ke-Koh, the Ifrit of Rebellion. Through emotion, he could empower and use the creature's mighty fire.

His eyes core was tethered to Kullthantarrick the Sneak. Through visualization he could unlock doors and avoid detection. However, he had completed her pact and could drop her magic at any time to bind something else to that core.

His soul core and loins core were untethered, and Finch didn't really want to change that. The soul core required inner tranquility and peace in order to use the magic tethered there, and the loins...

Finch didn't think he had it in him at the moment to delve into that magical power set.

No, he would need a creature who could bind with his eyes—and somehow protect him from bullets.

Enzo paced a small circle before walking back over. He didn't appear to be on the edge of rage any longer. His breathing was normal, his hand resting casually in his jogging pants.

"I know a lot of dwarves have magical powers over metal," Enzo said.

Bree's eyes went wide. "Papa knows all kind of dwarves! And he knows even more about metal. We should ask him. Please, Adair? I know he can help!"

CHAPTER
EIGHT

F inch strode back inside *Nico's Brew*. Enzo, not
feeling sociable, remained outside, and Bree opted
to stay with him.

The quaint little coffee shop was still deserted, except for
Nico behind the bar and Liam with Jessie at their table. It
smelled of freshly brewed coffee, which helped soothe
Finch's stress.

He went straight to the booth. Liam and Jessie were
having a quiet conversation and not paying attention to
their surroundings.

"I'm sorry to hear about your husband," Liam
muttered.

"It happened a decade ago," Jessie replied, barely above a
whisper.

"I, uh, recently lost my wife."

"Oh." Jessie fidgeted with her cup. "I apologize. I
shouldn't have said anything."

Finch slammed his hand down on the booth table. Liam
tensed and nearly slid out of his seat, but when Jessie
whirled on him, her eyes flashed red and the smell of brim-

stone overpowered the coffee aroma. Whatever demonic magic she had, Finch could sense it was quite potent. He made a mental note not to startle her in the future.

"Sorry," he said. "I need Liam's help."

"Mine?" Liam slid back up until he was correctly seated once more. "Really?"

"You know some dwarves, right? Do you know any who has a particular strength over metal? One that might help against bullets if I bond their magic to my eyes?"

Liam's eyes widened. "Bullets?"

"Maldonado has a lot of goons in his employ."

"I-Is Bree going to be safe with you? I mean, if you think you're going to get shot at—"

"Everything is under control," Finch interjected. "*And* I can make sure we're bulletproof if I find the right dwarf, so do you know anyone?"

Silence descended over the table. Liam fingered the rim of his mug, his eyes falling to the mocha brew within. Then he straightened his glasses and nodded. "Yes," he said, returning his attention to Finch. "I do know someone. *Heslop*. He's a Simonside dwarf. Or, uh, most people call them *duergars* now."

Simonside dwarf?

Finch had heard that name. The Simonside Hills in northern England were quite magical and filled with all sorts of supernatural phenomena. Fae gates littered the whole area, and it was common for people to go missing. Tosson Hill, specifically, was where the Winter King had their coronation.

"Are there any fae gates around here?" Finch asked. "Any way to get a hold of Heslop?"

"There are," Jessie quickly answered. "But there's only one naturally occurring gate—all the rest in Stockton were created by the local covens."

There were only three types of fae gates—mushroom circles, dream circles, and coven circles. Mushroom circles were naturally occurring gates that grew in places where wyld magic was in abundance. Dream circles could be opened by lucid dreamers if they knew what to look for—but that was rare.

Coven circles were gates made through the power of multiple witches pooling their magic together. In order to activate them, the coven had to come together at the same time. Finch didn't have the patience for any of that.

"Where's the mushroom circle?" he asked.

Finch didn't want to go to the land of the fae. He hated it there. However, if he traveled to a gate, he could use a summoning circle to call for Heslop's attention, and perhaps the duergar would walk through to the realm of mortals.

"The gate is difficult to find," Jessie muttered.

Liam offered her a slight smile. "It's a good thing we have an expert in seeing through fae trickery."

"W-Well, that would require me to leave the coffee shop and travel through Stockton again."

"Adair said this place wasn't even magical. Maybe it would be best if you stayed on the move."

Finch waited. If Jessie didn't want to go, he would handle this himself, but if she did, everything would go a lot faster. After a moment of mulling it over, Jessie sighed and left the booth.

"All right. I'll take you to the gate. It's located in McKinley Park."

Finch snapped his fingers and gestured for Liam to stand as well. "Let's go. If you know Heslop, this will make everything easier."

———

McKinley Park was the largest park in Stockton. Ten years ago, Finch would've said the place was dangerous—bums had taken over all twenty-two acres and turned it into a one-stop shop for your street drug of choice.

Finch parked his car next to the massive fence that had been erected at the perimeter of the park. It was mostly chain link, with several wooden privacy slats laced through the links to prevent people from climbing it. A large sign read: NO TRESPASSING. MCKINLEY PARK IS NOT OPEN TO THE PUBLIC.

"What's going on?" Finch asked, glaring at the unsightly fence.

"Back in 2023, the park closed for renovations," Liam said from the back seat. "It should've only taken two weeks."

Enzo snorted. "California only works at one speed, and that speed is *fuck you*." He pointed to some tiny print at the bottom of the sign. "Says there the park will be open again in 2025."

"You can read that?" Liam wiped his glasses clean and then squinted through them. "Incredible. I didn't know werewolves had enhanced sight."

Bree opened the back door and sprang out. She immediately went to the fence and attempted to climb it, but the wooden boards were busy doing their duty.

When Jessie exited the vehicle, her attention went to the sky. It was a little past noon. Witches disliked this time of day the most, but Finch never knew why. After gazing at the bright light for half a second, Jessie ambled around the car and then stood on the sidewalk, her attention on her boots.

Finch, Enzo, and Liam all approached the fence. Before anything else happened, Finch motioned for Enzo's arm and drew the Mark of Chronos.

"Bree," he snapped.

She stopped attempting to climb over and leapt to his

side. "Yeah?" When she spotted the pen, she smiled and held out her arm.

Finch drew the mark on her as well.

"Do I get one?" Liam whispered. "It seems like... I might need it? Whatever it is?"

"No," Finch drawled. "Find us a way over the damn fence."

"Well, I've made a pact with a mineral dwarf to help with crafting items. I, uh, don't have any magic that can get us through the fence."

Finch turned to Enzo.

He shrugged. "What? You want me to rip it apart? Because I can whup this fence's ass if you don't care who sees."

"I can burn it down just fine," Finch sarcastically replied. "I was hoping you had a subtler way of getting in."

"Climb it," Enzo said.

The fence was over ten feet high—likely to prevent the bums from re-infesting the place—and Finch was certain he wouldn't be able to get over. Perhaps, ten years ago, when he was still in his prime, he could've done it, but now... not so much.

"I can get us in," Jessie said. She stepped up to the fence and placed her palm flat against the wooden boards. "You all should be close."

Bree, Liam, Enzo, and Finch all gathered around her. At first, Finch thought Jessie would use more of her stolen demonic power, but when the air shimmered like a desert mirage, he realized it was just her normal half moon witch abilities.

A strange fog wafted over the sidewalk for a moment, and then the wood in the fence *moved* of its own accord. It shifted its shape, briefly forming into branches, as it twisted and strained the fence. The cracking of the wood, and the shriek of the metal, caused Finch to cringe.

He glanced over his shoulder. There were Stockton residents out on the streets—in cars, in nearby homes—but none of them seemed to see or hear what Jessie was doing to the barrier.

"What's going on?" Bree asked.

"I put up a glamor," Jessie said, her voice strained. She was focusing on her magic, controlling the wood and warping the metal. "It's a type of illusion that hides my magic use from magicless mortals."

Bree stared at the fence as a door was shaped into it. "And what's this?"

"My crown is filled with wyld magic." Jessie gritted her teeth. "All my witch training was to help me get to gates that would normally be difficult to find."

"You mean, these are your witch abilities?" Bree's eyes practically sparkled with delight.

Once a seven-foot door had appeared in the fence, Jessie lowered her hand and then ushered everyone through. "I'll leave the glamor up so no mortals notice this."

Finch and the gang walked through into the park.

To say it was a nightmare would indeed be an understatement. The park was a living example of what happened when ambition collided headfirst with incompetence.

The renovations, it seemed, had been abandoned halfway through, leaving behind an apocalyptic blend of unfinished dreams and uncollected trash.

The paths were a treacherous mix of loose gravel and half-laid paving stones. The benches were either upturned or mysteriously missing entire slats. The grass—no, it was just weeds—was at least knee-high.

A solitary swing dangled from a bent frame, its chain creaking with every faint breeze like it was practicing for a horror movie sound effect. As a matter of fact, the whole playground was so rusted it had an aura of tetanus.

At least the trees were tall and offered plenty of shade from the oppressive Californian sun. It was the only silver lining.

Finch motioned for Jessie. "Lead the way."

She hesitantly nodded and then headed down one of the neglected paths. The others followed behind her without a single word of conversation. The dilapidated environment gave Finch postapocalyptic vibes, and he almost didn't want to speak because it felt like nearby raiders would hear.

However, the silence didn't last long. Jessie stopped next to a concrete bathroom building.

"The mushroom circle is just behind this building," she said.

"O-Oh, before we go any farther, I should tell you something." Liam pushed his glasses higher up on his nose as he walked over to Finch's side. "Heslop is the king of the duergar, and he's a little fussy when it comes to interacting with the non-fae."

"He's the *king*?" Enzo snapped. "And you seriously didn't think to mention that until now?"

Liam grimaced. After a flustered moment, he added, "Well, I figured Adair could handle anything—interacting with fae royalty doesn't seem like it would faze him."

"Fae royalty are extremely powerful," Jessie whispered. Her gaze wandered off to the tops of the trees overhead. "They gain extra magic from those who swear fealty to them. So, whatever pact you make, it'll be useful no matter what."

"But a *king fae* always demands outrageous things to borrow his magic," Enzo said, his irritation thick.

Bree hurried to the corner of the bathroom building. "I can't wait. Let's go, Adair! I've never met fae royalty before."

CHAPTER
NINE

Finch and the others rounded the bathroom building. Finch had mentally prepared himself to see a rotting septic tank with strange brown puddles everywhere, but what he stumbled upon was far from that.

It was beautiful.

Behind the bathrooms was a large grove. There were trees growing in a circle and providing some shade. Pillars of sparkling light shone down on the emerald grass—grass of a reasonable height, and rather lush. Small patches of white flowers littered the bases of the trees, giving them a mystical feel.

A smell of spring hung in the air, making the whole area seem lively and vibrant.

There was even a bench and a place marked for doggie deuces, but it was covered in a bed of yellow flowers.

"Oh, wow." Bree spun in a circle as she moved forward. "I like this place."

Jessie half-smiled. The first time since she arrived. "It's wyld magic. This place is full of it. The whole park used to be entirely like this, but now it's only in a few small patches, such as this one."

"This reminds me of Vera's magic," Liam whispered to himself as he glanced around.

But Finch didn't want to sit around and admire all the life floating in the air. He walked to the center of the grove and investigated the grass. Mushroom circles were always on the ground, and at least three feet in diameter—any smaller and it wasn't a gate to the fae realm.

Enzo strode over to Finch and then crossed his arms. "You find it yet?"

"It's close," Finch muttered.

Jessie pointed to some of the greener grass. "It's right there. A glamor has been placed over the circle, to hide it. If you touch any of the mushrooms with your hand, you should be able to dispel the effect."

Finch walked over to the darker grass, knelt, and then ran his hand over the lush blades. Sure enough, white-capped mushrooms popped into sight, all in a perfect circle six feet in diameter.

A fae gate.

It was a portal to the realm of fairies, elves, dwarves, sprites, pixies, brownies, and everything else classified as *fae*. It wasn't as welcoming to other types of creatures—humans, demons, demi-gods, and all the other strange things out in the world.

Pleased with how quickly this was going, Finch stood and backed out of the ring.

"All right, stand back, everyone." He motioned them all away. "I'm going to draw a Mark of Summoning on the ground, and hopefully Heslop will sense it from the other side."

Bree skipped up to the edge of the mushrooms. "Oh! I

remember this. Just like how you summoned Kull, right? You're going to have to teach me how to draw these."

"It's pretty simple," Liam chimed in. "I know plenty of summoning marks that I could teach you and—"

"Okay, okay, Papa," Bree said with a sigh. "Not right now."

Jessie's eyebrows knitted. She glanced over at Liam, frowning. "She calls you *Papa*?" she quietly asked. "Not *Dad*?"

"Vera, her mother, was raised in the UK before coming to the US to become a witch," Liam whispered. "Bree spent a few summers there, and she's used it ever since."

"Ah. The UK is lovely. I've been there a few times."

Finch knelt again and used his finger to dig furrows into the dirt. Making a mark didn't require a pen or blood—it just needed to maintain its shape somehow. Making lines in the ground was how all the original witches and wizards had done it back in the day, so Finch knew this would work. He just didn't enjoy doing it.

After drawing the circle and filling it with the ancient symbols required to get the attention of dwarves, Finch stood.

"Um, do you mind if I help?" Liam shuffled close to the mark and altered a few of the symbols. "You want something that suits the duergar more specifically—and you want to make sure to write his name if you want Heslop instead of a random dwarf."

"Thank you," Finch said.

He hadn't dealt much with dwarves. Whatever worked, worked. Liam stood, smiling, clearly pleased with his work.

Everyone backed away from the mushroom circle and held their breath. The beautiful afternoon sunshine glittered with pollen. The world inside the empty park was rather peaceful.

Finch tapped his foot. Normally, a summoning circle worked pretty quickly.

"What're you going to say to Heslop?" Enzo asked. "I mean, fae royalty *hate* being summoned."

"I'm a warlock. I'm going to offer to do something for him in exchange for some powers. Conversations like that have a way of working themselves out."

Bree stared at the mushroom circle, unblinking. "Wait, if Heslop is in England, how are we going to find him through a gate in California?"

"The fae realm has several portals, and fairy winds, and all sorts of ways to teleport, basically," Finch muttered. "If you enter a mushroom circle in England, you can—in the blink of an eye—exit through a circle in Brazil. Well, as long as you know where you're going. That's why I'm summoning Heslop *to me* instead of trying to find him."

"Oh. But then, where is he?"

Nothing happened. The gate didn't activate. No one strode out. It was just a blissful day in an abandoned park.

Enzo snorted. "You might have to go get him."

Finch groaned. Then he glowered at Enzo. "You want to go instead?"

"I'm cursed, jackass. The fae hate me. They'll try to kill me immediately."

Right. Finch knew that. He exhaled as he turned to Jessie.

"I'm irrevocably bound to a demon," she said, running her hand through her pixie-short hair. "I can't even use this gate. The only gates I can get through are the ones made by covens."

Damn.

Finch gritted his teeth as he turned to Bree.

She was a child. The fae regularly stole children and either ate them or raised them in their courts for their sick games. Finch caught his breath—Bree *wasn't* a child. She was currently on her first shark week. She was an adult as far as the fae were concerned.

Finch shook his head, dispelling the thoughts. It was still too dangerous. He couldn't let her go wandering the fae realm.

That left Liam. When Finch turned to the man, all color drained from Liam's face.

"Uh, I have a lot of allergies." Liam shrugged. "It's not a good time for me, ya know?"

"Goddammit," Finch muttered under his breath. "*Fine*. I'll go into the fae realm and search for Heslop."

He quietly cursed the situation as he removed his shoes. Fae gates were a little tricky. They were open at dusk and dawn, on full moons, or during the solstice or equinox. However, if it *wasn't* one of those times, the gate could only be entered if the person walked barefoot into the center, with the intent to travel to the fae realm.

"Can I go with you?" Bree asked.

"No," Finch drawled.

"But you might need my help."

"I don't need any more unnecessary bullshit in my life. If you get kidnapped—"

"You can just reset everything," Bree interjected.

Both Liam and Jessie stared, their gazes intense. They said nothing, but Finch already knew they were piecing things together from Bree's many cryptic comments.

He gave the little girl *the look*, and she squished her mouth shut and made a motion to zip up her lips and lock them tight.

"Wait here," Finch told her.

Once his shoes were off, Finch pulled out his phone.

12:33 p.m.

The park was quiet, and seemed to be a safe place. In

order to make sure he could try the conversation as many times as needed, without having to redraw the circle or enter the park, Finch decided to re-mark the time.

He didn't like doing it too often, but since he wasn't chasing a murderer, he figured it would be fine.

Then Finch walked into the mushroom circle. He inhaled and then exhaled, and the sweeping magic of the fae swirled around him. It was warm, like the California summer heat, but then it faded into the cool chill of autumn. When Finch blinked, he was no longer in McKinley Park.

He had entered the fae realm.

The sky was impossible hues of pink, gold, and turquoise. The trees stretched taller than in the park, their bark shimmering with veins of light, as though they carried starlight within. Leaves whispered, not with the wind, but with words Finch couldn't quite make out—mocking, perhaps, or simply gossiping about the human idiot who'd blundered into their realm.

It was more a vast forest than a simple human park, and Finch stepped forward, painfully aware of the moss squishing between his bare toes.

The air tasted sweet and sharp, like honey laced with citrus, and every breath left him slightly dizzy. Finch knew he couldn't stay here long, or else he would start to act funny—similar to how humans acted when they were drunk.

Fortunately, dwarves stepped out from behind the magnificent trees—at least ten of them.

Finch held up his hands. "King Heslop?"

A duergar stepped into the moss-covered clearing, his heavy boots crushing everything underfoot.

His inky-black beard, long and woven with beads of what could only be described as *ominous metals*, caught the glimmering light of the mystic sky as though mocking lesser facial hair everywhere. His eyes, bright and calculating, flicked over the scene before him.

He stood four feet high, but was basically three feet wide with muscle and covered in heavy armor. The duergar's whole outfit appeared to be crafted of dark metals that didn't so much shine as they drank the light around them, and it clanked faintly with each of his steps.

On his head, he wore a hat made of dark green moss stuck with a blue feather.

"I am Heslop, King of the Simonside Dwarves," the duergar stated.

His ash-gray skin and onyx eyes were so stone-like that Finch could've sworn the man had been birthed by a mountain.

Finch bowed his head and stood straight. "I'm Adair Finch, Warlock for Hire."

"Are you the one who drew a summoning circle to call for me? A circle in the *human realm*?"

"I am," Finch said. "I'm in need of—"

"We can smell the demonic and cursed magic from here," one of the other nine duergar shouted. The man who had shouted wore similar armor, but was carrying a crossbow already loaded with a bolt.

He had it pointed at Finch.

Heslop grunted and then grazed his fingertips over the blue feather on his hat. "You have set up a trap, warlock— but you cannot deceive ol' Heslop."

"Wait," Finch said, lifting his hands higher. "I can explain."

Much to his surprise, because it *never* went Finch's way, Heslop tensed, held up a fist, and the nine duergar guards took a step backward. When he lowered his hand, he snorted. "Well, go on, warlock. Explain."

Finch exhaled and relaxed at the same time, unable to stop himself from smiling. Finally! Someone reasonable. "Okay, this isn't a trap. The demonic and cursed magic are from associates of mine—they didn't want the fate they currently have. I'm actually trying to help them. I don't know if I can cure them, but—"

"And you've come here for my assistance," Heslop said, smiling wide. "O-ho! I see now. It all makes sense."

"Uh, no." Finch lowered his hands. "I actually came here to bargain for your magic. I need to repel *metal*. Bullets, really."

Heslop narrowed his eyes. "You don't want help with the curses? Or demons?"

"Can you cure lycanthropy?"

"I can behead a wolf with a single swing."

"My werewolf is housetrained," Finch quipped. "No need for beheadings."

"Ha!" Heslop pointed and then waggled his thick finger. "In the Realm of the Fae, we still follow the old rules. And the old rules say you shan't allow curse carriers to live."

"Good thing he's not here, then."

"Papa!" someone shouted, shattering the conversation. "Is it safe to come out yet, Papa? I want to meet the warlock who was trying to kill you!"

CHAPTER
TEN

Heslop groaned. "It's never safe in the company of humans, daughter. And reveal yourself before you embarrass me any further."

From behind a thick tree with bark the color of night, a smaller duergar emerged—though *smaller* was relative. She had the same ash-gray skin as her father and hair like obsidian, braided intricately with shards of dark crystals that caught the light like they were hoarding it. No beard, just a face still chubby with baby fat.

Her armor was lighter but no less menacing, and she carried herself with the kind of confidence only someone who has never truly been challenged can manage.

When she reached her father, Finch could tell she was three feet tall, instead of her father's mighty four.

"Warlock, this is my daughter, heir to my title and magic." Heslop motioned to the girl. "You may address her as Princess Agneth."

"It's a pleasure," Finch muttered, half bowing his head.

"Papa, he doesn't appear to be very dangerous," the girl

duergar said, eyeing Finch. "You said warlocks were unpredictable. This one looks like he might carry business cards."

"You should listen to your father," Finch drawled. Warlocks could be bonded with anything—have any magic, including those found only in the darkest corners of the world—but he wasn't about to explain that.

She turned to Heslop with an expectant glare. "Well?"

"Well, *what*, Agneth?" Heslop asked.

"Aren't you going to behead him?"

"What was that?" Finch snapped, already tense. He inched backward, closer to the gate.

"You said you would behead him," Agneth said as she stomped a foot. "I want to see human blood spilt across our realm. It's been decades since we've properly watered this forest with crimson."

Heslop huffed and stroked his beard. "The warlock isn't here to kill me. He wants magic to repel bullets."

"*Bullets*?" Agneth asked.

"Yes, humans are kings of invention, and even without a hint of magic, they have devised ways to kill each other in an instant. Bullets are projectiles that put most evocations to shame."

"How droll." Agneth threw back some of her long, braided hair. "I say we behead him anyway. He didn't offer me a proper greeting when we met, and I don't appreciate his casual garb. How dare this human summon us. How dare he."

"I suppose," Heslop drawled.

Finch sardonically shrugged. "Really? That's it? You're going to sentence me to death because she doesn't like my outfit?"

"What can I say." Heslop chortled as he stroked his beard. "I have a soft spot for lil princesses. I'm sorry, warlock

—but you must've known fae royalty don't take kindly to being summoned."

The click of a crossbow reached Finch's ears right as he activated his magic.

The world around him ground to a standstill. Three crossbow bolts, each sharp and coated in a substance Finch knew would incapacitate him, were held in suspended animation, all inches from his chest.

This wasn't the first time Finch had experienced the realm of the fae—and this wasn't even the first time he had been shot at moments after entering it. He sighed as the colors drained from the realm of magic, and silently thanked Chronos he could instantly eject himself from such terrible situations.

When the shapes of the world finally faded, Finch blinked.

He was back in McKinley Park, standing before the mushroom circle.

12:33 p.m.

"Is everything okay?" Bree asked.

Enzo stepped forward. "What happened?"

Liam and Jessie, perpetually confused, lifted their eyebrows and remained silent. Finch silently cursed under his breath. He had drawn the Mark of Chronos on Bree and Enzo *before* he marked the time, which meant that—until the mark was removed—they would *always* remember when he rewound time.

It wasn't bad, per se, but it was annoying. Sometimes he liked to rewind time without anyone knowing. Unfortunately, that wouldn't be the case for a short while. At least until the ink from the markers wore off their skin.

"I'm fine," Finch said. "I made a tactical error."

"You haven't done anything," Liam stated, confused.

Finch sarcastically shrugged. "I made a tactical error in

my imagination." Then he pointed at Bree. "You—with me. You get to go."

Sucking in her breath in the longest gasp ever, Bree dramatically hopped to his side. It was cute, but Finch found it difficult to be amused by anything today. He was already on the world's longest side quest for one specific magical enhancement, and he still had to find Maldonado.

"Wait!" Liam stepped forward. "Are you... certain?"

"She'll be fine," Finch stated.

But then Enzo stepped forward as well, his arms crossed. "Really, Adair? The fae realm is unpredictable. Anything could happen."

"I've got this under control."

Bree rolled her eyes. "Since when did I get *three* papas?" She offered both Liam and Enzo a frown, and the two men backed away.

"Take off your shoes," Finch said, snapping his fingers at Bree.

She threw off her footwear and then spent a moment flexing her toes on the grass. "Now what?"

"Imagine you're going to find the land of the fairies when you walk into the mushrooms." Finch went first. "And don't freak out once you get to the other side."

Warm fae magic swirled around him, fading quickly to a cool autumn breeze. When Finch blinked, he was once again in the fae realm.

Bree appeared by his side a moment later. She fluttered her eyes open and then craned her neck as she took in all the sights. The strangely colored sky. The impossibly tall trees. The glittering vines.

Watching Bree, with her mouth hung open and her eyes wide, reminded Finch of his first time seeing the other-worldly lands. He had been impressed, too. He had almost forgotten what it felt like, but when he observed Bree, it all came rushing back to him.

This place *was* beautiful.

"The air tastes sweet," Bree said, smacking her lips once, her brow furrowed.

"Yeah, try not to breathe too deep," Finch quipped. "You're a lightweight, so we shouldn't stay here long."

Ten duergar stepped out from behind the trees. Many carried crossbows, but only one stepped forward. It was King Heslop, and this time, Finch was prepared to greet him.

"Salutations, King Heslop," Finch said, bending to one knee. "I am Adair Finch, Warlock for Hire, here seeking your aid in matters most dire."

He hated speaking this way. He hated formalities. But he swallowed his pride and did whatever was necessary to get out of the fae realm alive—and with the magic he wanted. After all, if Heslop didn't make a pact with him, what was his Plan B? He didn't currently have one.

Bree fidgeted with her hands before mimicking Finch. "My name is Bree Blackstone, Warlock-in-Training. Nice to meet you." She also knelt onto one knee and then bowed her head.

The mighty duergar king marched across the moss-covered ground until he was only a few feet from Finch. Then he waved his hand, motioning for everyone to stand. Finch and Bree got to their feet.

"You two drew a summoning circle to call for me? A circle in the *human realm*?" King Heslop folded his arms over his chest.

"You may have sensed demonic and cursed magic from beyond the mushroom circle," Finch immediately said, heading off the conversation. "But they are my poor compatriots, afflicted with terrible fates outside their control. I left them behind because I wish to make a pact with you—a pact to repel bullets and all other manner of metal."

Bree nodded along with his statement. "It's all true," she added, like she was determined to help in some way.

"O-ho! I see. I never expected to meet such an intriguing warlock," Heslop said, stroking his beard, one eyebrow raised.

"Intriguing?" Finch asked.

"What kind of warlock brings along their young apprentice, asking for specific magics, pulling behind him a gaggle of cursed and demonic wards? Is *intriguing* the correct word? Perhaps *chaotic*." Heslop chortled. "Back in the day they'd call you a loon, I daresay."

"Today we say *unhinged*," Bree said.

Heslop's eyes twinkled as he smiled. "Ah, yes. My lil princess will love to hear what words humans are thinking up next. Your weird antics delight her."

As if summoned by a mere mention, the girl shouted, "Papa! Don't tell them my secrets!"

"You must have a soft spot for your princess," Finch whispered.

Heslop kept his smile as he said, "Come, daughter! Introduce yourself."

Just as Heslop's daughter stepped out from behind a tree, Finch knelt again. Bree followed along, eagerness in all her motions. When Agneth had crossed the grove, she came to a stop by her father. It was only then that Finch and Bree stood.

"She's beautiful," Finch said. "A worthy heir to your title and magic."

Agneth's ash skin darkened on her cheeks. She threw back some of her black hair and then turned to Bree. "Oh, I didn't realize you were important enough to have an apprentice." She inclined her head. "You may both address me as Princess Agneth."

"Oh, Adair is super important," Bree said, standing a little taller. "He's the best warlock in the world—which means I'm going to be equally great one day!"

Agneth's eyes widen. "The *best*? He wears such plain attire... but perhaps that is to hide his true identity. Yes, a very fae-worthy tactic. Clever." She gently clapped her hands.

Already, Finch knew this interaction was better. Heslop and his daughter were nothing but smiles. No mentions of beheadings, no aggravation. Determined not to redo this conversation a third time, Finch mirrored their happy expressions.

"King Heslop, please allow me to make a pact with you."

The duergar snorted and then waved his hand. "Ah, yes. The reason for your summons. Very well, warlock. I will lend you a bit of my power, but in return, you must—"

"Agree to join my stable," Agneth interjected. She placed her hands on the sides of her cheeks and stared up at Finch through her eyelashes. "All royal male duergar have impressive concubines of all varieties of fae. I simply must outdo them, and what a better way than having *the most powerful* warlock at my beck and call?"

"Stable?" Bree asked, confused.

"*No*," Finch answered, speaking over Bree, ready to abandon this whole endeavor. "I won't—"

Heslop shook his head, the metal in his beard clanking against his chest plate. "Absolutely *not*. Firstly, he's a human. Secondly, you're too young, you know that. Thirdly, he's a *warlock*. They're unpredictable."

"I'm already two hundred and twenty-two," Agneth said, whining. "That's plenty old, Papa!"

"In seventy-eight more years, we'll circle back to this conversation, but not a year sooner, do you understand me?"

Agneth huffed as she crossed her arms. Then she dramatically turned her back to her father—a major sign of disrespect for most fae. Finch stiffened, wondering if Heslop was a parent who believed in corporal punishment.

Heslop exhaled and then turned his back to his own daughter. Half facing Finch, he rolled his hand to motion for the conversation to continue. "If you wish for my magic, you must do me a favor, warlock."

"What kind of favor?" Finch quietly asked.

"You must assassinate the king of the ruby dwarves. He is without heir, and once he's gone, I will take his hills for my own."

Bree gasped—but she didn't say anything. She turned to Finch, holding her breath.

This was a common request for fae royalty. They *always* wanted someone dead for some reason. It was to avoid all-out war. If Heslop killed the king of the ruby dwarves, *all* the dwarven tribes would be up in arms. But if Finch did the deed, and Heslop just happened to swoop in and claim territory, there wouldn't be such an uproar.

Fortunately, Finch knew better than to get involved in fae politics.

"Your magic isn't worth the lifelong vendetta I'll carry," Finch snapped. "If I do this for you, every ruby dwarf, from now until I'm dead, will hunt me. This pact isn't equal, and I reject it."

"You can do that?" Bree whispered.

"Never accept their first offer," he murmured back.

Heslop gritted his teeth so hard the noise echoed throughout the mystical grove. After pursing his lips for some time, he said, "Your rejection has merit. Very well, if you want my magic, you must provide me a vial of your blood."

Finch pointed at the duergar. "Listen—I'm not going to take a lifelong penalty for a sample of your magic. I know you fae will use my blood against me. You'll concoct some sort of brew to force me to comply, basically enslaving me. I'm not ignorant of your tactics."

Heslop inhaled and then fiercely exhaled. "*You* have come to *me*, warlock. I was not in search of some human to do my bidding. If you want my magic, the price may be steeper than you originally anticipated."

"I'm the most powerful warlock, remember?" Finch said with a half smile, motioning to Bree, who had made the claim. "Surely you can think of a task I'm capable of carrying out. One that won't brand me an assassin and enemy to a whole race of fae."

Heslop mulled over the request, his gaze growing distant as he turned inward. Bree held her hands together, watching him contemplate the request, but Finch wasn't as patient. He was half tempted to leave the fae realm, just so he could wait at *Nico's Brew*. Why did the fae always take so long to do anything? Their long-lived lives meant nothing was an emergency. Everything could be handled in a slow and methodical manner.

"I have it," Heslop finally said. "I will grant you my magic on one condition..."

CHAPTER
ELEVEN

ing Heslop stroked his long black beard. "You must craft me a firearm—one imbued with magic. You will present it to me within one full year has passed. Seems fitting for magic that will make you bulletproof, does it not?"

A gun?

Finch wasn't a gunsmith, but he knew how to imbue magic into already built firearms. Which meant he just needed to buy or find one that would be suitable for a king. This was an irritating pact, because it would require him to do a lot of things he didn't normally engage in, but it was a much more reasonable task than the others Heslop had mentioned.

"Do you have a specific caliber in mind?" Finch asked.

"O-ho! A question I don't have an answer to. All I want is a firearm fit for a king."

Bree leaned over to Finch. "When you summoned Kull, you accepted her first offer."

"I know," Finch quietly said with a sigh. He hadn't been intending on keeping Kull's pact. He had intended to rewind time at some point and undo the pact, so he hadn't cared how outrageous it was.

But this was different. Finch was fairly certain he was going to keep this magic for a while. He definitely needed to make sure he could follow through on the obligation.

"Very well," Finch said. "I accept the terms. I'll bring you a gun worthy of fae royalty."

"Then we have a deal!" Heslop chortled and then held out his right hand, palm facing the sky.

Finch placed his hand on top of Heslop's. To his surprise, dwarven hands were wider than a human's. The fingers were shorter and thicker, though. Heslop's were also calloused.

Before Finch accepted Heslop's magic, he exhaled, and Kull's trickster magic left him. It felt like popping his back, after it had been stiff for a long while.

Then, a surge of magic pulsed between Finch and the duergar king, linking them together like pieces of a chain. At the core of Finch's being, he felt the tie—the shackle. After another moment, his sight darkened, but it returned as quickly as it had gone.

When Finch next inhaled, power surged through his entire body, starting from his eyes. His nostrils filled with the scent of iron, and his muscles felt tighter, yet somehow more limber.

Finch pulled his hand from Heslop's.

"My magic is more than just *bulletproof* defenses," Heslop said. "It's the control of metal itself. You and the veins of the world are one. And since my magic is tied to your eyes, you must visualize what it is the metal can do for you. Do you understand?"

"I do."

Heslop stroked his beard. "Ah, now that you have a piece of my kingdom with you..." Heslop waggled a finger.

"I should warn you, that if any of the ruby dwarves meet you, they won't hesitate to strike you down."

Finch rubbed his right wrist. "You specifically waited until after we made the pact to tell me?"

"That's just messed up," Bree said. She crossed her arms. "Can they do that, Adair? Withhold important information like that?"

"The fae often do," he muttered, not surprised at all by Heslop's warning.

In truth, Finch had already known something like this would happen. The fae were rather... territorial. They held long grudges and hated humans who intervened in their affairs. Finch was fairly certain that *all other dwarves* were going to hate him from now on.

Well, so long as he had Heslop's magic. Once he completed the pact and let it go, Finch suspected no one would care then.

Agneth giggled as she stared up at Finch. "I can't wait to see you again, warlock."

"We depart at once," Heslop said. "Come, daughter. We have important business to attend to before this year's Midsummer Gala."

The many duergar positioned around the grove stepped back behind trees. Heslop and his daughter turned on their heels and practically glided over the moss-covered clearing. Once they turned around a tree trunk, they were gone as well.

Leaving just Finch and Bree standing in front of a mushroom circle.

"Do you know a lot about guns?" Bree asked.

"I know enough," Finch replied, his attention on the spot where the fae king had disappeared. He was worried they were still being watched. It felt as though eyes were upon them.

"What's a *caliber*? You asked the king about it."

"I was asking what kind of bullets he wanted to fire," Finch absentmindedly muttered. "The larger the caliber, the bigger and heavier the bullet."

Bree nodded along with his words. "Wow. Really? I thought all bullets fit into all guns."

Finch snorted back a laugh. He glanced down at her, his eyebrow raised. "Why would you think that?"

Bree shrugged. "I dunno. Video games."

"Well, *no*. Not all bullets fit every gun. Some are longer. Some have buckshot. Some explode."

"Some *explode?*" Bree gasped the last part.

She was acting... a little more excitable than normal. Finch exhaled. They had been in the fae realm long enough. Even if someone was watching, they needed to leave. Fast.

"C'mon." Finch took her shoulder and walked her back through the mushroom circle. The tug of magic brought them both back to Earth, the transition smooth and easy, but the scents of McKinley Park weren't as sweet or comforting as the fae realm.

Finch grabbed his socks and shoes and quickly tugged them over his feet. Bree put her socks on, but then stumbled with her shoes, almost falling over.

"How was it?" Enzo barked, glaring daggers at Finch. "Did you get the magic you needed?"

Finch nodded. "Thanks to Bree, everything went smoothly."

"Oh, I'm so glad you're both unharmed. I was worried." Liam walked over to his daughter and offered her a smile. "Are you okay, sweetie? You look... uh..."

Bree fell onto her butt and then giggled. "Wow. Do you see this, Adair? Look!" She waved her hand in front of her face, her eyes barely focusing. "I have, like, an afterimage. My hand... I have *many* hands. Weird."

Before Finch could respond, his phone buzzed. He reached into his pant pocket and glanced at the screen. Kull was calling. And according to his phone, she had called five other times before that. Was she in trouble?

Finch held up a finger as he answered.

"The air in the fae realm acts like alcohol when humans breathe it," Jessie said to Liam, keeping her voice low.

"My daughter is *drunk*?" Liam half-shouted, his tone indignant.

Finch turned his back to them. "Hello?"

"*Bree is drunk*?" Kull asked from the other end of the phone call. "Adair, what's going on?"

"Everything is fine. Why did you call so many times? Are you in trouble? Do you need something?"

"It'll wear off in fifteen to thirty minutes," Jessie reassuringly whispered.

Kull's voice, beautiful and full of life, was laced with a hint of concern. She half-chuckled as she said, "Adair, you released my magic. I tried calling you, and you didn't answer. I'm worried."

"I was just in the fae realm," Finch said. "No reception. I'm sorry."

"Wait... Are you on another adventure? *Without me?*"

"I've been working since you left for L.A. That's what I do. Did you think I was just going to vacation while you were away?"

"I thought you'd give me a call if you were about to do something exciting! You dropped my magic and gained something else? This must be super important." The hurt in Kull's voice quickly faded when she added, "I'll be there in a few hours."

"It takes six hours to drive from L.A. to Stockton," Finch snapped. "Don't bother, Kull. We have this under control. Just keep filming your YouTubes or your TikToks or whatever you do."

"I'll fly. Stockton has an airport."

"Do. Not. Fly here. Kull, I'm serious, I'm almost done with this. You know how I operate."

Enzo leaned over. "Tell Kull I said hi."

"Oh, is that Enzo?" Kull asked. *"Hi, Enzo!"* she yelled, hurting Finch's ear. He held his phone away from his head. *"I can't wait to see you again! I'll be there later tonight!"*

"Are you hearing any of the words coming out of my mouth?" Finch sardonically asked.

Kull laughed as she replied, "I heard them, but even though I'm human now, I'm still a little bit mischief spirit—and you can't control mischief spirits. That's just the rules. I didn't write them."

Finch pinched the bridge of his nose. "Kull—"

"Besides, I have something super important I need to talk to you about, and now that you don't have my magic, I think now is the best time to have this conversation. So, I'm definitely going to be there later tonight. Got it? No more arguing—I hate arguing."

"You can talk to me on the phone," Finch said. "You can tell me whatever you need to right now, in fact."

"Uh, no. This requires a face-to-face talking. See you soon!"

Beep.

The call ended.

Finch deeply sighed as he glanced at the clock.

12:57 p.m.

He slipped his phone back into his pocket. He had missed Kull, and he was happy to see her again, but he was actively worried about Maldonado's thugs. What if they were still prowling around Stockton when she arrived? Finch silently promised himself he would have everything wrapped up with the goons before Kull made her appearance on the scene.

Which meant he needed to kick things into high gear.

"Enzo, you're with me," Finch said. "Liam, you stay here with Bree and Jessie. I seriously doubt anyone is going to come looking for you in a closed park."

"Wait!" Bree held up a hand, but she still hadn't managed to stand. "I'm your apprentice. You can't leave me."

"I'm going to fight a bunch of idiots with guns," Finch said as he walked around the side of the bathroom building. "It's best you wait here. Trust me on this."

"Ah…"

Enzo leapt to Finch's side and walked with him through the rundown park. He kept his hands in the pockets of his sweatpants, but he walked with purpose. His bald head reflected some of the oppressive sunlight once they were out of the shade of the trees.

"You need to test out your magic before you have to use it on some thugs?" Enzo asked.

"I have this under control," Finch muttered.

"It seems risky to just use it without practice. Don't warlocks get better with their magic over time? Constantly improving?"

"I know how to use magic tied to my eyes," Finch said matter-of-factly.

"Didn't you tell me that you couldn't rewind time if you died?"

Finch was about to make a sarcastic retort, but he stopped himself. That was true. If he died, there would be no rewinding time. Despite that, he was still confident. He had used similar magics in the past. It was like riding a bike —wasn't it?

Before Finch reached the fence, his phone rang a second time. He answered without even looking at the screen.

"Adair Finch speaking," he said.

"It's me again," Kull replied with a laugh.

Sighing, Finch set his phone to speaker. Enzo glanced over and smiled. He had missed Kull, too, it seemed.

"Why are you calling again, Kull?" Finch asked.

"Uh, well, I wanted to know who you bonded with. I mean, they're not cooler than a mischief spirit, right?"

The odd nervousness in her voice almost made Finch chuckle. What was this? Jealousy? Finch had made pacts with hundreds of creatures, and *none* of them had ever been upset when he dropped their magic for something else.

"He made a pact with fae royalty," Enzo replied. "So, yeah, much cooler than a spirit."

Finch shot him an irritated glance as they continued to the edge of the park.

Enzo shrugged. "I calls it like I sees it."

"Some junior assistant you are," Finch quipped.

"Uh, so what did your pact entail?" Kull asked over the phone.

Finch was almost to the fence. He stopped, sighed, and then said, "I have to deliver the duergar king a magical gun worthy of a king. I have a year, so it's nothing to worry about."

Kull nervously chuckled. "Right. Okay. I understand."

Then she hung up. Odd. Finch kept his phone out, wondering if she'd call a third time.

She didn't.

Then they reached the fence, and Finch stepped through it onto the sidewalk. Before anything else happened, Finch decided to mark the time.

1:02 p.m.

CHAPTER
TWELVE

R e-marking the time was like his *save point*—he didn't want to have to do the conversation with the duergar king all over again, or his multiple conversations with Kull. After all, he wasn't trying to catch a murderer, or gather evidence as quickly as possible, unlike the last few cases he'd had. This was different. He could advance his mark on the time with each perfected encounter.

Finch got into his vehicle, and Enzo casually slid into the passenger's seat. Finch drove his Toyota away from the park, not wanting to waste any more time now that he was bulletproof. Enzo barely had enough time to buckle himself in before Finch was already on the road.

Kull's phone calls weighed on his mind. Wasn't she going to speak to him face to face soon enough? Why call if that was the case? Finch shook it from his mind and focused on the road.

The drive went by in silence. Enzo stared out the window, his own thoughts seemingly far from his body.

Then they arrived at the parking lot with the thugs.

Finch found a parking spot and turned off the car. He was parked all the way across the hot, dry lot, far from the two armed men still waiting in their own vehicle.

"Can you transfer some of your bulletproof magic to me?" Enzo asked.

"I'm not entirely certain," Finch muttered.

Enzo whirled around in his seat so he could glare at Finch. "So you *should have* practiced. Goddammit, Adair."

"Listen, this is just faster. I'll master all the ways to use this later. Right now, I'm going to walk over, rough these guys up, and then get some information from them. You watch the car."

Enzo snorted. "You remember I used to be a cop, right? I've had to handle worse situations."

"Again, it's just easier if I don't have to worry about anyone else getting shot." Finch opened the car door and stepped out. "This won't take long."

There were no further arguments, which Finch appreciated. He closed the door and crossed the unreasonably hot parking lot until he arrived at the driver's side door of his target.

1:15 p.m.

The man in the driver's seat—the one wearing a bright white shirt, baggy pants, and more tattoos than reasonable for one human being—glanced up. His mouth hung open for a long moment before he rolled down his window a tiny bit.

"*What the fuck do you want?*" he shouted.

"I want to know who you work for," Finch stated. "I'm here to give your boss a message—leave Jessica alone. Or else."

The second guy was the first one to exit the car. His black shirt and gold jewelry almost made this rumble in the parking lot look like B-roll for a rap video. Both men wore sunglasses, but they both took them off and tucked them away.

When the driver got out, he already had his gun in hand, the Colt Emiliano Zapata. Finch briefly thought about taking one for the duergar king. It was a needlessly fancy handgun, with all sorts of detailing on the side.

But it didn't feel like a weapon fit for royalty—not after so many street gangs had made it their mascot.

"Do you know who you're messin' with?" the white-shirted buffoon asked.

Finch ignored him. Instead, he activated his magic. Using abilities tied to the eyes core meant he had to visualize what he wanted the magic to do. Seeing the gun made it easier. He pictured the bullets, the alloys most guns were made of, and kept it all visualized as the conversation progressed.

So long as Finch pictured the bullets bending to his will, they would. Which meant he had to keep that in mind for as long as he was around Maldonado's goons.

If he slipped up, and stopped thinking about the metal, he could accidentally get himself shot, which he wanted to avoid at all costs.

"Did you hear me, *old man*?" the thug barked. Then he shoved the barrel of his handgun into Finch's chest. "Do you know who you're messin' with?"

"A couple of midwits at the bottom of their criminal hierarchy?" Finch quipped.

The black-shirted goon narrowed his eyes, his last two braincells fighting for dominance. He processed the conversation like English was his third language.

"He called us *midwits*?" he finally said. "Fuck this guy."

The other thug snorted back a laugh. "You're right." He took a step back and kept his gun pointed at Finch's chest.

Then the man pulled the trigger.

The sound wasn't a mere *bang*, but a violent exhalation of power that shoved everything else aside. The vibration roared through Finch's chest, rattling his ribs and stealing the rhythm of his heart. His ears reverberated, ringing with the sharp echo that followed.

But half a second later, a busted bullet clinked onto the parking lot asphalt.

It wasn't the metal that killed people when it came to bullets—it was the force from which they were fired. Fortunately, the duergar king's magic redirected everything connected to the metal. Once Finch visualized it, the bullet was brought to a halt by fae sorcery and shattered, as though a whispered command of "no" had been enough to strip it of all its violence.

Finch's skin remained unbroken, though his pulse still raced from the raw, primal energy of the gunshot. Once he mastered this magic a little better, perhaps he could even redirect the bullet and its force, but that was something to practice later.

As the two goons stared, wide-eyed, at the hole in Finch's shirt, a cocktail of gunpowder odors wafted through the air.

"Man, you somehow screw up everything," the black-shirted guy said as he pulled his own Zapata from the waistband of his pants.

Without any warning or preamble, the man shot three times at Finch. While the sound was just as loud as the first time, Finch was prepared. His magic protected him from the bullets—they all hit the asphalt afterward, smashed as though they had been fired directly into a steel wall.

Finch's clothing wasn't within the purview of his new magic, however, so his shirt was startling to resemble Swiss cheese. Fortunately, he didn't care. It was more amusing to watch the look on both the thugs' faces.

Once the goon was done shooting, Finch just stood there.

The two idiots stared, taking in the fact that Finch had suffered no injuries. Finch then casually slipped his hands into his pockets.

"That's all you got?" Finch asked.

The black-shirted thug lowered his weapon. "What is this Superman bullshit?"

His companion took another couple steps back, his breathing shallow. "I'm out. I don't get paid enough for this shit."

"*You can't nope outta here*. We have a job to do!"

But the white-shirted goon had already whirled on his heel. He took off running—he didn't even try to get back in his vehicle.

Before his accomplice wised up and followed suit, Finch lunged for him. The black-shirted thug only had a fraction of a second to react. He pulled the trigger of his gun again, but the only damage it did was to Finch's ears when the *crack* rang out.

Finch slammed the man against the hood of his car. Then he ripped the handgun from his grasp and tossed it away.

The thug tried to wrench Finch's arm to the side, but Finch activated his other magic—Ke-Koh's flames. A burst of fire erupted from his palms and scorched some of the thug's forearm.

The man screamed, and then Finch slammed him onto the asphalt, back first. The man's head bounced once after hitting the hard surface, and his gaze was unfocused for a moment, but he quickly regained it.

"What the fuck?" he asked as Finch pinned him with a knee to the chest.

"Where's your boss?" Finch asked.

The man blinked one eye and then the other, completely out of sync. "Who are *you*?"

"I'm Adair Finch, Warlock for Hire."

"I—"

Finch grabbed the gold chain around the man's neck and lifted him up slightly. "Where's your boss? Tell me, or I'll burn you so bad they're only going to find your ashes."

"I-I... All right. It's Maldonado. The wizard. I work for him."

"No, dumbass," Finch said through gritted teeth. "Who do you answer to directly? I need to find whoever is leading Maldonado's hunt for Jessie. I need them to clear out of Stockton."

The thug blinked again. After a breath, he regained more of himself. "Maldonado. I answer straight to him. He's... He's here. Looking for Jessica himself."

"*What*?" Finch asked, his voice barely audible.

No. That couldn't be right. Maldonado ran most of his operations out of Mexico City. There was no way he was in California—and it was damn near an impossibility that he would be in Stockton.

The goon brought a hand to the back of his head. He touched his hair and then glanced at his fingers, as though he had thought he might find blood.

"You answer directly to Maldonado?" Finch relaxed his grip on the necklace, and eased the man back down onto the ground. "And he's here? *Where?*"

"He's holed up in his vacation house. In some fancy area called *Spanos Park*, or something." The thug exhaled. "He's paying quite a bit to bring that dumb bitch in. That's why he's here. He said he doesn't want her to get away this time. He wants this witch hunt over for good."

CHAPTER
THIRTEEN

Spanos Park was the rich section of Stockton, complete with gigantic houses and a massive golf course. It was the pet project of a billionaire real estate developer—Alexander Spanos—and considered the best area to live within the city.

Finch had been there a handful of times, but only to pass through.

After a long exhale, Finch got off the thug and brushed himself off. Enzo crossed the parking lot a moment later, jogging over with a serious expression. Once he was close, he grabbed the black-shirted goon and dragged him to his feet.

"What's your name, son?" Enzo asked.

The thug sneered. "What're you? *A cop?*"

"Not anymore," Enzo snapped. "Which means if you don't cooperate, I'll just beat your ass."

When Enzo cracked his knuckles, he also flexed his bulging arms, his tank top barely contained all his muscles. He had the type of physique that said, "*Yes, I could suplex an oven, why do you ask?*"

The thug, intelligently, took in all the information and

quickly nodded. "My name is Vince, but people on the street call me *Shredder*."

Enzo snorted back a laugh. "Did you think up that name when you were thirteen?"

"More like thirteen beers deep," Vince muttered. "I thought it was cool."

"Uh-huh." Enzo turned to Finch. "And this went better than I expected. You really do know how to just *use magic* you've never trained with before. Most warlocks have to, ya know, fiddle."

Finch shrugged. "This isn't my first rodeo." He rubbed his ear. "But I probably shouldn't just run head-first into every gun we see."

Enzo snorted. "Probably."

"All right, *Vince*," Finch said, "you're going to take us to Maldonado's house, got it? Do as I want, and we'll let you go once we get there."

"His *house*?" Enzo turned to face him. "He's here?"

Finch nodded. "Apparently."

"Feh. This just got thirty times worse."

———

1:42 p.m.

The road through Spanos Park stretched ahead like some sun-blasted purgatory, shimmering with heat waves that made it look as if the asphalt itself were melting. While most shrubs in Stockton looked like overcooked broccoli, all the greenery in Spanos Park glistened with life.

Finch drove where Vince pointed, but it was difficult, as the thug sat in the back seat with Enzo. It was safer this way —Enzo always kept one hand on the man's shoulder.

The air conditioning chugged along like an asthmatic on mile three as Finch pulled his car up to the gate of a massive estate. The black wrought-iron bars were at least seven feet tall, and the accompanying brick fence went all the way around the property.

"This is it," Vince muttered. "Maldonado stays here."

"Looks small for a wizard of his caliber," Enzo said, staring through the gate at a tiny building positioned on the other side.

"That's the pool house, *fool*. The mansion is way down the driveway and far from the street."

Enzo huffed. "What's the gate code?"

"Sixteen ten."

Finch punched in the code on the access pad, and the gates slowly groaned open. Beyond them, the driveway stretched toward a sprawling mansion. As Finch drove forward, he counted at least a dozen vehicles parked near the garage. They were all makes and models, some roughed up, some clean.

A lot of people were here, but no one was waiting outside.

Finch didn't blame them. It was too hot to have a bunch of thugs standing around out in the sun. There were likely plenty of cameras around, though. Finch almost regretted ditching Kull's mischief magic—he could've avoided most security measures if he still had it.

The mansion itself had a brick façade. It sported columns and balconies so large and spotless they probably required a whole team just to clean them. Finch suspected the house was at least ten thousand square feet. At least.

"When I first learned about wizards, I figured they'd live in ancient towers or some shit—not McMansions," Enzo said.

"Ancient towers don't have Jacuzzies," Finch quipped.

Then he killed the engine, the sudden silence filled only with the faint hum of the distant air conditioning vents. He turned to Vince, who was already sweating more than anyone sitting under a perfectly functioning AC should.

"What orders did Maldonado give you?" Finch asked. "Specifically. What were his exact words?"

Vince rubbed the side of his neck as he mulled over the question. Then he finally said, "We were supposed to find Jessica Finch and bring her back—even as a corpse. We'd get a bonus if we brought her back alive, though."

"Did Maldonado mention me?" Finch asked.

"Uh... Who are you?"

After a short sigh, Finch opened the door. "Good enough."

He had been worried Maldonado might've sent his goons out with specific instructions to harm him or to make sure he didn't get involved. Most wizards knew of the Finch brothers, after all. Well, they *had*. Finch was reminded yet again that it had been nearly a decade since he was last active in the supernatural community. Perhaps Maldonado had forgotten all about him.

Probably for the best.

Finch stepped out of the car into the unforgiving rays of the sun. Enzo and Vince exited a moment later, with Enzo firmly holding the thug by his upper arm. Together, they all walked to the front door.

It was unlocked.

Finch pushed one of the double doors inward and then walked into the mansion. Upon stepping foot into the building, he felt a wave of magic pass over him. It was a sort of suppression magic—the kind meant to trap noises and smells.

Anything that happened inside the mansion would not be heard outside, and vice versa.

To his surprise, there was no one waiting to greet them. Finch heard laughter and glasses clinking deeper within the abode, though, and decided to head toward the sounds of partying.

"Who all is here?" Enzo whispered.

Vince shrugged. "I dunno. The boss. His associates. Some other hired guns."

Enzo sneered. "What's going on? Why here?"

"I told you. The boss is on vacation." Vince shrugged. "He's enjoying himself."

Finch motioned to the nearest hallway, toward the noise. "Let's go find him."

The mansion was, in a word, excessive.

The floors were polished to the point of being reflective. Intricate patterns were carved into the surface, swirling and spiraling in ways that probably meant something profound, but mostly just made Finch worried about tripping.

Columns lined the halls, each one covered in carvings of snakes and jaguars glaring downward. The shadows they cast were dramatic, undoubtedly intentional. The occasional glint of gold broke up the gloom, decorating vases and sun disks that looked more like props from a museum than actual décor.

The walls were plastered with murals. Feathered warriors posed heroically, while Aztec priests held their arms up under bright red skies. The colors were almost too vivid —it hurt Finch's eyes to stare at any of them for too long.

When they entered a massive living room, Finch immediately spotted something odd.

Positioned in the center of the room was a stone altar squatted like a forgotten god. It was a table slab where humans would lie down to have their hearts carved out. Its surface was worn smooth in places, but the edges still bore the sharp precision of deliberate craftsmanship. Around it, the furniture—oddly modern—looked out of place.

"Jesus Christ," Enzo whispered, glaring at the altar.

"Maldonado has taken *Aztec chic* and made it his entire personality."

Above the fireplace mantel loomed a massive sculpture of an eagle eating a snake, because subtle metaphors were for the weak.

"I like it," Vince muttered. "Once I sell my crypto, I'm going to buy a crib just like this."

Enzo snorted. "Sure you are."

The living room was large enough for a whole soccer game, and Finch was intending to pass through, but the sounds of celebration were nearing. Were Maldonado and his associates heading to this very living room? Finch held his breath and glanced at his phone.

1:55 p.m.

"*Let me go*," Vince hissed. "I don't want the boss to see me like this." He tried to jerk his arm out of Enzo's grasp, but he was completely incapable. He just flailed for a moment until the far door to the living room opened.

And in strode the wizard they were looking for.

Maldonado.

Finch could tell it was him by the thick stink of magic that wafted in with the man like incense. And even if he couldn't, the man's clothing gave it away.

The foundation of Maldonado's outfit was a sleek black suit, custom-tailored to perfection. The fabric had a subtle sheen, like polished obsidian, catching just enough light to suggest luxury without crossing into gaudy. He had a toned physique—someone who took care of themselves.

His lapels were embroidered with intricate golden patterns that mimicked Aztec glyphs, but only upon closer inspection—at a distance, they simply looked like a unique, elegant design. His shirt beneath was a deep crimson, the color of dried blood, its collar sharp enough to cut.

Instead of a tie, he wore a thin gold torque around his

neck, shaped like the feathered serpent deity, Quetzalcoatl. The cuffs of his sleeves were edged with golden thread, and his cufflinks were tiny obsidian skulls, gleaming darkly whenever he moved his hands.

But beneath all the pageantry, there was no denying he was sharp. His eyes, dark and calculating, missed nothing.

Maldonado slicked back his inky hair and then glanced between Finch, Enzo, and Vince.

Five other individuals walked in behind the wizard, but two of them—in suits as well—took one look at the scene and immediately ducked out of the room.

Of the remaining three, two were gunmen—likely guards—and one was a woman in an emerald bikini. Her skin was perfectly tanned, her black hair perfectly silky, and her eyes perfectly glittering.

She was, without a doubt, beautiful beyond the norm. Only the magic of Photoshop or the fae could make a woman appear so flawless, and Finch could smell the elf on her.

"Well, what do we have here?" Maldonado asked, amusement in his dark tone. His voice had the lyrical edge of a native Spanish speaker—someone who hailed from Spain, specifically.

Finch stepped forward. There was still a gulf between them, since the living room was so massive, but Finch didn't really need to change that. He knew Maldonado had plenty of magic, and he didn't want to put himself in unnecessary danger.

"I'm Adair Finch, and I've come—"

"You?" Maldonado barked, half laughing. "*You*? You're *the* Adair Finch?"

Not bothering to hide his smile, the wizard strode into the room. His unbelievably beautiful lady walked over to the nearest couch and lay down, needlessly stretching as though she were posing for a photo shoot.

The two gunmen spread out. One went to the north wall, and the other to the southern wall. They went straight for the most shadowed areas of the room, like they were trying to melt away, out of sight, but Finch never allowed them to leave his mind.

He had to keep his visualization perfect if he wanted to maintain his bulletproof magic.

"You're not bad-looking, but I expected someone a little more... sophisticated," Maldonado said, giving Finch the once-over. He walked over to the altar in the room and stood next to it. His smile only widened, but it didn't actually reach his eyes. "You're shabby, *brujo*."

"I might be a little rusty, but I'm still the best warlock out there," Finch stated.

"Hmm. And who is your cursed associate?" Maldonado turned his sharp attention to Enzo. "I don't remember hearing that you kept pets."

Enzo growled. "My name is Elijah Harris, ex-detective for the Oakland PD. You can call me Enzo."

"And you can call me Master Wizard Alonso del Maldonado XIV, the River Coatl."

"Yeah, but what's your real name? *Todd* or *Gary* or some shit?"

Finch snapped his attention to the other man. He mouthed, "*Don't provoke him.*"

"Fine." Enzo shrugged, his grip still tight on the thug, Vince. "I'll play nice."

Maldonado never replied to Enzo. He either didn't care, or simply didn't consider werewolves people deserving of respect, which was quite common for the upper echelons of the magic-wielding community.

"Why have you come here, Adair?" Maldonado asked.

"Upset about your sister? Because you should know—*she* betrayed *me*. I was perfectly happy to make deals with her, but actions have consequences. No one double-crosses me."

Finch nodded once. "She told me what happened. I want to know what it will take to pay off whatever debt she owes you. I have money."

"It's not about *money*. I have more money than you can possibly fathom."

Maldonado strolled across the living room, inching his way closer and closer to Finch, his gaze never straying. As he neared, Finch detected a faint hint of brimstone and sulfur. Maldonado's magic was intense, but it was obvious the wizard was trying to hide it—like how a whore bathes in perfume to hide the stink of musk—and it just wasn't working.

"Is there any sort of deal we can make?" Finch asked, never moving from his spot. He wasn't about to back away from this lunatic. He was here to help Jessica, and he couldn't do that if he was on the run. "I understand Jessie took a demon from you, and that you want it back, but let's be real. Wizards are long-lived. Witches aren't. She'll die on her own, and you'll get your demon one way or another."

The reason wizards were so powerful, and feared across the supernatural world, was because they poured their magic into mortal sources. They refreshed the magic, made it new, and then return it to their cores, keeping them young. They kept coteries and close contacts, and while most people only had their five cores to fill with magic—their eyes, crown, heart, soul, and loins—wizards could use the cores of mortals to house more and more magics.

That was how wizards lived so long. Because they tethered their magic to so many beings, they leeched life from them, maintaining themselves far longer than they ever should. So long as their mortals survived—wizards often called them *servitors*—they would not only be powerful, but in their prime.

The wizard Merlin had kept the knights of the Round Table as servitors, using them all to store his magic.

Mimir had kept students in his school, up until he was beheaded, his body gifted to Odin.

Rasputin had kept his magic in the royal family of Russia, but his reputation soon caught up with him.

In addition to siphoning life from their servitors, wizards could cultivate their magic in their cores, becoming stronger and stronger. The humans received access to some of the magic as well, which was why so many of King Arthur's knights had so many miraculous stories surrounding them.

And this all had to be the case with Maldonado—the man was well over five hundred years old. He would outlive Jessie, so long as he didn't get himself and his servitors killed in dramatic fashion, so Finch was fairly certain there was *something* he could negotiate to spare Jessie the wizard's wrath.

Maldonado stopped in front of Finch, leaving just a foot of space between them.

"I love negotiating," he whispered, far too darkly for Finch's taste. "I'll allow Jessica to keep my demon, and I'll recall all my hits on her, so long as you agree to serve me in her stead."

CHAPTER
FOURTEEN

"Y ou can go fuck yourself," Finch said. He hadn't needed to mull it over—he just spoke the first words that came to mind.

"Oh, so, *you* can provoke him?" Enzo sardonically whispered.

Maldonado huffed out a laugh and then took a step back. "You and your brother were legendary nearly a decade ago. I could put your skills to real use."

But Finch didn't reply.

He couldn't allow someone like Maldonado to have access to his magic. Chronos, the Titan of Time, was thought to be dead by most individuals. No warlock—other than Finch and his brother, Carter—had ever made a pact with the titan, and Finch wanted to keep it that way. If someone like Maldonado had access to such powerful time-altering abilities...

"Your sister's life isn't very important to you, I take it." Maldonado shrugged. "I understand. Her life isn't worth much to me, either."

Finch shook his head. "I won't work for you, but surely there's something *else* you want that I can trade for Jessie?"

With casual, unhurried movements, Maldonado continued to slink away, his tone bordering on uninterested. "I need a few men assassinated. Are you willing to trade other lives for your brother's wife?"

"I'm not going to be your killer," Finch said.

"Then what good are you, *brujo*?" Maldonado slyly smiled. "I'm old enough to know that when someone has a problem with me, and they're powerful enough to be a thorn in my side—they need to be disposed of."

A man appeared next to Finch.

He hadn't teleported. He hadn't leapt down from the ceiling. The man had simply stepped out from invisibility, handgun already at Finch's temple. Within a split second, and at point-blank range, the surprise gunman pulled the trigger.

The *bang* rattled through Finch's ears, but thankfully, the bullet didn't. Finch had maintained his magic—visualizing the metal being repelled from his body—and the bullet bounced away upon fire, blowing back the handgun.

The shooter was some infernal-blooded human, and when his gun blew back, he managed to keep hold of it with supernatural strength, his red eyes flashing. He leapt away from Finch and seemingly melted from sight, wrapping himself in invisibility once more. He had only been visible for a second or two, not long enough for Finch to get a great look at him.

The two visible gunmen lifted their weapons, their aims shaky.

"Firearms aren't effective?" Maldonado tore off his black suit jacket. "Tsk. I should've known that's why you have holes in your clothes."

Finch only heard him through one ear. His other buzzed with a sort of static white noise.

The wizard threw down his coat. The moment it hit the floor, the fabric erupted into a swirling black mist, as if shadows themselves had been trapped within the threads, desperate for release. In the blink of an eye the dark cloud expanded until it filled the whole living room with darkness.

The two human gunmen opened fire. The flash of their guns' muzzles pierced the magical shadows, sparking orange for just a fragment of time.

Finch leapt in front of Vince and Enzo. He shielded his eyes, irritated by the imposed blindness. The bullets, once controlled by Finch's magic, fell to the floor, flattened or shattered.

Clawed hands reached out of the unnatural darkness and slashed Finch across his side and shoulders. The spindly fingers were familiar—they belonged to shadow imps.

Dozens of imps.

They had been hidden, just like the infernal assassin, all waiting for their master's command to strike. Their claws tore at Finch's clothing, slicing through skin and gouging muscle. It all happened so fast, Finch almost stopped his mental visualization of the metal in the room. Thankfully, he had been through worse stresses in his life.

Enraged, Finch swept his arm out to the side.

A torrent of pure white flames burst from his palm and shredded the darkness. The *whoosh* of heat and destruction rushed through the living room, incinerating more than a couple shadow imps. They had no mouths, but the way their thin bodies twisted as they turned to ash conveyed their suffering just fine.

When the fire licked the windows, they cracked or shattered. His magic spread over the furniture and up the walls, crawling across the ceiling.

A feminine scream broke through to Finch's thoughts, and he remembered there was a young woman in the living room. He instantly pulled back his magic, snuffing out the flames at the far ends.

Most of the unnatural darkness had been burned away, allowing Finch to once again see.

Enzo, bleeding from dozens of cuts, was already in his werewolf form. Pieces of shadow imp melted from his canine maw. He had been tearing them apart like only a wolf could.

Vince—poor, stupid Vince—was not safe from his boss's orders. The imps had flayed him alive. His skin was missing, as were his eyes and the tips of his fingers. Somehow, he was still squirming and alive, but not for long.

Shadow imps were cruel.

Enzo leapt at the nearest gunman. The man was flailing, trying to pat off the fire on his clothing, and never even saw the massive eight-foot-tall werewolf until it was too late.

With precision befitting a surgeon, Enzo backhanded the man so hard, the sound of cracking bones echoed through the living room.

"You're in control?" Finch quickly asked.

"I knew a fight was coming," Enzo growled.

The other half-burnt gunman shot at the wolf, his aim terrible. Enzo flew across the room and handled that thug as well, slamming the man's hand into a bookshelf so hard the piece of furniture was rendered useless.

A few remaining shadow imps attempted to draw their claws through Enzo's black fur, but Finch held out his hand and drowned them in fire. His rage was lessened, though, and with the dulled emotions came redder, cooler flames.

With the immediate threats dealt with, the flames slowly died. The smoke and ash almost smelled like a BBQ, but the lingering scent of brimstone destroyed that illusion.

Maldonado stood on the other side of the living room. That end hadn't been burned, and the couch with the woman was entirely untouched. She was trembling, her knees to her chest, her eyes large.

After a deep breath, Finch patted himself off. The imps had sliced him, and his blood ran in small rivulets down his arms before dripping off his fingers onto the scorched floor.

The invisible gunman was still in the room, Finch was certain, but he wasn't attacking. Finch maintained his visualization of metal being repelled from his body, just in case.

"That wasn't very polite," Finch angrily quipped.

"Neither was entering my house without an invitation," Maldonado casually replied.

In werewolf form, with shiny black fur and dark intelligent eyes, Enzo stepped over to Finch.

Vince, without any skin or dignity, was dead on the floor, his blood pooled around him. His body had been spared the fire, but the imps had carved him up too fast for Finch to save. They were dangerous creatures in groups, like any swarm.

"What's the plan?" Enzo whispered, his voice rough with anger, blood dripping from his injuries.

Maldonado hadn't gotten involved in the fight. He had stood away from it all, observing. Could they rush him? Kill him in an honest-to-goodness fight? Finch wasn't so sure. Finch knew next to nothing about Maldonado's personal capabilities—he knew the man dealt with magical creatures and demons. And as a wizard, Maldonado's magic was quite potent. The best way to harm him would be to know all his capabilities, his servitors, and his weaknesses, and then use that against him.

But specific weaknesses were things that wizards kept hidden at all costs. Most supernatural beings, really. Finch didn't have any of that information.

"You're making an enemy of the wrong person, Adair Finch," Maldonado said. He walked over to a nearby wine cabinet, one untouched by the chaos that had been swirling around the room a few seconds ago, and poured himself a glass of something deep red. "I wasn't the one who killed your brother."

"You're trying to kill my sister-in-law," Finch stated. "That's close enough for government work."

"If you keep this up, you're going to fail to keep her alive, too."

Finch *had* calmed himself down, but all his rage was slowly boiling back up through his chest.

Maldonado swirled his wine before taking a small sip. "Don't you want help catching your brother's murderers? I mean, they've been on the loose for ten whole years—you clearly have no idea how to track them down or hurt them. *I* know where they are. *I* know all their tricks. It's in your best interest *not* to fight me."

"I'm not going to let you kill Jessie just because you have some information."

"The coven you're after—they incubated the egg that hatched into the magic-eating god, Gixmoth the Desolate. That's the beast that ultimately got Carter Finch, isn't it? I heard it all went down in Paris."

Finch tensed, a knot forming in his gut.

It was all true. Carter had died in the catacombs under the city of Paris. Gixmoth—the monster who could nullify magic—had been the one to get him.

The coven of full moon witches had been the ones using Gixmoth, but Finch hadn't known they had hatched the thing. Was it really a god? Chronos had called himself a god, and in terms of power, he wasn't far off. Did that mean Gixmoth was just as strong as Chronos?

Finch wanted to dwell on these questions, but intrusive

thoughts and memories kept interrupting. Memories of the catacombs haunted Finch, even to this day—even though he thought he had gotten over it.

"Clara Voss, Elena Voss, Anya Falk, Mira Hartmann, and Isabella Moreau," Maldonado said, rattling off the names with a disinterested tone. "All five witches are still alive and call their coven the *Sisters of the Deavan Grimoire.*"

Finch had never heard their names.

He and Carter, along with other witches and warlocks, had been hired by the supernatural department for Paris. The Sisters of the Deavan Grimoire had been murdering magicless mortals for some sort of ritual, or perhaps to create artifacts, he wasn't entirely certain. Finch and his brother had been tasked with bringing the coven to justice.

"I heard the coven was so delighted they had killed one of the Finch brothers that they paraded the body around at one of their parties." Maldonado sipped his wine. "They decapitated his body, and then carved out his spine so they could fashion it into something. A cane, I think."

His... spine?

"*You shut your lying mouth,*" Enzo barked, his fur on end, his claws plainly visible. When he moved, it was with restrained power, like he wanted nothing more than to fly across the living room, losing all control.

Maldonado shrugged. "I wouldn't lie about something like that, dog. All I'm trying to emphasize is that it's *odd* that Adair hasn't hunted down this coven. As a matter of fact—" the wizard swirled his glass again, "—the coven relocated, and their baby god monster has been on the loose, killing and terrorizing. You could say that all those deaths are on Adair's head. If he had stopped these witches sooner, this wouldn't have happened."

That coven had killed hundreds of innocent people before Finch and his brother had gotten involved. They were powerful, and now that they were vampires, probably three times as dangerous as when they were in Paris. Not too many people would be able to stop them.

Enzo placed a canine-like hand on Finch's shoulder. "Don't listen to this fuck-face's mental gymnastics."

"Don't you want revenge?" Maldonado sounded earnestly baffled. "Surely you do, yes? Come. Let's make a deal. I have the information you want—I control the assassins after your sister—I could give you everything. Just offer me *something* of real value."

CHAPTER
FIFTEEN

"Master," the elven woman on the couch whispered. "May I go? I'm frightened and—"

"*Did I say you can speak?*" Maldonado hissed. He gave her a narrowed glare, far icier than any winter.

The beautiful woman shivered, looked away, and returned to being as silent as the furniture.

"We shouldn't make deals with a devil wearing a man's skin," Enzo said under his breath. His canine face wasn't as expressive as his human version, but when he flashed his fangs, his ears lying back, it was clear his rage was building.

"You should really keep your dog on a tighter leash." Maldonado shook his head and half laughed. "Fighting me is tantamount to suicide."

Enzo snapped his jaw and took a step forward. "You ordered a surprise attack on us, and all your little minions got their asses handed to them. You have no idea how powerful Adair is—or else you wouldn't have made such a bitch mistake."

This amused Maldonado more than irritated him. He

chortled and then shrugged before sipping his wine. "We can settle things like civilized men. I can create a spellrift right here, right now. Effortless."

A *spellrift* was a type of duel where both participants offered their soul. It was mostly used by demon- and oni-summoning lunatics who wanted to enslave infernal forces for their own twisted desires. Once a spellrift was formed, both entities who entered would have their souls tied to the other. Whoever won the duel would have control of the other. Forever.

Demons and oni happily agreed to spellrifts, as every human soul they consumed only made them stronger—and they could only consume those freely offered or won. If the demons or oni triumphed in a spellrift, they would consume the idiot who had summoned them.

Maldonado had won many spellrifts. That was how he first created his empire of crime. He relied on demons, and many other infernal beasts, to give him the edge he needed to defeat the lawful witches, warlocks, and wizards all throughout Central America.

If Finch entered a spellrift with Maldonado and then lost the fight, his soul would be forever bound to the wizard.

But if Finch won, he could force Maldonado to drop the hits on Jessie, release his demons, and even provide Finch with all the information he had on Gixmoth and the Sisters of the Deavan Grimoire.

It just required Finch to win.

"I'll do it," Finch stated.

Enzo turned on his heel. "You will?"

"Yeah." Finch walked around the muscled werewolf and then motioned for Maldonado to proceed. "C'mon. Let's go. Make your spellrift."

Maldonado's eyes lit up like a young child on Christmas morning. When he smiled, his canines seemed longer than normal, his teeth freakishly white. The man pulled a small marble from his pocket and then tossed it to the floor. It hit the semi-charred floorboards with a *thud*.

Then the marble began rolling on its own. Slowly at first, but then it picked up speed. The marble left a trail of white behind, marking the ground. It spun in a little circle, but then widened its path, writing strange words in a language unknown to Finch.

It was creating a spellrift mark—drawing faster and faster, widening the diameter of its circle until it was about ten feet across.

"What're you so happy about?" Enzo growled.

"I've *never* been able to figure out how the Finch brothers managed to do so many miraculous things," Maldonado said with a chuckle. "For years, Adair and Carter Finch seemed able to pull off the impossible—all with the limited power of mere warlocks. Everyone had speculated they formed a pact with a god, but no one could figure out which."

It was true. Finch and his brother had kept that information hidden, even from Jessie. Only a small handful of individuals knew. And some of the fae. But the fae never gave up secrets if they could help it.

The marble continued to draw the intricate spellrift, rolling as fast as it possibly could.

"I can't wait to see what magic you have hiding up your sleeve," Maldonado said, his smile genuine. "Because once I own you, I'll also be able to sell the secret of your power—telling the world how the Finch brothers were so successful. Your hubris will make me a small fortune."

"Hubris?" Enzo asked.

"You're both fools who overvalue yourselves. You can never beat *me*. You're trash. I'm a master wizard."

"The only thing you've mastered is wasting everyone's

time with your third-rate theatrics," Enzo yelled, spittle flying from his fanged maw.

Finch placed a hand on his shoulder. After a moment, Enzo calmed enough for his fur to settle down. His tail angrily swished from side to side as he huffed.

"I'll handle this," Finch said, turning his attention to the floor. Several blunted bullets lay at his feet. He knelt and gathered a handful of them. When he stood, he visualized the metal as something moldable—malleable.

The duergar king's magic meant he was a master at manipulating metal, and Finch took advantage of that. The bullets in Finch's hand bent to his will. He shaped them like putty and quickly pinched an edge until it was flat and sharp. Once he was done, he had a six-inch knife made out of a lead alloy.

Enzo snorted and then motioned him forward. "Make this lowlife scumbag regret he ever met us, Adair."

Once the marble finished creating the mark, it hit a floorboard, bounced, and then bounced again, straight up into Maldonado's hand. He tucked the magical object back into his pocket, placed his glass of wine down, and then stepped into the drawing on the floor.

The chalky white marks deepened into an insidious red. The air around the spellrift shimmered as faint crackles of power hissed and snapped like the first sparks of a fire catching hold. Crimson lightning flickered in sharp, jagged flashes, illuminating Maldonado's face in fleeting bursts, casting him as something monstrous.

Then Maldonado casually lifted his hand and then bent his fingers in quick succession to motion Finch forward.

Without hesitation, Finch strode into the spellrift. The lines on the floor glowed enough to fill the living room with an infernal aura. Unseen power gripped at his chest, and the rattle of chains echoed throughout the massive house.

A faint chain appeared tethered to Finch's sternum, though it only appeared occasionally, like an image at the corner of his vision. It snaked its way over to Maldonado, also connecting to the man's sternum.

But Maldonado was different—seventeen other phantom chains occasionally became visible, flashing for just a brief moment and then disappearing from sight afterward. One of the chains ran from Maldonado to the elven woman on the couch, while the others went in all other directions, the ends of them far from this building.

Obviously, Maldonado was no stranger to spellrifts.

Once two people were within the mark, the spellrift crackled and sealed itself. Once one of the participants was knocked to the verge of death, the binding would be complete.

Of course, there was always the possibility that one combatant went too far, and the other died. But in that circumstance, they didn't get the individual's soul. Therefore, *death* was never the goal in a spellrift. Just incapacitation so the chains could secure themselves to an individual.

Enzo stood outside the mark, watching intently, his ears erect.

The elven woman also watched, trembling the whole time, her brow furrowed.

"Let's get this over with," Finch muttered.

He lifted his hand and thought about Carter—thought about what the witches had done to his body. The moment he pictured his brother's face, he had all the bottled-up emotions he needed to create fire that rivaled the sun. The flames that burst from his palm were just as white-hot as before, only this time, they couldn't escape the boundaries of the spellrift.

The inferno washed over Maldonado and then crashed into an invisible barrier. The heat swirled around in the arena, washing back over Finch and charring his clothing in a matter of moments. He ended his magic, hoping the fire would've done *something*, but he caught his breath when he realized what had happened.

Nothing.

Not even Maldonado's clothing was singed. His silky blood-red shirt was unharmed. His pants were still crisp with a line from ironing. His black hair was slicked back in an immaculate fashion.

"You have an ifrit's fire," Maldonado said. "Whose? Ke-Koh's? Sin-Rava's? One of the powerful ifrits." He shook his head. "I have the protection of a demon prince. Your flames won't harm me."

After exhaling embers, Finch lunged forward. Though he figured this wouldn't work, he knew he had to try.

This was about gathering information, after all.

Maldonado's lips curved down at the corners in a sharp frown as Finch slashed at him. Finch went for his neck, but when his knife connected, it was like striking a brick. The blade didn't cut Maldonado—it barely made a scratch.

But at least Finch had learned something valuable.

Magic swirled around Maldonado. Not infernal forces, but something more natural. The air grew heavy, thick with the earthy scent of rain-soaked moss and the crisp tang of ozone. It was the smell of a storm gathering its strength.

Lightning flashed across Maldonado's body, jagged and white-hot. It arced outward, striking Finch. The light burned into Finch's vision, numbing his limbs, even as the impact drove him back. He slammed into the barrier that kept them both in the spellrift, stealing his breath.

He slumped down onto one knee, his muscles refusing to obey. He couldn't breathe, not for a full thirty seconds, his body overwhelmed by the power that had surged through him.

"You've never fought a coatl," Maldonado said, with no irritation, just smug confidence. "You don't understand the sheer ferocity of nature under my command."

Once Finch was able, he took several deep breaths. The lightning fucking hurt. Why did he always get himself into situations where people wielded the most torturous of magic? Why couldn't he fight people who used their magic to smell good? Or something equally as manageable?

"*Get up,*" Maldonado hissed. "I know you haven't shown me your best. Your childish metal trick wasn't even worth my time. Fae magic can't compete with *me.*"

Finch forced himself to stand. He had known he didn't have the tools to beat Maldonado in a duel, but at least he had figured out a few things.

"What're you hiding?" Maldonado stepped forward, glaring. "Show me."

"All right," Finch muttered.

He activated Chronos's magic.

Everything around the room froze. Enzo stopped moving. The crackle of power from the spellrift stopped. The woman on the couch no longer trembled.

But for a few short seconds, Maldonado could still move. Chronos's magic took the longest to hold him in place. His eyes widened, and he took a nervous step backward.

"*You can manipulate tim—*"

But Maldonado never finished the sentence. He was frozen in place, just like everything else.

Then the colors drained from the world. The living room became black and white, like an unused coloring book. Finally, all the shapes melted, leaving Finch in a void of pure white.

When he next blinked, he found himself outside McKinley Park, Enzo—in human form—standing by his side. Finch's car was in front of him, the broken fence behind him. Finch thanked the good stars he had "saved his progress" after speaking with Heslop because he didn't want to negotiate with the fae king ever again.

His hearing was back in both ears, and the claw marks across his body were healed.

1:02 p.m.

CHAPTER
SIXTEEN

"D amn," Enzo muttered as he turned to Finch. "I really wanted you to just whup his ass. That man has it coming."

Finch sighed.

Even talented warlocks and witches would've been killed by an invisible assassin appearing out of nowhere with a gun pointed at their temple. And the imps afterward—they could tear a person to shreds in a matter of seconds. But Finch had done this song and dance before. He had been prepared for the worst. And he wasn't like most witches or warlocks.

Which was good, because if he died, there would be no more rewinding time...

He couldn't afford to slip up. Not on this case.

"Well," Finch said, "now that we know Maldonado *will* engage in a spellrift, he's already lost."

It was only a matter of time. If Finch could figure out a way to beat him—and there *was* a way, no magic came without its disadvantages—then this whole nightmare would be over. And Finch found it ironic that Maldonado had made fun of him for hubris. It would be Maldonado's pride that ultimately brought him down.

"I get it," Enzo said, clearly coming to the same conclusion on his own. He chortled. "What're we going to do, then? How do we figure out Maldonado's weaknesses?"

"The best place to start looking would be his little vacation home."

Enzo crossed his arms over his chest. "You mean... the place we just came from?"

"Yeah. Maldonado enters his living room at 1:55, so we can probably enter at the opposite end and search around without too much trouble."

"And what're we looking for?" Enzo shook his head. "Because I don't normally keep a list of all my fears sitting around my house."

Finch walked to his Toyota. "No, but Maldonado probably created wards, or has witch's brews to counteract any weaknesses. If we find those, we'll have all our answers. So, let's search his place. Gather all the information we can. Then I challenge him again—and win."

Enzo walked over to the passenger-side door. "All right. Let's do it."

"First, I need to stop by the office. I can't magically unlock doors anymore, so we'll need some tools..."

———

Finch drove through the hot California sun all the way back to his office. When he arrived, he glanced at his phone.

1:25 p.m.

Once he stepped out of his vehicle, however, he noticed three individuals all waiting around outside the front door. They were men, each one increasingly more formal than the last.

The first was a man in shorts and a T-shirt. He wore a pair of bright green crocs and held a folder full of paperwork under one arm. Of the three, he was the youngest, likely in his late twenties.

The second man wore a black suit with a black button-up shirt and a black tie. He was the most emo-looking attorney Finch had ever seen in his life, and actively hid in a narrow patch of shade cast by the tall building. His dark hair was unkempt, the dark bags under his eyes matched his outfit, and his unusually pale skin couldn't even be considered Caucasian—it could only be classified as "undead." Perhaps he was.

The final man wore a dark blue suit with a white shirt and a red tie. He was tall, athletic, and his blazer was slightly too large—which meant he likely had a shoulder holster. Finch was positive the man was packing heat, so Finch immediately activated his duergar magic. Just in case.

Enzo exited the car and stepped close to Finch's side. They walked over to the office door as a team, which seemed to intimidate the youngest man. He moved away, his crocs squeaking as he went.

"Can I help you gentlemen?" Finch asked as he unlocked the front door.

Ironically, it was croc-man who spoke first. "Oh, I'm an intern at *The Law Offices of Tibbedeaux & Pimentel*. I'm here with the paperwork."

"What paperwork?" Finch snapped. He shoved open the door and stepped into the delightfully air-conditioned office.

"We called your office earlier today," the man said as he followed Finch inside. "You agreed to serve paperwork, right?"

"Oh, goddammit," Finch muttered under his breath. He had completely forgotten about Bree's random acceptance of a minor job. After a long exhale, Finch said, "*Fine.* Hand it over."

The two suited men also walked inside, followed closely by Enzo, who gave them both an intimidating once over. The goth lawyer frowned and the man with the shoulder holster tensed but didn't otherwise react.

And then a kitten walked into the office, just barely sneaking in through the door as it shut. The feline playfully scampered by everyone and then ran around the reception-ist's desk, an odd baggie and a wallet in its mouth.

The only person who reacted to the strange kitten was croc-man. He stared, flabbergasted, and then motioned like he had just witnessed something amazing. No one else shared in his enthusiasm, which only deflated him.

"You didn't see that?" the man asked.

Everyone in the room, including the goth lawyer and Enzo, all shook their heads.

"Well?" Finch held out his hand, hoping to distract the man from the obviously supernatural. "The paperwork?"

"Uh, right." The man handed over the file. "You need to give this all to a man named *Seth Rivers*. It's a subpoena. He's a key witness and we need him to testify in court tomorrow."

Finch flipped through the paperwork. A criminal case. Drug dealer. Other than the name of the defendant—which was *Pedro Nine Fingers*—the entire case was utterly mundane. Apparently, Seth Rivers was one of the only people willing to testify. They needed his testimony to pin the crime on the real culprit and get their client's charges dismissed.

"Mr. Rivers had been extremely cooperative with us, but then he went missing a couple days ago," the croc-man said. "We're hoping you can find him before tomorrow."

And this was urgent? Finch placed the paperwork on the

receptionist's desk, making a mental note to never allow Bree to answer the phone ever again. "I'll handle it."

"This is extremely time sensitive. We were hoping that—"

"I said, *I'll handle it*," Finch interjected. "Trust me, as long as Mr. Rivers isn't dead or out of town, I'll find him."

Finch's confidence seemed to convince the man. He smiled, nodded once, and then headed for the door. "Thank you so much! If you have any questions, please call our office." Then he left.

But the other two strange men were still here. And they reeked of magic. The goth lawyer was undead, no doubt in Finch's mind, and the other man was something divine.

Before Finch could call on one of them to state their business, the kitten with the baggie and wallet wandered out from around the receptionist's desk. The little feline reached up with a paw and pushed at its own chin until *pop!* Its head became a hat and a brownie stood before them, the baggy held in his hand, the wallet under his arm.

"Ugh, I thought the human would never leave," the little brownie said, his voice adorable but also masculine and clearly German. He shot Finch an irritated glance. "I have stuff." He shook the baggie.

"Put it on Liam's desk," Finch said.

The brownie huffed and then hurried across the office floor.

But it didn't faze either the lawyer or the divine man with the gun. They barely gave the brownie a second glance.

"My name is Harlan Kane, Attorney at Law," the undead goth said. He swept back his black hair, his eyes a deep red, though Finch hadn't noticed before when he was in the shadows. "I heard you're the famous Adair Finch?"

"So what if I am?" Finch asked.

Mr. Kane took a moment to glance around the office.

When he was done, he returned his attention to Finch with a sneer. "I heard you were legendary, but I must admit, you're not impressing me."

Enzo stepped forward, practically between Finch and the lawyer. "Did we barge into your law office and talk about how much you stink like the grave? No. Because our mamas raised us right."

"I'm one of the most successful attorneys in the entire San Joaquin district," Mr. Kane stated. "I only want to work with the best. Are you, or are you not, *the best?*"

Finch narrowed his eyes. "Wait, I think I know you. Are you that vampire who defended that chupacabra in a murder case?"

"I am," Mr. Kane said. When he forced a smile, his canines were curved and sharp—more than a normal human's, but not exaggerated like in movies.

Most folks didn't like vampires, and it was for the same reason they didn't like werewolves. They carried a curse that infected a person's cores. Fortunately, the vampire curse was difficult to contract.

"Isn't it the middle of the day?" Enzo turned his attention to the bright light shining in under the curtains. "Don't vampires explode in the sunlight or some shit?"

"Sunlight hurts us," Mr. Kane stated. "But I have ways around it, thank you very much."

Finch didn't care how successful or amazing this man was. He had bigger problems to worry about. He waved away the vampire. "Listen, I'm not taking on any cases right now. If you need something, try again later."

Mr. Kane gave the place one last scan before heading toward the door. Then he left without another word. No goodbye. No observation. Finch was surprised the vampire had come personally, but other than that, he didn't give the man a second thought.

"And you?" Finch asked the last remaining visitor to his office.

"I'm Agent Jack Steele," the man said as he reached into his blazer and pulled out a badge. "I'm a member of the *Supernatural Hazard Analysis and Defense Operations Wing*. You're familiar with my department, yes?"

The badge had a seven-pointed star, a snake, and sword, with a banner underneath that held the words: *Custodimus Arcana*. If Finch remembered correctly, it meant *keepers of secrets*, or *guardians of the arcana*, something of the sort.

The man's name was clearly stamped on the badge, along with a number.

He was a SHADOW agent. Finch hadn't been expecting one to turn up on his doorstep.

"I'm familiar with SHADOW," Finch said. "What can I do for you, Agent Steele?"

The man tucked his badge away. In all ways, he reminded Finch of an Eagle Scout. His blond hair was cut short and neat. His face was clean-shaven. He stood with proper posture. Neat, neat, neat. Nothing out of place.

Agent Steele didn't waste any time, either. He got straight to the point when he asked, "Have you seen your sister-in-law, Jessica Finch? We have reason to believe she might be trying to reach you."

"I haven't heard from her in years," Finch replied, confident and casual. "Is something the matter?"

"She's wanted for the attempted murder of a federal agent," Agent Steele bluntly replied. "If she hasn't contacted you yet, we were hoping you might aid us in finding her."

Finch almost rewound time to get out of this conversation. He wasn't going to help SHADOW get a hold of Jessie, so what was he supposed to tell this man? He reeked of divine magic, and Finch knew that creatures like angels and kami—both of which were very divine—had ways of reading minds or sniffing out the truth. Not all the time, but frequently enough that it bothered him.

"I'm busy," Finch said. "I apologize."

"You're not the least bit curious about your *sister-in-law*?" Agent Steele asked.

Finch shook his head. "Like I said—I haven't seen her in a long time. We were never close to begin with, so I seriously doubt she's trying to get a hold of me."

"Her motorcycle is in a nearby parking lot." The agent forced a smile, his posture tenser than before. Then he motioned to the helmet sitting on the edge of the receptionist's desk. "And I'm pretty sure that's hers, too."

CHAPTER
SEVENTEEN

For a prolonged moment, the office was silent and tense. Then Enzo snorted out a laugh. He slapped Finch on the shoulder, shaking his head.

"He saw through you like a clean window." Still chortling, Enzo added, "Oldest trick in the cop playbook. I can't believe you didn't notice that helmet when you came in."

Finch sighed. "It's already been one hell of a long day. You think I'm supposed to remember minor shit like her helmet?"

"I saw it the second we entered."

"And why didn't you put it away, *junior assistant*?"

That got Enzo laughing harder. Finch couldn't help but half smile himself. It *had* been a long day already, and they were only officially a few hours in.

Agent Steele observed the interaction with a slightly perplexed expression. He chuckled along with them, but it was forced. Finally, he pulled a pair of handcuffs from a pocket inside his blazer and then motioned to Adair with a jut of his chin.

"I'm glad you two are having a great time, but lying to a federal agent is a felony," Agent Steele stated. "Adair Finch, you're under arrest for obstructing justice. If you refuse to cooperate with my orders, you'll also be charged with resisting arrest."

Enzo's laughter became deeper and more genuine. He rubbed at the corner of one eye, wiping away tears of mirth. "I can't believe you're about to get arrested. Right *after* you got out of a spellrift. You're so unlucky."

Agent Steele frowned. "A spellrift? It's a felony to create a spellrift on United States soil."

Which only got Enzo laughing harder. Finch hadn't known about the law, but he wasn't surprised. The legislation on whether spellrifts were allowed constantly went back and forth.

"You're getting *extra* arrested," Enzo quipped.

"Wouldn't be the first time," Finch sardonically muttered.

But instead of going through the charade, Finch decided now was the time to activate his magic. The world around him froze, including Agent Steele, who had his handcuffs held out toward Finch. Then the colors drained, and finally, the shapes all melted away like a sped-up time-lapse of a candle being burned down to a nub.

Once the world around him was completely white, Finch blinked.

1:02 p.m.

He was outside the park, Enzo at his side, his car parked on the street, just feet in front of him.

Enzo continued laughing. "We have to deal with a criminal wizard *and* avoid the feds. Fantastic."

"It's one of those days," Finch replied as he walked around to the driver's side door. "C'mon. Let's go."

"Go?" Enzo leapt over to the passenger door. "Where now?"

"We're going back to the office, but this time we're going to do it right."

————

Finch pulled up to his office. Just like before, all three men were waiting, despite the oppressive heat. When Finch stepped out of his vehicle, he went straight for the croc-wearing delivery boy.

"You're from *The Law Offices of Tibbedeaux & Pimentel*?" Finch asked. Before the man answered, Finch snatched the file from under his arm. "I'll deliver your subpoena in time for your trial."

"Uh..." It took the man a whole second to process what had happened. "Th-Thank you. Let us know if you can't find Mr. Rivers? He's been really cooperative, and—"

"I know, I know," Finch interjected. "I'll handle it."

"Right. Well, thank you again." The man half heartedly turned and walked down the street to his bicycle. More than once he glanced over his shoulder like he couldn't believe how the conversation had gone down.

Then Finch turned his attention to the vampire hiding in the sliver of shade. "Mr. Kane? If you want my help with one of your cases, you'll need to come back tomorrow. I'm currently too busy to entertain you at the moment."

"You knew what I was here for?"

"I did. I know a great many things."

The vampire licked one of his fangs and narrowed his eyes. "Let me just say—I'm impressed."

Finch didn't bother responding.

Then the attorney raised a perfect eyebrow. He didn't take long to mull over the situation and come to a conclusion. "Very well. Can I schedule an appointment for tomorrow at one?"

"I'll see you then."

The vampire smirked as he slunk his way out of the shadows and toward a black vehicle. The undead didn't sweat, nor could they suffer from heatstroke, but Mr. Kane still acted as though he could. He shielded his face as he got into his car and then drove off, his windows tinted.

Finch didn't open his office. Instead, he rounded on Agent Steele.

"You know why I'm here, too?" the SHADOW agent asked, his voice low, his gaze discerning.

"Of course I do," Finch casually replied. "You're looking for my sister-in-law."

Agent Steele dutifully flashed his badge. "I'm here on official business. Jessica Finch is wanted for attempted murder on a federal agent." He tucked the badge away. "Do you know where she is?"

Enzo finally stepped out of Finch's Toyota. He smiled as he walked over, almost like he was suppressing a laugh. He didn't say anything, though. Finch was grateful.

"I didn't know she was in trouble with the feds." Finch placed his hand on the office door. "She came by here this morning wanting my help, but we're estranged, and I told her I didn't want anything to do with her. She left shortly afterward."

Agent Steele loosened up after that statement. Then he reached into his blazer and pulled out his phone. With some deft taps, he made a few notes. "Can you tell me anything else? Like where she might be heading? Or if she plans on staying here in town?"

That was the true way to lie—telling half a truth first, so the person believed you. Since Agent Steele already knew Jessie had been here, Finch couldn't lie about that, or else it would be suspicious. However, now that Finch had the man's attention, he had more pressing questions.

"Does it really matter where Jessie is?" Finch asked. "Because I just heard that the wizard Maldonado is in town. Shouldn't you SHADOW boys be handling *him* rather than some lone woman?"

Agent Steele stopped typing on his phone. He glanced up at Finch, his blue eyes a light shade of ice. "Did you just say *Maldonado* is in town? The wizard from Mexico City?"

"The same."

Enzo stepped over to the office door and leaned against the glass. "It's true. He's over in Spanos Park. A little crazy he can just come and go without anyone noticing. What're you feds even doing?"

"Our taxpayer dollars at work," Finch quipped.

While Agent Steele never became flustered, it was obvious he was becoming less confident. He tucked his phone away, his gaze distant. "I see. We'll have a team over there shortly. We have reason to believe Jessica Finch was operating under his orders, so perhaps this is all one and the same."

"Good luck," Finch said.

Before he left, the agent reached into his pants pocket and pulled out a black business card. It had his name, a phone number, and a seven-pointed star. "If your sister-in-law contacts you a second time, please call me. It would be extremely helpful. We have reason to believe she's extremely dangerous."

Finch snatched the card and tucked it away. "I'll let you know."

With that, Agent Steele forced a smile and then turned on his heel to leave. Finch waited a long while—all the way until the agent got into his car—before he opened up his office. A wave of cold air washed over him as he stepped inside. Enzo and the little kitten weren't far behind.

Finch glanced down at the disguised brownie, wondering where the little fae had been hiding the entire time they had been speaking.

The brownie peeled back his magic hat and *poofed* back into a tiny person.

"Ugh! I thought they'd never leave." Then he frowned at Finch, a baggie under one arm, and a wallet under the other. "Where do you want these?"

"On Liam's desk." Finch hurried to his office—but before he went in, he made sure to tuck Jessie's helmet underneath the receptionist's desk, just in case. Then he unlocked the door to his office and stepped inside.

He had plenty of lockpicking tools, he just hadn't had to use them while he had Kull's mischief magic. Now that he was planning to snoop around a wizard's temporary hideout, he decided he would also need a few precautions.

He went to his desk, opened one of the lower drawers, and pulled out a small bag of supplies. He counted the brews inside. He had five.

Two would allow whoever drank them to see in the dark —even through magical shadows.

The next two would allow whoever drank them to survive thirty minutes without breathing.

The last one was a brew that would accelerate healing. It was the most expensive of the bunch, and could prevent an otherwise fatal injury from killing someone, but only if administered immediately.

Each little brew was in their own metal vial complete with a cork stopper.

Then Finch sifted through his lockpick set and sighed. It would work for all mundane locks and some magical ones, but it certainly wasn't a complete kit.

And he had absolutely no ability to see through illusions or invisibility. And since Maldonado had an invisible gunman following him around, Finch knew other things in the house would also be hidden.

He needed some way to deal with that.

Carrying his small duffle bag of tools, Finch exited his office. Enzo waited for him by the front door, his arms crossed, a smile on his face.

"I can't believe you made a joke about taxpayer money," Enzo said. "When I was a beat cop, that would've gotten you in a world of hurt."

Finch shrugged. "I have to get my jollies somehow."

"Weird that SHADOW agent didn't know a full-blown wizard was in town. Makes me think these guys aren't bringing their A game."

"Maldonado's vacation home has a lot of magical protections," Finch muttered, thinking about the barrier he had passed through when entering the house. At first, he had thought it just sealed in noises, but he suspected it must prevent magical detection.

"Still," Enzo said, opening the front door so they could both leave. "I was hoping the feds would be a little more competent."

"It doesn't matter." Finch headed out toward his car. "I'll deal with Maldonado."

The kitten exited the office with him, and then hurried down the sidewalk, no doubt off to look for more materials.

"Before we head to his house, we should probably pick up Jessie." Finch slipped into his vehicle. "She can see through all manner of illusions, after all. And I think we'll need that skill."

CHAPTER
EIGHTEEN

Finch drove back to the park, his duffle bag in the trunk and ready to go.

1:42 p.m.

They'd have to hurry to get to Maldonado's. He would enter his living room at 1:55 p.m., and Finch wanted to use that knowledge to help move through the house unseen. There were still thugs, and guards, and shadow imps, but Finch could handle all those things if a problem arose. He wasn't worried about that.

Together with Enzo, Finch hurried across McKinley Park and then walked around the bathroom building to find the magic-infused grove. Liam and Jessie sat on the dog bench, locked in conversation, while Bree stood at the edge of the mushroom circle, staring at the fungi. They were all too preoccupied to even register that Finch and Enzo had returned.

"All right, you're up, Jessie," Finch said.

She jumped to her feet, her body tense. When she was upset, she looked like a woman who carried multiple knives and maybe even a small gun in her prison wallet. Her leather jacket, pixie-short hair, and boots gave her an intimidating aura, but once she calmed down and realized it was Finch, she relaxed, and the aggression faded.

"Adair... Where did you even go?" Jessie shook her head. "You weren't gone long."

Bree leapt over, exuberant. "Is it time to do some real *hard-core* investigating? Because I'm ready!" She playfully smacked her own cheek a couple times. "All the fae world air has worn off."

"Actually, I just need Jessie on this one." Finch motioned her over. "C'mon."

"Where are we going?" Jessie asked.

"We're going to investigate Maldonado's vacation house and see if we can find anything interesting."

"*What?*" Bree gasped. "I'm perfect for this! You gave up Kull's trickster abilities, right? I haven't, which means I can still unlock doors. You'll definitely need that if you're going to investigate a house."

Finch hadn't thought of that. Kull's trickster abilities were far superior to any lockpicking tools he had. With a half shrug, he said, "Okay, fine. You're with us."

"*Yes,*" Bree whispered under her breath, a smile on her face.

Enzo slammed a heavy hand down on Finch's shoulder. "Wait." Then he pulled Finch to the side, away from the others. When he lowered his voice, he sounded like he was growling. "We can't take her."

"Why not?" Finch asked.

"She's twelve."

"Okay. And? We're sneaking into a place and avoiding everyone. She'll be fine."

Enzo gritted his teeth. His tone darkened. "What if someone finds us? What if there's a gunfight?"

"Oh, *no,*" Finch said, over-the-top sarcasm thick in each

word. "We've never gotten out of a situation *that* scary before. Whatever will we do?"

Enzo twisted his fingers into Finch's shirt and yanked him closer, his anger a little more visible, his eyes more canine. "You'll traumatize the girl."

"How?" Finch asked, cold and serious once more. "Bree's already seen people get offed—including her own mother, just in case you forgot. And she's been shot. Plus, like I said, we're not aiming to fight anyone. She'll be fine. This is a *sneak in, and then sneak out*, situation."

"What if there's..." Enzo huffed and half shrugged. "What if there's coke in the house?"

Again, sarcastically, Finch frowned. "Oh, no—not a pile of cocaine! How traumatizing."

Enzo shoved the man away with a forceful push. Finch stumbled back a step, only slightly surprised by his friend's anger. Finch brushed himself off and then met Enzo's gaze. While they said nothing, Finch knew he had won the argument, but not the war. This wasn't over.

"Is everything okay?" Liam asked.

Finch whirled around on his heel. He had almost forgotten the other man was here. "Yes. I'll be taking Jessie and Bree, and you'll wait here."

"Why?" Liam glanced around the grove. He pushed his glasses up to the bridge of his nose as he asked, "Is this place important?"

"I don't think any of the SHADOW agents or Maldonado's thugs know about this place. I just want to avoid you getting hurt while we're gone."

"SHADOW agents?" Liam asked.

"They're here?" Jessie asked at the same time.

Finch grabbed his sister-in-law's arm and pulled her toward the park exit. "Yes. You're wanted for attempted murder. But it's fine—I sent the agent on his way. Now we just need to get some information, and I need your magic to help with that."

"Don't get into too much trouble, Papa," Bree said as she stayed by Finch's side.

———

The drive to Maldonado's vacation house in Spanos Park was quieter than usual. The radio remained off, and no one bothered to speak. Bree sat in the front passenger seat, her attention on the world beyond the window. Jessie sat behind her, leaning back in her seat as much as possible. Enzo sat beside her, but he leaned forward so much he might as well be on the center console.

Halfway to the house, Enzo cleared his throat. "So, Bree. Wouldn't you agree that guns are frightening? Maybe you've had nightmares about them?"

Bree turned away from the window and then slowly faced him. She crossed her arms. "Why are you acting weird?"

"Okay—first off, I'm not acting."

Finch held up a hand. "Enough, enough. We don't need to discuss this. Everything is fine. If there's even a hint of a gunfight, I'll make sure we're all out of there. Does *that* satisfy you?"

Enzo snorted but said nothing.

"Why does Maldonado have a vacation house in Stockton, California?" Jessie asked, her voice distant, like she hadn't heard any of the previous conversation.

"Because he's here in town looking for you," Finch replied.

Jessie shot forward in her seat, once again so tense, she smelled of brimstone. Whatever demon she was bound to had a powerful reek, and the demonic magic seemed to seep through her whole body whenever she was agitated.

Which meant it was probably bound to her heart core.

"Everything is fine," Finch said.

"We're *going to his house*?" Jessie reached for the door handle in the back. "We can't. We can't get anywhere near him. He'll find me. This is a terrible idea." She pulled the handle, but thankfully—and Finch had never expected to think this—the child locks prevented anyone from leaving.

Enzo grabbed her arm. "What's wrong with you, woman? You can't leap out of a moving vehicle."

"You don't understand." Jessie jerked away from him, and then pressed her back against the car door. "Maldonado is extremely powerful. He'll kill us. He won't even hesitate."

Finch remembered the invisible gunman and the dozens of shadow imps. "Oh, I know," he sardonically quipped.

"Adair has this handled," Enzo stated.

Bree nodded. "Yeah, you don't need to worry. Everything will be fine as long as Adair is with us."

The chorus of confidence in Finch's abilities seemed to baffle Jessie more than reassure her. She glanced between everyone, her brow furrowed, her hands trembling. In that moment, Finch almost told her about his pact with Chronos, and how he could manipulate time, but he held back.

Later.

———

Finch pulled his Toyota up to the gate of Maldonado's private McMansion. He leaned out his window and poked the keypad outside.

Sixteen ten.

The gate groaned open, squeaking a bit as it went. Finch

drove up the long driveway, past the pool house, and up to the fleet of parked vehicles. Once he was situated among them, he glanced at the time.

1:52 p.m.

Perfect.

He stepped out of his car into the suffocating heat. Bree and Enzo quickly joined him, though none of them appeared happy about it. The oppressive temperature killed all enthusiasm.

Jessie didn't exit, however.

Finch walked around to the car to her door and opened it for her. Jessie had her gaze locked on the massive house. When she turned her attention to Finch, her lip quavered. Then she managed to point at the front door.

"Can't you see all the wards and protections?" she whispered.

There was nothing to see—Finch wasn't capable of detecting the protections until he walked through them. He shook his head. "Is something wrong?"

"Maldonado has elves in his employ. This whole place is secure. We'll never be able to sneak in."

Finch glanced at his phone again.

1:53 p.m.

"We'll be okay to slip in on the western side of the house in just a couple minutes," he muttered. Then he motioned her out. "C'mon. I promise, nothing will happen to you while I'm here."

"You don't understand how strong he is."

"Listen—let's pretend that's true. I don't know." Finch knelt to see her better—and to also get within the tiny amount of shade the car cast. "I have a way to get us out of here in a pinch, okay? It's more effective than teleportation."

"Nothing is more effective than *teleportation*," Jessie said, glaring. "It's instant."

Finch didn't bother responding. He motioned to the house. "Trust me. I can get us out of this. But we need to go. And I need your help—specifically, I need your ability to see wards and protections."

Without that, he knew he would never uncover all Maldonado's secrets.

Despite his urging, Jessie still needed a long moment. She took several deep breaths, her shoulders bunched at the base of her neck. Finally, she whispered something to herself before stepping out of the Toyota.

"Okay," she said after a hard swallow. "I'll trust you. Just, *please* make sure Maldonado doesn't catch us." She threw her jacket into the vehicle, sporting just a simple black T-shirt underneath.

"He won't." Finch grabbed his duffle bag from the trunk and then headed for a pathway around the mansion on the western side.

CHAPTER
NINETEEN

The four of them crept around the house, the sun hammering down like it had a personal vendetta. Finch wiped at the sweat threatening to slide into his eyes, while Enzo muttered something under his breath about heatstroke. Jessie fanned herself with one hand.

And then there was Bree—still wrapped in her hoodie like it was a second skin, completely unbothered by the temperature. California kids were built differently. Finch wasn't sure whether to be impressed or concerned.

As they neared a window, Finch raised a hand. The others froze in place. He leaned forward, just enough to peek inside. A kitchen. Several goons. Finch ducked below the windowsill and kept moving. The others followed without instruction.

The next window? A palatial bathroom. Floor-to-ceiling marble, gold-plated fixtures, and a shower so large it probably had its own echo. Thankfully, it was unoccupied. Finch moved past it.

When Enzo crept by, he chanced a glance inside. That

was when he huffed and whispered, "I hate that crime pays so well."

They moved on. The third window revealed something far more useful: a personal study. Dark wood shelves lined with books, a heavy desk that had likely seen more than a few dubious dealings, and most importantly—no people.

Finally. A way inside.

Finch grabbed the window and attempted to lift it. He almost ripped a fingernail off on the frame. Biting his tongue, he held in a string of curses as he backed away.

"It's locked," he finally said through gritted teeth.

Bree leapt forward like she had been waiting for her name to be called. "I've got this." She placed her hand on the frame of the window and concentrated. Enzo, Jessie, and Finch just waited, no one saying a word, everyone keeping an eye on their surroundings.

"Uh, Adair?" Bree whispered.

"Yes?"

She motioned him over. He stepped close and half bent over to listen better.

"How do you do this again?" she asked.

"Kull's magic is bound to the core of your eyes. You have to visualize how you want the magic to work. Picture the window's latch undoing itself." Finch tapped his temple. "See it all in your imagination."

"R-Right."

Bree returned her attention to the window. Finch stepped back, content to allow her to try—he had infinite time, after all—but Jessie grew restless. She rubbed her upper arms, practically scratching through the sleeves of her T-shirt.

Click.

The window latch inside clicked upward. Additionally, a light flickered off, and Finch was extra thankful for Bree.

He hadn't thought about the electronic surveillance around the property. Kull's magic could trick machines and computers, though, so it was unlikely anyone would know they entered the house.

Bree slid the window open and hopped over the sill. Enzo and Jessie followed after, with Finch taking up the rear. Once inside, Finch took a deep breath of air-conditioned glory. As icy relief washed over him, Finch threw his duffle bag onto the desk.

There was only one door out of the room, and it was at the opposite end. While most studies were smaller personal rooms, this one could've doubled as a living room in a normal house. It was spacious, and even had a couch and two reading chairs.

"We're looking for anything that may lead us to Maldonado's weak point," Finch stated. "Magic isn't flawless. Iron undoes fae magic, for example—silver harms curses. As a wizard, Maldonado absorbed his first magic from a coatl, and then he cultivates it. We need something to counter his specific brand of magic."

"Wizards cultivate magic?" Bree asked, her brow furrowed.

Finch walked over to the nearest bookshelf and began scanning the spines. "That's right. They absorb it, change it slightly, empower it, reabsorb it. It's a long weird process."

"Sounds like bees with honey."

"Uh, sure. Yeah. Whatever. Bees and honey. Wizards are..."

"The queen bee?"

Finch sighed. Somehow, this analogy had gotten away from him.

Quickly and quietly, Jessie investigated her surroundings. Enzo paused, doubled over, and transformed. It was noisy—his bones made cracking and popping noises as he shifted—and his fur blossomed across his body in an aesthetically pleasing way.

When he stood straight again, he had tall wolf ears, a long canine snout, and fangs dangerous enough to rip out someone's throat.

"Are you okay?" Bree whispered, her eyes wide.

Enzo patted the fur on his arms. "I'm fine. When I'm not angry, I can control the curse enough to transform. And when I'm like this—"

"Wolfed out?" Bree interjected.

"Yeah, *wolfed out*. When I'm like this, I can smell better, hear better—I do everything better."

"Except control your rage," Finch quipped. "You get easier to piss off."

Enzo's ears went back as he shot the other man a glare. With a swish of his bushy tail—his sweatpants seemed to have a seam loose enough for it to poke through—Enzo turned away.

"I'm fine," he said. "Let's just get to searching."

Enzo went for the desk, carefully opening each drawer and checking for things like false bottoms, while Jessie went to the opposite end of the room and rifled through another bookshelf.

"What are wizards, exactly?" Bree asked. She stuck close to Finch, staring at the books with knitted eyebrows.

"Wizards are men born with a special spirit core that allows them to absorb ambient magic," Finch absent-mindedly said. "Their magic spreads to the other four cores, and then they can implant magic in people they call *servitors*, and the more people they do this to, the longer they live, and the more powerful their magic becomes."

"Only *men* can become wizards?"

Finch nodded. "That's right."

"That's not fair." Bree fidgeted with one of the books, frowning.

"Only *women* can become witches—and there are thousands of them compared to wizards. Maybe even more than that."

"Still." Bree rolled her eyes. "I wish it were equal."

"The world won't be nice, so you need to get stronger," Finch said. "Only your best self can face the inequities of reality."

"That doesn't mean I can't wish for things."

"Sure. Just don't rely on wishes. The power to change things starts from within."

Those were words Finch had heard from his father. He spoke them without much thought as he continued his work.

There had to be *something* of use in the study. Unfortunately, most of the books were either encyclopedias—who even owned those anymore?—or they were thick tomes on world history. Neither of those were useful.

"So, Maldonado absorbed some magic, and now he's cultivating it until it's really strong," Bree slowly said, taking her time to thoroughly grasp the concept.

"That's right."

"And whatever magic he *first* absorbed is the magic we're trying to find a weakness to?"

"You're quick," Finch quipped.

It was difficult to read the spines of books while Bree continually asked questions, but Finch didn't complain. Since she was his apprentice, he needed to give her all the information she could handle.

"Oh, Mother Moon," Jessie said, half gasping.

Finch whirled on his heel. His sister-in-law was kneeling by the far bookshelf, a book open in her hands, her eyes wide. Everyone hurried over to her location.

"What is it?" Finch whispered as he got close. "You found something useful?"

To his confusion, Jessie held a book about geography. The book was open to a page that contained a map of the Grand Canyon.

"What is this?" Finch asked.

"It's a record of activity," Jessie said, her hand trembling as she touched the page. "This whole book contains information on the world's most powerful covens, including the bitches who killed Carter."

Enzo leaned over her shoulder. He sneered as he turned to Finch. "She's not high, right? That's a map?"

Jessie shook her head. "The contents of the book are hidden by illusions. Just... give me a moment." She pressed her palm on the page and concentrated. Slowly, like a snake shedding its old skin, a sheen of magic sloughed off the book, finally disappearing before it hit the floor.

The contents of the book became clear. It was a record of information—where witches were located. What the covens were doing. Any secret locations, and their exact coordinates.

Bree's eyes brightened. "You just did that on your own? With your own magic, I mean?"

"Yes," Jessie said, exhaling. She held the book closer. "And look here. Do you see this? All the witches in the *Sisters of the Deavan Grimoire*. Didn't you hear me? They're Carter's killers."

"That's great." Finch straightened his posture and turned away from her. "But we don't need that right now. I told you—we need to find what Maldonado is weak against. Look for that."

"Who cares about Maldonado?" Jessie leapt to her feet. When she turned, she was glowering. "This is far more important! Let's just leave this place—let's go straight for this wicked coven and finally avenge Carter once and for all."

"We'll do that *after* we stop Maldonado." Finch returned to his section of the bookshelf, but then stopped once he realized all the books would be illusioned. What was the point of searching if Jessie was the only one who could see through the trickery? "Jessie, please. Once we're done here, we can plan to go after that coven. I promise."

She didn't reply. Instead, she stepped closer to the bookshelf, her gaze down. When Bree motioned to a couple nearby books, Jessie touched them and their illusions melted off, revealing new books entirely, some with handwritten spines.

Then she turned away and just read the record book— she made no effort to look through any of the other tomes.

Enzo and Bree hesitantly removed the few books without illusions from the bookshelf. They flipped through the pages, though occasionally they glanced up to look at Finch. There weren't any more books for him to search, so he moved closer to the door and played watchman.

This search would've been easier if Jessie had cooperated —and removed the illusions on all the books—but it was clear she had no interest in doing that.

Jessie flipped through the record book, taking her time as she read.

Trying not to storm his way over, Finch crossed the room. He cleared his throat when he was close.

"I doubt that book has the information we need," he said.

"You don't even know how vile these witches are," Jessie whispered. She glared at the current page, her hands trembling. "Do you see this? Do you see what they've done? *They're birthing new gods.*"

Finch clenched and unclenched his fists, trying desperately not to get visibly angry. He knew. Maldonado had told him as much. Gixmoth—his brother's real killer—was some new "god" brought about by the lunatic coven.

But he couldn't change that.

"Wait, did you say *gods*?" Enzo asked. "Not just one? How many are we talking about?"

Jessie poked the page. "It says right here that this coven is birthing *modern gods of downfall*. Five in total."

Bree wrung her hands. "Modern gods? What does that mean?"

"When gods are born, they take on characteristics of the world," Jessie whispered. "So, thousands of years ago, gods were of nature, or emotions, or basic concepts. Gaia is the goddess of life. Aranyani is the goddess of forests. Ares is the god of war."

"And Chronos is a god of time?" Bree asked.

Jessie nodded once. "Yes. But... these *modern* gods were born just a few years ago, so their powers are based on the world of today."

"So now we have a *god of twerking*?" Enzo quipped. "I didn't have that for my 2025 bingo card."

"*Don't joke.*" Jessie grabbed the book and held it close to her chest. "Eleven years ago, they hatched Gixmoth the Desolate—*a god of anti-magic*. Don't you realize how terrible that is? Nine years ago, they somehow brought about Yyroh the Black Flood—a goddess of pollution. Seven years ago, it was Automnix the Clockwork Revenant—a god of machine warfare."

No one said anything.

Finch turned the ideas over in his mind, the pieces clicking into place with a sudden, undeniable clarity.

Many millennia ago, magic had once been an undeniable truth. The fae had been part of society, their presence as natural as the wind in the trees or the stars in the sky.

Monsters and dragons had roamed the countryside. Every town had had a local witch who offered brews to solve simple problems.

After a while, the magicless grew jealous and unhappy. They sought to rid the world of magical beings, citing they were a nuisance. Superstitions grew like wildfire, until such beings were distrusted and chased from town.

And now? Now, belief in magic had crumbled beneath the weight of progress. The modern world had no patience for what it could not measure, dissect, or control. Elves and dwarves were fairy tales. Dragons never existed. Witches were to be burned.

Magic had not faded, not truly—it had been rejected. Forgotten, not by its own failing, but by those who no longer wished to see it.

That was why *anti-magic* was such a modern concept.

It could only exist in a time where magic itself was treated as myth, where entire societies had scrubbed magic from their understanding.

Pollution, machine warfare—they were the same.

In the past, there had been no need to name them because they had not yet existed. A thousand years ago, no one would have spoken of smog or acid rain, of rivers choked with sludge or skies thick with poison. Such things were the birthright of industry, the byproducts of a world that had outgrown its old gods and built new ones—factories, refineries, cities of metal and glass that churned and consumed without restraint.

And war—war had always existed, yes. But not like this.

There was a vast difference between warriors clashing with swords and shields, and the cold, mechanical slaughter of drones and automated weapons. Once, war had required hands, had demanded blood and sweat. Now, it could be fought from a distance, waged with machines that did not fear, that did not hesitate. The battlefield was no longer soil and stone—it was circuits and algorithms, cold efficiency replacing the brutality of human hatred.

These things were modern because they had to be. No one had needed such gods before. But now? Now, they might redefine the world.

"So they've created *three* gods?" Enzo finally asked.

Jessie shook her head. "There's more."

"And what? You stopped listing them for dramatic effect? Just give us the whole damn list."

After a deep breath, Jessie said, "Five years ago, the same vile witches gave life to Sielas the Hollow Witness—a goddess of isolation and disassociation. Three years ago, it was... Elroth the Gilded—a god of celebrity, vanity, and the need to be worshipped." Jessie turned her glare to Finch. "Don't you know what this means?"

"What?" he asked.

"It means if you had killed these witches *ten years ago*, like you should have, none of these other downfall gods would've been born!" She had spoken every word louder than the last, practically shouting.

Someone had most definitely heard them.

CHAPTER
TWENTY

"K eep your damn voice down," Enzo growled, flashing his fangs. "This isn't the time for family drama." He moved closer to the door and then sniffed at the gap near the floor. "Someone's coming."

He locked the door and then sighed.

"Jessie," Finch said. "Just find us a book about Maldonado's magic. I don't care how many gods the witches have created—I'll deal with them afterward."

"I've waited *years* for this," Jessie shouted, clutching the book close. "I've been trying to avenge Carter, and you've done nothing! You're still doing nothing! I'm not going to wait any longer! I'm going to—"

"*Don't you fucking dare tell me you're the only one doing anything*," Finch yelled, far louder than his sister-in-law. The whole damn McMansion knew they were here now.

Jessie, stunned into silence, didn't move when Finch stepped close.

"When I told you about Carter's death, you told me you wanted nothing to do with me! You blew out of my life so fast I didn't even know where you went!" Finch continued at the same volume, consequences be damned. "For half a decade it was radio silence—it was just *me* thinking about what I was going to do for Carter. I'm the one who saved the citizens of Paris who were kidnapped by the witches. I was the one who went to the ifrits for the strongest fire!"

Bree watched the argument from the corner of the room, glancing back and forth between Adair and Jessie, her brow furrowed. She held on to one of the books like it was a talisman that would shield her from the confrontation.

"It was only *after all that* that I came home," Finch said, his tone turning to cold, precise anger. "Yeah. I couldn't find the witches. Yes, I was overwhelmed. Yes, I fell off the horse. But don't you dare think that your self-destructive crusade is somehow more noble. You reached out to a magical cartel leader! You bound yourself to a demon! And then you have the audacity to say that *I'm* the one who has failed Carter? That *I'm* the one fucking up?"

"There are like ten guys in the hallway beyond this door," Enzo muttered, his ear twitching. He pressed the side of his canine head to the wood. When the door handle jiggled, he growled a deep and guttural growl. Whoever was on the other side stopped immediately.

"*I needed time*," Jessie shouted back, no regard for Enzo and his warning. "And I did reach out to you! E-Eventually —after a few years—but you never replied! You were just *dead* as far as anyone knew! I had to do *something*! I couldn't just wait for you to get your shit together!"

"They're preparing to break in," Enzo muttered.

"Well, I'm here now!" Finch snapped. "And I'm going to fix this. I'm going to deal with Maldonado, your demon, those witches—and it would go a lot fucking faster if you helped me!"

Jessie shook her head, her lip quavering, her whole body shaking. Hot tears ran down her face, though her expression never changed. She glared at Finch, her teeth gritted. "I-It's too late now. We're not going to fight our way out of here. We messed up."

"They're sending people around to the window." Enzo's ears twitched again. "And they're loading rifles." When he turned to Finch, it was with a frown. "You promised me no gunfights."

Finch cursed under his breath, ripped open one of the desk drawers, and then grabbed a pen. With restrained rage, he walked over to Jessie, grabbed her arm, and then drew three lines—like tally marks—and then a fourth line through them all, as though creating lowercase Ts.

Jessie didn't struggle, she just watched, her eyebrows knitted, her breathing shallow.

"They're coming," Enzo shouted.

That was when Finch activated his magic. Everything froze. The colors drained from the world. And once everything looked like an unused coloring book, all the shapes melted away, leaving Finch utterly alone in a void of white.

Then he blinked, and he was back in front of McKinley Park, his Toyota straight ahead, the broken fence at his back, Enzo—in human form—right at his side.

1:02 p.m.

"Fuck me," Finch said with a sigh.

A hot breeze rushed over them. Enzo rotated his arms and then swiveled his neck to stretch. "You never told me the details of Carter's death."

That was true. Finch had only told him the bare minimum. He didn't like recalling the story, but he supposed after that argument, it was best to let Enzo know.

"We were in Paris," Finch said. "We were looking for a coven of full moon witches, because they had kidnapped some people and were killing them in ritualistic fashion. Our search led us to the catacombs under the city..."

The chill of that evening remained in his bones. Despite the California weather, he still felt the damp cold whenever he thought about that night.

"But that magic-eating god, Gixmoth, was down there. We didn't know. We just... ended up in a fight with it, in the dark." Finch closed his eyes. "We hadn't reset our mark on the time in over twenty-three hours, and Gixmoth prevented us from using magic, so... When Carter died... I couldn't rewind time to save him."

"And you blame yourself?"

"If I had been more cautious..."

Finch knew if he had reset his mark on the time before entering, he could've saved his brother. But he hadn't, and now everything else was history.

"Ya know, cops deal with a lot of *survivor's guilt*." Enzo laced his fingers together and then placed both hands on top of his bald head. "Best piece of advice I ever heard was to live life great enough for two people—that way, when the person you lost peeks down at you from behind the pearly gates, they're proud of what you've done."

Finch slipped his hands into his pants pockets. He hadn't wanted to get into an argument with Jessie. He had wanted to mend their relationship and start again. But hearing her anger—and voicing his in turn—had helped get something off his chest.

He felt better, though he didn't know how to articulate exactly why.

"We didn't find out Maldonado's type of magic, did we?" Enzo sardonically asked.

"I don't think so."

"You want to head back there?"

Finch let out a powerful exhale. "Not right now. First, let's go back and get the paperwork I need to serve."

"Why?" Enzo asked with a laugh. "Who cares about that paperwork?"

"It'll give me time to just drive," Finch muttered. "I think best when I'm driving."

"But why even deal with that paperwork at all? Let's just go grab a burger or something."

"Bree accepted this assignment and I don't want to disappoint her by not doing it." Finch walked around his vehicle and opened the driver side door. "So, let's get it—I can find out where this loser is at some point during all these rewinds."

Enzo rolled over to the passenger side door. "You don't want to speak to Jessie? She's in the park right now, probably confused. She's never remembered a time rewind before, right?"

"Bree is with her. She can explain it. I'll... speak to Jessie once I've cleared my head, so there's no chance we get into another argument."

"All right. Whatever you want, man."

———

Finch drove straight to his office and then parked on the street directly outside. The same three individuals were there waiting for him, but this time, Finch had no fucks to give.

He stepped out of his car, practically hitting the croc-wearing delivery boy in the process, and then snatched the paperwork from the man's arms.

"I'll find Seth Rivers," Finch said, monotone.

"Uh, thank you," the man replied. "He's been elusive lately, so—"

Completely ignoring the man, Finch directed his attention to the vampire lawyer. "I'll speak to you tomorrow, Count Chocula."

The lawyer frowned, but otherwise remained silent.

Finally, as Finch stepped around the SHADOW agent, he said, "I don't want any Girl Scout cookies, Mr. Irons."

"My name is Agent *Steele* and—"

"I don't care."

To his surprise, the agent grabbed Finch's upper arm and held him back from getting to his car. In that instant, Finch weighed the consequences of just lashing out, but instead he contained his rage.

The croc-wearing delivery boy and the vampire stayed to watch the confrontation, both seeming interested in how it would all play out.

Agent Steele—with his free hand—pulled out his badge. "I'm an agent in the Supernatural Hazard Analysis and Defense Operations Wing of the United States government. I'd like to speak with you about your sister-in-law and her current whereabouts."

In a cold and quiet voice, Finch asked, "Do you have a subpoena, warrant, or national security letter?"

"*No*," Agent Steele drawled.

"Then get your hands off me and go fuck yourself."

Technically, as long as you weren't making threats, you *could* insult federal agents. Telling a SHADOW agent to *go fuck himself* wasn't a crime, but it also wasn't the greatest idea, either. Most likely, the agent would escalate things administratively, meaning they would come back with all the appropriate paperwork to make an arrest or detainment for questioning. At worst, the agent would get local authorities involved and make everyone's life a living hell.

Finch didn't care about any of that. He didn't need to play nice.

So, when Agent Steele released him, Finch shot the man a glower and then got into his vehicle without another word.

Once he was seated, with the door shut, Enzo clicked his tongue several times. "Tsk, tsk, tsk. You're yangling for a strangling."

"I'm not afraid of that Eagle Scout," Finch said as he drove away from the office. All three of his guests were still standing in front of the door, each seemingly in shock that the encounter had gone down like it had.

Enzo relaxed back in his seat. "So, now you have your paperwork. You ready to speak with Jessie?"

"No."

"It's probably been lonely for her as well, ya know. All those years, no one to turn to."

"I don't want to be angry when I speak with her," Finch quickly said. Then he glanced down at the paperwork he had tossed onto the center console. "Let's go find this loser and serve him his subpoena."

Enzo sat up. "What? *Right now?*"

"Why not." Finch poked the first page. "Here's his address. You can use your werewolf nose to track him, right? We'll just follow his scent, discover his location, and keep that information until I'm finally ready to really live through this day."

With a chuckle, Enzo relaxed again. "All right. Let's knock this side quest out of the way and get back to the others."

CHAPTER
TWENTY-ONE

After a short scent-chase across town, Finch's Toyota rolled to a stop with a tired groan. He and Enzo stared at a house that sagged under the weight of its own neglect, its peeling white paint curled like sun-scorched skin, its warped porch slats gaping. Someone had once cared about this place, long ago. Now, it simply endured.

"This is the place?" Finch asked.

The window was down on the passenger side, allowing the California heat to seep into the vehicle.

Enzo sniffed at the air. "It's faint, but I'm pretty sure our boy is here."

"Good." Finch glanced at the time.

2:37 p.m.

It hadn't taken them too long to find this man, though Finch had no idea why he would be hiding out on the outskirts of Stockton. Why wasn't he at his own home? Was he avoiding debt collectors?

Did it matter? Finch just needed to serve the subpoena, and then he could forget about this.

The sun wasn't shining—it was looming. Finch stepped out of his car and immediately regretted it. The air shimmered above the cracked pavement, making even the broken weeds at the edges of the driveway look like they were writhing.

The street was silent in that eerie midday way, where even the stray dogs had enough sense to hide from the sun. There was movement, though—something scuttled under the porch, something with too many legs and no interest in being seen. A curtain twitched in the neighboring house, just enough to confirm that someone was watching but not enough to suggest they'd ever admit it.

Enzo got out of the car and joined Finch as he entered the porch and headed for the front door.

After cracking his knuckles, Enzo smiled. "All right—what's our plan?"

"To make some bad decisions," Finch quipped.

"Unconventional, but I'll allow it."

Finch knocked on the door. Then he poked the doorbell. When he stepped back, he folded the paperwork in half and stuck it in his back pocket.

"They're cooking something here," Enzo whispered, his nose wrinkled.

"Like pasta?"

"Like *meth*."

Finch groaned as he pinched the bridge of his nose. "It's always meth," he muttered under his breath.

The door didn't so much open as it cracked, just wide enough to reveal a bloodshot eye and a strip of sweaty, sunworn skin. The man behind it was thin in that brittle, overcaffeinated way, jittery but trying to play it cool, failing spectacularly.

"H-Hello?" he said.

He smelled like burnt plastic and a long criminal record.

"My name is Adair Finch, Private Investigator. I'm here to see Seth Rivers. Is he around?" The house exhaled a breath of hot, chemical air, thick enough to coat the back of Finch's throat.

"You're an investigator?" the guy rasped, licking his lips. "We don't got any Seth Rivers here."

Enzo snorted, and the man's pinprick pupils gave him the once-over.

"You're lying," Enzo said.

"We can do this the easy way, or the hard way," Finch chimed in.

And in that instant, he visualized the metal of the house, of his surroundings, of his body—basically forming a barrier in which he would repel anything that threatened to take his life.

The jittery man coughed, laughed, and then slammed the door shut. A moment later, three harsh *clicks* echoed inside.

"He picked the hard way," Enzo said.

Finch smirked. "I was hoping he would."

Without need for any further instruction, Enzo reared back and kicked the front door at full force. As a werewolf, even in human form, he was stronger than the average human. Add on top of that the fact he had muscles in places most people didn't even *have* places, and the door never stood a chance.

It flew inward, breaking the three locks, shattering the doorframe, and busting the hinges. The drug-addled lunatic on the other side was so shocked, his eyes so wide, it looked like he might suffocate on his own gasp.

He hadn't been expecting the might of the supernatural.

And then the man pulled a 9mm handgun from his waistband and opened fire. One bullet went straight into Enzo's bicep before Finch could leap between him and the shooter. The next couple shots did nothing—the bullets hit Finch's magical barrier and then clinked onto the floor.

"*What is going on?*" the man hysterically shouted, his reality having been shattered twice in quick succession.

Finch stepped forward and threw a quick right hook. He punched the man on the side of the jaw. When the meth addict hit the floor, he dropped his gun. Finch grabbed it and then fired twice, once in the man's chest, one in the head. The quick *bang bang* echoed throughout the house, followed by movement in the attic.

While growling, Enzo transformed into his werewolf form, fur erupting across his body, claws sprouting from the tips of his fingers, his ears moving across his newly-canine-shaped cranium.

When he stood straight, he grazed the bullet wound on his arm with two of his claws.

"We always find the violent ones," Enzo muttered.

Finch checked the 9mm's magazine. Ten shots left. "Let's find Seth."

"You just going to shoot your way through a meth house?" Enzo eyed the bleeding body on the floor.

"What? Is that going to cause it to explode?"

Enzo snorted. "Unlikely. You'd have to be pretty damn unlucky. Me and the boys had a few shootouts in meth labs."

He spoke with the kind of confidence that only came from working as a cop in Oakland. He had probably seen more meth labs than he had beer cans.

"Then let's get this done," Finch stated.

"That's a little more mercenary than you usually roll."

"I'm going to rewind time—so this might as well be a video game." Finch strode forward. "All I want is to know where we can serve our subpoena."

The front room was a disaster zone of half-empty fast

food containers, crushed soda cans, and the kind of stains that told stories no one wanted to hear. A cheap TV flickered static in the corner, its glow giving the room a sickly, artificial heartbeat.

Finch went straight to the kitchen door and listened. Two individuals were frantically moving around, their shoes squeaking on the tile floor. The unmistakable loading of a gun told Finch everything he needed to know about the situation.

He motioned to Enzo, and although Enzo was injured, he gave Finch a fang-filled smile and then kicked in the door worse than he had with the front door. The resulting *crash* and *crunch* of wood splintering in dramatic fashion made it sound like a bomb had gone off in the house.

A cloud of dust and debris filled the kitchen. Two men opened fire. Finch, visualizing his immunity to the bullets, casually walked inside and took aim at the first gunman. He fired twice—one in the chest, the next for the head. *Bang bang.* The man crumpled to the floor.

The other man, panicking, fired as fast as his gun would allow. His aim was terrible. He shot the wall and ceiling more than he managed to hit Finch's barrier, his arms shaking.

Finch turned and shot twice again, striking the man in the neck and dead between the eyes. When this man collapsed, there was no more movement.

After a few seconds, Enzo strolled in. "Where'd you learn to shoot?"

Finch waved the dust and foul odors away from his nose. "Carter and I had this old-school marksman teach us a few tricks. That was back before I made a pact with Ke-Koh. Now that I have his intense fire, I rarely use guns, but it's nice to know I haven't gotten too rusty."

Finch glanced around, frowning.

The kitchen was a disaster.

Clouded glassware all over the table. A bottle of drain cleaner knocked onto its side, the liquid inside still seeping onto the counter. The sink was full of blackened coffee filters and god-knows-what residue, the smell sour and caustic.

He turned his attention to the stove. There were pans and beakers on the top, but he wasn't sure if they were cooking. Anxiety got the better of him.

"How quickly do meth labs explode if they're unattended?" he asked.

Enzo snorted out a laugh. "Depends. If someone is mid-cook, and not paying attention to the pressure buildup, it could be a couple short minutes for an explosion." He held up a very canine finger. "If vapors are leaking, it could take, like, a few hours—maybe even days—before it explodes. And if it's just degraded chemicals, probably weeks."

"Are we in danger?" Finch asked.

"We should probably check the bathroom," Enzo stated, a little nervous himself.

Finch immediately went for the hallway. Four doors. Banging from the attic sounded above him. It was rhythmic, like someone was kicking at a timed interval.

The bathroom door stood open.

Inside, the bathtub was stained a deep, resinous orange, the kind of color that didn't come from rust. The mirror over the sink was cracked down the center. But there wasn't any meth cooking.

Finch moved to the bedroom. *This* was the real heart of operations. Rows of Mason jars, plastic tubing, a hot plate still on, its coil glowing a faint, menacing red. A table in the middle of the room was littered with powder-crusted Pyrex dishes and plastic containers with labels scratched off.

"Let me just get this," Enzo said. He moved forward and

rearranged some of the cooking. Finch wasn't entirely sure what he was doing, but he trusted the man.

Finch opened the door to the next room and instantly regretted it. He found it filled with cat litter. Just... all over the floor. Hundreds of pounds of it, like someone had just thrown fresh litter on top of old litter whenever it was too soiled—and they had no litter box.

The acrid smell of urine was worse than the cooking meth, and hundreds of poops filled the disgusting sandbox had once been a bedroom. Old curtains covering the windows were a dark yellow, but it was clear they had once been white.

Somewhere in the room, a cat faintly meowed.

Finch quickly shut the door before he vomited.

When Enzo joined him in the hallway, his wolf-like ears were twitching. "Did I hear a cat?"

"It's a prisoner of war," Finch sarcastically said. "Beyond saving. We should go."

"There's a cat locked in this room?"

"It's not a room. It's a biohazard. Trust me—let's get to the attic."

"Why not just let it out?" Enzo asked.

Finch sardonically motioned to the door. "You can have the pleasure."

Without hesitation, the werewolf opened the door.

Then all the fur on his body stood up on end. Enzo quickly slammed the door shut, his nose wrinkled in disgust, his ears pressed backward, flat against his skull.

"Do you understand now?" Finch asked, still all sarcasm.

"Fuckin' meth addict logic," Enzo muttered under his breath. He shook his head, his nose still twitching. "But I spotted the cat. It's still in there. I think... it's too weak to move. I don't think they've been feeding it."

"You saw all that in the half second you had the door open?"

Enzo motioned to his eyes. "I'm a werewolf. I have magic, too. I smell life."

"Well, sucks to be the cat." Finch motioned to the hallway again. "Let's go."

But Enzo didn't move. The man glanced back at the door, his fur still half spiked. Was he contemplating going into the room to save the cat? Finch knew that was foolish. Firstly, Enzo's nose was more sensitive than a normal human's. Being in that room would be a torture, even if Enzo held his breath.

Secondly, the litter...

It would get stuck in Enzo's fur. He'd never smell the same again.

"I'm going to rewind time," Finch stated. "Saving the cat isn't going to matter. Let's. Go."

"Remember how you said we were here to get information?" Enzo asked. "What if the cat will live if we save it? We won't know until we examine the little guy."

Finch didn't understand how people kept roping him into saving random animals. Why were there so many critters around? Why didn't people spay and neuter their pets? After a long sigh, Finch pushed all that irritation aside.

"Fine," he said. "I'll save the damn cat. Wait here."

CHAPTER
TWENTY-TWO

After a short sigh, Finch tucked his 9mm into the waist of his jeans. Then he opened the door and stepped onto the first mound of cat litter. It crunched underfoot, the clumps making each footfall precarious. The cat was in the far corner—of course it was, why would anything be easy?—and Finch held his breath as he carefully made his way over.

The cat was elderly—over the age of twelve, at least—and skeletally thin. It had dark stripes, gray, patchy fur, and gigantic yellow eyes that were crusty at the edges.

The cat meowed, softly, desperately, as half its body was covered in dirty litter. Finch pulled off his shirt and used it to cover his hands before lifting the feline from the waste. The second he had the cat in his arms, the purring started. Loud. Appreciative. The feline pressed itself against him as Finch hurried out of the room.

Once he was in the hallway, Enzo slammed the door shut.

"I got it," Finch said, showing off the tabby.

"You're a braver man than me," Enzo playfully replied.

Finch snorted out a laugh. Then he walked back into the kitchen and placed the cat on the counter. He had bigger fish to fry. But the instant he turned away, the cat started crying louder and more frantic than before.

The elderly cat's back legs weren't working. It tried to stand but just couldn't. It fell several times in its attempts to chase after Finch.

Yanked back by his heartstrings, Finch used his shirt to cradle the cat once again.

The purring was so loud, it practically echoed throughout the house.

"You can't leave him now," Enzo said.

"*Him*?"

"You can't smell that he's a little boy cat?" Enzo shrugged. "It's a wolf thing."

Finch thrust the cat over, shirt and all. "You hold him. I'm going to check the attic. Hopefully Seth Rivers is there, or else we're going to have to be creative with our searching."

"He's definitely there." Enzo took the cat. Then he wiggled the tip of his canine snout. "I'm telling you—my ability to smell is unrivaled. Our man is up there."

"Good."

Finch didn't want to waste any more time. Multiple gunshots had gone off in the house, and while that should have guaranteed a 911 call, this neighborhood played by different rules. Someone might have heard. Someone might have cared. But more likely, no one wanted the cops sniffing around too hard—too many skeletons rattling in too many closets. Around meth-infested neighborhoods, silence wasn't just golden; it was self-preservation.

Still, Finch wasn't about to gamble on it. The last thing he needed was sirens rolling up and turning this already bad day into a worse one. He just wanted to serve this damn paperwork.

He searched the ceiling in the hallway until he found the ladder up. Finch yanked it down and headed into the attic, but the moment he was halfway there, the little cat cried and cried. The urge to return and quiet the animal was strong, but Finch ignored it.

"Hey, hey, little man," Enzo whispered to the cat, patting his tiny head. "Everything will be okay. You're safe now. Adair will be *wight* back." He spoke the word *right* with a hard W, imitating the speech of a baby.

Holding back a chuckle, Finch continued up the ladder.

He pushed open the attic hatch, and a wave of pure, unfiltered hell blasted down at him. The air wasn't just hot —it was aggressive, clinging to his skin, crawling into his lungs, making every breath feel like he was inhaling the inside of a hair dryer.

The attic itself was a graveyard of forgotten junk, where things were left to be ignored and melt in peace. Old furniture and plastic bins that looked like they were seconds from liquefying. A single, bare lightbulb hung from the ceiling, its chain swaying slightly.

And there, in the middle of it all, was a man whose arms were bound behind his back. He was lying facedown on the dusty floorboards, his breathing ragged. Blood stained the floor around him, mostly in smears and droplets, but it was all dry, not fresh. How long had he been here?

Finch stood and carefully made his way over.

"Seth Rivers?" he asked.

The man glanced up from the floor. His eyes were spaced so far apart they looked like they were in the process of filing for divorce.

"What?" Seth said. "Who are you...?"

"Oh, Jesus Christ." Finch pinched the bridge of his nose.

The name *Seth Rivers* had sounded familiar, but Finch hadn't placed it. Now that he was face-to-face with this loser, it all came rushing back. Seth was the pathetic warlock who had been involved in the witch's feud back when Finch was solving the case of Bree's murdered mother.

Seth had been so pathetic that Finch had defeated him almost accidentally.

But Finch had rewound time after that. Seth likely didn't remember their encounter.

He still looked mostly the same, though. The sides of Seth's head were shaved close, while the sad, wilted remnants of a mohawk drooped to one side like it had given up on life. It was unmistakable. Finch recognized it immediately.

Seth wore a pair of bloodstained jeans, and he had enough metal pieces on his face to set off airport security from a mile away. Studs, hoops, bars—if there was a piece of flesh that could be punctured, it had been.

Except for his ears. He had had several piercings there, but they had all been ripped out, leaving his earlobes shredded and covered in clotted blood.

Finch knelt next to the man. Then he grabbed the paperwork out of his back pocket and placed it on the floor next to Seth's face.

"This is a subpoena," Finch said.

Seth groaned. "You came to... serve me paperwork?"

"Yes. Your presence is requested at the courthouse tomorrow so you can testify."

"That's why I'm in this mess, man," Seth said, half sobbing into the floor. "I turned on them, man. They knew I was gonna rat them out, so they tried to keep me here, keep me away from the prosecutors."

"Hmm."

Finch flipped to the last page of the paperwork. It was an *Affidavit of Service*—a piece of paper Finch needed to fill out and file with the court to officially claim the subpoena had been served.

He quickly jotted down all the relevant information.

RESPONDENT—Seth Rivers
DATE & TIME—September 10, 2024, 2:50 p.m.
LOCATION—An attic above a meth lab
DIRECT SERVICE?—Yes
RECIPIENT REJECTED DELIVERY?

Finch gently pushed the paperwork under Seth's chin.

RECIPIENT REJECTED DELIVERY?—No

"Consider yourself served," Finch said with a groan as he stood and tucked the affidavit into his back pocket. Then he turned to exit the attic as quickly as possible.

Seth squirmed. "W-Wait! You can't... you can't *leave* me. Please."

Finch stopped at the ladder. "Don't worry. When I do this again, I'll save you for real, but I'm not feeling it right now."

"What...?"

As he placed his foot on the first rung of the ladder, Seth thrashed harder.

"Wait!" Seth rolled to his side. "Please! I'm t-trying to get my life straightened, man. I'm trying. I have a daughter, I want to do right by her. I'm clean, man. I'm clean. My buddies wouldn't stop hasslin' me, though. Kept tryin' to sell me shit. I had to turn them in—or else I'd never be clean. *Please*. I had to do this. I need your help. They're killin' me."

There really was no point in saving Seth at this moment. Finch knew he was just going to rewind time at some point, and all his work in this nightmarish meth lab would be undone. But he thought back to Bree, and how she had wanted to save Seth the last time they had seen the man.

If she were here, she would argue to help him, even if it wasn't real.

So Finch cursed under his breath, turned back around, and then undid Seth's restraints on his arms. That was when Finch realized Seth wasn't standing because his ankles were broken.

The meth heads really had been torturing him.

After a long exhale, Finch physically lifted Seth up into his arms. The man wasn't too heavy—he had the physique of a drug addict—but Finch was still worn out after everything that had happened, and he already dreaded the ladder.

"Thank you, man. Thank you. *You're an angel.*"

"Don't mention it," Finch muttered as he awkwardly made his way down out of the attic, half holding Seth on his shoulder as he did so.

"Why are you shirtless?" Seth whispered.

"Because I was just at your mom's."

Despite his injuries, Seth chuckled. Was it the heat that was causing him to be so delusional and happy? Or was he really just ecstatic to be saved? Finch couldn't tell.

When he reached the bottom of the ladder, Finch could detect a faint amount of magic wafting off Seth, like a sort of perfume. He was a warlock—but it seemed the man only had a pact with one weak creature.

"If you have magic, why didn't you fight these druggies?" Finch asked as he hauled the man down the hall and into the front room.

"I'm... I'm not a very good warlock, man."

Enzo followed, all his attention on the cat. He was no

longer in werewolf form—he was a human, complete with the most human smile—and he was massaging the cat's little head.

"Let's take this buffoon and that cat to the office," Finch said.

Enzo finally glanced up. "Why?"

"I have extra clothes there. And we can leave them there with the brownies."

CHAPTER
TWENTY-THREE

W hen Finch arrived at his office, it was 3:15 p.m. and delightfully deserted. There were no vampire attorneys, feds, or croc-loving delivery boys. Finch breathed a sigh of relief.

Enzo carried Seth inside, and Finch carried the elderly cat. The little feline purred the whole way into the building, but as soon as the air-conditioning washed over his dirty fur, the cat went into overdrive.

Enzo unceremoniously placed Seth on the concrete floor before turning and gently taking the cat from Finch. "We need to give him a wittle bath."

The baby speech was almost too much for Finch, but he decided not to say anything. Enzo looked genially happy as he took the cat, swaddled in Finch's shirt, into the nearby bathroom. Seth groaned and writhed around on the floor, but Finch just stepped over him and went straight to his office. Once inside, he shut the door and headed for his desk.

Finch reached for a drawer and froze.

The air smelled of magic. It was faint, but he detected *something*.

Had someone been in his office? Finch glanced around. Unfortunately, his office was extremely barren. Nothing was out of place because there was nothing in this place.

Reluctantly, Finch returned his attention to his task. Out of paranoia, or perhaps years of instinct, he kept his bulletproof magic in place by maintaining the visualization. Just in case.

After throwing on a black T-shirt, Finch headed out into the main room. Enzo and the cat were waiting. Well, and so was Seth. The man was still broken, lying in the middle of the room, breathing through his mouth straight onto the floor.

"This little man is in bad shape," Enzo said—about the cat. Not the literal man on the floor.

And he was right. The feline was damp, his fur clinging to his emaciated body, his yellow eyes huge, his stripes barely visible with the matting. At least he was clean—but he looked more like a skeleton than before.

"Do you smell anything magical?" Finch asked.

"All I've been able to smell for a while is *ass* and *cat*. That litter box room was a doozy."

"Fair," Finch muttered.

"We should give him a name," Enzo said, cradling the cat gently.

Finch frowned as he stepped over Seth and headed for the door. "Aren't you a wolf? Shouldn't you hate cats? Shouldn't it hate *you*?"

"First off, everyone loves me." Enzo stomped after him. They both exited the office, and Enzo used a hand to shield the cat's elderly eyes. "Even cats. Even babies. I have natural charisma."

Finch snorted back a laugh. "Who's a good boy? *You're a good boy!* Yes, you are. *Yes, you are.*" He locked the front door and headed for his car.

"You're a son of a bitch," Enzo muttered as he followed.

"Just admit that one of your werewolf powers is a *good boy aura*. People find you trustworthy, and inexplicably want to throw things for you to chase."

When they entered the vehicle and finally sat down, Enzo patted the cat. "You ready to talk to Jessie now?"

Finch let out a long, contented sigh. After fighting a whole meth lab's worth of villains, saving an idiotic man and an elderly cat, the world seemed just a little bit brighter. "Yeah. I'm ready. Let's go talk to Jessie."

———

Finch parked his car in front of the illusioned fence around McKinley Park. Jessie's magic worked wonders. No humans could see the hole she had created, and so it went completely ignored. Finch and Enzo—and the damn cat—went straight in without any problems.

As Finch went around the bathroom, he braced himself for Jessie's fury. He was ready, and confident he wouldn't lose his temper. Enzo was correct—Jessie had been through a lot, and Finch didn't want to be one more problem in her life.

They made their way through the park, following the cracked pathways to the bathroom. When Finch rounded the corner, he froze.

No one was there. He glanced around, his breath held. When Enzo approached, Finch motioned to the clearing with the mushroom circle. "Can you smell where they went?"

Enzo sarcastically held up the cat. "I smell a lot of dander."

The cat pitifully meowed.

Irritated, Finch turned his attention to the ground for

clues. He *could* rewind time, and they would all be back in the park, right back here, where he had left them, but that would result in Jessie losing her memories of the time rewinds. Finch had managed to draw the Mark of Chronos on her arm before he rewound time in Maldonado's McMansion, but if he didn't redraw it before he rewound time again, Jessie wouldn't remember their argument in the house, or the information on the witches and modern gods.

Finch pulled out his phone and called Jessie. His heart almost stopped when he realized *she still had her phone*. No wonder the SHADOW guys were able to stay so on top of her. They knew she was here in Stockton.

He poked her number in his contacts list. It didn't even ring. It went straight to voicemail. Off.

Perhaps Jessie wasn't as foolish as he had originally thought. Turning off the device would make it much harder to track—and if she only turned it on for calls, that explained why the feds were in Stockton. They knew she was here, they just weren't sure *where*.

Finch called Liam.

It rang and rang, but no answer. Were they in trouble? Finch's heart raced with uncertainty.

"Let's split up to look for them," Finch said.

"I'll head east to the fence, you go west. We'll meet up in the middle." Enzo started in the direction he indicated.

"Right."

Finch jogged westward. He wove between new play equipment that had yet to be set up, and then made his way across a busted tennis court. Why would Jessie, Bree, and Liam leave the safety of the grove they had found? Finch shook his head. Perhaps Jessie had needed time to clear her thoughts, too.

But as he neared the western fence, he spotted Bree in

her black hoodie. She stood beside a bench, where Liam and Jessie sat. They were right in front of a park drinking fountain, one that was clearly broken and the water continuously shot out of the spout.

"Jessie?" Finch called out.

She leapt to her feet, spinning with the sharp, instinctive tension of someone expecting a fight. Her hands curled into tight, ready fists, shoulders squared, eyes hard. But then— recognition.

The instant she saw Finch, the stiffness ebbed from her posture. Her hands relaxed, a ghost of a smile tugged at the corner of her lips. A quiet thing. But there.

That sight relieved him. Finch didn't stop jogging until he was at the bench, and the moment he arrived, he exhaled and said, "I'm sorry for shouting back at Maldonado's. Listen, I need to talk to about—"

"Bree told me everything," Jessie said, cutting him off. "You and Carter bonded with Chronos. You can rewind time." Some of her harshness returned.

"Yes. About that... I didn't—"

"Bree told me about Paris as well. How you and Carter didn't mark the time before chasing Gixmoth..."

Finch held his tongue. He had just explained this to Enzo, and he didn't feel like being tormented by the memory a second time in one afternoon.

But Jessie didn't continue. She paused, the silence growing thicker. *This* was what Finch had feared. The only conclusion to draw was: Finch had fucked up. He had let Carter die. This was all his fault. *If only he hadn't been so careless.*

Of course, Jessie would blame him.

When she remained quiet, Finch reached into his back pocket and withdrew a pen. He motioned for her arm, and she complied. As he drew the Mark of Chronos, he murmured, "I'm sorry. About everything."

"You *do* blame yourself, don't you?" she whispered as she grazed her fingers over the mark. "Adair... I..."

"Adair and Jessica Finch—you're both under arrest."

Finch recognized the voice, but he couldn't immediately place it. When he whirled on his heel, everything fell into place. There was Agent Steele, the SHADOW agent, only twenty feet away, no firearm in hand.

He didn't look happy, though. Agent Steele stood with the stillness of a man who had never known uncertainty. His suit—a crisp, government-issue black—clung to his frame with the severity of a uniform. It was a blatantly expensive outfit, but it was his wings that commanded attention.

They were not feathered.

No soft plumage, no comforting stretch of white against his back. Instead, they burned, constructed not of matter but of something pure and unyielding, as if someone had sketched the idea of light itself into the air. The edges of them flickered and curled, not flames, not electricity, but something not of Earth.

They were made of divine golden light.

Because he wasn't a kami or an angel—he was a nephilim. A half-angel, half-human immortal. Finch hadn't guessed that because they were so rare. How many were in the United States? Fifty? One hundred? A vanishingly tiny amount, and they mostly kept to themselves.

"What're you doing in the park?" Finch asked.

"You were acting strange at your office, so I followed you," Agent Steele said, no mirth in his voice, no warmth. "You've been busy, Adair. Murdering men in cold blood within their house. Dragging an injured warlock to your office. And now consorting with a known criminal. You've become a higher priority than your sister-in-law.

I'm almost impressed with the speed you accomplished that."

Murdered people?

Finch wanted to laugh.

Agent Steele had followed them to the meth lab. He knew messing with federal agents was risky, but he hadn't thought one of them would make it his personal mission to stalk his every move over a couple of snide remarks.

"Uh, can my daughter and I leave?" Liam asked.

Finch had forgotten the man was even there. How was he so supernaturally quiet? He might as well have been a wooden plank on the damn park bench.

"We're not part of this," Liam said with a nervous laugh.

Bree shook her head. "Quiet, *Papa*. Adair will solve this. Just watch."

Agent Steele's hands—long-fingered, efficient—rested at his sides, but there was no mistaking the heavy brass knuckles glinting on his fists, each one etched with markings that did not belong to any human language. Not decorative. Functional. Deadly.

They were likely etched with words of binding and disruption, to cause pain and to break concentration. Most magic needed some amount of concentration. Not all, but most.

Finch knew he had a firearm as well—all agents had one —but it was obvious the man wanted to take everyone in alive.

"Lie on the ground and place your hands behind your head," Agent Steele commanded. "If you refuse to cooperate, I will use force."

Where was Enzo when he needed him? Finch shook the thought away, and then gave serious consideration to playing along, just so he could learn more about Agent Steele's capabilities. As a nephilim, perhaps he would have—

Agent Steele's wings shuddered slightly, and he zipped forward, propelled by divine magic. Then he threw a blow right at Finch's body.

The punch cracked at least two of Finch's ribs. Might've been three. Hard to count when pain was chewing its way up your side like a starved dog.

Finch staggered back, boots skidding through wet grass, and barely ducked in time to avoid the next swing. The fist passed so close he felt the heat of it, the air pressure thrumming in his ears. The damn knuckles—they were too magical.

Brimstone and malice filled the park. Darkness pooled around the agent's feet, and chains flew up to tether him.

"Bye, bye, birdie," Jessie quipped, her eyes blazing red, her demonic magic connecting to Agent Steele's wrists and ankles.

When the chains went to pull him under, however, there was a problem. His wings blazed white, shining so brightly, Finch had to look away, though the intensity was so much that he could practically see the wings through the thin skin of his eyelids.

A tremble in the air was the only warning before the blast of hot air. It felt like a small explosion, and Finch shielded his face with his forearm and managed to keep on his feet, but just barely.

Bree screamed and fell to the ground. Liam leapt on top of her, shielding her as best as his thin physique could. Jessie was the most affected. When infernal and divine magics clashed, it was the infernal at a disadvantage. It suffered the most under divine light, and the backlash caused Jessie to hit the ground and tumble.

"You're resisting arrest," Agent Steele growled, adjusting his blazer, which—miraculously—still looked crisp despite the charring on it. His wings twitched at his back, shifting like they were itching to spread, but he kept them half closed.

Finch wiped his mouth. Blood. When had that happened? During the explosion? "Brass knuckles aren't the kind of thing they teach you in Sunday school," he said. "I don't even think they're standard-issue weapons."

Finch had about two seconds to think before another punch came his way—this one aimed right for his jaw. Fast. Too fast.

No dodging. Block or get knocked out.

He got his forearm up just in time, and even managed to visualize with his new fae magic. Repelling metal would save him, wouldn't it? Agent Steele's knuckles hummed half an inch from Finch's arm, unable to connect.

Repelled.

That meant no more punching.

But then Agent Steele's wings glowed a brighter gold, and a blast of force hit Finch across the front of his body. The impact rattled his bones, sent his own fist slamming into his own damn face, and before he could regain his footing, Agent Steele drove a knee straight into his gut.

Everything inside Finch rebelled at once. Stomach. Lungs. Soul.

He hit the dirt with a wet thud, gasping like a fish left on the dock too long.

Well, at least this was a lot of useful information. He wheezed as he rolled onto his side. Agent Steele wasn't a sadist, it seemed. The agent waited, looming over Finch, his blue eyes narrowed, his wings twitching at the points.

"You're making this harder than it needs to be," Agent Steele stated.

Finch groaned. "That's sort of my thing."

"I didn't want this to turn violent in front of a child. Stop resisting."

"That's my apprentice," Finch said as he managed to get to one foot. "I'm teaching her everything I know."

"Then you're forcing my hand," the agent said as he spread his feet, taking a stance for a strike.

Finch snapped his fingers, and a puff of flames exploded from his hand. The *whoosh* of flames caused Agent Steele to flinch, and the man blinked. In that moment, Finch lunged.

CHAPTER
TWENTY-FOUR

Finch shot up and caught the agent square in the throat, his momentum carrying him into a full-bodied lunge. With his other hand, Finch punched the agent's ribs, and the two stumbled back, Agent Steele momentarily forgetting Finch was immune to his knuckles. When the agent tried to punch Finch in the side of the head, his blow was deflected.

Flames burst from Finch's palm, scorching part of the agent's throat. The man fell backward, and they both crashed to the ground, the half-angel gasping in pain.

Not invincible. Good to know.

The angel's wings began to glow brighter, and Finch wasn't about to deal with that shit. Finch leapt up and then curb stomped the agent's head, a brutal *crunch* following his blow, and Agent Steele's wings flickered. Then they disappeared, the light dissipating.

The fed was knocked out. Or worse, Finch wasn't entirely certain. The man wasn't moving—but that's what happened after a curb stomp, after all.

Finch inhaled and then exhaled.

A hot wind rushed through the deserted park.

"You beat him?" Bree shouted, gleeful. She dashed around her father and then went straight to Finch. "You beat a crazy angel? That's so amazing!"

"He's a nephilim." Finch tried to stand straight, but then he groaned, grabbed his side, and gritted his teeth hard. Agony lanced through him, his cracked ribs rebelling. So Finch ambled over to Jessie, half hunched over. "Are you okay?"

She picked herself up, trembling as she went. "I... have a terrible headache... but I'll be all right." Once she stood, she brushed off the dirt. "Sorry I wasn't much help. The demon I have has sometimes managed to stop these divine weirdos. His power is just that overwhelming."

"Which demon? You never told me the name."

Jessie sighed. "His name is *Sabnock*, and he's—"

"A marquess of hell," Finch muttered. Then he sighed, hobbled over to Agent Steele's motionless body, and knelt next to it. "I can't believe you took control of a *marquess*. Unbelievable. No wonder Maldonado wants you back."

Bree wandered over to the other side of the agent, sticking close to Finch. Her father also came over, his glasses cracked and crooked. He endlessly attempted to adjust them, but every position he tried obviously irritated him.

"What's a *marquess*?" Bree asked.

Finch patted the unconscious agent, feeling his pockets and even pulling out the man's handgun. A Glock 19. Then Finch placed it to the side. He wanted to know everything the agent had on him, just in case.

"Marquess is a title given to demons who control armies and minions," Finch answered absent-mindedly.

"And you know *all* demon marquesses just off the top of your head?"

"There's only fourteen of them. It's not a difficult list to keep track of."

Unable to fix his glasses, Liam approached the downed agent and watched as Finch sifted through the man's belongings. Jessie also watched, her brow furrowed, as though confused and concerned both.

Finch reached into Agent Steele's front pant pocket and withdrew a receipt from a Taco Bell, where the time of purchase was 12:01 pm. He rolled his eyes and wondered how a man this pale could have the digestive tract necessary to handle such "food."

"So, when you and the marquess demon merged, uh, like what happened?" Bree scooted closer to Jessie. "Like, what did it do to your magics?"

There was a short moment of silence before Jessie crossed her arms and then exhaled. "Sabnock is grafted to my heart core—which means I draw on the magic of *his* heart core as though it were my own. He's a demon known for imprisoning people and torturing them with festering wounds."

"Wow. What about your witch magic in the heart?"

"I lost it forever," Jessie intoned, so devoid of warmth she almost sounded robotic.

Bree rubbed her arm and cringed. "O-Oh. Sorry."

The silence returned. As if to save them from the awkward moment, Liam cleared his throat and turned to Finch. "What are you looking for, Adair?"

"Anything interesting," Finch replied.

The agent's jacket had his badge, a phone, a second phone, a gold chain necklace that smelled of divine magic, and a blank piece of paper. Finch wasn't stupid, though. The paper didn't smell of magic, but that was because it was hidden.

He ignored that and continued to search.

"Robbing the dead isn't very... dignified," Liam said, frowning.

"He's not dead." But Finch wasn't entirely certain anymore. He placed two fingers on the man's neck, pressing hard on the carotid artery. The pulse was weak, but there. "Yeah, he's still alive. This is fine."

Liam fidgeted nervously. "S-So Bree explained to Jessie and me that you rewind time. We aren't going to get in trouble for this, correct? This will all disappear? No one will ever know? All the evidence of our crimes will vanish?"

Finch nodded once, most of his attention on his task. "You got it."

"Oh, thank the old mountains," Liam murmured. He wiped sweat from his brow, either from the heat or his nervousness, Finch didn't know.

"What magics do you have in your *other* cores?" Bree asked out of nowhere, facing Jessie with a forced smile. Perhaps she was trying to make the moment between them less awkward, but Finch couldn't really tell.

"The core of my crown, pure wyld magic, is how I see through illusions, glamors, and invisibility," Jessie said. She kept her eyes on the motionless body of the nephilim. "The core of my eyes holds the power to remove illusions. So long as I visualize them being peeled away in some manner, I can dispel them."

"Oh."

"My heart... you already know. The core of my soul allows me to easily break free of fae magics and charms. I can free myself or others. And the core of my loins makes me immune to poisons, venoms, and inebriation, especially from fae sources."

"Like the fae *air*?" Bree asked.

Jessie nodded, but otherwise remained silent.

"When you became a witch, why did you get those

magics specifically?" Bree hastily added, "I'm just curious. M-My mum was a witch, and I didn't talk to her too much about, uh, how witches pick the things they want."

"When you drink from the moon, you must only imagine your deepest desires," Jessie whispered. "They manifest in your cores, becoming your magic. You must focus on what you want—what makes you happiest—for if you allow your thoughts to stray, your magic will be forever weaker."

"So don't think of the Stay Puft Marshmallow Man at the wrong moment," Finch quipped.

No one laughed.

Bree gave Finch an odd and confused look before inching even closer to Jessie. "What were *your* desires?" she whispered.

"My human mother took me from my elven father when I was young." Jessie's gaze was unfocused, unseeing. She "stared" at Agent Steele, though it was obvious she saw nothing in front of her, just images in her mind's eye. "My greatest desire was to return to the fae realm and find him."

"And that's why you have all your magics?" Bree asked.

Jessie didn't reply.

"Are you done yet?" Liam curtly asked. He knelt next to Finch. "I think we need to go. What if there are other SHADOW agents nearby? What if one of them shoots you before you can rewind time?"

"Just let me—" Finch cut himself short. He found a hidden pocket inside the agent's jacket, and inside that was an ancient nail. And not just *any* nail, but a covenant nail— an object imbued with divine magic and used to seal away other types of magic. Someone had to slam the nail into someone's body and keep it there, but as long as the nail remained, the person's cores wouldn't activate.

Well, unless they used divine magic of some sort. Then the covenant nail wouldn't work.

Finch turned the nail over in his hands. "I found what I was looking for."

It was dark in color, except for the tip, which seemed rusted.

"So now you'll rewind time?"

Finch stood, shoved the nail into his pocket, and then grabbed Liam's arm. "You're not allowed to tell anyone about my magic. Got it? Not under any circumstance. Ever."

"I understand," Liam muttered.

"And we're going to need to find a way to keep your mind from being invaded and your thoughts being read."

As he spoke, Finch drew the Mark of Chronos on Liam's arm. The other man didn't protest, but he did fidget with his glasses the entire time.

Then, without warning, Finch activated his magic. The world froze. The leaves stopped swaying. The wind no longer blew. And then the colors drained, seeping into the ground until they vanished. Finally, all the shapes in the black-and-white world melted away until there was nothing.

Finch blinked.

He stood outside McKinley Park, his Toyota straight ahead, the broken fence at his back, Enzo—in human form, and without a cat—right at his side. And his ribs weren't shattered. Breathing was easy, as was standing straight.

1:02 p.m.

"Dammit, Adair," Enzo growled.

Finch wheeled on his heel to face the man. "What?"

"I didn't get a chance to say goodbye to *Methusepaws*. You need to give me more warning before you just rewind time."

"*Methusepaws*? Are you serious?"

"Don't you get it? Methuselah plus *paws*. Plus, it's actually the most perfect name for the cat." Enzo leaned in and sardonically said, "His nickname can be *Meth*. Ya, you heard me. The. Perfect. Name."

Finch let out a long exhale. Methuselah was the first wizard—and the oldest human being who ever lived. He was eventually killed, but only after everyone hunted down all his servitors. Naming a cat after him? Finch shook his head.

Although, the more he mulled it over, Finch had to admit it *was* the perfect name. The cat was elderly, so naming him after a notoriously old wizard was fitting.

Enzo punched Finch's shoulders. "Admit it. It's perfect."

"Sure," Finch said with a groan. He turned and headed into the park, the sun beating down on them like it was a spiteful landlord and they hadn't paid the rent in three months.

"I'm thinking we can give the cat to Bree," Enzo said as he followed. "You didn't tell her about it, did you?"

"No, I was too busy fighting Agent Dumbass. He's half nephilim, half boxer, so it really took all my concentration to best him."

Enzo chuckled, showing off his white teeth. "Oh, so that was all that light and noise. Sorry, I was too busy with Meth to run over." He snorted at his own inadvertent joke. "Ugh. Maybe we shouldn't call the cat *Meth*. A lot of conversations could sound bad out of context."

"Focus," Finch snapped. "I have a new plan. Our half-angel buddy has a lot of interesting weapons on him—and I think it would be amusing to use them ourselves."

CHAPTER
TWENTY-FIVE

Before Finch could head straight back to his office, he wandered into the park and headed for the bathroom building. He barely saw the dilapidated slides or cracked walkways, as the park was now becoming a familiar space.

When he reached the others behind the bathroom building, Jessie was waiting for him. She rushed forward, frowning.

"Adair," she breathed.

He stopped in front of her, his words trapped in his throat.

"You really can't rewind time further?" Jessie's voice was a whisper, fragile as thin glass. "Back to when Carter was alive?"

She already knew the answer. Finch could tell from her voice.

He shook his head. "I can't. I'm sorry."

Her eyes flickered, searching his face as if she might find some trace of a lie, some hidden loophole he hadn't considered. Her fingers curled at her sides.

"Can Chronos?" Her question came out sharper, edged with desperation.

Finch hesitated.

Visiting Chronos had been his first desperate act after Carter's death. But Chronos had barely entertained the request before shutting the door on it completely.

"*Ask me for more power again*," Chronos had warned, his voice as hollow as the space between stars, "*and I will unravel you from all time.*"

Finch had believed him.

The fraction of power Chronos had granted him—the ability to turn back the clock just one day—was all he was willing to give. Not a moment more.

"Can Chronos?" Jessie asked again.

"He said *no*," Finch replied. "I'm sorry."

Jessie's breath hitched, and for a second, she looked ready to argue. To demand that he try again, that he fight harder, that he trade whatever was left of himself for a different outcome. But then she closed her eyes.

She already knew—it wouldn't work. Finch didn't have the power to force an ancient titan to do his bidding.

Silence descended.

Enzo slowly walked by Finch and Jessie and then headed for Bree. "You okay, kid?" he whispered as he gave her the once-over.

She pressed a finger to her lips and shot him a sharp glare. "*Shh.*"

Bree turned her attention back to the conversation happening just a few feet away, her posture tense with focus. She and Enzo leaned in, listening intently, but Liam remained distracted, uninterested. Instead, he held up his glasses, tilting them this way and that, inspecting the places where they had once been cracked.

Since time had rewound, everything was restored. And that fascinated him.

This was the first time he had remembered going back in time, and it showed. The quiet marvel in his eyes, the way his fingers traced over the flawless glass, as if half expecting to find fractures that no longer existed.

"What kind of pact did you make with Chronos?" Jessie's voice cut through the moment, direct and insistent. "What did you and Carter promise for this power? Can't you promise more? Do more?"

The words hit Finch hard.

Because the pact had never left his mind—not since they had found the records on the modern gods in Maldonado's study. It had weighed on him. Gnawed at him.

Because Chronos had not given his magic freely. The Titan of Time had named his price.

"*New modern gods will be born,*" Chronos had told them. "*They will rise. They will fight. They will forge a new pantheon.*"

And he had seen every possible outcome of that war.

So when Finch and Carter had come recklessly pleading for his power, Chronos had given them only one request in return:

Protect one of the newborn gods. Not just *any* god— one of Chronos's choosing. One he would name when the time was right.

And Finch had agreed. They both had.

But Chronos had never come to him. Not with a name. Not with a sign. And after Carter's death, Chronos had been irritated. Not grief-stricken. Not angry. Just... displeased. Like a man watching a carefully built clock lose a gear. A necessary piece removed too soon.

Had he miscalculated? Had Carter's death disrupted something even he hadn't foreseen? Finch didn't know. But he did know one thing: Chronos had ordered him to tell no one about the details of the pact.

"Chronos won't give me more of his magic," Finch finally said with a sigh. "Trust me, I know. And my pact isn't something I can *do more of*. It's a one-time thing. A single mission."

Jessie chewed her bottom lip. Her gaze fell to the ground as a rush of hot wind swept by. Her pixie-short hair barely moved, even as the gust twirled in the grove before moving on.

No one spoke for a few minutes. The quiet solitude of the deserted park was a welcome change from the fighting they had done, but Finch didn't want to stew in his dark thoughts any longer. He wanted to move on—he wanted to put an end to the wizard and save Jessie.

"I'm going to head to the office," Finch said as he turned to leave.

Jessie grabbed his arm. "Wait."

"Hmm?"

"I'm sorry," she said.

"For what?"

"For leaving. After... After Carter's death." Jessie exhaled, her tension clearly fading with her breath. "We should work on this together. You want to defeat Maldonado, right? That's step one before we move on to killing those witches?"

Finch slowly nodded. "Yeah. Exactly."

Jessie forced half a smile. "Well, now that I know you have infinite amounts of time, I understand why you did what you did back in the study. Let me help you."

"First, I need to go to the office," Finch stated. "But that weirdo half-angel is there, so you should wait here until I get back."

"I get to go, too, right?" Bree interjected.

"All apprentices get to go—who else is going to carry all our things while we search?" Finch teased.

"*Hey*! That's not funny." She crossed her arms and frowned.

"I'd rather wait in the park," Liam said, holding up a single finger. "You said this place needs to be guarded, right? I'll keep doing that."

Bree rolled her eyes. "Papa! You should come with us. We need to find out all the information we can. Having a fifth person search would make things go faster."

Liam, unable to say no to his daughter, just stood from the bench. "All right. I'll go."

"When I get back from the office." Finch pulled a pen from his back pocket and quickly drew the Mark of Chronos on both Jessie's and Liam's arms. "Until then, wait right here." But with a quick motion of his head, he turned to Enzo. "Except you. You're with me."

———

The two of them arrived at Finch's office to find the same three men waiting.

The delivery boy.

The vampire attorney.

And the nephilim SHADOW agent.

Now if they would all walk into a bar, Finch was certain it would make a great joke, but he pushed his tangential thoughts aside to focus on his mission. He stepped out of his vehicle, into the blazing sunlight, and then went straight for the delivery boy.

Finch snatched the paperwork from him. "I'll give these to Seth."

The man opened his mouth to speak, but Finch had already turned away from him.

Mr. Kane, the goth vampire, smiled as Finch faced him. "You seem preoccupied."

"I am. So you should come back later." Slapping the vampire on the shoulder, Finch walked past and sarcastically asked, "Besides, don't you have a love triangle with a werewolf and a girl you need to get back to?"

Mr. Kane's flabbers had been gasted because all he could do was huff and sputter and utter angry words under his breath as Finch continued to the agent.

"You smell like old tacos," Finch casually said as he continued past Agent Steele. "How embarrassing."

The agent, momentarily stunned by the statement, didn't grab Finch this time around. Instead, Finch walked halfway around his vehicle before Agent Steele managed to whirled around on his heel.

"Wait! I need to speak with you about—"

"Come back with a warrant, subpoena, or national security letter, boy scout," Finch yelled back with a wave of his head. Then he got into his car, shut the door, and started the engine.

"What's wrong with you?" Enzo snapped. He lowered his voice as he added, "The last time you threw insults at this guy, he followed us to the meth lab. Or have you forgotten?"

"I've forgotten nothing," Finch replied. Then he drove away from the office with a slight smile. "I *want* him to follow us."

———

Finch drove up to the gate of Maldonado's McMansion and punched in the entry code. Sixteen ten. Once he was finished, the gate groaned open, and Finch drove up the long driveway to the front of the house.

1:52 p.m.

They only had a few minutes if they wanted to enter the McMansion while Maldonado was in the living room.

Liam practically pressed his face against the back window as he ogled the surrounding area. He glanced from the pool house to the dozens of flashy cars, his expression growing more and more incredulous.

"A wizard is really here? In Stockton?" Liam nervously laughed. "I can't believe a little resort estate exists inside the city's boundaries."

"Spanos Park has a lot of places like this," Finch muttered.

"Professors don't get paid enough…"

"None of us get paid enough," Enzo quipped.

Once parked, Finch stepped out of the vehicle. Everyone hurried out a moment afterward. Without a word between them, they crept around the same side of the house. Finch was more flippant this time, hurrying under a windowsill without bothering to scope out the area. While he had only done this once before, it had been so easy that he didn't care to stress about the details this time.

He kept his magic operating, though. He visualized metal being repelled from him. If some invisible lunatic with a gun popped up out of nowhere, Finch would be ready.

Bree, Jessie, and Enzo kept pace, familiar with the surroundings and quickly heading to the window they had entered the house through before. Only Liam lagged behind, his eyes wide as he crouch-walked to avoid detection. Finch waited for him, holding back a whole line of sarcastic commentary.

When Liam finally reached Finch, he stood straight and then whispered, "Didn't you say there were gunmen around here? Should we really be moving as a group?"

"You're fine," Finch said through gritted teeth. "Besides,

you're a warlock. You don't have any magical abilities to help you out in a fight?"

"Uh, no," Liam stated, lamely. But then he perked up a bit as he reached into his pocket. "But I do still have one of those items I had made for the police department. Y-You know. The ones made with some of Gixmoth's magic. I can, uh, see through illusions and invisibility."

Finch grabbed his shoulder and shoved him toward the study window. "Fantastic. You can be one of the lead investigators."

Bree placed her hand on the window and stared at the glass. A soft *click* alerted everyone that her trickster magic was successful. She glanced over at Finch with a smile. "I got it my first time!"

"Excellent," Finch replied. "Keep practicing. You should be able to unlock any door if you're good enough."

"Wait, is *this* what you're teaching Bree when you take her on a case?" Liam whispered.

Everyone ignored the man as Bree opened the window and then slid inside. Enzo and Jessie followed soon after, and Finch practically pushed Liam inside before entering last.

"How often do you break into places?" Liam indignantly asked.

"*Shh!*" Finch shut the window and then shot the man a glare. "Will you keep your voice down? Just help us search the goddamn study for Maldonado's weakness. We can talk about the legality later."

"Uh, A-Adair?" Bree said.

"What?"

"She wasn't here before, right?"

Finch turned.

Inside the study was none other than Maldonado's elf woman.

CHAPTER
TWENTY-SIX

"She shouldn't be here," Bree whispered.

The elf woman sat by the bookshelf, perched on the edge of a chair like a doll that had been placed there and forgotten. She was still dressed for a pool party, her emerald bikini catching the dim light, glittering every time she shifted—which wasn't often. She didn't stand. She didn't scream for help.

She simply stared.

Her eyes were too deep, too dark, beautiful in a way that was almost haunting. There was something wrong in that stillness. Finch didn't like it.

Was she okay?

Bree swallowed and tugged up her hoodie, retreating a step. "I-I mean, every time you rewind stuff, things don't change. Why is she here?"

She was right.

When Finch rewound time, everything reset—exactly as it had been. No one remembered anything. No one could alter their actions. The only time things deviated from the original timeline was when he changed something.

And yet here the elf was.

Finch's gaze flicked to Liam.

Liam hadn't been with them last time. He hadn't snuck in, hadn't moved with them like a silent ghost. Could he be the reason the elf woman was here now?

That didn't make sense.

Enzo moved forward, his presence filling the space like a gathering storm. "We're with the police," he announced, tone flat, hard. "This place is surrounded, and I hope you all know some good RICO lawyers, because you're going to prison for a very long time."

Then he stepped even closer to her, looming over her seat.

The elf gasped, flinching before she could stop herself.

"Unless," Enzo continued smoothly, "you cooperate. Then we'll go easy on you."

The elf hesitated. For a moment, Finch thought she might actually break, might beg for protection—but then she inhaled, her voice slipping out so softly he almost missed it.

"I... I can't cooperate. I can only do what my master instructs."

Damn. She had forfeited her soul to Maldonado. Finch remembered seeing the chain from her soul to his.

"What did he tell you to do?" Enzo pressed.

"He told me to wait in the study until he was done with the intruder."

The intruder. Singular.

Not *intruders*.

Something clicked in Finch's mind, the realization like a bolt of lightning straight to the skull. He knew why things were different. He knew why the elf had been sent here instead of playing out the same loop as before.

"It's Agent Steele," Finch said, the certainty settling over him like iron. "He followed us. A little faster and sloppier than I expected, but I'd bet any amount of money he's the one who has Maldonado's attention."

Enzo turned toward the door. As he moved, his body rippled and shifted, fur bursting from skin, wolf ears jutting from his skull, his mouth elongating into a canine snout. He grew a few feet, and his sweatpants and tank top could barely contain him, but they maintained. A tail slipped from the seam of his pants, bushy and unmistakably *wolf*.

He moved to the door and listened.

Everyone was quiet for a long moment.

"You're right," Enzo eventually muttered. "The guys in the house are prepping for some sort of ambush on a single guy. It seems they know our SHADOW agent is nearby."

Jessie's eyes widened. "You brought an agent from SHADOW here?" She shook her head and cringed. "Of course Maldonado would sense them! He *hates* them. He wants them to leave him alone—or better yet, he wants them all dead. Don't you remember why he hired me? To assassinate the ones he hates the most."

Finch remembered. He just hadn't counted on Maldonado having such specific defenses. Apparently, he had some sort of magic to detect these guys. Or maybe something they wore? Like their badges or their guns?

He wasn't certain, and it didn't matter.

"It's okay," Finch said, gesturing for everyone to calm down. "This was what I wanted. Admittedly, I had hoped Agent Steele would've given us more time before showing up, but this is ultimately the plan."

Enzo snorted out a dark laugh. With his fangs showing in a smile, he asked, "You *want* him to fight Maldonado? Is that it?"

Finch nodded and half shrugged. "Yes. It'll give me more

information. Like how useful divine magics will be against him."

"You're a sick son of a bitch." Enzo laughed again. "I like it. This is your best plan yet."

"So, we're *not* going to search through the books?" Bree asked.

With a wave of his hand, indicating most of the room, Finch said, "You all search that area for clues about Maldonado's magic and weaknesses. Jessie, you take point to dispel illusions. I'll take this one bookshelf near the door. As soon as the fighting starts, I'm going to watch—for research purposes. You all continue here, and once I restart everything, we'll discuss what we found. Got it?"

Everyone nodded.

Except for the elven woman. She nervously rubbed her arms up and down, glancing between each individual in the room. Finch pointed at her, and she froze.

"You're not going to do anything?" he asked.

She shook her head, her silky black hair gorgeous as it swayed with her movements.

"Because you can't?" Finch added. "Maldonado has control?"

"He told me to wait," she whispered. Then she visibly grimaced as she asked, "You're here to *fight* him? Can you please... leave me out of this?"

Bree leapt to Finch's side. "You don't have to worry! We're going to save you. That's what we do—we save everyone."

"Not *everyone*," Finch muttered under his breath.

"And we'll definitely make sure you get out of here, *especially* if there's magic controlling going on," Bree continued, ignoring Finch's sardonic remark. "Don't worry. Adair is going to kick Maldonado's ass."

"*Language*," Liam scolded from the other side of the room.

"Ugh." Bree narrowed her eyes and whispered, "Okay, mental note—let's *not* take Papa on any of our cases."

Jessie quickly touched the books, their protective illusions sloughing off a few seconds after her fingers left the spines. Enzo and Liam grabbed a few and flipped through the pages. Finch was poised to join them, but he stopped himself when he noticed Bree watching the elf.

"You're not hurting, are you?" Bree asked.

The elf narrowed her eyes and scooted back in the chair as far as she could go. "Please, stop talking to me. I want nothing to do with you."

"But we're going to save you."

"*I want nothing to do with you.*"

Bree huffed and placed her hands on her hips, her cheeks growing red. Finch stepped between her and the elf, his attention divided by the events in the room and the ever-growing scent of magic. Clearly, a fight was going to break out in the middle of the McMansion.

"Leave the woman alone," Finch commanded.

Bree frowned. "Did you hear what she said? She said she didn't want to be saved."

"Yeah, okay, let's believe her. Leave the woman alone."

"B-But that doesn't make any sense! Did you say she was being controlled? Maybe she was forced to say that."

Finch grabbed Bree and pulled her away from the elven woman. He leaned down to whisper, "Listen, there's nothing I can do about it right now, all right? So let's not waste our energy on dealing with this. This is lesson number one of apprentice training, understood?"

"But you've already taught me tons of things," Bree muttered, "so this is like *lesson number eighty.*"

An explosion rocked the McMansion, ending the

conversation with a violent tremor that knocked most of the books off the shelves. The elven woman threw her arms over her head, shielding herself from the ensuing chaos. Jessie, Liam, and Enzo stumbled away from the mess, none of them even remotely harmed.

"I'm going to go," Finch said. "You all stay here. I'll either be back, or I'll reset everything."

"Don't worry, I'll make sure it gets done," Jessie replied.

Finch threw open the door while visualizing his metal-repelling duergar magic. The long hallway was filled with smoky debris and dust, and another tremor through the floor told Finch the fight was raging close.

Covering his mouth with the collar of his shirt, Finch rushed forward. He made it to the kitchen—a massive room with enough stovetops to feed a whole army—and then froze. Two gunmen stood by the large kitchen window, each with handguns firmly held with both hands. They were pressed up against the wall on either side of the glass, carefully peering outside.

They hadn't spotted him.

Another explosion, and the window rattled, as did most of the pans in the cupboards. Finch had to steady himself.

"This is not the day for this," one thug said. He was rail thin and shaking, his teeth black, his fingers cracked.

The other gritted his teeth. "Shut up, asshole. Just shoot if the weird angel gets close to the window." He was aggressively normal, with an average build and plain clothes.

"Brah, I can barely see straight. The colors are dancing."

"*Keep it together.*"

Clearly, the thin man was so high he could smell his own brain.

Which meant he was the weak link. Strung out, twitchy, barely standing upright. The other one? Solid, calm, reliable. The kind of man who actually aimed before he fired. To make sure the fight went as fast as possible, Finch would start with the weak link first, and get himself a gun.

Finch lunged.

He grabbed Thin Guy's wrist and snapped it sideways. The man screamed. The gun clattered to the tile floor.

Normal Guy reacted faster than Finch liked. A sharp intake of breath, a pivot, the gun swinging up toward Finch's head. But he wasn't fast enough.

Finch drove his elbow into the guy's throat before he could fire. The bastard staggered, choking, his shot going wide and blasting through a rack of hanging pans. The resulting *bang* and *clatter* didn't compare to the battle outside, thankfully.

"I knew this was a bad day," Thin Guy frantically muttered. "*I knew it.*"

Thin Guy, despite his utterly useless motor skills, was still in the fight, pawing for his gun with his one working hand. Finch kicked it away, sent it skidding across the tile.

Normal Guy lunged, throwing a wild punch, wheezing. Finch caught his wrist and twisted, wrenching him around and slamming him face-first into the steel countertop. People didn't understand how vulnerable wrists were. Finch had learned, years ago, to aim for them in close combat, as it would often disable the opponent faster than many other locations. And they were often easy to reach.

Normal Guy slumped and rolled over the countertop, a wet, bloody smudge left behind on the surface.

Then Thin Guy did something stupid. He grabbed a kitchen cleaver and lunged, arm trembling, sweat pouring off him.

Finch sidestepped.

Thin Guy tripped over his own feet. Finch shoved him —just a little push, barely anything—and the idiot went headfirst into the open pantry door.

"I hope Maldonado isn't paying you two much," Finch quipped.

Normal Guy, half-conscious, slurred out, "Shit... *Shit*..." Blood poured down his face.

Finch scooped up both handguns and went for the exit. He followed the sound of distant fighting, the smell of brimstone and jasmine flowers in the air.

CHAPTER
TWENTY-SEVEN

Finch slammed through a door and found himself in a spacious parlor room. The bay window was smashed, the hot summer wind blowing across the sofa, love seats, and coffee table. Papers on the nearby shelves fluttered and flew to the ground.

Outside, there was a literal battle between divine and infernal. Agent Steele, the half-angel, with his golden wings of light, faced off against a man who was clearly half demon.

The half-demon moved like a puppet on tangled strings, body jerking and twisting in ways no human should. His skin—where it wasn't blackened and cracked—shimmered like hot coals, and his eyes were pits of ember and ruin, blazing as though hungry. The "man" lifted a clawed hand, and an explosion erupted forth, shaking the estate.

So *that* was where it was coming from.

From the smoke and debris outside, a chair came flying into the parlor room.

"*Dammit,*" Finch grunted as he barely dodged to the side.

The chair splintered against the bookshelf behind him.

A glance told him it had been a nice chair once. Hardwood, well-crafted. Someone had probably spent a fortune on it. Now it was expensive kindling. Why had it been outside?

"Kill him, Zarvul," a man commanded, his voice familiar and sinisterly confident. "I can make use of his blood."

Finch whirled on his heel to find Maldonado strolling into the parlor room. Their eyes locked a moment later, with Maldonado's expression shifting to amused confusion.

"Are you *Adair Finch*?" he asked. "In my vacation home?"

"This isn't where I parked my car," Finch sarcastically said as he backed up toward the door.

"You dare make a joke at a time like this?"

Finch shrugged. "What was that? I don't speak Spanish."

"*Tsk*." Maldonado sneered. "You're not a clown. You're the entire circus."

Normally, Finch wouldn't make such jokes, but now he learned something new—Maldonado could be easily frustrated. More information he could use.

Maldonado ripped his suit jacket off and threw it to the floor, just as he had done the last time they fought. However, unlike last time, the jacket transformed into something large, clawed, and extremely pissed off. It was like twenty shadow imps had fused into one gigantic imp, its body massive and corded with obvious muscles.

The giant shadow imp hunched low, its charcoal-black limbs coiling like stretched tar, its eyes glimmering. It had entirely too many teeth.

Finch exhaled, flexed his fingers around the two handguns. He was tired. Pissed off. But still standing.

What was one more fight?

The massive imp moved first, too fast, a blur of black

sinew and hunger. Finch barely shifted in time, twisting out of the way as claws raked the air where his side had been a second before. The thing had reach, and it knew it.

But Finch had something better than reach.

He stepped in, too close for it to adjust, and fired one of the handguns three times straight into the monster's throat.

The imp gurgled—a sound like water over hot coals—and Finch followed up by dropping the gun and blasting the beast with orange flames. The heat burst from his palm, fueled by his amusement of the situation, and his desire to wreck this filthy den of thugs. This wasn't the hottest fire he could produce, but it was enough to melt the skin of the shadow imp, and practically liquefy its insides.

A normal shadow imp would've gone up in smoke, but this fat monstrosity somehow clung to existence.

When Finch stopped incinerating it, the beast staggered but didn't drop.

Of course not. That would be too easy.

The imp lunged again, just as something else came crashing through the broken window.

Agent Steele and the demon-man slammed into the parlor floor, splitting the coffee table in two, wood and glass flying in every direction. The demon-man rolled, already recovering, laughing as blood dripped from his split lip, steam curling from his wounds.

Steele pushed himself upright, breathing heavy, golden wings dimmed slightly, his eyes locking on Finch just as Finch blasted the shadow imp with more fire, finally killing the beefed-up monster.

Maldonado slicked back his black, oiled hair. "*Zarvul*, what did I tell you about fighting in the house?" He spoke the question with his teeth gritted, every word on the edge of rage.

Without giving Maldonado any warning, Finch lifted

his remaining handgun and fired two shots. One bullet hit Maldonado in the forehead, the other in the chest. The first bullet struck the man hard enough to stagger him, and the other bullet ripped through his crimson silk shirt—but neither of them pierced Maldonado's skin.

They left divots, as though his body were too tough for a bullet.

Maldonado sneered as he rubbed the dent on his forehead. Then he snapped his fingers and pointed at Finch.

Zarvul, the half-demon, turned and flashed his fangs.

But that was when Agent Steele shot forward, wings flaring like a war banner. He struck the demon-man's jaws with his brass knuckles. The thing reeled back, then grinned, lips splitting too wide.

Steele grabbed the half-demon, kneed him in the side and then slammed him into the floor, cracking floorboards with his superhuman strength. Zarvul, unfazed, kicked up into Steele's gut, sending the man stumbling backward. Steele fell to one knee, grabbing his stomach, trembling visibly from the pain.

Zarvul slowly got to his feet.

"You're not going to help your friend?" Maldonado asked, eyeing Agent Steele.

"Nah." Finch casually walked over to Steele and reached into his suit jacket. "I'm just going to mug him real quick."

"What... are you... *doing?*" Agent Steele hissed, pink spittle coming out with his words.

But Finch didn't care about his anger—all he cared about was the *covenant nail* the man was hiding. Finch found the hidden pocket, plucked the nail from its hiding spot, and then quickly used his ability to manipulate and mold metal to reshape it.

"How did.... you know?" Agent Steele's brow furrowed. "How?"

"Magic," Finch quipped.

In a matter of moments, Finch popped a bullet out of the magazine and mixed some of the covenant nail with the tip of the bullet. He had to take away some of the original metal to get it to work, and the bullet wasn't quite as aerodynamic afterward, but it would do the trick.

Finch slipped it back into the mag and loaded the round.

"Zarvul," Maldonado drawled. "*Kill both of them.*"

Finch fired.

His divine-infused bullet wasn't as accurate as he wanted, but he still struck Maldonado in the arm. The man grunted, his sleeve torn... but the bullet didn't pierce his skin. Maldonado brushed it off, his expression angrier than before.

"I will make you *suffer*," Maldonado spit.

Damn.

Finch had really thought that was going to work.

When the half-demon lunged, Finch knew it was his time to exit stage left.

He activated his magic. Chronos's hold on time froze everything in place, including Zarvul, who was suspended in midair, maw open, black ember-skin mid-burn.

Maldonado, just like last time, was the final thing to be frozen in place. His power was so substantial that it took Chronos a few extra seconds to freeze him, but it eventually happened.

Then the color drained.

The shapes melted.

Finch blinked.

There he was. Outside McKinley Park, his Toyota straight ahead, the broken fence at his back.

1:02 p.m.

Enzo, back in human form, rubbed his bald head. After

a few moments of glancing around, he turned his full attention to Finch. "You didn't give us much time."

"I know," he muttered.

"There are eight hundred books in that study."

"I know."

"We had five minutes to read. I barely got through the fucking foreword, let alone to the juicy bits of the interior."

"*I know.*" Finch exhaled and then headed into the park. "But you're thinking about this all wrong. You're talking to a man with an infinite amount of time."

Enzo snorted out a laugh as he followed. "Sure, yeah, but how much patience you got? Because sneaking back into a gilded shack for the hundredth time isn't how I imagined spending eternity."

"Listen, *junior assistant*—you need to learn to go with the flow." Finch shot him a grin. "Besides, this is why I hire people. So I don't have to do the jobs that suck."

Enzo lifted an eyebrow, but didn't comment.

When they reached the concrete bathroom building, Finch rounded the corner to find Liam, Jessie, and Bree all chatting about what they had found. Liam, surprisingly, was the most animated. His glasses kept slipping down the bridge of his nose, the sweat making it easy.

"And there were books about magics long thought lost," he said. He gestured to the south. "There were civilizations who killed humans to make magical items, and apparently, they had ways to infuse the person's personality into the item."

"The Aztecs did that?" Jessie shuddered. "Creepy."

Bree nodded. "Wow," she said, slightly slurring the word. "I wish I had gotten to read that book. I was just reading about the locations of flowers. It was so dull." The moment she spotted Finch, her smile widened. "Oh! Adair! There you are. Is everything okay? No one hurt you, right?"

She was still tipsy from the air in the realm of fae. Finch had forgotten he marked the time just directly after that. Bree would be back to her normal self soon—but she moved a little wobbly as he approached.

"No one hurt me. This time, I did all the hurting." Finch stopped next to them and then crossed his arms. "I take it you all didn't find anything that would directly link to Maldonado's weakness?"

Liam half lifted his hand. "I did, actually."

"Oh, really?" Finch was honestly surprised. "Okay. Let me hear it."

"Apparently, Quetzalcoatl, one of the Aztec gods, felt such guilt after incestuous relations with his sister, Quetzalpetatl, that he killed himself. The book specifically stated that coatls are extremely difficult to kill, but that Quetzalcoatl finally devised a way."

Enzo motioned for Bree. "I think you need to go."

"What? *Why*?" She crossed her arms. "I'm here to help, too."

"This story is too graphic for you. C'mon. Wait around the other side of the building until we're done."

"*What*? It wasn't too graphic! I can handle suicide." She stomped over to her father. "Besides, you're not the one who gets to decide. Right, Papa? I can stay?"

Enzo shot the man a glare. "*Incestuous relations*?" he mouthed.

Liam's face brightened, practically glowing red. "Uh, forgive me. I said that purely academically." Then he hesitantly turned to his daughter. "Don't worry, Bree. The worst part of the story is over, but please don't try not to repeat anything from it."

She jerked away from her father and then marched over to Finch. "Why are you all treating me like I'm *five*? I can handle this." Bree huffed. "Tell them, Adair."

"Leave me out of this," Finch stated.

Jessie stepped forward. "You're all acting insane. She's old enough to become a full witch. Liam, just continue your damn story." She had a bout of fiery sass that hadn't been there before.

Bree visibly relaxed and offered her a small smile.

"Uh, well, it turns out that turquoise drained Quetzalcoatl of his powers," Liam said. He nervously laughed as he faced Finch. "And you said Maldonado was coatl-like, yes? Or that was how he got his magic? You might be able to weaken him if you have enough."

CHAPTER
TWENTY-EIGHT

"So any turquoise will do?" Finch asked.

Liam half-shrugged and shook his head. "Well, there are four types of turquoise, one is magicless, while the other three have innate wyld magic. The thunder turquoise is located in Australia, but whispering turquoise and skyfire turquoise can both be found in North America."

"There are magic rocks?" Bree asked.

Enzo shrugged. "Don't look at me."

"You think one of the magical variants is what harmed the coatl?" Finch asked.

Liam waggled his hand back and forth before eventually nodding. "I mean, it makes more sense. So, yes."

This was what Finch had been fearing. There were so many damn magical rocks, he had never even bothered to learn them all. Normal humans sometimes stumbled upon them. That was how *new age medicine* was born—where one rock they stumbled upon *genuinely* had an effect on their body, and then for the rest of their life, they sold normal rocks to poor saps because they couldn't tell the difference.

Rocks that contained trace amounts of magic were known as *aetherite*, and if Finch had paid more attention when he was learning about ambient magic in the world, he would've known where to find it easily. However, since he had little interest in geology, most of that information had slipped from his mind like water through a colander.

"If I had more time in the study, I could narrow it down for you," Liam finally said.

Finch ran a hand down his face. He had exhausted most of his other options for Maldonado. He needed to find a way to counter the man's personal magic if he wanted any hope of defeating him. Knowing which type of turquoise was their best option.

But that wasn't the worst part.

Even if Finch knew the specific type of turquoise, he still had to get his hands on it. So, in order to maximize productivity—and his mental health—Finch decided the team needed to split up.

"Come here," he said to Liam.

The spectacled man hesitantly walked over. "Y-Yes?"

Finch pulled out his pen and drew the Mark of Chronos on Jessie's arm and then Liam's forearm. "You're going to return to the study to keep reading. You should be able to sneak back into Maldonado's at 1:54 p.m. like we did before —using the same route and same window."

"By myself?" Liam asked.

"No. Enzo will go with you."

After rubbing sweat from his brow and fixing his glasses, Liam turned to Enzo. "Ah. Yes. Well, let's hope he doesn't turn on me."

Enzo shot the man a heated glare. "*Have I turned on you yet, mother—*"

"Language," Bree sarcastically injected. "Don't want me, *the child*, hearing such foul words."

Enzo swallowed his tirade and shoved his hands into his sweatpants. "I'm in control most of the time, dammit. And I've never attacked you."

"Lycanthropy is a curse that affects your ability to control yourself," Liam stated matter-of-factly. "There's a reason most people don't associate with werewolves."

A pained silence followed that. Enzo said nothing, though Finch was fairly sure he was clenching his fists in his pockets.

"Enzo has made remarkable progress in controlling his temper," he said. "Besides, I'm just gonna rewind time, Liam. Get with the program. Even if something happens, you'll be completely safe. Just read the books, get me the answers, and everything will be fine."

The man rubbed the Mark of Chronos on his arm. "Didn't you say you *couldn't* rewind time if you died?"

"You find the cloud to every silver lining, don't you?" Jessie whispered.

Liam's face reddened. "I apologize. I... can't help myself sometimes."

"If something goes wrong, just call me," Finch said. "I can rewind time anywhere, and you'll be back in this damned park, got it? You're overthinking this."

Bree leapt over to Finch's side, her expression hard, her eyes twinkling. "If Papa and Enzo are going back to the study, does that mean that you, me, and Jessie are going to do something different?"

"Bingo," Finch said. "We're going to visit a local coven and see if they have some aetherite for sale."

———

"He doesn't have to treat me this way. I *am* old enough. I've seen enough. Even Papa doesn't think I need to be coddled."

Bree leaned back in the front passenger seat, her arms crossed, her glare pointed at the window.

The drive through Stockton was hot and unforgiving. The AC worked overtime to shield them from the worst of the weather.

Jessie sat in the middle back seat, quiet as the dead. Whenever Finch glanced at the rearview mirror, he noticed her staring at him. He wasn't entirely certain why, and he didn't feel like asking.

"Is Enzo just picking on me?" Bree huffed. "He keeps buying me candy, and saying nice things, but then when we're out on this case he's snapping constantly. I don't understand. I'm a warlock. He likes you—he should like me, too."

Finch turned on the radio. Even if it was only playing commercials, anything was better than this.

Bree leaned forward and turned off the radio two seconds afterward, cutting off a perfectly innocuous commercial about Dove soap.

"Adair—are you even listening? Enzo's not treating me right!"

Thankfully, Finch knew Stockton intimately. He could drive the roads, guided by various landmarks, with a fraction of his attention and never get lost.

He turned to Bree, mulling over her teenage puberty-fueled outburst, and responded as earnestly as he could.

"Enzo lost his daughter," he said.

Bree stiffened, her eyes wide. "W-What?"

"When he became a werewolf, the Oakland PD faked his death. Because—at some level—your father is right about the violence. Werewolves have outbursts. Gruesome outbursts."

"It's true," Jessie intoned from the back seat.

Finch continued. "The police chief thought it best that

Enzo's wife and daughter be kept away from him, so they were told he was, in fact, dead."

The interior of the Toyota was silent as they drove down a narrow roadway, toward the more suspicious shops in town.

"Enzo's daughter—her name is Zuri—has grown up without him," Finch said with a sigh. "So maybe you should cut him some slack. He might just... see a piece of his daughter in you. I don't know how he would handle it if you were hurt."

Bree was quiet the rest of the drive, her gaze falling to her feet. Thankfully, it didn't take them long to arrive at what appeared to be a new age medicine shop plus thrift store named: *Potion Notions*.

Finch groaned at the terrible pun. Once parked, he immediately stepped out into the sun and hurried for the front door. Bree and Jessie flanked him, and they entered as a trio.

A wave of *smells* washed over Finch like a wave on the beach.

Not the sterile, lavender-scented air of modern spas, nor the artificial sweetness of a candle shop, but something older, layered, and unsettling. The sharp tang of dried herbs, the musky undercurrent of burnt resin, the faint trace of something metallic.

Shelves lined the walls of the old shop, each one crammed with bundles of sage and rosemary. Glass jars filled with powders, dried petals, and glimmering minerals sat neatly labeled, their names written in too-perfect calligraphy. Names like:

Health Moon Sparkle
Quartz & Joy
Tiger's Eye of Recovery

A few older women wandered through the aisles, inspecting jars and picking up sticks of incense. They seemed unbothered and unhurried, completely content to live life as they wanted, with little regard for anyone else's judgment. Finch could respect that.

Unfortunately, he wasn't fond of such shops, and decided the best course of action was to get the information he needed and then leave immediately.

Finch passed a wooden display of crystals, all sorted by supposed magical properties—harmony, protection, wisdom—but he ignored them all and went straight to the register. Bree grabbed his elbow, and he gave her half a glance.

"Shouldn't we be inspecting their turquoise?" she whispered, pointing to a blue display in the corner of the store.

"No, we're just going to speak straight to the coven," he replied.

Finch went straight to the counter, his gaze drifting to a dream catcher hung in the corner. Its woven webbing was too intricate, and the knots were too tight and too deliberate. It was meant to trap more than bad dreams. Finch suspected it would alert the witches who worked here if he had ill intent.

Fortunately, the dream catcher gave no subtle indication as Finch returned his attention forward.

The woman behind the counter looked the part of a modern wellness guru—flowing linen dress, silver rings stacked on every finger, a necklace strung with a dozen different talismans. She was rail thin, her brown hair down to her waist, but her skin glowed with health and her eyes were alight with life.

"What troubles you?" she asked in a singsong voice.

"I'm here for aetherite," Finch stated. Even if the magic-less humans overheard his request, they wouldn't know what he meant, so he didn't bother to conceal his intent any further.

The woman barely gave any indication he had asked for something strange. "Let me speak to Maradith," the woman said. "I'll be right back. Please, make yourself at home and relax."

She walked off to a backroom door, which was covered in a curtain of beads, no hurry in her step. Finch watched her go and sighed.

"Was *that* a witch?" Bree whispered.

Jessie—who had been utterly silent until this point—interjected with, "She's a new moon witch."

"She doesn't seem very powerful."

"New moon witches specialize in healing. They're not usually powerful—but they are frequently rich."

Bree perked up at that statement. "Why?"

"Because no one pays premium prices like those who are sick," Jessie darkly replied.

"Are new moon witches more powerful than warlocks?"

Finch thought that was a bizarre question. There were too many variables to factor in to determine which would be stronger. Warlocks could be bound to any type of creatures, and while new moon witches typically had powers that healed and sensed the world, they could also do the reverse —and spread sickness.

So, it was nearly impossible to say which was *stronger*.

"It depends," Jessie said. "But what does it matter? You're safe with us."

Bree sighed and turned away. She didn't elaborate on her question, but she eventually turned back.

"The type of witch you are depends on the moonlight when you ascend, right?" Bree tilted her head. "But you also said that your magic is based on your desires. Why do all new moon witches have healing powers, then? Wouldn't they all have different desires?"

Jessie shrugged. "Witches choose what night they want to ascend. People who have strong desires to heal typically perform their ritual on a night of the new moon. If *I* had performed my ritual under a new moon, I probably... would've had magic that healed people from fae tricks and traps. Or made them immune to such tricks, to help them get into the fae realm."

"Oh. I see. The light of the moon influences your desires..."

"What kind of witch are you?" Finch whispered. He felt embarrassed for forgetting. She had told him. He should've remembered.

"I'm a half moon witch," Jessie replied, seemingly unbothered by the question. "The light of the half moon represents the ability to see both the light and the dark—to see things as they really are. To detect magic. Unravel magic. Bend magic."

She had such a haunting way of describing it that even Finch felt his curiosity piqued. He hadn't learned much about witches, other than their various flavors and what they generally represented, and he supposed—just like with aetherite—he should've paid more attention.

"I didn't know that about the moon," Bree whispered. "Can you tell me what the other phases mean?"

But before Jessie could give her that lesson, a woman who dressed like a 1970s hippie exited the back room and then approached the counter. She wore a necklace of turquoise, at least a dozen of the stones trapped in decorative copper that hung from a thread tied around her neck.

CHAPTER
TWENTY-NINE

"My name is Maradith Clairwood," the hippie woman said. Her brown hair was laced with white, but her skin was rather smooth. Only laugh and smile lines marked her face, which put Finch at ease. "I'm the matriarch of this coven. I heard you need a special kind of rock."

She walked around the counter to be on the side with Finch and the others. The woman moved with slow, deliberate grace, as though she were walking through water, her many layers of fabric whispering with each step. The turquoise at her throat caught the dim lighting, flashing blue-green like something alive.

Jessie fell silent. She even took a step away when the witch neared.

"My name is Adair Finch, and I'm looking for aetherite," Finch said. "You have any for sale?"

Maradith scented the air, a barely-there inhale to taste the magic that lingered like a smell. She scrunched her nose and narrowed her eyes. "A warlock. Yes, you might just very well be *the* Adair Finch. This must be important."

Eh.

Finch already hated where this was going. New moon witches loved making an easy buck whenever they could—and if Maradith knew he was desperate, she would charge extra.

"I need to know if you have whispering or skyfire turquoise," he said.

Maradith touched the necklace that lay on her collarbone. "Oh. Whispering turquoise is my signature stone. I see now—you must've heard of my magnificence and incredible powers."

Finch had never heard of this woman in his life.

"I've heard so much about you," he said, trying to hide the sarcasm in his tone. "I really do need your help. There's a criminal in town—a sociopath, really—and your turquoise might be the only solution."

Yes, he was buttering her up, and it was probably the opposite thing to do at the moment, but he figured it was just better to get the rocks and test them than try for a perfect negotiation.

The woman's cheeks flushed a bit. Then she fanned herself, a sly smile appearing. "I knew it. I'm the most discerning and gifted lapidary in Stockton. Me and my ladies have only the finest of materials."

"What is a *lapidary*?" Bree whispered.

"Someone who engraves, cuts, and polishes stones and gems," Jessie replied, equally quiet.

Maradith placed a hand on Finch's bicep. She gave him a little squeeze as she said, "I heard tales years ago that you were an astounding warlock who never failed to catch a criminal or solve a murder. That's quite impressive..."

Finch forced a tight-lipped smile. "Yep. That's me. A real legend. Now... back to the stones?"

Maradith squeezed his arm again, lingering just a little

too long. Finch fought the urge to yank it away, but he also didn't want to provoke the "most discerning and gifted lapidary in Stockton." He would just nod and go along until this was over.

"Strong, too," she murmured. "And such a sharp jawline. You know, warlocks of your caliber used to court witches of great renown."

Jessie let out an audible snort. Bree shot her a glance, holding back her own giggle. They were a little peanut gallery, Finch could tell.

"I'm flattered," Finch said dryly, resisting the urge to glance toward the nearest exit. "Really. But I'd be even more flattered if you could sell me the whispering turquoise before I end up married into your coven."

Maradith pished and poshed and waved her hand for a moment. Then she motioned to a stand not far from them covered in crystals that were labeled *aphrodisiacs*.

"We aren't the type of coven to believe in such hetero-normative ideals. Marriage? No, no, no. We have *group nights* every Thursday, for those who are adventurous and want to explore themselves, and others, in a safe, comfort-able location."

Sometimes, Finch wondered how he got into situations like this.

He hadn't been trying to get invited to an orgy when he first entered the rock shop, and yet here he was. Completely at a loss for words. Wondering if it would be best to just rewind time now to save himself the embarrassment of finishing the conversation.

"Uh, hello?" Bree waved her hand, gaining the woman's attention. "I know I'm only twelve, and people think I don't understand what you're talking about, but I've been on the internet since I was, like, six. Would you mind not hitting on my mentor while I'm right here? That'd be great—thanks."

"He's my brother-in-law, so it's also embarrassing for me to see this, too," Jessie sardonically chimed in.

"You all wound me," Maradith stated, pressing a hand to her chest as if he had just turned down the love of a lifetime. "I didn't realize I was dealing with such Karens. But fine. You may purchase my finest whispering turquoise. The real question is—can you afford it?"

"As long as the cost is *money*," Finch replied.

Maradith hummed, then turned on her heel, the layers of her gauzy skirt swishing dramatically as she disappeared behind the rickety curtain of beads.

"You should've just flirted back," Jessie whispered. "It would've been awkward, but we'd probably have our aetherite by now."

Bree shook her head. "Adair isn't like that. He's ace."

"Stop saying that," Finch muttered. "I don't need bizarre modern-day labels."

"It just means you don't want to be intimate with anyone."

"*I never said that.*"

"Labels help tell people what you're into—since you won't talk to anyone about your feelings. Maybe you're demi? That would make sense, if you really do want to be with someone."

Finch almost fell for her trap and asked what that meant, but he managed to hold back. He really didn't want a relationship with anyone until *after* he had handled his brother's murderers. The agony of failing, even just for a split second, was too much to experience again.

What if he did find someone he loved? What if they, too, were taken from him because of a mistake *he* made?

Finch almost never recovered from the first mistake.

He knew damn well he'd never come back from the second.

Every fiber of his being told him not to get intimately involved with anyone until he was done with the wicked coven and their modern gods. Once that was over, perhaps he could focus on labels—and what it meant to find someone to share his life with.

But not now.

And *definitely* not on *group nights* in a local new age medicine shop.

"You and her would've made a cute couple, though," Jessie teased, half giggling.

"I'd rather be castrated."

Bree folded her arms over her chest. "See? I might be right. Demi people only feel attracted to someone after they've formed an emotional attachment to them."

Wasn't that just normal love? Finch really didn't understand the modern need to define everything. He also didn't want to talk about it. Ever.

He had a wizard to defeat, for fuck's sake.

The beaded curtain rattled, and Maradith reappeared, a small, ornate wooden box cradled in her hands. She lifted the lid, and inside sat a cluster of whispering turquoise, faintly pulsing, as if the stone itself were breathing.

"For you," she said, voice dripping with satisfaction, "ten thousand dollars."

Finch nodded. "Deal."

Maradith nearly choked. "O-Oh. Well, I thought you would negotiate more and—"

"I'm in a hurry, so if you wouldn't mind wrapping up this transaction, that would be great."

She walked around to the register. "There's no need to rush, my fine warlock."

"Maradith, I am literally trying to stop a criminal

maniac from using dark magic to commit horrific crimes. Few situations are as urgent as this one."

Perhaps it was his sarcastic attitude, or the way both Jessie and Bree were whispering to each other, but Maradith hardened her expression as she punched out the price and asked for his card. Finch paid, though he didn't much care. He had plenty of money in his account—and this would all be undone anyway.

She might as well have charged him fifty thousand. He still would've paid.

Finch took the box of rocks, gave her an appreciative nod, and then headed for the door of the shop. Bree and Jessie followed close, both of them glancing over their shoulders as they went.

———

As they drove back to the park, Finch continually checked his phone.

2:35 p.m.

Enzo and Liam hadn't called. That wasn't a problem, it was just curious. They had only been reading books for about forty minutes, so perhaps they were still preoccupied with the task at hand. Which meant Finch either had to find a place that sold skyfire turquoise or he had to return to the McMansion to test his newfound rock immediately.

As he debated, Bree turned her attention to Jessie, who once again had decided to sit in the middle back seat.

"So... what does the light of a new moon mean for witches?" Bree asked.

Jessie's voice took on an almost reverent tone. "The new moon is shrouded in darkness, hidden behind the Earth's shadow. It represents how healers give away pieces of themselves to help others. That's why new moon witches are gifted in curing poisons, warding off sickness, and shielding people from dark magic."

Bree tipped her chair back, turning more fully toward Jessie. "What about waxing crescent moons?"

"The waxing crescent is the first return of light after darkness—it represents rebirth, renewal, and time's endless march forward. Witches who ascend under its glow don't age like others. Some say they can choose their age, slipping between youth and old age as easily as changing clothes. They are untouched by entropy, free from time's hold."

"Wow." Bree's eyes widened. "I had no idea."

Neither had Finch. Though, thinking back, it explained why so many waxing crescent witches never looked as old as they claimed.

Bree hesitated, then lowered her voice. "What about waning crescent moons?" She paused for a moment. "My mother performed her ritual under their light."

"The waning crescent is a phase of endings, of quiet retreat. It symbolizes isolation, death, and ultimate freedom. Witches born beneath it never join covens. Instead, they build households—small, tightly woven families they protect fiercely. Their magic is crafted to keep outsiders at bay. They are suspicious by nature, gifted in piercing through lies and deception."

Silence settled between them, thick with thought.

Then Bree asked, "What about full moons?"

Jessie hesitated.

The full moon was the most potent. Its light was unlike any other.

Jessie finally spoke, her voice softer now. "The full moon is the culmination of all struggle. Its light is intoxicating—it promises power. That's why so many witches are drawn to it, why they crave the magic it offers." After a moment, she added, "But everyone knows full moons drive witches mad."

Bree blinked several times. "Really?"

"If you can't handle the power," Jessie continued, "it will shatter you."

She let that sink in.

Finch knew the light of a full moon drove even normal magicless men crazy, but he hadn't realized it would sometimes shatter witches, too.

"That's why, despite the temptation, most witches choose another lunar phase. It's safer." Jessie rubbed her upper arms. "I couldn't bring myself to perform my ritual under a full moon. I just... I couldn't."

Power always had a cost.

And some witches paid for it with their sanity.

"Adair?" Bree asked.

"Hmm?"

"If you were a girl, and you got to be a witch, what would you pick?"

Finch remembered what Liam had said. Liam desperately wanted Bree to follow in her mother's footsteps. But if Finch was being honest, he never would've picked the waning crescent light. It didn't sound like something that would suit him.

"You shouldn't listen to me," Finch said. "I'm not a witch."

"*Hypothetically*," Bree said with a groan. She made her seat go up. "Please. Just tell me... what would you do?"

Finch exhaled. Fine. If she wanted to know, why not tell her?

"I'd go for the full moon." He gripped the steering wheel of his Toyota firmly. "Carter and I always said—we should be the best. We'd do whatever it took to rise above any challenge. Any problem. And if the light of the full moon is the most powerful, then I'd be a full moon witch, no doubt in my mind."

Jessie's brow furrowed. She didn't follow up his words with a statement or question, but it was clear she was intrigued.

"I see," Bree muttered. Her gaze drifted to the side window. "That... makes a lot of sense."

Had he made a mistake in telling her the truth of his theoretical intentions? Finch didn't know, but he also didn't want to think about it any further. He drove toward Maldonado's house. He had made up his mind. He'd test out his newfound rock now.

CHAPTER
THIRTY

Halfway to Maldonado's.

2:55 p.m.

Finch went over his battle plan in his head. How would he use this whispering turquoise? What was the best method? Finch cursed himself for not speaking to Maradith about the properties of this aetherite. Should he throw it at Maldonado? Punch him with it? Hold it to his face?

At some level, Finch could test all his theories, but he much preferred to be efficient. He had a lot to do in this one day, so it was best he didn't have to jumble all his thoughts with useless hypotheses.

"Uh, Adair?"

Finch barely glanced away from the road. "Hm?"

Bree sat beside him, fidgeting with her fingers, twisting them together, knotting them up, then unraveling them, only to start over again. "Could I ask you a favor?"

"What is it?"

"If I wanted to go do something... not related to the case?"

Finch eased his foot off the gas, slowing just enough to take the nearest turn—one that didn't lead toward Maldonado. "Where are we heading?" he asked.

Bree hesitated. "You don't mind?"

There were a dozen things Finch could've said. That he wanted to get the job done. That the case was urgent. That every second wasted could mean losing whatever lead they had. But there were things more important than this job.

Half the reason he had taken Bree on as his apprentice was because she had already lost too much. Her mother had been murdered in front of her, in the place that was supposed to be safest. Her home.

No one should have to learn so young that safety was an illusion.

Finch couldn't change what had happened. He couldn't undo the loss, the violence, the way the world had broken apart right in front of her. But he could make sure she knew one thing:

People wouldn't just leave her anymore. Not while he was around.

Sometimes that meant taking a detour—to make sure she was mentally prepared for the rest of the adventure.

But Finch didn't really know how to say that all to her.

"I don't mind," he eventually said. "Where do you want to go?"

"My mum said she had become a witch by the wooded area near the American River. I was wondering if, maybe, we could go look at it?"

While Finch hated that stupid river, he wasn't about to tell her no. He turned again down another road, and headed for the nearest route out of town. It wasn't far from the edge of Stockton, but it would add an hour to their trip, at the very least.

3:14 p.m.

Finch just hoped Liam and Enzo were fine without him.

———

Finch stood at the edge of the American River, on top of a small levee that overlooked the rushing waters.

The river was long, wide, and twisty, and there were several places for camping. The trees around most of the river were tall and grew so close together, it felt like a dense forest. The webs in the branches reminded Finch the place mostly belonged to spiders.

It would be a beautiful location—if everything wasn't mud brown, anemic yellow, or sickly tan. Even the water. It was a grayish brown, because of course it was.

This was the perfect place for witches, though.

"I didn't know covens still used these woods," Jessie said as she strolled between some of the thin trunks, her fingers grazing the bark. "It's like a little piece of history here."

Finch turned to Bree. She was slowly searching, keeping her gaze on the ground, and occasionally picked up palm-sized stones.

"It's around here somewhere," she muttered. Then she glanced over at Jessie. "Where did you perform your witch ritual and drink in the light of the moon?"

"It was far from here, in the mountains near Lake Tahoe." Jessie ran a hand through her pixie-short hair. "It was gorgeous. Especially at night."

Bree picked up a stone and stared at the bottom. With a smile, she presented it to Finch. "Look! This is a marker. It says we're on the right track." Bree tapped at markings on the stone. It was a cryptic map, though Finch wasn't entirely certain how to read it.

The leaves of the cottonwoods rustled in a breeze that

was apparently too good for Finch. He wiped the sweat from his brow.

"This way," Bree said, leading them further downstream.

———

5:53 p.m.

Liam and Enzo still hadn't called. At first, Finch had thought his phone just wasn't getting reception, but whenever he glanced at the bars, it showed him topnotch strength. The American River wasn't as in the boonies as he had thought it was.

As they walked, Bree picking up stone markers along the way, Finch tried to relax. The river's edge glinted, tempting him with a cool, rippling promise. But he knew the water would be disgusting. He held off getting anywhere near it.

A heron stalked the shallows.

Bugs fluttered through the air.

This was the wilderness, all right. They were far from any road.

"Why do witches go *so far out*?" Bree asked, exasperated. "Mum said it was out here, but I didn't think it would be *this* out here!"

"Witches of old would dance naked under the moonlight during their ritual," Jessie said matter-of-factly. "Obviously, you don't want anyone around to see that."

Finch turned on his heel. "I'll be waiting in the car."

"They don't do it anymore," Jessie said, rolling her eyes.

After a long moment of consideration, Finch turned back around and rejoined the others. The box with the turquoise weighed heavy in his pocket, but he kept reminding himself this was for Bree. He just needed to be there for her.

"I'm not actually doing the ritual." Bree gave him a long glower. "You know that, right? I just wanted to see the site. To, uh, be familiar with it."

Finch shrugged. "Why not?"

"Well, first off—I want to be a warlock, remember? Second off—it's a bad night. The moon tonight is *waxing gibbous*." For some reason, Bree scrunched up her face in a look of deep contemplation. Then she glanced over at Jessie. "Why aren't there any waning or waxing gibbous witches?"

"Those are the phases of the moon before and after the full moon." Jessie recited all the information as though it was second nature to her. Her calm and educational demeanor reminded Finch of old school videos he had been forced to watch as a teen. "It's said they're the *wings of the full moon*, and their power is only for the full moon itself. If you perform the ritual on the night of the gibbous, you'll lock your cores, and become magicless, sacrificing your power to the lunar phases."

That sounded ominous.

Finch frowned.

He also remembered his promise to Liam, and how he had said he would nudge Bree in the direction of becoming a witch.

"Why do you want to be a warlock again?" he asked. "You know we need to make pacts, right? That sometimes those are dangerous and require a lot of work or effort? And if you fail them, it could cost you your life?"

Bree stomped through the undergrowth of the brown forest, her lips pursed. "I know, I know. But I want to be magical and powerful and have all the options."

"Why though?" Finch insisted.

After a short moment, Bree stopped dead in her tracks. She wheeled on her heel, her shoes crunching dead leaves with every movement. "My mum was a witch, and she *died*." Bree hardened her expression and stared at Finch. "And then *you* came along and made everything better. I want to be like... like *you*. I want to be strong enough to stop bad people from..."

Her voice trailed off. It had been growing weaker, though it was clear Bree felt passionately about what she thought. Perhaps *too* passionately. Some of her emotions leaked out the corners of her eyes, and she had to wipe them away with the sleeve of her black hoodie.

Jessie crossed her arms and turned away, examining the nearest trunk with a look of discomfort. She had nothing to say. That was fine—Finch had known he would have to have this conversation at some point.

He stepped closer to Bree and placed a hand on her shoulder.

"I'm honored you want to be like me," he said, his voice quiet. "But being a warlock won't mean you'll be strong enough to handle every bad guy who comes your way."

"*You always handle everything*," Bree said, though she didn't pull away. Her voice was raised, and it echoed throughout the trees, but Finch could tell the anger wasn't directed at him. "You defeat every criminal and s-solve all the crimes. You—"

"I didn't save Carter," Finch stated, cutting her off.

A chill ran through the woods, followed by silence. It seemed even the critters of the American River didn't want to disturb the conversation.

Finch gently squeezed her shoulder. "Power is important, but so is skill, experience, and... people you can rely on. Being a warlock won't solve everything. If anything, it'll cause you more problems, because you'll need to look for magic—like I did with King Heslop."

After rubbing her face for a solid thirty seconds, Bree

met Finch's gaze with red eyes. "You don't think I should be a warlock?"

"I think only a lucky few girls are born with the ability to become a witch, and perhaps you shouldn't be so quick to throw it away. Lunar magic is a special source of power."

Then, at the most inopportune moment, Finch's phone rang. At first, he was going to set it to silent, but when he glanced at the screen to make sure it wasn't Liam, he realized it was Kull. With a sigh, he backed away from Bree.

6:05 p.m.

"One sec."

He turned around and answered the call.

"Adair?" Kull asked. "Are you there?"

"What is it, Kull? This is a really bad time."

"O-Oh, yes, well, I was calling to tell you that I'll need a few days before I arrive, actually. I thought I could get there quickly, but then something happened, and now I'm a bit behind."

"You didn't have to call and tell me that," Finch snapped into the phone. "I already told you not to rush in getting here."

"I just wanted you to know so that maybe you limit the number of amazing cases you're taking while I'm away," Kull said with a smile in her voice. "Because I have something for you, and you'll definitely love it, all right?"

Finch pinched the bridge of his nose. "Kull. Focus on TikTok or YouTube or whatever it is you do. I have my hands full here. I don't need updates on your every move."

"I *am* focusing on my career—and becoming more human. That's important to me. But it's also important that I see you soon. So, just know, in a couple of days, I'll be there." Kull's voice took a turn for the serious. "And we need to talk." Then, with a happy giggle, she concluded, "Okay, bye!"

And then she hung up.

Right as Finch was tucking his phone into his pocket, it rang again. He answered, annoyed, and ready to tell Kull that she needed to wait twenty-four hours to call.

"Kull—" he began.

"It's me, Enzo," the man on the other end growled. "*Rewind time!* We got it. All the information, but we're in deep shit."

"Tell him to rewind time!" Liam frantically said in the background of the call.

"I did." Enzo grunted. "Get off me!"

Finch turned back around. Jessie was kneeling next to Bree, rubbing her upper arm and whispering to her. Bree had seemingly recovered most of her moxie. Her tears had dried up, and she was nodding along with whatever Jessie had to say.

Exhaling a long exhale, Finch felt the box in his pocket one more time before rewinding time. He had never gotten to test it, and as the colors drained from the sad brown forest, he realized it wasn't that big a deal. He had simply purchased it from Maradith. If he wanted it again, he could easily get it again.

But still. As the world faded away, he thought it sardonically funny.

Then he stood in front of his car, right outside McKinley Park.

1:02 p.m.

Enzo turned to face Finch, smiling like a fool. "You're never going to believe this."

CHAPTER
THIRTY-ONE

"What happened?" Finch asked.

Enzo slapped his shoulder. "We were there in that study, Liam reading books, when some goons wander in. They thought we were some of Maldonado's hired men, so they rounded us up, brought us to a party and—"

"They brought you to a *party*?" Sometimes Finch stood baffled by the endless possibility of time travel.

The simple act of just Enzo and Liam breaking in had somehow led to a thug blowout. Having Agent Steele get anywhere near the house led to a full-on war out on the lawn. The slightest change had drastic outcomes.

"This is one of Maldonado's vacation houses," Enzo said. "And it was everything you ever see in a movie. Coke. Hot tubs. Ladies. Topless ladies. More coke. Music so loud I was going deaf."

"And *Liam* was at this party?"

"Guy looked like a cactus in the middle of a dance floor."

Finch could picture it perfectly.

"And then the craziest shit happened," Enzo said, holding up both his hands. "They brought out, a, uh, creature. A goblin or something. Then Maldonado *liquefied it*." Enzo clapped his hands to emphasize the suddenness. "Poof! Liquid." He shook his head as he continued, "And then he just served that to everyone. People *drank* it."

"What kind of goblin?" Finch asked.

There were several goblin tribes that lived underground in the North America region, all of whom had their own weird magical properties. They hated humans, though, and all spoke their own unique language that was mostly made of grunts and snorts.

"They said it was... a... puke-wedge-something."

Finch narrowed his eyes. "A *pukwudgie?*"

Snapping his fingers and pointing at Finch, Enzo nodded. "Yes. A pukwudgie. Everyone drank it. And then they were so high. I've never seen people act so insane. Even Maldonado had a few sips."

The story had definitely taken a crazy turn. Finch knew Maldonado dealt in weird mystical creature goos, but he had had no idea the man was sucking down his own product.

"Maldonado saw you?"

Enzo shook his head. "Liam and I kept out of his sight, but I sensed other cursed individuals and warlocks, so I suspect we were blending in fairly well with the crowd."

"Did you drink it?" Finch asked, cringing.

"Me? No. I've seen what weird substances do to people —*meth, don't even try it once*. I pretended to take a swig and then tried to get Liam out of there. He insisted on looking around the house first, though."

Now Liam's panic was making more sense. "Let me guess. You two were caught."

"Oh, yes. And they weren't happy when they found us in Maldonado's bedroom, let me tell you."

"Wait, wait, wait." Finch glanced at his phone and then glared at Enzo. "What time did the party start?"

Enzo, thrown off his stride, had to scratch his head for a moment. He squinted as he stared off into the distance. "I want to say it happened around five."

"Do you know specifically when Maldonado liquefied the pukwudgie?"

"Maybe thirty minutes after the party began?"

"*Maybe*?" Finch stressed.

"I don't know." Enzo snorted back a laugh. "I'm not a time-wielding lunatic. I was just playing bodyguard for a book-loving coatrack."

Finch tucked his phone away. "In the future, it would be helpful if you recorded the time for interesting events. That way we can exploit them."

Enzo replied with a sarcastic salute. "I will strive to be a better junior assistant."

This time, Finch hadn't been expecting the joke. He coughed and laughed at the same time. "Goddammit," he muttered under his breath.

Then he sighed, and his imagination kicked into overdrive.

Could he use this party to his advantage?

What if he challenged Maldonado to a spellrift *after* the man had ingested some of the pukwudgie? Maldonado was prone to reckless moves, Finch had already proven that, so perhaps the best way to deal with the man would be while he was high as a kite.

Enzo patted Finch's shoulder again, drawing him out of his thoughts.

"C'mon. Let's go speak with Liam."

Together, Finch and Enzo entered the dilapidated park and made their way to the stone bathroom building. When they rounded the corner, they saw Liam was already engaged in an animated retelling of the entire party scene.

"Have you ever seen the movie *Gremlins*?" Liam waved his hands around in circles. "The pukwudgie appeared just like one after it had gotten ugly. He was snarling, but when Maldonado entered the room, it cowered in the corner of its cage."

Bree's blue eyes widened. "Did you save it?" she asked, her words slightly slurred.

That took the wind out of Liam's sails. He nervously chuckled as he continued. "Well, no, because I didn't actually know what was going on."

"Maldonado didn't hurt it, right? The pukwudgie was okay in the end?" The concern in her voice was so genuine, Finch dreaded the rest of the story.

"Uh... Yes. Nothing bad happened to the pukwudgie. Everything was fine." Liam cringed a bit as he added, "Maldonado just gave everyone drinks that made them feel funny."

Jessie lifted an eyebrow. "That doesn't sound like Maldonado. He kills all sorts of creatures to—"

"*That's what happened*," Liam interjected. "And once everyone was fuzzy, I took Enzo and went to Maldonado's personal room."

"Why did you do that?" Finch asked as he walked over.

That caused Jessie, Liam, and Bree to jump. Their surprise quickly turned to elation as Finch joined them. Enzo immediately went to Bree, and gave her the once-over.

"Everything okay with you, kiddo?" he asked.

Bree brightly smiled. "Yes! Adair kept me safe, and we successfully located whispering turquoise. Our mission was a big success." She offered Enzo a thumbs-up.

"Good, good. That's what I wanted to hear."

But Finch wasn't interested in distractions. While

everyone was gathered together in the calm magic-filled grove behind the bathroom building, he pulled out his pen and quickly drew the Mark of Chronos on both Jessie and Liam. Then he stood in front of Liam and stared him dead in the eyes.

"Why did you head for Maldonado's bedroom?" he asked.

"In the books about Quetzalcoatl's death, they talked about how he was the father of all coatls. His magic controlled the others. I thought it was interesting, because I remembered hearing a while back about coatls dying all over Central America."

Finch lifted an eyebrow. He didn't interrupt the story, because he no longer knew where it was going.

"Then I realized it made sense." Liam motioned his hands around as he spoke. "Maldonado is known for hunting mystical creatures, after all." He held up a finger. "But that's besides the point. What I figured is that Maldonado would like to have a contingency for any kind of attack—including an attack that pinpointed his weakness. You see, the scales of Quetzalcoatl control coatls. He'd like to have some of those scales, I think."

"In his bedroom?" Finch asked.

Liam shrugged. "Well, I'm *also* a warlock—I know everyone keeps forgetting—but I made a pact with one of the brownies, and—"

"D'aww," Bree said, stepping closer to her father. "Really? You made a pact with those cute little guys in the office?"

"Y-Yes." He fixed his glasses and continued. "Because they have magics for finding rare materials. I used said magics, and it led me to his room, but before I could find the scales, that was when we were caught."

"And then you called me," Finch concluded.

"Exactly."

Clenching his hands into fists, Finch asked, "Does that mean the whispering turquoise was for *nothing*? Because getting it was... an ordeal."

"It was pretty easy," Jessie muttered. "Just awkward."

"We'll need *both* actually." Liam ignored Jessie's commentary. "We'll need these scales, and the turquoise. Just normal turquoise, by the way. You see, once you cut Maldonado with the scales, you should be able to absorb a lot of his raw magic with the turquoise, but the rock must be devoid of magic to fully take in Maldonado's power."

"So I don't need whispering turquoise?"

"Uh, no."

A long moment of silence passed between them. Finch contemplated cursing, but then he just exhaled and allowed his irritation to leave him. This wasn't too big a deal. The *Potion Notions* shop sold regular turquoise as well.

"So, the plan is to stab Maldonado with some scales and then throw normal turquoise on him?" Finch asked. "Am I getting that right?"

"Yes. You'll weaken him, and then you'll suck away his magic. After that, he'll be defenseless... in theory."

Finch didn't love the way Liam's voice took a severe downswing with the last two words, but in his mind, it didn't matter. Maldonado was going down no matter what —it was just a matter of time. And Finch had *plenty* of time.

"So, what's the plan?" Bree asked.

"I think I need to see this party," Finch sardonically stated. "And get myself a few scales."

CHAPTER
THIRTY-TWO

5:15 p.m.

Finch pulled up to the gated entrance of Maldonado's private estate, the metal bars looming tall and unwelcoming against the darkening sky. He punched in the access code, and the gate slid open.

As Finch eased the car forward, up the long driveway, he passed through the magical barrier that protected the property.

The effect was instant.

One moment, there was nothing but the hushed whisper of wind through the trees. The next—a heavy, rhythmic bass line pounded through the air, vibrating through the car doors, shaking through Finch's chest. The barrier had kept all sound from escaping, shielding the outside world from whatever debauchery lay within.

It was a perfect defense against the magicless. No one outside would ever hear the strange things happening in Maldonado's so-called vacation home.

Finch slowed the car and then parked well away from

the main entrance, careful to stay within the shadows of the surrounding trees.

Liam and Jessie sat in charged silence, glancing at each other in that unspoken way that told Finch they were thinking the same thing.

Liam adjusted his glasses, looking at the house with academic disapproval. "Do I have to go inside?"

"Yes," Finch replied.

"But couldn't I just tell you where his bedroom is?"

"You'll be perfectly fine," Finch snapped. "Just help me locate the exact position of these damn scales, all right?"

"R-Right..."

Jessie shifted in the back seat. Finch needed Liam to locate the scales, but he wanted his sister-in-law to dispel any illusions or protections that might be in the way of his prize. Hopefully, there weren't any, but just in case—he wanted to get in and out as quickly as possible.

Enzo and Bree weren't with them.

On Bree's insistence, she had taken Enzo to go get the turquoise, since she was determined for him to meet Maradith and her special coven. Finch wondered if Bree was going to try to sign him up for "group nights" without explaining what it was. If she did, it would be amusing, but probably the last thing she'd ever do in this world.

Finch stepped out of his vehicle, Liam and Jessie close behind. He snuck around the side of the house as the oppressive sun began its downward descent. The orange and red glow of the sky washed everything in a sinister color palette.

Once at the study window, Finch stopped.

Bree wasn't with them. She had been the one to open the window.

"Wait, how did you and Enzo get inside?" Finch whispered to Liam.

"Enzo just manhandled the window." Liam shrugged. "It wasn't particularly difficult for him."

"Tsk."

Finch sighed, grabbed the window with as solid a grip as he could, and then grunted as he yanked upward. The window rattled, but held in place. He did it a second time, putting more effort into his attempt.

Werewolves were supernaturally strong. Of course Enzo could do it without breaking a sweat. Still, it bothered Finch that he couldn't do this. It was a *window*, for fuck's sake. How could the most powerful warlock in the world be stopped by a simple window?

He gritted his teeth as he yanked upward a third time. The window creaked, the latch on the inside splintering the wood of the sill. It was breaking.

"C'mon, you son of a bitch," he muttered under his breath.

"We could probably find another way in," Jessie said. "An easier way, for certain."

No.

Finch was going to break this window by fucking punching it before he went somewhere else. Instead, he yanked a fourth time and finally shattered the flimsy latch on the inside, breaking a part of the sill as he managed to lift the window open.

The music inside blared louder. The place smelled of so much brimstone, it might as well have been a house in a suburb of hell.

Finch smiled and took a few deep breaths before he stepped inside. "I got this."

"I'm impressed," Liam said as he slid inside afterward.

"Men," Jessie sardonically said as she came in last.

The study was dark, the lights completely off. The

scarlet glow of the sunset gave him enough illumination to make it to the door and then enter the hallway.

Bass from the speakers hit him like a physical force, rattling in his chest, shaking the floor beneath him. The air was thick with smoke, the kind that clung to his clothes, stung his eyes, and made him wonder how many brain cells he was sacrificing per breath.

"Where to?" Finch asked, coughing once.

Liam waved a hand in front of his face—constantly—as he motioned to the end of the hall and then through a door. He led the way, his shoulders bunched at the base of his neck, his head low.

Jessie didn't seem to mind the smoke. Her expression remained hard as they continued forward.

They turned into a massive open-plan living room. A dozen thugs lounged on white leather couches, their weapons casually strewn over coffee tables cluttered with playing cards, crushed beer cans, and powder-dusted mirror trays. Liam came to an abrupt halt, and Finch almost ran into the man. Then they both quietly made their way back into the hall before anyone spotted them. Jessie waited for them, frowning.

"We have to go through there?" Finch whispered—though it wasn't necessary. The music was loud enough to cover the sound of an elephant gun being discharged.

"His bedroom is through this room, and then the hall, past the kitchen." Liam shrugged. "I'm sure there's another way, but this was what Enzo and I did. It's just... these guys weren't here already."

That was the problem with Enzo's vague directions. If he had remembered exact times, Finch wouldn't have had to guess.

"We can walk through," Finch muttered.

"They might recognize me," Jessie stated.

Damn. Finch hadn't thought about that. He glanced back into the living room, assessing the danger.

One guy—shirtless, rail-thin, eyes completely black—was attempting to "levitate" a cigarette into his mouth and failing spectacularly. It was obviously a parlor trick, but he couldn't pull it off without dropping his smoke on the floor. Every time it got close, the guy next to him—built like a bulldozer, blue veins visible across most of his muscled body—was too busy laughing his ass off to help.

"You're a shitty magician," the big one said, slapping the thin one. "*And you work for a wizard!*" He was wheezing, laughing so hard. "It's so ironic!" His face was purple. Finch was certain he couldn't breathe.

In the far corner, a shaky man with razor-sharp nails was snorting something off a book, which felt like the kind of decision that had consequences.

"Hide in one of the bathrooms," Finch said to Liam and Jessie. "I'll handle this."

He entered the room, moving with purpose but not too much purpose—confidence was key. *Act like you belong, and no one questions you.* That was a simple rule that had served him well over the years. But, just in case, he visualized himself as bulletproof, keeping mental note of the many handguns in the room.

He approached the coffee table.

Half the men glanced up, most of them in irritation. One even gave Finch the once-over, his annoyance shifting to confusion as he slowly reached for his firearm.

"Maldonado has a treat for tonight," Finch said. "He's giving out *essence of pukwudgie.*"

"What the fuck is a *pukwudgie*?" one of the men asked, loud enough to pierce the din of the party music.

The rail-thin magician rubbed his nose. "It's a goblin, ya douche. Magical. Makes you hallucinate." When he smiled, he showed off a full mouth of blackened teeth. "I bet it makes for one hell of a drink."

"It'll fuck you up," Finch said, smirking. "But he's not going to have much. He only has one pukwudgie."

The men at the coffee table all shouted and grunted things about not missing out. They slapped each other on the shoulder or pushed each other out of the way in their haste to stand. The bulldozer even shoved Finch to the side as he made his way out of the living room.

The idiot snorting stuff off the book had already disappeared—the moment Finch mentioned any sort of new drug, it was clear the man needed it in his life.

Then, once the room was empty, Finch hurried to the nearest bathroom and tapped on the door. "C'mon," he snapped. "Now's our chance."

Liam and Jessie quickly exited, and then the trio went straight for Maldonado's bedroom.

They slipped down the hall, past the excessive gold trim on the crown molding, and a mirror so large Finch was convinced Maldonado used it to stare lovingly at himself.

The *thump-thump* of bass vibrated through the walls, drowning out most sounds—except for the moment something screamed.

Not a normal scream. Not human.

A high-pitched, warbling shriek that curdled in Finch's gut right before it was abruptly cut off.

The three of them froze mid-step, exchanging uneasy glances. Finch turned his attention to a set of grand double doors that led to the kitchen. They were cracked open a bit, and he glanced through.

The gigantic industrial-sized kitchen had a couple dozen of Maldonado's goons. On the massive island in the middle of the room was a silver cage with a hideous little goblin inside.

The pukwudgie.

It was small—no taller than a child. It sat hunched in the cage, pressed into the farthest corner, a tiny amount of hair on its head standing on end. Its gray-green skin shimmered unnaturally under the fluorescent light, damp with sweat or something worse, its wide, intelligent eyes darting between the goons who stood around it. They laughed, pointed, passed around small vials.

Maldonado stood next to the cage, smiling and waving his hands to calm everyone down.

The pukwudgie trembled, but it did not cower.

It pressed both clawed hands together, a pleading motion universal across all languages, and let out a series of high, warbling sounds, part chitter, part growl. It shook the bars, rattling them as if shaking them hard enough might convince them to let it go.

One of the goons—the same bulldozer from the living room—grinned down at the goblin. "What's that, little guy?" he said in a mocking baby voice, tapping the bars with the barrel of his pistol. "Too stupid to speak?"

The pukwudgie bared its teeth—sharp, yellowed, made for crunching bone and snapping through roots. It hissed, flicking its fingers through the air, tracing patterns with its claws. Not an attack—a sign, an attempt. A desperate effort to communicate, to appeal to something human in these men.

Goblins were intelligent. Finch knew—even if they could be vicious at times.

The pukwudgie pointed to its own chest, then toward the door.

Me. Out.

It reached through the bars, palm open, hopeful, trembling.

One of the goons laughed. "I think it's begging!" For some reason, that garnered a lot of laughter.

Maldonado stepped closer, his presence icy.

The pukwudgie's movements grew more erratic, more panicked. It clawed at the bars again, tapping out an urgent, rhythmic beat—the last frantic plea of something that knew it was about to die.

Because it knew.

It could smell the sour, acrid magic clinging to the air. It could see the greedy hunger in their eyes.

It wasn't leaving this cage alive.

And still—*still*—it begged.

"We're just... letting that happen?" Jessie asked.

She stood directly next to Finch, though he didn't know when she had come over.

"Do you want me to fight every asshole in this house to save the goblin?" Finch sarcastically asked. "Or would you like me to figure out how to defeat Maldonado, so I can rewind time and save the goblin in an easier fashion?"

The way Jessie turned to face him—it made Finch think she wanted the former.

CHAPTER
THIRTY-THREE

inch wondered how he had become the designated *Savior of Literally Everyone*, but a piece of him thought back to Bree and how she had been upset by the thought the goblin might be harmed.

"You're right," Jessie whispered. She stepped away from the double door. "It's not logical to save him now. We should wait for the perfect moment. I'm... not used to thinking about things like they're... all a practice run."

"It's fine," Finch replied.

But then the moment came. Maldonado reached out a hand, and the scent of acrid magic filled the house. He grazed a single finger over the upper arm of the little goblin.

The pukwudgie twisted in agony, its tiny arms flailing as its body melted into a shimmering, sickly green sludge, evaporating into the air like someone had just boiled a toad alive. Its eyes ruptured one at a time, like bubbles exploding.

Halfway between life and death, with its body falling off in chunks, it reached again for someone—anyone—to help. It mouthed words in a goblin language, but then its teeth fell from its skull, and all the skin on its body sloughed off.

Maldonado watched, unbothered, as the creature sputtered and oozed away through the cage's bottom. Then he lifted the cage to reveal a tray that had caught all the pukwudgie's goo. It shimmered green, almost like Jell-O.

The thugs in the kitchen cheered. Maldonado did the honors by taking his vial and getting himself a small sip. Some of the green ooze stuck to his lip, and he licked it off.

"Enjoy," he said, toasting with the vial.

And then everyone rushed forward, their little vials at the ready, all trying to scoop some of the goo for themselves.

Worried that Maldonado might see them, Finch pulled Jessie and Liam away from the door and continued through the house.

They reached the bedroom door, Finch barely slowing as he shoved it open, ushering them inside before clicking it shut behind them.

For a long moment, none of them spoke.

Then Jessie bit her lip. "I hate how callous some people can be."

Liam nodded, rubbing his temples. "Is there a magical ethics committee we can report this to? I feel like there should be."

"You two have never interacted with criminals before, have you?" Finch shook his head. "Forget about that. We'll take down Maldonado—we just have to make sure we have the means to do so. Liam, find me those means."

The room, much like Maldonado himself, was an absolute exercise in overcompensation.

The four-poster bed was so absurdly oversized it looked like a king had commissioned it but never actually used it. The headboard alone was a masterpiece of unnecessary luxury, hand-carved with swirling Aztec serpents and smoke motifs.

The walls were lined with custom shelves, each holding

relics, trophies, and artifacts—some of which were probably cursed as hell. Finch made a mental note to not touch anything unless absolutely necessary.

Jessie ran a hand over the soft bedspread and scowled. "There are illusions even on the bed... Everything in here isn't what it appears to be."

"Is it just a less expensive bed?" Liam asked. "Because that would be hilarious."

Finch snapped his fingers. "Enough bantering. Liam, tell me where the scales are. C'mon, c'mon."

Liam drifted toward a locked glass case, frowning at the various boxes held within. "This is where I got last time. I didn't want to break the glass or mess with anything too much, so I struggled to open it. Then someone entered the room..."

"Just break the glass. All I need to know is where the scales are exactly."

Finch dashed over to the bedroom window. Thick curtains blocked out the dying sunlight, so Finch threw them open and stared at the backyard. The pool, the long patio with a BBQ set, and the many outdoor couches could accommodate at least a hundred people. But Finch didn't care about any of that. He took in the exact location of the window, and then he attempted to open it.

Locked.

"Jessie, come take a look at this," Finch said.

As she hurried over, the sound of shattering glass filled the bedroom. Finch glanced over his shoulder. Liam's arm was wrapped in a silk blanket, but he had still managed to cut himself on the broken glass of the case.

"Someone heard that," he muttered.

"Then *hurry*," Finch snapped. When he returned his attention to the window, he tapped on the glass. "Is there anything protecting this?"

Jessie placed her palm on the glass. "No."

"Just what I wanted to hear."

That was all he needed. He knew now how to get into Maldonado's personal room from the outside. As soon as he knew where the Quetzalcoatl scales were, he'd be set.

The door handle rattled. Finch barely had time to whirl around on his heel before whoever was trying to get in decided force was the best option. The door burst open as the bulldozer stumbled inside, his eyes fully dilated.

"Oh, shit," the guy slurred. "I *did* hear something."

A second guy lurched in behind him, slower, veins visibly pulsing. Pukwudgie goo was clearly not FDA-approved. He cracked his knuckles, grinning wide enough to show blackened teeth.

Finch had three seconds to process the situation before the guy swung a sloppy right hook.

Instinct took over. Finch ducked low, grabbed a fancy-ass decorative bowl off a nearby table, and smashed it straight into the guy's face.

The ceramic shattered. So did the man's nose.

The thug reeled back, stumbling into a shelf, sending artifacts and expensive-looking junk clattering to the floor. What was one more fight? Finch's body loosened up as his focus sharpened.

The bulldozer guy roared and charged, but Finch had been in enough stupid back-alley fights to know that when a giant moves, he commits. Finch sidestepped, letting all that momentum carry the guy forward, and then slammed an elbow into the base of his back.

Big guy didn't go down, but he did slam into the glass case, sending even more priceless trinkets to the ground.

Liam, still clutching his arm, hissed, "*I'm not done searching that!*"

"Then hurry, you donut!" Finch threw up an arm just in

time to block a wild swing from the first thug, who was now bleeding but probably too high to notice.

The guy grabbed a candelabra off a nearby table and swung it like a baseball bat. Finch ducked the first swing, caught the second against his forearm, and ripped it out of the guy's hands.

"What kind of medieval bullshit—"

Before he could finish, the bulldozer recovered. He then lunged at Finch like a goddamn linebacker. Finch had one second to react before they both went down, crashing into Maldonado's obscenely oversized bed.

Finch landed hard, the air knocked from his lungs, the weight of the thug pressing him into overpriced silk. A part of him wanted to use his fire, but another part of him didn't want to use magic, in the fear it would attract Maldonado himself.

However, with all the noise they had made, he knew they had seconds, at best, to find what they needed.

Jessie, her eyes glowing red, her body fueled by demonic magic, kicked the big guy in the side, sending him rolling off the bed. Smoke wafted off her, filling the room with a charred smell.

Finch sucked in a breath and sat up just in time to see the first thug getting back up, still swaying but determined.

"*Liam*," Finch barked. "Do you have it?"

Finch grabbed the nearest decorative pillow and hurled it at the thug's face. It didn't hurt him, but it did throw him off just long enough for Finch to grab a lamp and smash it over his head. There was no shortage of improvised weapons in this fancy bedroom.

The guy finally collapsed.

Bulldozer tried to rise—Jessie kicked him again, her boots crunching down on something.

This time, the man stayed down.

Liam, standing amid a sea of broken glass and expensive garbage, held up a wooden case, his fingers shaking. "I have it! Here they are."

Shouting in the hallway outside the room got Finch's heart going faster. He hurried over to Liam, snatched the box out of his hands, and then flipped it open.

Inside, nestled in velvet, Quetzalcoatl scales shimmered in gold and blue, each the size of a human thumb. When Finch grazed his fingertips over them, he realized something intriguing.

They were metal.

Perfect.

Finch snapped the case shut, and then carefully examined the exterior of the box. It was simple. Brown. Made of maple wood. No prints or markings. The metal brass.

"More are coming," Jessie shouted.

"Don't worry, we're leaving," Finch muttered right as he activated his magic.

Everything froze.

Colors drained.

Shapes melted.

Then Finch was standing just outside McKinley Park.

1:02 p.m.

Enzo snorted and breathed out a soft chuckle. "Well, how did it go for you? Liam finally find those damn scales?" He fixed his sweatpants and then ran his hand over his tank top. "Because Bree and I got so many turquoises you could drown in them."

Finch let out a long sigh. "Yeah, we found them."

There was no mirth or happiness in his tone, though. Finch was too busy trying to connect a perfect path for him to take once he entered Maldonado's abode. What plan would save him the most trouble? Which would be the safest?

"You look like you've been worn too thin," Enzo stated. "You want to grab a bite to eat and discuss the plans with everyone?"

Finch turned to him, an eyebrow raised. "I'm not worn out."

"I used to be a bartender for a couple years. I know what burnout looks like. Did you get into another fight or something?"

"I get into a lot of fights."

Enzo chuckled. "Lucky." He slapped Finch's upper arm. "Come on. We'll relax, share all our information, make a plan, and then go from there. You need it."

Perhaps his friend was right. Finch did feel stiff from the fights, and he wanted nothing more than to relax just for a little.

"All right. Where should we eat?"

"*Casa Flores*. Best Mexican food in all Stockton."

CHAPTER
THIRTY-FOUR

There were technically several *Casa Flores* restaurants in Stockton. They were all generally the same, yet no two were identical. They were nestled in buildings that were at least fifty years old, the décor and furniture from roughly the same time period.

Enzo took them to the one located on Hammer Lane, its store front almost lost between a gigantic *Dollar Tree* and a *Pay For Less*.

Despite the wear and tear, *Casa Flores* was lovingly cared for by the owners. All the tables were clean, the floors vacuumed, and the smell of homemade tortillas filled the air.

It had all the welcoming warmth of a grandmother's house.

To Finch's amusement, the walls were covered in romanticized artwork of the Aztecs. A burly warrior man with rippling, oiled muscles holding a woman in a white dress that didn't quite cover her long, sculpted legs hung proudly on the western wall.

Soft mariachi music played throughout the restaurant, its upbeat and joyful tunes helping Finch's mood. He didn't speak Spanish, but he had taken many years of French, and sometimes he caught words he understood.

Finch, Enzo, Liam, Bree, and Jessie all took a seat at one of the larger booths. Finch took the time to draw the Mark of Chronos on Jessie and Liam, before he forgot.

The waiter, an older gentleman with an absolute unit of a mustache, came to greet them and get their drinks orders. Then he returned to the kitchen, where the cook was happily singing along with the music.

A moment later, he brought water for the whole table, as well as a gigantic basket of fresh chips.

"I love this place so much," Bree said as she munched on a complimentary chip. "It's so good. We used to go here all the time, just me, Mum, and Papa..." Her voice trailed off a bit, her gaze threatening to fall to the table. But then she snapped it back up to Enzo. "It's a shame we couldn't keep all our turquoise. We had too many."

"It was a practice run," Enzo stated.

"And it was a *super* shame you didn't want to spend more time with Maradith. She really liked you!" Bree ended her statement with a little giggle.

Jessie hid a smile by taking a sip of her water.

"I'm married," Enzo stated.

Bree scrunched up her nose and frowned. "I thought you said your wife thought you had died. And hasn't she married someone else?"

A chill came over the table. Enzo crossed his arms, his hands gripping his own biceps. He didn't reply, but his aggressively neutral expression spoke the truth—Bree was correct. His wife had moved on after Enzo's "death."

"She has a new life, maybe you should, too," Bree finally concluded. Then she bit into another chip.

Liam pushed Bree's water closer to her. "Maybe we shouldn't offer unsolicited advice to people about their personal lives, hm? I think everyone has their own problems, and they can deal with them as they see fit."

"I wish Kull were here," Bree muttered. She sipped her drink and concluded, "Kull always talks about *love* and finding something that *lasts forever*, and it's so hopeful. We need more of that energy. Everyone here is so..."

She glanced around, her eyes darting from one person to the next, only lingering a short time. It was obvious from her ever-deepening frown that she thought the whole table needed a therapist.

Then again, everyone, including Bree, had lost someone —or multiple someones—close to them.

Now that Finch really thought about it, maybe they all *did* need a therapist. He drank some of his water, his dark thoughts like quicksand, a trap he couldn't escape.

But then Jessie reached out and touched his forearm, bringing Finch back to reality—to this moment in the *Casa Flores*—away from his doubt.

"Weren't you always popular in all the clubs whenever you and Carter traveled?" she asked. "He was always concerned you'd never settle down, because you never really stayed with one individual for very long. I bet if you went out clubbing again, you'd find lots of luck."

"He found lots of luck at *Potion Notions*," Bree giddily chimed in.

Enzo loosened a bit as he leaned back in the booth. "Yeah, Adair. What the hell? You should definitely get back out there. Plenty of fish in the sea—especially at *group nights*."

Why was everyone so obsessed with his love life? Again, Finch couldn't really bring himself to discuss the specifics, or why he wasn't as eager to deal with the situation, but just to amuse them all while they waited for their food, he played along.

"Maybe I should get a dating app," he sardonically stated.

"I've heard great things about *Tinder*!" Bree leaned on to the table, her excitement so real, it was almost contagious. "And there's *Bumble*, too! And *Grindr* is the fun one."

"Why do you know so many dating apps?" Liam whispered, his brow furrowed.

"Yeah," Enzo barked. "You're way too young for this. What're you even doing looking at those apps?"

Bree scooted back in her seat. With a glare, she lifted a finger. "I learn about them from YouTube. Everyone talks about them. Dating apps are the only way you meet people nowadays, duh."

Liam shook his head. "Still..."

"Please, Adair! Please get a dating app. You should definitely fill out the profile and try a few dates. Jessie is so right."

When Finch glanced up, he spotted Jessie's mischievous grin. For a split second, it felt like Finch was ten years younger, hanging with Jessie when she was first with Carter. She had loved to play games like this—causing people to get flustered. She had learned it from the fae, who loved to mess with humans and delighted in their social dramas.

Jessie seemed more relaxed now that they were all joking —even if it was at Finch's expense.

"Fine," Finch said, again just rolling with the punches. "I'll get one, and I'll fill it out, but I don't promise anything more than that."

Bree clapped her hands as though she needed an encore. "*Yes*! Okay! I'm so excited." Then her eyes widened, and her smile doubled. "Can *I* fill out your profile? Please? Pretty please?"

That got everyone at the table chuckling. Before Finch could answer, the waiter brought their food—a gargantuan serving of tacos, enchiladas, and quesadillas, all covered in glorious red sauce, each cheesier than the last. It smelled divine.

And while Finch would've been happy to ignore the current conversation and just eat, Bree held out a hand, her fingers curling and uncurling in a grabby motion. While Finch thought it ridiculous, he ultimately decided to humor her.

He handed over his phone.

Bree practically squeed in delight. She ignored all the food on the table and quickly began typing away with the frantic energy of someone on too much coke. Liam watched, a hint of concern on his face, but eventually he exhaled and ate one of the saucy enchiladas.

While Finch took a bite of a taco, Bree snapped a picture of him.

"You should have a dating app, too," Bree said, glancing at Enzo.

The man shoved half a quesadilla into his mouth. "No."

"You would get *so many messages!* Do you see your muscles? Everyone would swipe right, even most of the men."

"I told you. I'm married."

Bree sighed, though she never took her eyes off Finch's phone. She continued typing away, delighted by whatever she was crafting.

Right as Finch was finished with his food, Bree giggled maniacally and then handed him back his phone. "Okay. You're all set. Now you just have to wait for the messages to pour in."

Finch opened the app to look at his own profile. He groaned the moment he read through the first half.

His pictures were of him eating. One with a taco, and

two more taken secretly while he was attempting to scoop up the sauce from a particularly ornery enchilada.

Adair Finch
Age: 38
Gender: Male
Orientation: Demi

I'm a man of mystery, power, and a totally normal amount of brooding. I've got the brains of a detective, the reflexes of a panther, and abilities that'll blow your mind. If there's a problem, I fix it. If there's danger, I face it. If there's an unfairly overpriced burger at my favorite restaurant, I complain about it and buy it anyway.

Fun Facts:
I can pull off a trench coat in any weather.
I'm a Greek mythology nerd.
Cats love me, dogs respect me, and a pigeon is one of my closest friends.

What I'm Looking For:
Someone who thinks Batman's attitude isn't something that needs to be fixed, is totally okay with "adventures," and loves intelligent conversation. Also has to be okay with casual acts of heroism. And also can't be too worried about schedules and getting places on time.

"I'm not using this," Finch said, deadpan.

Enzo plucked the phone out of Finch's hand before he could delete anything. "I've got to see this." He quickly read through the whole thing, a smile growing the entire time. Once he reached the end, he was snorting back laughs and shaking his head.

Jessie took the phone next and immediately let out a laugh. Something in the first line or two really set her off.

"Well, now I have to see," Liam said as Jessie handed it over.

It garnered a few chuckles from him before Finch finally got his phone back.

"It's pretty accurate, actually," Liam said.

Finch narrowed his eyes into a glare. "I sound like an arrogant jackass in this profile."

"People like bad boys," Bree said as she stabbed one of the enchiladas with her fork. "You have to roll with it."

Jessie finished her meal and pushed her plate to the edge of the table. "You know, there's an app called *Bewitchr* that's for witches, warlocks, and other magic-wielding individuals. It's a little awkward to get on, though, because you have to be approved before your profile will show, but maybe that's something you want instead?"

Finch regretted ever going along with this. He shoved his phone into his pocket and then leaned back in the booth. "No. Thanks."

"I didn't know about *Bewitchr*," Bree said in awe.

"Maybe you can look at it in six years," Liam said, sterner than normal.

"Let's try *ten* years," Enzo added.

Since most everyone was either finished or halfway finished, Finch held up a hand. "Okay, enough. I don't care about any of this. Let's get back on track."

The others turned and nodded.

"This is the new plan," Finch said. "We're going to get

the turquoise first. How many rocks do you think I need, Liam?"

"I would say *five*, but I would also recommend you grind them down into a sand-like substance. You see, the turquoise has to remain on his body for at least a few moments, and if you just throw rocks, or even hold them on him, he could fight back." He nervously laughed as he added, "But sand is harder to dislodge, so it'll stay on longer."

"Fine. Once we've ground up some rocks, I'll grab the scales from his room, challenge him to a spellrift, and then hopefully end this madness."

Bree's eyes widened. "You really think you'll win?"

"That's the plan, at least."

Right as Finch said that, his phone buzzed. Finch pulled it out, half expecting to see Kull's number, but was surprised to see a message on Tinder. He opened it up and noticed a woman named *Stephanie Ackerman* had contacted him. In her profile pic, she wore her blonde hair long, and her tank top tight to her athletic body. She had also taken a photo of herself from the top down, acres of cleavage on full display.

Her message:

Hi! I saw your profile. You sound hilarious.

Finch, still a little shocked someone had replied so quickly, found himself at a loss for words. Was this really happening? Did Tinder really work that fast?

He wrote:

Hello

The woman replied quickly. Was this an encouraging sign? She messaged:

> Did you get on Tinder because you're thinking about the future?

Finch responded:

> That's one way to put it.

Stephanie replied:

> If you really want to improve your future, try investing in bitcoin. I can help you get started today.

With a groan, Finch tossed his phone onto the booth table. He leaned back his head until he was staring at the restaurant ceiling. "I fucking hate the internet," he mumbled under his breath.

"Well, what are we waiting for?" Liam rubbed his hands together. "We should test out our new theory."

Jessie nodded. "I couldn't agree more. Adair, if you really think you can face down Maldonado, I say we do it."

After snatching his phone off the table, he sighed. "Everyone good and relaxed? We're prepared for the confrontation?"

"As long as you are," Enzo quipped.

And that was all Finch needed to hear. He rewound time.

And once the restaurant had disappeared in a haze of black and white, Finch found himself standing in front of McKinley Park.

1:02 p.m.

Time to deal with Maldonado.

CHAPTER
THIRTY-FIVE

Finch and Enzo returned to the others behind the bathroom building. From there, Liam and Enzo opted to retrieve the turquoise. Finch and Jessie decided to stay behind with Bree while the air of the fae world wore off. Just as Finch suspected, it was gone in a few minutes, her speech normal, her movements her own.

While they waited for their turquoise to arrive, Finch constantly glanced at his phone.

1:30 p.m.

Breaking into Maldonado's room from the outside would be difficult, but since the wizard was going to be in his living room at exactly 1:55 p.m., he knew he had an opportunity to get the scales without being caught.

"Adair?" Bree asked.

He removed his gaze from his phone and turned his attention to the girl. "Yes?"

"Can I talk to you over here?"

Bree gave Jessie the side-eye, and then tugged Finch's sleeve until they were at least fifteen feet away. She didn't take him around the corner of the bathroom, or even out of the magically dense grove, but it was far enough away to hide a conversation through whispers.

"What is it?" Finch asked.

"I just wanted to talk to you about being a warlock," Bree whispered.

"You can't do that in front of Jessie?"

Bree shook her head. "It's *my* decision. I don't want everyone giving me advice. I have too much of it from Papa and now Enzo—who I should just start calling *Papa 2.0.*" She crossed her arms, but then stifled a giggle. "But I appreciate him being worried about me."

"What did you want to ask?"

She stared up at him, her blue eyes glassy. "Do you think... once all this is over... you could let me become a witch, and if I don't like how it feels, you could rewind time? That way I can *know* before I make any final decisions?"

"If that's what you need to make up your mind, I'll be there for you," Finch stated.

He understood what it was like to be young and uncertain, standing at the edge of a future that felt endless and full of possibility. How many twelve-year-olds had sworn they would be veterinarians, astronauts, artists—only to change their minds the next year? At that age, every path seemed open, every choice valid, every dream within reach.

Was being a witch better than a warlock? That depended entirely on one's tolerance for bargains and fine print. Bree wasn't afraid now, but she hadn't yet seen the worst of it—the kind of deals that twisted people into something they had never meant to become.

Still, Finch liked her thinking. If he could give her a glimpse of what it meant to be a witch, maybe she'd be able to choose her path with certainty. No regrets. No second-guessing.

Most people didn't get that luxury. Most people made their choice and lived with it, whether they wanted to or not.

But Bree would be different. She would be the rare exception—someone who got to stand at the crossroads and see both paths before she took a single step.

"Thank you," Bree whispered. She tugged on the cuffs of her hoodie sleeves. "For helping me, and being my mentor, and everything." A smile twitched at the corner of her lips. "You'll still teach me warlock stuff if I decide not to be a witch, right?"

"Right," Finch replied.

Bree exhaled. "Oh, good. Thank you, Adair." She stepped away from him and gave a confident nod. "No matter what happens, I'll be the very best I can be."

"That's all anyone wants."

She turned and began pacing around the grove, her gaze distant as her thoughts clearly turned inward. A few times she walked around trees, one hand on the trunk as she swung herself around, still barely paying attention to her surroundings.

Jessie walked over to Finch and lowered her voice to barely a whisper. "Everything going okay?"

"It's fine," he replied.

"Listen, I've wanted to tell you that I'm sorry." Jessie gritted her teeth and hardened her expression. "I wasn't thinking about this situation correctly, and I never should've taken my anger out on you."

Finch shook his head. "You don't have to mention it."

"You... almost seem like your old self, Adair. I think I'll finally know peace once we've ended that vile coven, but...

seeing you like this has brought back a piece of myself that I thought lost. So, thank you for not being angry with me."

While there were a million things that could be said, none of them came to Finch. Perhaps it was for the better. The silence that followed felt like a comfortable one. Best not to break it.

Until Enzo and Liam came jogging around the bathroom building, both with joyful grins.

"We did it," Liam announced.

Enzo held up a baggie of what appeared to be blue sand. "Turquoise. All ground up. Ready for duty."

Finch jogged over, grabbed the bag, and smirked. "All right. How about the four of you wait here, and I'll see if this works?"

"*What*?" Enzo barked. "You can't leave me. I'm going with you."

After a second's worth of consideration, Finch rolled his eyes. "Fine." Then he drew the Mark of Chronos on both Liam and Jessie. "If this works, I'll be back with good news."

"And if it doesn't work out?" Liam asked.

"I'll be back with a new and improved plan."

Finch and Enzo entered the wizard's property right on time at 1:51 p.m. and went straight for the usual parking spot at the end of the driveway. Instead of heading for the study window, Finch got out of his vehicle and went around the property, ducking beneath windows to avoid detection and sweating up a storm so much he was basically leaving a trail of water behind for anyone to follow.

Enzo stuck close, occasionally stopping to stand a bit straighter and listen. Sometimes, he just had the mannerisms of a canine, but Finch kept that comment to himself.

They made it around the corner of the McMansion, and into the backyard proper. The Olympic-sized pool glistened in the sunlight, tempting all who gazed upon it with the relief of cold water on a hot California day.

Finch recognized the many outdoor couches and the BBQ set. His attention eventually fell to the wall with the window that led to Maldonado's bedroom.

"Over there," he said, pointing. "Let's try to keep things quiet. The goons around here aren't high on goblin juice yet, and I'd rather not get into *another* fight."

Enzo rotated his head, and then cracked his knuckles. "I would've been fine fighting. I've got a little extra spunk in my step."

"I feel like I've fought everyone here at least once already," Finch sardonically replied. "We don't need any unnecessary repeats."

Together, they made their way over to the large window. Finch attempted to lift it.

Locked.

Enzo ushered him away and then tore open the window with little effort. Finch grumbled something under his breath as he slipped inside afterward. He wondered what kind of creature it would take to make a pact with to get that kind of strength.

Inside, the bedroom was just as Finch remembered. Oversized four-poster bed, plenty of custom carved shelves with decorative artifacts placed strategically about. The glass case with all the boxes sat on the opposite side of the room, and Finch immediately went for it.

On his way, he realized one tiny detail that hadn't been there before—the pukwudgie. Its silver cage was in the darkest corner of the room, the goblin hunkered down in the corner, trembling. Finch froze and stared at it, and the pukwudgie turned to meet his gaze with giant yellow eyes.

"Uh, *shh*!" Finch held a finger up to his lips.

The pukwudgie scrambled to the edge of the cage, desperation in its movements, its lips quavering. It shook the bars and then made gestures of escape. It was obvious the pukwudgie couldn't speak English, but it uttered a few goblin words.

Finch had no idea what it was saying.

"*Shh!*" he hissed again. "I'll save you. I promise. Just not right now."

The pukwudgie must've understood a tiny bit, because it fell silent.

After a long sigh, Finch refocused himself on his mission. The pukwudgie was obviously stored in this room until it was time to parade it around—and then melt it. That wasn't a problem, it was just a mild distraction.

He shook his head, pushing the goblin from his thoughts.

The box Finch needed sat dead in the center of the glass case. Unfortunately, the case was locked as well.

"You think you can strong-arm this open?" Finch asked, keeping his voice low.

"Of course."

Enzo sauntered over and took a long hard look at the case. Then he placed both hands on the glass and yanked.

In theory, he should have torn off the case's door. Unfortunately, in reality, he jerked the whole case to the side, and only took off half the hinges. The case tumbled to the floor, shattering on impact, the boxes within tumbling about, rattling as they hit the wood, like the whole case was one gigantic maraca.

The cacophony was so loud and so thorough, Finch was absolutely certain everyone in the house heard. And if Maldonado hadn't set up an anti-sound barrier, the neighbors would've heard this as well.

The pukwudgie shook the bars of its cage, its eyes wider than ever. It said something in Goblin. Finch still had no idea.

"Oops," Enzo playfully said.

With a sigh, Finch knelt down and sifted through the broken glass. He just needed the contents of the box. Everything else didn't matter.

As he searched, he realized several of the other boxes also contained things that were probably rare and bizarre. There was a pair of glass vials, one with pink sand, one with tan sand. They reminded Finch of his turquoise, though he wasn't entirely certain what they were. There was also a wrought iron chain link in one box—a single chain link—and what appeared to be a sliver of a unicorn horn. Lastly, there was a knife with a handle carved to look like a mermaid.

Then a chill entered the room.

Finch grabbed the box of scales and quickly stood. He visualized his anti-bullet protections, though his heart hammered when he whirled on his foot and saw no one else besides Enzo in the room.

Someone was here—even if the door hadn't opened.

The pukwudgie knew it, too. The goblin shook the bars of its cage hard, and then wildly pointed all around. It was too frantic to understand.

With a guttural growl, Enzo transformed. Black fur sprouted across his body, exploding from his skin in a quick wave. His face elongated, fangs jutting out of his new jaw. His legs curved, and claws burst from his fingers and toes.

When he stood, he was a few feet taller, and now he had a bushy tail and pointed ears.

"Someone's here," he muttered through gritted teeth.

"I felt it, too," Finch stated. "Maybe we should—"

A man appeared next to Enzo, invisibility dropping from him like a coat thrown to the floor.

He was the same half-demon who had attempted to one shot Finch. And he used the exact same tactic. His handgun was already pointed at Enzo's noggin, and within a split second, before Enzo could even fully turn to face his new opponent, the man fired.

Bang.

The bullet pierced straight through Enzo's skull, sending a splatter of blood and gore across the wall, the ruined glass case, and a good portion of the floor. And it had to have been a silver bullet, because it met with basically no resistance.

Enzo's skull had ruptured like a watermelon.

As Enzo slumped, his body like a puppet cut from its strings, the infernal man stepped backward, invisibility wrapped around him like a blanket. His red eyes flashed as he turned his attention to Finch, as though letting him know—*you're next.*

Tensing for the blow, Finch was ready. But the seconds ticked on, painfully slow. Had the assassin left?

Shouts in the house told Finch that everyone was now alerted to what was going on. This wasn't how he had imagined fighting Maldonado. He had imagined it a little... quieter.

Then, without warning, the man appeared next to him, his invisibility leaving him whenever he committed a violent action.

Like lifting a gun to Finch's temple and pulling the trigger.

Bang!

The bullet pinged off Finch's temple like a rock skipping across a lake, but the sound rattled in Finch's ear, the ringing constant and painful. But Finch didn't think about that. All he could think was, he was a liar—he *hadn't* fought everyone in the house yet, because he hadn't yet fought this son of a bitch.

The assassin glared, stepping back, his gun still raised.

"You should be dead," he said, his voice unnaturally deep, his teeth freakishly sharp.

"People keep saying that," Finch quipped as he turned on his heel.

Then he lunged forward. The man was shimmering—once again becoming invisible—but he wasn't fast enough. Finch grabbed the barrel of the gun and slammed it sideways, twisting it out of the assassin's hand. The man was fast. Too fast. He twisted with the motion instead of resisting, using the momentum to drive his knee into Finch's ribs.

White-hot pain exploded through his side.

Oh, yeah. That was broken.

Funny how he could be bulletproof, but not immune to a simple kick straight to a floating rib.

Finch barely had time to process it before the assassin vanished again. Finch turned his back to the wall, chest rising and falling too fast, blood pumping loud in his ears.

"Coward," Finch spat, listening. Sensing.

The man had a *lot* of demonic blood in his system.

Something crunched glass underfoot.

Finch struck out with a punch in the direction of the sound, his fist connecting with something solid. A crack on impact, a gasp of pain, and the assassin flickered back into view.

"You son of a—"

Finch cut him off with a punch to the gut, driving the breath from his lungs. The man doubled over and backed away, smoke streaming from between his teeth and out the sides of his mouth. His magic... it built like a storm.

But before anything else could happen, the door to the bedroom opened.

Maldonado stood just beyond the threshold, his eyes narrowed.

"Are you... Adair Finch?" he asked, both annoyed and slightly intrigued.

CHAPTER
THIRTY-SIX

The assassin grunted, shrouded himself in invisibility, and then crunched over more glass as he retreated to his master.

With one ear ringing, and his rib throbbing in agony, Finch stood as straight as possible. He could still win this. That was why he was here, right? To put an end to this—to figure out if his plan would actually work.

"Maldonado," Finch said.

The pukwudgie tucked away in the corner of the room hid in its cage, trying to get as far from Maldonado as possible at all times.

"You broke into my humble abode," Maldonado said, a hint of bafflement in his voice. "And destroyed my bedroom." His eyes flicked down to Enzo's corpse before returning to Finch. "Did you think you would infect me with lycanthropy? That's... *new*. What a bizarre tactic from someone of your caliber, brujo."

The hallway behind Maldonado was filled with his thugs, most of whom were brandishing firearms. The smell of brimstone filled the building, and Finch knew that the invisible assassin still lingered. Close by. Probably waiting for the perfect opportunity. Outside the window, out near the patio furniture, gunmen were getting into location, though Finch only spotted them in his peripheral vision.

"Maldonado, you're so pathetic," Finch said. When he took in a deep breath, agony lanced through his side. His side was having none of it. Finch held back a grimace and continued. "A vacation house in Stockton just to stalk my sister-in-law? This is *my* home. I won't suffer a wizard to live —not when they're scum like you."

There was a pause in the tension, as though the whole collection of Maldonado's goons had to absorb what was going on. After a prolonged moment, some of them chuckled. Quiet at first, but then it picked up.

Maldonado himself smirked, unable to hold back a chortle. "You... came here to end me?"

"Actually..." Finch rocked one of his hands back and forth. "I was a little hasty there. I'm not going to kill you. I came here to challenge you to a spellrift."

His sarcastic tone and irreverent statement clearly agitated Maldonado. The man sneered, his glare icy. "*You*? A simple warlock? Challenge *me*? A master wizard? *To a spellrift*? Are you are out of your mind, brujo?"

There was laughter from his men as Maldonado chortled.

Then he continued in an angry growl. "Clearly, the death of your brother has left your whole family desperate and pathetic. First your sister, now you?"

The gunmen outside moved in closer, and the men packed in the hallway behind Maldonado fanned out to the other rooms, probably trying to make sure there was no possible escape.

Finch was a little taken aback, though. When he had faced down Maldonado in the living room, the wizard had offered the spellrift and had seemed eager to do it. Now he didn't want to? Was it because Finch had made the challenge? Or was it because Finch didn't seem like a challenge? In the living room, he had defeated all Maldonado's minions one by one, but this time Finch appeared to be on the ropes.

Maldonado was all about appearances, it seemed.

If Finch wanted him to engage in a spellrift, he'd have to play that up.

"Fine," Finch stated. "We'll do this the hard way."

He reached into his pocket and fiddled with the latch of the box. Once some scales were in his hand, he tested out his metal-molding magic. Could he rearrange the scales?

To his delight, the scales shifted in his fingers like clay, moving as he wanted them to, fusing together into something new.

"I've always wanted to know what magic made you powerful." Maldonado smiled, flashing his sharp canines. "Why don't you show me right before you die, hm?"

He snapped his fingers, and the illusions in the room all shimmered and fell off. Jessie was right—most of the furniture had some sort of illusion over it, and that was to conceal the snakes. Massive barbed snakes, each with four eyes, two on either side of their head. They were ten feet long, and brilliant emerald green in color.

They were magical creatures found in the wild—they were *nagas*. Powerful serpents that could be trained like a dog to guard people or places. Apparently, they were just waiting in Maldonado's room until he gave the order to attack.

Normally, they were found in East Asia, but this must be Finch's lucky day.

Because they were also highly venomous.

Maldonado's laughter hadn't even fully died down before the first naga struck.

A blur of scales and muscle, fangs flashing as it lunged for Finch's throat. He barely had time to jerk sideways, feeling the snap of jaws so close to his ear that he heard the wet click of fangs meeting empty air.

Then the second one lunged.

Finch held up his hand, and white-hot flames erupted from his palms. He hadn't realized how angry he was in that moment—how much he hated himself for allowing Enzo to get hurt—until the fire basically scorched the whole damn bedroom in a matter of seconds.

The serpent practically screamed as it caught flame, its body charring right before Finch's eyes.

A third one came in low, fangs aiming for his calf, and Finch staggered backward, lifted his foot, and then kicked the bastard straight in the side of the skull. When it was thrown back just a foot, he blasted that snake with fire as well.

The room was chaos now—hissing, snapping, the shuffle of feet as Maldonado's men ran from the other rooms and got near outside, by the window. The pukwudgie was shouting, its cage rattling.

"Would you look at that," Maldonado said smoothly, watching like it was all a fun show. "You're a little harder to kill than expected."

This was it.

Before Finch could rewind time, before he could devise a better plan, he had to make sure these scales would work. He stopped his fire, whirled on his heel, and lunged for Maldonado, recklessly throwing himself at the wizard.

With a look of disgust, Maldonado barely took a step backward. From his pocket, Finch pulled out the scales—which he had fashioned into a crude knife—and slashed at Maldonado's neck.

The rough blade sliced through Maldonado's skin, effortlessly drawing blood.

Yes!

Finch's eyes went wide, his delight palpable.

Maldonado, in the split second that Finch flew past him, had a look of realization and horror. He hadn't thought anyone knew about the scales, that much was obvious from his expression.

Finch turned quickly, but it wasn't fast enough to avoid the next serpent. The naga shot from the floor up to his face. Finch brought his forearm up just in time to protect a vital spot, but the monster managed to sink its fangs straight into his arm.

Pain. Hot, fast, and screaming through his veins.

Venom.

Shit.

Finch grabbed the thing by the throat and twisted, forcing it downward. As he did so, fire exploded from the creases of his palms, practically melting through the serpent's scales and destroying most of its insides. The naga thrashed, opening its jaw in the process.

Finch slammed it to the floor, reached into his pocket, but felt his hand shake and the edges of his vision blur.

He had wanted to test the turquoise, too, but if he didn't use his time magic immediately, he suspected he'd never be able to again.

"Goddammit," Finch said through gritted teeth.

"*Kill him!*" Maldonado shouted. "*Do whatever it takes! Mátalo!*"

He concentrated. Through the pain, through the heat rushing around his body. He thought about his magic, blocked everything else out, and then...

The world froze.

Finch let out a gasp of relief.

The colors drained. Finch started to laugh. The agony in his veins vanished with the colors, draining out of him like everything else faded away.

That had been close.

Too close.

When Finch blinked, he was back at McKinley Park.

1:02 p.m.

Enzo ran both hands over his bald head, his gaze straight ahead at Finch's car. For a long while, he said nothing, he just stared.

Finch didn't know what to say. In all the many times he had rewound time with Enzo, the werewolf had never died before. Was it a surreal experience? It was something Finch hadn't himself encountered before, even when both he and Carter could rewind time.

"Sorry about that," Finch eventually muttered, unable to find better words no matter how long he struggled.

"It was like everything became calm." Enzo let his arms fall to his sides. "Just... all at once. And then nothing."

Finch rubbed his face and then half shrugged. "You want to punch me or something? To make you feel better?"

Enzo slowly turned to face him. "The only thing I want from you is—don't you ever fucking die after me. You got it? Don't. You. Dare."

After a snort and laugh, Finch nodded. "Fair. I don't plan on dying anytime soon."

"Okay. So, what happened with Maldonado?"

"The scales worked." Finch took in a deep breath and then exhaled out all his hesitation, all his anxiety, all his half-assed plans. "Which means we need to do this right. Enzo, go get the damn turquoise with Liam. I'll get all the other tools we need."

"Right now?"

"Fuck yes, right now."

———

Finch really was done dickin' around.

While Enzo and Liam went to get the damn rocks, Finch went back to his apartment. He picked up his material cutter. It wasn't like a wood cutter or a glass cutter found at a *Home Depot*, but a special kind of tool made with the talon of a griffin. It could cut through anything except diamond and fae redwood, and Finch had used it on more than one windows in the past.

Afterward, he grabbed his Glock 17, a pistol with a seventeen-round capacity, and tucked it into his bag.

Then he picked up a pair of goggles. He would need these.

He gathered three pairs of handcuffs as well. He didn't always need them, but today would be different.

Additionally, he grabbed a can of mace. Always useful.

Then he also took a pair of bolt cutters. Unlike his other tool, this one was an ordinary as it came. Just a standard *cut through strips of metal* type of tool—and that was all he needed.

Finally, Finch drove back to his fucking office.

He politely took the paperwork he needed to serve Seth, then he told the vampire he would talk to him next week, and finally Finch turned to face Agent Steele.

"Can I help you?" Finch asked in the most casual tone possible.

Just like in their first meeting, Steele flashed his SHADOW badge. "I'm Agent Jack Steele. I'm a member of the *Supernatural Hazard Analysis and Defense Operations Wing*. You're familiar with my department, yes?"

"I'm familiar with SHADOW," Finch said. "To what do I owe the pleasure of your visit?"

The man tucked his badge away. "Have you seen your

sister-in-law, Jessica Finch? We have reason to believe she might be trying to reach you."

"She called me a couple times this morning, but I haven't had time to speak with her yet." Finch held up the paperwork he needed to serve. "Work is never ending."

"She's wanted for attempted murder of a federal agent," Agent Steele stated. "I would appreciate it if I could get your cooperation on the matter."

"Really?" Finch knitted his eyebrows together in a look of concern. "That doesn't sound like her, but I haven't really spoken with her in years, either. She was very... solitary... after my brother's death."

Agent Steele softened a bit and nodded once. "I can understand."

"Do you have a card or a phone number? Once I'm done dropping this off, perhaps we can talk? I'd like to hear more about the situation."

Without hesitating, Steele reached into his pants pocket and withdrew a business card. He handed it over to Finch.

"We found your sister's motorcycle parked nearby," the agent said. "So I'm going to assign men to watch it—and your office. Just so we're on the same page."

"I understand." Finch tucked the paperwork under his arm. "This shouldn't take long, and then we can chat."

This seemed to please Agent Steele, because he nodded again, stepped aside, and allowed Finch to enter without any other interruptions. Finch hoped that meant Steele wouldn't follow him this time. His plan required Steele to wait here until Finch was all done.

Finch got in his vehicle and drove off, but he circled the block a couple times before returning to the office. He entered, quickly grabbed his bag and the five witch brews he had. Two to see in all darkness, two to survive not breathing for thirty minutes, and one to accelerate healing.

There would be no more tests. No more games.

He left the office quickly, muttering aloud about how he had forgotten something just so the SHADOW agents who were listening wouldn't get too suspicious.

Finch regretted not getting his brews sooner, though he had managed to get around any obstacles without them until this point, but it was clear to him that playing things loosey-goosey wasn't the appropriate angle anymore.

As soon as Enzo and Liam were done gathering the turquoise and crushing it up, Finch grabbed his werewolf buddy and drove for Maldonado's estate.

With singular focus, he drove up the driveway, parked, got out, and made his way around the building. Enzo followed him, stalking his steps like a shadow, being vigilant as they went.

"You seem angry," Enzo whispered as they rounded the corner.

"I can be patient, or I can burn everything to the ground —and I'm all out of patience."

When Finch reached Maldonado's bedroom window, he threw down his bag, pulled out his material cutter, and held the tip to the glass. To the uninformed, the material cutter appeared to be an oversized X-ACTO Knife, but the magic stored within the griffin talon fragment made it easy to cut through even reinforced glass.

And Finch was lucky—when his material cutter had been made, a Pacific sleeper shark had been used to adhere the magic, giving it a lifespan of over a hundred years. He'd have his material cutter when he was on his deathbed.

He placed the tip of the cutter on the glass and then made a crude circle, dragging the talon freestyle until he connected the loop. The glass was still held together from pressure, and Finch had to press on the circle before it popped out of place.

Then there was the second pane. A thicker, more irritating obstacle, but Finch cut through that as well, the *scrape* of his cutter barely loud enough to be heard from twenty feet away—and absolutely no way it was heard from somewhere inside.

Once the second hole was cut, Finch reached a hand in and unlocked the window. Then he slid it up, allowing himself and Enzo a way in without breaking anything or causing a ruckus.

"Why didn't we do this from the beginning?" Enzo sardonically asked.

"I don't usually keep my tools in the car," Finch mumbled as he stepped inside.

"Why not?"

"Most of the time, I'm not breaking into places. These are meant only for emergencies."

But Finch made a mental note to always keep them in his trunk from now on. If he needed them, they'd be within arm's reach.

Once inside Maldonado's extravagant bedroom, Finch turned his attention to his phone.

1:52 p.m.

There was no commotion in the house, which meant Agent Steele hadn't followed him.

The rattle of the pukwudgie's cage drew him back to the immediate. He strode over, pulled out his bolt cutter, and snipped his way through the silver bars of the cage. The pukwudgie, trembling, watched with giant yellow eyes. They were so round, they could've been little plates. Once a hole had been made, Finch took a step back.

"You're free," he said.

The pukwudgie sat frozen in the corner.

Finch gestured to the hole in the cage, then to the open

window where the hot air wafted into the room. "You. Go. Quickly."

Understanding dawned over the pukwudgie. It hissed some words, leapt from the cage, and then dashed over to the window. It was too small to reach the sill, however. When it reached up with its bony hands, it was just inches away from making it. The poor thing appeared emaciated, and without the energy to heft itself upward.

Enzo stepped over. "You need help, lil guy?"

The pukwudgie hissed louder and pressed its back flat against the wall. It flashed its sharp teeth and trembled ten times harder than before.

With a sigh, Enzo moved away. "It knows I'm cursed."

"Let me." Finch strode over and knelt. The pukwudgie hesitated, waiting, watching. Then Finch gently grabbed it by the armpits and lifted it to the sill. "Get out of here before everyone drinks your goo."

Which was not a sentence he had thought he'd ever utter, but here he was...

Once the pukwudgie had an opportunity, it took it. The creature flew out the window, and then hit the ground running. It was only a matter of seconds before the creature was beyond the swimming pool and headed for the wrought-iron fence. It could easily squeeze between the bars.

But right before it disappeared, it turned around, its pointed ears twitching.

Then *poof*—it was gone. Vanished beyond the fence.

Finch tucked away his bolt cutter and then made his way to the glass case. Just like with the window, he carved his way inside and grabbed the wooden box with the scales.

Easy. Effortless. And without a cacophony of noise to alert the whole house.

"That was fast," Enzo said, straightening his sweatpants. "Now what?"

Finch pulled out two vials of witch's brew from his bag. The ability to see in the dark. He handed one to Enzo before pulling off the cork on his own and throwing it back. He drank the thing in one gulp. It tasted like seaweed.

After a shiver and a sneer, he said, "Let's go fuck up Maldonado."

CHAPTER
THIRTY-SEVEN

F inch and Enzo made their way out the bedroom window and then to the front door. Like the first time they visited Maldonado's estate, they just walked straight to the living room. They hurried past the Aztec decorations and the gaudy paintings until they were right where they were supposed to be.

Finch visualized his bulletproof self, keeping his magic running by dedicating a portion of his thoughts to this one task. Then he grabbed his Glock and tucked it into the waist of his pants, so it was snug against the small of his back.

He also patted his pocket, making sure he had his baggie of turquoise sand ready.

1:55 p.m.

In strode the wizard they were looking for, wearing his sleek black suit, trim and perfect. And just like before, five other individuals walked in behind Maldonado. Two gunmen, two men in suits, and one outrageously beautiful elf woman wearing an emerald bikini.

The two men in suits took one look at Finch and Enzo and then immediately fled out the door they had arrived through. Who were they? Finch was almost curious. The more he thought about it, the more he suspected they were local businessmen. People Maldonado was paying to make sure no one would bother him in this little slice of paradise.

"Well, what do we have here?" Maldonado asked, amused. "A man in my living room? Why?"

Finch stood his ground. In almost a lazy tone, he replied, "Waiting for you." He unslung his bag off his shoulders and tossed it to the side. "Took you long enough to arrive."

Finch's arrogance obviously bothered the wizard. He gave Finch the once-over, his eyes narrowing. Then he ran a hand over his black oiled hair. "You must be *Adair Finch*. I should've known you'd eventually show up to greet me, what with your sister's predicament."

Then Maldonado took a few steps forward, his expression neutral, but his eyes were intense. His elven lady walked over to the nearest couch and lay down. The two gunmen, just like before—they were probably trained to do just this—spread out. One went to the north wall, and the other to the southern wall.

"You're not bad looking, but I expected someone a little more... sophisticated," Maldonado said. He walked over to the altar in the room and stood next to it. "You're shabby, brujo."

"And I expected you to have more defenses around your vacation home," Finch said with a shrug. "Really, it was almost too easy to get in here, snoop around, and wait for you. Have you ever considered hiring henchmen through an agency or something? A place that trains guys to be a little more perceptive than *not at all*?"

Maldonado's jaw tightened. He wasn't amused, and growing angrier by the second.

"Why have you come here, *Adair*?" Maldonado

snapped. "Upset about your sister? Because she'll be a corpse by nightfall. No one double-crosses me."

"I've come here to pay off her debt," Finch stated. "Or, if you're not willing to let me do that—we'll have to do things the hard way." He smiled, though it was dark. "I don't mind whatever you pick, just do it fast because I have places to be."

The elf on the couch, as well as the two gunmen, seemed unnerved by this. They gave Maldonado hesitant glances.

"Pay her debt?" Maldonado forced a laugh. "You? *A lowly warlock*? You don't have the kind of money that would interest me, but I suppose I've always been curious about your magic. You and your brother were legendary... So, if you agree to take your sister's place, and serve me, I'll recall all the hits on her life."

This was what Finch had been waiting for.

His smile became genuine. "You can go fuck yourself, Maldonado. I'll never work for you—not even as an Uber driver."

"Then what good are you, *brujo*?" Maldonado growled. "I'm old enough to know that when someone has a problem with me, and they're powerful enough to be a thorn in my side—*they need to be disposed of.*"

The assassin appeared next to Finch, his invisibility dropping.

But he was ready for it.

Finch pulled his Glock and turned at the same time. The assassin fired, his bullet grazing Finch's hair, giving him a little trim, the *bang* of the shot still drilling into Finch's ear. But, as the assassin recoiled, startled, Finch brought his weapon up and basically played the *Reverse Uno* card.

Finch shot the man right between his red eyes, the bullet piercing flesh, skull, and brain matter. He was part demon, but that didn't make him immortal. Gore splattered backward, splattering across a beautiful bookshelf.

The assassin actually stumbled backward before hitting the floor on his back, his legs twitching as though his body was still trying to follow through with a whole host of commands before dying.

The other two gunmen in the room stared, stunned, clearly taken aback by the sheer turnaround they had just witnessed.

Finch straightened his posture, ran his fingers over the slice of hair he was now missing, and then frowned. "You really need to hire better men."

Unable to stop himself, Enzo snorted out a laugh. It drew the ire of Maldonado, but only for a fraction of a second. He seemed determined to ignore the werewolf.

"Tsk," Maldonado said with a click of his tongue. "No warlock can withstand all the power I can bring."

The wizard threw down his coat with a huff. The moment it hit the floor, the fabric erupted into a swirling black mist, as if the shadows themselves were bubbled upward. The dark cloud filled the room with shadows—but Finch didn't care.

He saw everything, thanks to his brew. So did Enzo.

Instead of being panicked, or waiting for the imps to arrive, Finch lifted his gun and took aim.

Maldonado's two gunmen were blind. They had no idea they were even being targeted. Finch shot the first in the chest and then the head, and then quickly swung his weapon over and did the same with the other man.

Four shots. *Bang, bang, bang, bang*! And they were down.

Then dozens of shadow imps came, but Finch was ready for those, too. He swept his hand out, and red fire gushed from his palm. The flames *swooshed* through the living room, culling the darkness and lighting all the imps on fire.

The demons screamed and attempted to flee, but it was too late for them. Finch kept his flames roiling over the room, burning the floor, the bookshelves, and some of the furniture. He was careful not to attack the elf woman, though.

In a matter of moments, the darkness died.

The imps were mere ashes.

The goons were dead.

It was just Finch and Enzo versus Maldonado and his elf. No one else was here.

Finch rotated his shoulder and sarcastically glanced around, as though he were surprised by his own destruction. "That's it? Or do you have another surprise you're hiding from me?"

"You think you're tough?" Maldonado forced half a smile. "Your arrogance will be your undoing."

"It hasn't been yet," Finch quipped.

"Master," the elven woman on the couch whispered. "May I go? I'm frightened and—"

"*Did I say you can speak?*" Maldonado hissed. He shot a glare, and the woman fell silent.

Finch knelt down and grabbed his bag, He fished around for the box and covertly removed some of the metallic scales before secretly slipping them into his pants pockets. Then he stood, took a few steps closer to the wizard and shrugged. "How do you think we should solve this?"

This clearly amused Maldonado more than irritated him. "We can settle things like civilized men. I can create a spellrift right here, right now. Effortless."

Here it was. The correct path.

Finch had realized if he wanted Maldonado to suggest the spellrift, he had to demonstrate he was a capable opponent—one who couldn't be defeated any other way. Now that Finch had this path, he wouldn't mess around.

"I'll do it," Finch stated.

Enzo, with a tone that bordered on fake, turned to him. "You sure, Adair? He looks pretty tough. I don't know if you can make it through this fight."

Finch gave him the *stop hamming it up* stare, and then replied, "I'll be fine."

"All right." Enzo held up both his hands and backed away. "Whatever you say."

Maldonado's smile grew wide. The man plucked a small marble from his pocket and dropped it to the floor. It hit with a *thud*.

For a split second, it sat there, still and unremarkable against the semi-charred floorboards. Then it moved. Slow at first, almost a lazy roll, but then it picked up speed.

The tiny sphere whirled across the floor, leaving behind a trail of white, its movements impossibly precise. It spun once in a tight spiral, then widened, sweeping across the floor in sharp, deliberate curves.

The marble wrote and etched—strange, looping symbols burning themselves into the wood. A spellrift. The marble sped up, carving faster and faster, its path expanding outward until the entire room pulsed with static energy. The sigil it traced grew wider, pushing past furniture, gobbling up space until it stretched a full ten feet across.

"I've *never* been able to figure out how the Finch brothers managed to do so many miraculous things," Maldonado said with a dark chuckle. "For years, Adair and Carter Finch seemed able to pull off the impossible—all with the limited power of mere warlocks. Everyone had speculated they formed a pact with a god, but no one could figure out which."

Once the marble was finished creating the mark, it hit a

floorboard, bounced, and then bounced again, straight up into Maldonado's hand. He tucked the magical object back into his pocket, and then stepped into the drawing on the floor.

The air crackled.

The floor began to glow an insidious red.

Maldonado casually lifted his hand and then bent his fingers in quick succession to motion Finch forward.

Finch stepped into the spellrift. He knew what to expect, and he was ready.

The lines on the floor flared, flooding the living room with an infernal glow. A pressure gripped Finch's chest, unseen but undeniable, and the rattle of chains echoed through the massive house.

A phantom chain flickered into existence, tethered to Finch's sternum. It snaked forward, stretching toward Maldonado, linking them together.

But Maldonado was different.

Seventeen more chains flickered and vanished, appearing for a heartbeat before slipping out of sight. Finch hadn't forgotten about them. He knew Maldonado was a piece of shit—he used this technique frequently, and had many under his control.

Then the spellrift sealed itself.

It was time to fight.

Finch pulled the magazine from his Glock, molded the scales in such a way as to coat the tips of the bullets, and then reloaded.

"What special technique do you have?" Maldonado asked, his smile genuine. "What's the secret to your success?"

Finch tapped the side of his gun. "American magic."

Then he aimed and fired.

CHAPTER
THIRTY-EIGHT

The bullet pierced through Maldonado's shoulder and then shattered against the dome of the spellrift.

Completely taken aback, Maldonado stumbled backward, his hand shaking as he reached it up to touch the injury. Red-hot blood flowed onto the shirt and down to his belt and slacks. It was such a shock, Maldonado was clearly at a loss for words.

"You..." He gritted his teeth, eventually standing straight.

As Finch watched, he realized Maldonado's wound was already healing.

"Actually, the real secret to my power is... *pocket sand.*" Finch threw a handful of crushed turquoise straight at Maldonado's face.

Maldonado roared, stumbling backward into the edge of the spellrift. He coughed and sputtered, his tone turning to rage. His hands scrabbled at his face, bloodied fingers smearing dust and sweat across his skin as he glared at Finch.

Then he thrust out a hand—but Finch was ready.

Maldonado had used electricity before. In a split second, Finch threw himself to the ground just as the air sizzled and a bolt of lightning flew from Maldonado's palm and struck the magical dome that kept them in conflict. The crackle of power, and the static in the air, caused Finch's hair to stand on end.

But something was wrong.

The lightning flickered and faded. The turquoise sand on Maldonado's suit, face, and hand were all glowing—absorbing the wizard's coatl magic. Maldonado gasped, clutching at his chest as if he could physically hold on to his magic, as if he could keep it from slipping away.

"How?" Maldonado said with a grunt. "*How could you possibly know?*"

Finch smirked as he leapt to his feet. "You think I gained *legendary* status by being a chump?" He clenched his fists, eager to use his own magic. "You underestimated me, wizard. And that mistake is going to cost you."

Maldonado snarled, lifting a hand, fingers curled to release some sort of evocation...

But nothing happened.

The turquoise continued to glow, practically radioactive, and nothing from Maldonado seemed to work. Even his healing was halted, and the injury to his shoulder continued to bleed.

"I think you got a little something there," Finch sarcastically said as though to his shirt. "Might want to lie down. Don't strain yourself so much. I hear you're an old man, after all."

Maldonado pulled a thin knife from the side of his pants —how he kept it hidden, Finch had no idea—and then lunged. The space was small, and by the time Maldonado was on top of him, Finch had only begun to summon his flames. Maldonado stabbed at Finch's stomach, but Finch managed to twist his body so the blade merely grazed along his side, drawing only a line of blood.

Then Finch placed a palm on the man's injured shoulder and unleashed all the heat he could.

Technically, the heart core drew power from *all* emotions. Anger was the fastest and easiest to feel—especially with intensity—but happiness, sadness, fear, disgust, and even surprise could be used to fuel the magic tied to the heart core.

So, even though Finch wasn't feeling particularly enraged, he was feeling rather delighted. His fire was empowered by that, burning hotter and brighter.

Maldonado screamed as he stumbled away, his shoulder charred, but at least the bullet wound was no longer bleeding. Finch shoved him, hard, sending him staggering toward the edge of the spellrift. Maldonado caught himself, panting, sweat dripping from his brow. His nose was still dusted glowing blue, his pupils blown wide.

"You bastard," Maldonado rasped, barely holding himself upright. "You think this means you've won?"

Finch cracked his knuckles. "Oh, you silly lil wizard." He stepped forward, rolling his shoulders. "I know I've won."

Then he swung. A brutal right hook, his full weight behind it.

Maldonado didn't dodge. How could he? He had no magic to aid him, and he almost didn't even have a body that could, either. The punch landed clean, snapping his head sideways with a wet crack.

After a second, Maldonado hit the floor, blood weeping from his nose and the edge of his mouth.

The spellrift crackled and brightened, the pressure of the magic weighing down on him as it closed in a surreal feeling. Finch waited, his breath held, as the dome closed inward, Finch at the epicenter. Then, all the magic filtered into the phantom chain that rattled between them.

The magic of the spellrift flooded Finch, giving him control—over Maldonado.

Once the spellrift had transferred all its energy to Finch, it vanished. The lines on the floor became blurred, the crackling red energy of the dome gone. The living room was still a complete disaster area, but it was no longer an arena of conflict.

"Really?" Enzo asked as he walked over. "*Pocket sand?* That's what you said? 2004 internet humor wants its joke back."

Finch snorted back a laugh. "It was the first thing that came to mind. And it was appropriate—you can't deny that."

And while Finch wanted nothing more than to joke about the situation, something strange happened. The seventeen chains that were connected to Maldonado faded from sight—and then reappeared on Finch. The transfer of authority felt like drinking burning hot coffee, the sensation of the liquid scalding one's insides.

Finch doubled over, watching in confusion as the chains came into existence on him before once again fading from sight.

"Goddamn you," Maldonado said as he pounded a fist on the floor. "*You worthless maggot.* How could... how could you ever..."

After a few moments of steady breathing, Finch stood straight. He rubbed his sternum through his shirt, the feeling of the chains detectable but only when he focused. Had he inherited all Maldonado's victories? Could he release them?

"I'll kill you," Maldonado hissed, bloody spittle coming out with his hate-laced words. "I'll—"

"Shut up," Finch said.

And like that, the rattle of the chain echoed in Finch's ears, but nowhere else. Maldonado was silent. The binding of the spellrift was absolute.

The elven woman on the couch stood. Her eyes were wide, her body shaking. She seemed seconds from running for the door or simply fainting. Finch wasn't entirely certain which.

"You're okay now," Finch said, holding up a hand.

The woman shook her head. "I... I don't know what's going to happen to me."

"I'll... uh... release you." Finch half shrugged, because he wasn't even entirely certain if that was possible. "All right? You're safe, because Maldonado can no longer hurt you."

"I need to get back to the realm of the fae. Right away. But I don't know where I am." She cautiously made her way over to Finch. "Will you help me, human? I can owe you a debt."

"No. No debts. I'll just take you to a mushroom ring I'm familiar with."

Finch was certain the woman wouldn't be thrilled to discover it was behind a public restroom, but he couldn't change that fact. It was either that mushroom circle or bust. However, he was glad one was so close. This woman could be home with her family by the end of the day, so long as everything else Finch wanted managed to happen.

"My name is Yu'Teyril," she said. "Thank you, warlock. Thank you." The elven woman bowed her head.

Which reminded him.

Finch pulled out Agent Steele's card and then dialed the number. It only rang once.

"Adair?" the agent asked. "I'm surprised you're calling me already."

"Well, I was out doing my normal routine when I discovered that the notorious wizard, Alonso del Maldonado XIV the River Coatl, was here in town. Turns out, he's moving narcotics, both mundane and magical, enslaving local elves, and generally doing evil stuff. So I stopped him."

"*What*?" Agent Steele barked into the phone.

"That's right. I was hoping you and your SHADOW boys might be able to come over here and arrest some thugs."

"You..." The agent's voice trailed off, his bewilderment at an all-time high.

"Just listen carefully so you can get the address, will you?"

———

There wasn't much time to waste, Finch thought. So once Finch was done making arrangements with Agent Steele, he commanded Maldonado to recall all his goons from around town. He had to amass them all within the walls of the estate, and in thirty minutes or so when the SHADOW agents would arrive, Finch would order Maldonado to immediately surrender.

Then, Finch decided to get some information.

"Is there any way for Jessie to unmerge herself with the demon marquess?" Finch asked.

The wizard looked like he had been hit by a bus, and then hit by a train, and then lit on fire. He wasn't his normal suave, cold, and collected self—he was barely alive. It was almost comical to see him so busted and broken.

Maldonado exhaled, his lips curling into a thorough sneer. "Just as fae come from the fae realm, demons come from the infernal realm. You can banish them back to their place of origin—that's the only way I know of for a person to unbind themselves from a demon."

Banishment?

Finch had heard of things like that, but he had never used it before. Typically, someone with enough divine magic could perform such a feat, but they were rare. Finch doubted Agent Steele had the ability—he was clearly a pugilist. What they needed was someone strong of faith and will.

He made a mental note of that. He'd help Jessie no matter what.

"Next question," Finch stated. "Do you have any magical guns that would be fit for fae royalty?"

That question seemed to throw Maldonado for a loop. He narrowed his eyes and eventually shook his head. "No, brujo. I don't care for *American magic*."

Enzo snorted back a laugh.

That was unfortunate. Finch had hoped to wrap up all loose ends. After all, since Maldonado had lost the spellrift, all his possessions were now considered Finch's. Well, that was how they had dealt with things hundreds of years ago. Finch was certain the feds would confiscate everything in the house as soon as they arrived.

But maybe he could leave with just one or two things...

"What're your most powerful magical items you have with you at this estate?" Finch asked.

Maldonado's hateful expression never changed. "I have a statue of Yacatecuhtli, which makes all within fifty feet more likely to make deals, for good or bad."

More likely to make deals? That could be useful, though it was circumstantial.

"Is he a god of trading or something?" Enzo asked.

"He's the Aztec god of merchants, yes," Maldonado sardonically replied.

Finch crossed his arms. "What else do you have?"

"I have the *Ashes of the Fourth Sun*, known as *Nahui Quiahuitl*. They... empower all your magic so long as they're on your person."

"Are you holding them right now?" Finch asked.

Maldonado shook his head.

"Why wouldn't you use them for our spellrift?"

Maldonado spit blood on the floor and then exhaled. "I would've—had you been a wizard. But you're just a warlock. I never suspected—never imagined—I would ever need them for someone of your standing."

But why wouldn't he just use them all the time? Why wait for someone who was a threat? If he had a magical item that could supposedly empower himself, why would he ever take it off? Finch suspected he already knew the answer.

"What's the downside?" Finch asked. "I assume the ashes are cursed or something?"

"The *Ashes of the Fourth Sun* take from your own life force. The longer you hold them, the shorter you'll live. And..." Maldonado smirked. "They're quite addicting. Most individuals kill themselves because they refuse to give them up."

Finch nodded. "All right. Tell me where the statue and the ashes are. I'm taking them both."

Yu'Teyril, the elven woman, hovered close. She fidgeted with her slender fingers, her gaze constantly flicking over to the window. "We'll leave soon, yes?"

"We're grabbing our loot and we're going," Finch said. "After that—we get you to that mushroom circle."

But before any of that, Finch went to Maldonado's study and grabbed the ledger that had all the information on the *Sisters of the Deavan Grimoire*—as well as their fell gods. He wasn't leaving without this, especially since it included where he could likely find the witches who had killed his brother.

He'd soon pay them all a visit.

CHAPTER
THIRTY-NINE

The statue of Yacatecuhtli was a modest effigy carved from dark stone, worn at the edges as though it had passed through many hands over many years. It was not gilded, not encrusted with jewels, not crafted to dazzle the eye like Finch would've suspected. Instead, it was practical, utilitarian—fitting for a god who was a merchant, he supposed.

It was only two feet tall, so Finch buckled it in the back seat next to the elf. The statue appeared to be a lean and wiry man, his face lined but not aged. Slung across his back was a bundle, tied with a rope—a trader's load, not sacred offerings but the goods of everyday commerce.

Finch sort of liked it.

The ashes, on the other hand...

They were stored in a tiny glass vial and attached to a leather string. They were effectively a necklace, meant be worn. But Finch didn't trust himself to wear the Ashes of the Fourth Sun. Maldonado had been truthful—he had to be, because of the properties of the spellrift—which meant these ashes *were* dangerous. They *would* reduce Finch's life.

On the other hand, they sounded like a fantastic tool to use in an emergency. How would they empower Finch's time-rewinding abilities? He wasn't certain. He could easily imagine his fire and metal-controlling magics, though. The stronger they were, the more Finch could do with them.

He kept the necklace in the trunk for the time being.

Once they arrived back at McKinley Park, Finch and Enzo took Yu'Teyril to the fence. At first, she couldn't see through Jessica's glamor, but once Finch walked right through, she understood.

They walked, in the heat, all the way to the bathroom building. When they rounded the corner, the grove was deserted. Liam, Jessie, and Bree were currently waiting for them at *Nico's Brew*.

"Here you go," Finch ceremonially said as he gestured to the mushroom circle. "Have fun."

Yu'Teyril smoothed her long black hair. "You... You're just letting me go?"

"Yeah."

"What about the chain? Your magical control? Are you releasing that, too?"

Finch rubbed the back of his neck and half shrugged. "Yeah, about that... I know there are ways to break the magic of a spellrift, but I haven't researched that in years. I'll need time to look it up."

"Won't you break all the chains?" Enzo whispered. "Are you sure you want to give up your control over Maldonado?"

Finch had given thought to this, but he wasn't entirely certain of the solution. On the one hand, he didn't want to have so many controlling chains linked to his person. He didn't even know where sixteen of them went. On the other hand, releasing Maldonado was a terrible idea. The man was insane, and until he was fully in custody, Finch knew he couldn't release his hold.

"I'll free you eventually," Finch said to the elven woman. "But don't worry about it. I won't ever come looking for you, I don't care what you do, and I really need to be going, so can we hurry this up?"

"I'm a *poplar river elf*," she whispered.

Enzo rubbed his bald head. "Does that mean something to you, Adair?"

"Sure," he muttered. "It means she belongs to a group of elves who are dying out. There's less than seven thousand of them alive today, and they have mostly separated themselves from the rest of the supernatural world."

Now Finch knew why Maldonado had kept her. It was like keeping a white rhino around in a zoo—a trophy to display. The rarity of the elf species meant Maldonado had likely gone way out of his way to capture her.

"You know of my people?" Yu'Teyril asked, her eyes knitting in confusion.

"Yes." Finch dramatically gestured to the mushroom circle, practically imitating Vanna White. "I bet you miss them. Good thing the portal to your world is *right there*."

"If you know of my people, then you know they won't take kindly to..."

But she didn't finish her statement. But Finch didn't care. He wasn't intimidated, and he certainly wasn't about to change his behavior because some elves wouldn't like how he handled things.

This still seemed to confuse the elven girl. She tiptoed to the edge of the circle and then glanced over her shoulder, her expression betraying the fact that she thought this was all an elaborate prank.

Finch shooed her again.

Without any more coaxing, Yu'Teyril leapt into the

circle. The shimmer of magic—the veil between worlds—was subtle and swift. She was gone in the next blink of an eye.

"You don't think anything bad will come of this, right?" Enzo asked, stroking his chin.

"No. Why?"

"I don't know. I got a bad feeling when she left. Like she wasn't telling us something crucial."

Finch shrugged. "It's fine. I'm not interested in fae politics or schemes. They can keep all that shit to themselves."

Enzo growled and then shook his head. "The elves in Oakland got angry over everything, so I just assume it's going to be the same with... whatever she was."

Completely uninterested in dwelling on the subject, Finch motioned for Enzo to follow him. "Come. It's time to grab *Seth Rivers*."

"And *Methusepaws*," Enzo quickly added. "We can't forget him."

Finch rolled his eyes. "Just stick close, because we're about to speedrun this bitch."

———

Finch parked his Toyota in front of the house-turned-meth-lab. Before he exited his vehicle, he pulled out one of his witch's brews. He drank the one that would allow him to operate at full capacity without breathing for thirty minutes.

Then he grabbed the handcuffs, and his goggles. He slipped the goggles over his head and hung them around his neck.

Finally, he stuck his can of mace in his pocket and tucked the paperwork to serve Seth under his arm.

"I'll handle this," Finch said to Enzo. "Watch the car."

Enzo lifted an eyebrow. "Last time we did this, it was a gunfight. You sure you don't want me?"

"This time it's going to be worthy of *America's Funniest Home Videos*."

With a chuckle, Enzo replied, "You're dating yourself with that reference."

"Yeah, yeah, yeah."

Finch threw open the door to his car and headed straight for the front door of the meth house. The moment he was on the porch, he banged on the door. Then he slipped his goggles snug over his eyes and poked through his phone until he was recording. Finally, he slipped the phone in his pocket, microphone up.

The door cracked open just enough to reveal a single, bloodshot eye, blinking like it was processing five different realities at once. Below it, a strip of sweaty, sun-scorched skin peeked through.

The man behind the door was all jittery limbs and nervous energy, like a squirrel that had just discovered energy drinks. He was trying to play it cool, which only made it painfully obvious he was the exact opposite of cool.

"H-Hello?" he asked.

Finch tilted his head, letting the moment stretch just long enough to make the guy sweat harder. Then, deadpan, he asked, "Are you cookin' meth?"

The man blinked hard. "What?"

"Because everyone in the neighborhood wants you to stop." Finch sighed, as though personally exhausted by the entire situation. "It's not good for your health."

The guy's bloodshot eyes twitched. His tongue flicked out to lick dry, cracked lips. "Who are you?" he rasped.

Finch took a slow step forward. "I'm here to tell you to get out of this neighborhood. Or else."

The door creaked open another inch, revealing more of

the man—stringy, sweat-stained, visibly vibrating with a cocktail of fear. Then, with a jerky, overcompensating movement, he yanked a 9mm from his waistband and pointed it straight at Finch.

"Listen, ya little bitch—" His voice cracked mid-threat, but he barreled through anyway. "This is *our* house. *Our* meth. *Our* business. You and those nosey neighbors b-better leave us the fuck alone or—"

Finch maced him.

No hesitation.

No theatrics.

Just a sharp hiss of *aerosol justice* straight to the eyes.

The man screamed like a wounded animal, reeling back, clawing at his face as if he could physically remove the burning. His gun clattered to the floor.

It was a full-body reaction, the kind of pain that made a man reevaluate every life choice that had led him to this moment. His knees buckled, and he half-stumbled, half-fell into the doorframe, gasping as though he'd just been personally cursed by a vengeful god.

"*What the fuck?*"

Finch kicked his gun into the corner of the living room as he let himself inside. The man flailed around, whining and flailing, tears rushing down his red cheeks.

Mace was designed to incapacitate by hitting the eyes, skin, and lungs. It caused burning, tearing, swelling shut of the eyes, coughing, and a gagging reflex—nasty stuff. Those who used it against others could sometimes be affected, since the mist hung in the air, got into the mouth and could easily stick to the eyeballs of people nearby.

But Finch was just one step ahead. His goggles made it so the mace wasn't a bother, and since he didn't need to breathe, he wasn't in danger of sucking down the harmful aerosol irritant.

"What's going on?" someone from the kitchen shouted.

Before Finch was attacked by the other two men in the house, he knelt next to the jittery guy and handcuffed him to the front door. The man was too busy flailing and whimpering to put up a real fight.

The two goons from the kitchen ran into the living room. It was a swamp of half-empty fast food containers, crushed soda cans, and gross stains, but they barely glanced at any of it. Their attention went straight to Finch, their bloodshot eyes just as red as the first guy's.

They both lifted guns.

"Who are you?" one asked.

The other shook his head. "*Are you a cop?* You're dead!"

They opened fire, but their bullets were meaningless. Sure, Finch's shirt wasn't immune to the hailstorm of metal, and his shirt got a few new holes, but it was only a couple. Finch quickly maced these two idiots as well.

Just like the first guy, they screamed and thrashed as though this had never happened to them before. Both dropped their weapons, and Finch rushed the nearest guy. He threw the man to the floor and handcuffed him to the TV stand in the corner of the room. It was heavy—and perhaps it could be moved—but probably not before the cops arrived.

Then Finch grabbed the other meth addict and wrenched his arm behind his back. The man shouted and screamed as Finch slowly brought him to the floor.

"You're fine," he said. "Stop being a baby."

After handcuffing him, Finch got up, stopped his phone from recording, went to the sweltering hot attic, and found Seth Rivers in the same shape as last time—bleeding, tied, and held captive. His arms were bound behind his back; his face pressed hard against the dusty floor.

Finch stomped over.

"W-Who are you?" Seth asked, tilting his head to the side to get a better look at Finch. "Are you, like, the boss here? You gonna kill me?"

Finch grabbed the man by his shirt and hauled him to his feet. Then he unceremoniously carried him to the attic ladder, down into the hallway, and then toward the kitchen.

"I have a d-daughter! Don't do this!" Seth flailed and thrashed, but his effort was weak, and fresh blood bloomed from an injury on his side he had clearly torn back open. "*I don't wanna die!*"

"Shut up, you'll be fine." Finch set the man down on the kitchen table. "Wait right here—I got to save one other."

Then he grabbed a hand towel hanging on the stove and walked out.

Since he didn't need to breathe, Finch had no concern going into the cat litter room. He swung open the door, navigated his way over the pee-soaked mounds, and went straight for the crying cat who couldn't free himself from the feces grave he found himself in.

Finch wrapped the hand towel around the cat and pulled him free. The poor elderly cat shook as Finch cradled him.

"You're fine," Finch muttered. He sighed before he said, "Everything will be okay, Methusepaws."

He carried the cat out, slammed the door shut, retrieved Seth, and then awkwardly carried them both out of the nightmarish health code violations that had once been a house. Finch had to step over the writhing meth addicts, but that wasn't as difficult as he had feared.

Enzo waited for him outside the car, the door open and all ready for new passengers. Finch threw Seth into the back seat and then handed the cat over to the werewolf. Most cats would've had a problem, but this cat seemed elated he wasn't dying the most dishonorable death possible, so he just purred and purred and purred.

"Neither of these two look good," Enzo stated.

"Where are you taking me?" Seth demanded, his voice raspy. "Where?"

"I'm saving you," Finch snapped.

"R-Really?"

Finch reached into the car, grabbed his bag, and then pulled out the witch's brew for expediting healing. He uncorked the vial, motioned Enzo over, and then carefully gave the cat a tiny drop of the brew.

Methusepaws meowed loudly after taking the liquid, but then his pupils quickly widened into circles and he fidgeting.

Finch pulled off his goggles and rotated his shoulders. Almost done.

When Finch walked over to Seth, he yanked the man into a sitting position and said, "Drink this." He poured the rest of the brew into the sad warlock's mouth. Then he set him back on the seat.

While the cat and Seth were silent, Finch pulled out his phone and called the police. He informed them of a meth lab, and three individuals who had attacked them. He had everything recorded—he had feared for his life, and they were currently under citizen's arrest.

The neighborhood probably didn't want cops snooping around, but Finch wasn't about to leave it this way. The crime had to be cleaned up.

"Adair, look at this!" Enzo said.

Finch turned and glanced at the cat. When he had pulled the cat from the litter, he had gray fur with dark stripes, and his back legs weren't working correctly.

Now, the cat seemed... healthy. And had a few *white* stripes alongside his dark ones.

"Paws is all better," Enzo said, holding him up.

"Witch's brews work wonders," Finch muttered. The moment he heard the cat's motorboat purring, he half smiled. "I'm glad the cat is okay."

"I'm okay, too!" Seth said from the back seat. He was sitting up, his eyes wide, the bleeding on his side no more. "I can't believe this! I feel amazing."

Just like the cat, Seth had a white stripe of hair through his dark mohawk. Was that a side effect of the healing? Or the brew? Finch wasn't entirely certain.

But that didn't matter much. Finch grabbed his subpoena paperwork from the front seat—along with a knife he kept in the glove compartment—and then cut Seth's restraints so he could finally be served.

"Here," Finch said, shoving the papers into his hands. "You have to show up to court tomorrow."

Seth examined the papers. "I do?"

"And you better fucking be there. I didn't come save you just so you could skip town."

"R-Right. Yes. Thank you, man. I appreciate you, man. You're the best. I'll be there. I swear it, on my daughter's honor."

Enzo, too focused on Paws to hear what was happening with Seth, took a seat in the front passenger seat. He patted the elderly cat, whispering encouraging things.

"We'll get you a bath soon," he whispered.

Seth leapt out of the car and nodded several times. "I'll do this."

Finch filled out the *Affidavit of Service*. "Sure. Good luck."

"And... And who are you again?"

"Adair Finch."

"O-Okay. I'll remember this name. I will. Thank you!" He took off jogging down the street, giddy and smiling.

While Finch was grateful this was taken care of, he also couldn't wait to get back to the office...

CHAPTER
FORTY

By the time Finch was done speaking with the police, it was already 3:45 p.m. and he needed to get back to Maldonado's estate. He drove straight there, arriving a little after four.

The place was swarming with federal agents. Most of them wore suits, but others were in street clothes, milling around just outside the gate to the estate. Finch could always tell them apart from actual civilians—they were always a little too alert for their own good. And in shape.

When Finch drove up to the entry pad, one of the feds was there to greet him.

"Adair Finch?" the man asked. He wore sunglasses so opaque; Finch was surprised the man could see through them. "I'm Agent Murdock. Agent Steele has been waiting for you."

"Good," Finch replied.

"Please park by the door. I'll take you inside."

Finch did as instructed, though he wasn't thrilled to be chaperoned.

Almost all Maldonado's thugs had been arrested and

carted away, but a few of them still remained. All the men who were part infernal or obviously fused with demons weren't taken—they were being held by SHADOW agents, carefully secured with all sorts of restraining items to make sure they couldn't flee.

Finch got out of the car, but Enzo made a motion that he couldn't follow. Paws was asleep on his lap, and he didn't want to move the poor elderly cat. Rolling his eyes, Finch continued and met Agent Murdock at the front door.

Up close, Murdock was fairly barrel chested, and his shoulders gigantic. The man's suit was struggling to contain him, and Finch wondered what a big boy like him did for most meals. Three dozen eggs? Four? Hell, he probably ate chickens whole.

"This way," Agent Murdock said.

The two of them strode into Maldonado's home.

Agent Steele was already waiting in the foyer, his hands held together at the small of his back, his posture stiff, though he stood tall.

"Adair Finch," the agent said. "I'm so glad you could finally join us."

Murdock stood behind Finch and didn't indicate he would be moving anytime soon. His lingering presence, half in Finch's view, and half outside it, didn't sit well with Finch, but he decided to ignore it. SHADOW agents were a lot of things, but they weren't assassins.

"You've been a busy man today," Agent Steele said, lifting an eyebrow.

"It happens," Finch replied.

"Care to tell me how this all happened?"

"Well, I was out doing my job, when I came across some goons looking for my sister-in-law. I questioned them, they led me here, and the next thing you know, I'm face-to-face with one of the most notorious wizards in North America."

Agent Steele's face remained aggressively neutral. "Go on."

"I couldn't let him get away with all his crime dealing, so when he illegally trapped me in a spellrift, I kicked his ass."

Agent Murdock half hacked out a cough. "Aren't you a *warlock*?"

"*Shh*," Steele hissed. "Please, Adair, continue."

Finch shrugged. "I won the spellrift, didn't I? *Ipso facto*, I kicked his ass." Finch shot Murdock a sardonic glower. Then he continued. "But I couldn't stick around, because I'm a busy man. So I saved a goblin, brought an endangered elf back to the fae realm, took down a meth lab, rescued a cat that was about to die, served paperwork on a man who needs to be in court tomorrow, and prepped myself mentally to help a witch complete her ritual."

"Uh-huh." Agent Steele frowned. "And you did all that *after* you took down Maldonado?"

"More or less, yes," Finch said with a shrug.

"You did all that in *one afternoon*?" Murdock interjected, aghast.

Again, Finch shrugged, this time with sarcasm. "What can I say? I'm a busy man." He patted Steele on the shoulder. "I'm sure you all get as much done on a daily basis, right? I mean, that's what my tax dollars pay for, right?"

"But have you found your sister-in-law?" Steele asked.

"I have," Finch replied. "And I intend to bring her to you all. *However*, I think it's important for her defense that you speak with Maldonado about the situation. It turns out, he was forcing her into most of this, and that she betrayed his orders and went on the run rather than kill anyone. I'm hoping that my swift compliance and assistance in the matter might also be taken into account."

Agent Steele relaxed a little. He released his hands

behind his back and sighed. "So, you really have wrapped up everything here?"

With a single nod, Finch replied, "I'm always happy to help out SHADOW."

"Have you considered joining us? We could use a warlock of your caliber—it's not every day we find someone capable of taking down a wizard."

Finch shook his head. "I'm going to pass. I prefer being my own boss. However, if you need help, you can always call *24-Hour Investigations*." He smirked. "We specialize in handling things quickly."

The disappointment in Steele's face was genuine. "Perhaps I'll stop by your PI firm at some point." He held out his hand. "Until then."

Finch shook it. The grip was firm—maybe aggressively firm—but he didn't care. Agent Steele wasn't so bad. "I look forward to it, Boy Scout."

———

Finch, Liam, Bree, Jessica, and Enzo sat at a booth inside *Nico's Brew*.

5:51 p.m.

There were no other customers, no murmur of conversation, no clatter of cups or hiss of steamed milk. Just the scent of coffee, rich and dark, clinging to the air like an old friend who refused to leave. Finch loved this place.

"Where's your new cat?" Bree asked, turning to Enzo.

The man shrugged. "He's getting cleaned up by the brownies back at the office. Little buggers apparently want *everything* clean, which I appreciate."

"Are we... going to keep him?"

"Damn straight."

"Offices aren't for cats," Finch muttered, narrowing his eyes.

Enzo waved the comment away. "I'll take care of him. Me and Methusepaws are already close. *And* how can you say he can't stay? He loves you. The little shit gets jittery when you're not around."

This was already a lost cause. Finch knew, in his soul, he couldn't turn the damn cat away. He was too old, and had been in too much distress, for him to put back out on the street. He would probably only live for a few more months at the max anyway. He truly was an ancient feline, probably only holding on to life through sheer spite.

Everyone sipped their drinks, quiet settling over them. But then Jessie leaned forward. Her expression had been hard for some time, ever since Finch told her his plans for SHADOW.

"So, you're turning me in?" Jessica asked, her brow furrowed.

Finch took a sip of his freshly brewed coffee. "Well, technically, yes."

Jessie scowled. "Why would—"

"Just listen," Finch cut in, setting his cup down. "Here's how this will go. They'll question you, give you a lawyer, and then they'll go easy on you."

Bree blinked twice. "Why would they do that?"

"Because I handed in Maldonado."

Which, of course, wasn't the whole truth.

The real reason was buried in the fine print of a spellrift command—the part where Finch had subtly, casually, and entirely on purpose nudged Maldonado into giving a statement full of convenient lies. Lies that painted Jessie as an unwilling pawn, blackmailed into compliance, forced to turn on Maldonado at the last second to avoid harming SHADOW agents.

And Finch knew how these things went. They'd take Jessie in, process her, make a big show of it, and then, after the right amount of bureaucratic hand-wringing, they'd let her go. Maybe on probation, maybe under "observation," but in the end? She'd walk free.

They always did when Finch played his cards right.

Jessie exhaled, glancing away. "After they're done with me... what should I do?"

Finch leaned in, resting his forearms on the table. "Help me track down all those witches."

Jessie's head snapped up. "But... But how?"

Finch grinned, probably a little smugger than was healthy. "I took Maldonado's ledger." He tapped his fingers against his temple. "You didn't think I'd leave it behind, did you? I told you I'd get it. And I never go back on my word."

Jessie stared, her wide eyes somewhere between shock and reluctant admiration.

"And now that Maldonado isn't breathing down your neck, and the feds aren't tracking your every move, we can do this." Finch leaned back, crossing his arms. "Together."

"Ah, yeah!" Bree pumped her fist and smiled wide. "We're going to be a team? A big, amazing team? And we're going to hunt evil witches and modern gods?"

Liam waved a hand, obviously trying to settle his daughter down and failing. "Remember that you still have school and other responsibilities that don't involve life-endangering globetrotting."

"You should listen to your father," Enzo chimed in. He tilted his head and gave Bree a stern look. "You're an apprentice still. We can't be throwing you into any unreasonably dangerous situations."

Bree threw herself back in her seat with a groan. Then she crossed her arms and rolled her eyes. "You two are overprotective. If Adair is with me, I'm totally safe."

Before Finch could get involved in the argument, Jessie placed a gentle hand on his shoulder. He turned to face her. When she smiled, his whole chest unknotted.

"Thank you, Adair. I think... I want to work with you. I want to end this chapter of life. And I really want you in the next one."

He slowly nodded along with her words. "That's what I want, too."

"And since we have all the information we need, I think this will go faster than I ever could've hoped. So, thank you for that as well."

Then Finch's phone rang. He pulled it from his pocket and glanced at the time.

6:05 p.m.

And Kull was on the other end. Just like last time. Finch answered it.

"Adair?" Kull asked. "Are you there?"

"Yeah, it's me," he replied.

Kull's tone changed to one of pure delight. "Okay, I know I said I'd be there tonight, buuuuut.... I'll need a few days before I arrive. I thought I could get there quickly, but then something happened, and now I'm a bit behind."

"Everything is fine here," Finch said. "No need to rush anything. Take your time."

"I have something for you, and you'll definitely love it, all right?"

Finch couldn't stop himself from partially smiling. "All right. I'll see it when you get here."

"Oh, and..." Kull's voice grew more serious. "And we need to talk." Then, quickly, and with a snappy little giggle, she concluded, "Okay, bye!"

She hung up, leaving Finch no time to reply.

"Well, it seems this case is all wrapped up." Liam pushed

his glass of water away. "Perhaps we should all head home and get some much-needed rest after all that excitement?"

"Actually, the next thing we need to do is meet up again on the full moon," Finch stated. He turned his gaze to Bree. "I believe a certain someone wanted to test out becoming a witch, right?"

"The moon will be full tomorrow," Jessie muttered.

Bree sat up straight. Then she pulled the strings on her hoodie, swallowing hard. "You think it's time? You think I could... become a witch and see how it feels?"

"Seems like a great reward after all your help on the case."

Bree's face reddened a little bit as her gaze fell to the booth table. Liam was quiet, but he gave Finch a hopeful smile.

"Okay," Bree whispered. "Let's do it."

CHAPTER
FORTY-ONE

At night, the American River was a creature of two faces—one moment placid and silver, the next black and unknowable beneath the shifting clouds.

The full moon hung heavy overhead, its glow bright enough to illuminate the wilderness, even if some of the clouds attempted to darken it. The trees lining the banks of the river stood as dark sentinels, their branches stirring only faintly, whispering to one another in the breeze.

11:45 p.m.

Finch marked the time.

"You ready, kiddo?" Finch asked.

Bree stomped by him, her head held high, a thick book in her arms. "I'm basically an adult now, thank you very much."

"Hm. Sorry. Are you ready, *Miss Blackstone*?"

She stopped, turned, and smiled. "Yes, I am. Thank you, gentle sir."

Liam and Enzo stood around not too far away, lingering in the moonlight shadows of the nearby oak trees. It wasn't cold, but Liam shivered anyway. The man probably had less than five percent body fat, and should be dead, but somehow he kept himself operating.

Standing next to Enzo, who had enough muscles for two people, he looked even smaller than usual.

Normally, other witches would take the young ones out to greet the moon, but since Jessie was in custody, and Bree's mother was gone, there really wasn't a witch who could take Bree. So Finch, Liam, and Enzo had decided to step in as a "foster coven." It wasn't traditional, but that didn't seem to matter to Bree.

"You know what to do?" Liam asked. "Because if you're uncertain, we can go over it again."

Bree held up the book. "Mum wrote it all down." Her tone had become dour, but her expression was neutral. "I read it over... I know what to do."

Then she continued forward.

According to Liam, witches either wore special clothes for the ritual—or nothing at all. The clothing was meant to come from a witch closest to the girl undergoing the ritual, but that was obviously impossible.

So Bree had dressed herself.

She had done her best—which was to say, she had done terribly.

The dress she wore had been her mother's. It was meant to be elegant, the flowing kind that draped off the shoulders and cinched gracefully at the waist. On Bree, however, it was... not good. The neckline sagged too low, the sleeves swallowed her hands, and the hem pooled around her feet in a puddle of fabric that trailed behind her like a mourning veil.

To make it worse, the dress was a deep, somber blue.

Again, according to Liam, for the ritual of witches, the girls were meant to wear rich blacks and purples.

Perhaps in an attempt to fix her color mistake, Bree had added accessories.

A cheap Halloween witch's hat, bought from a drugstore, its floppy brim bent at an odd angle.

A beaded necklace with a too-large faux-crystal pendant, swiped from her mother's jewelry box because it looked mystical enough.

Fingerless lace gloves, borrowed from an old costume.

A belt of dried herbs, awkwardly knotted at her waist.

Striped stockings that made her look less like an ancient sorceress and more like a lost extra from a children's play.

Bree was an amalgamation of everything Hollywood thought a witch should be, and everything Bree thought her mother had been. Finch hadn't said a damn thing about her outfit, though. Whatever made Bree comfortable was actually the perfect thing to wear.

After a few steps away, Bree stopped. Then she shifted uncomfortably, the too-big sleeves slipping down her arms, the hat tilting dangerously to one side.

"Adair," she whispered.

Finch walked over to her. "Yeah?"

Bree kept her voice low—quiet enough that no one else would hear. "You won't be angry with me if I become a witch, right?"

"Why would I be angry?" he asked, matching her volume.

"Because then I won't be learning how to become a warlock. I can't be your apprentice anymore."

After a short moment of silence, Finch said, "You'll still be my PI assistant, right? What does it matter if you're a warlock or not?"

Bree glanced down at the ground. "I feel strange," she whispered. "I don't... like thinking about my mum. My chest hurts. I... always want to cry. But I don't *want* to cry. D-Does that make sense?"

"It does."

"If I'm a witch, I'll have to think about her all the time. People will ask me about her. People will ask me to join their covens. But they'll also say I'm not right. I'm weird. That's why... I thought being a warlock would be better. I thought you'd be there, and people wouldn't... question me. Judge me. They'd leave me alone."

"Judge you?" Finch asked. Had he lost the thread of the conversation? What was Bree talking about?

"Young witches are supposed to follow their mum's footsteps. I'm supposed to be a *waning crescent witch*, but I don't want that. I *want* to be as powerful as I can be—to stop criminals. And murderers. Like you."

She glanced up at Finch, her eyes bright blue, especially in the light of the full moon. They were also glazed with tears, her lips quavering.

At first, Finch just wanted to say, *well, fuck those other witches*, but he held back. This was probably a moment that required a bit more tact.

So, he picked his words wisely. Or at least, as wisely as he could.

"One of life's hardest lessons is realizing that others' opinions only have as much power as you give them," he said, slow and clear. "Most people don't care about your happiness—they just want control. So take that power back. Choose happiness for yourself."

After a long few moments, Bree wiped the corners of her eyes. "R-Right. I have to be brave."

This was obviously not how she had imagined her initiation.

"Your mother would be proud of you no matter what

you picked," Finch said. He placed a hand on her shoulder. "I guarantee."

Hot tears streamed down Bree's face as she nodded. Then, she dramatically took in a deep breath, and turned on her heel. It was now or never. Midnight fast approached.

She strode forward, into a thicket, off to find the perfect spot to drink from the moonlight and accept her place among the many witches of history.

Or just test it out. If she asked Finch to rewind time, he would.

Whatever she wanted.

Finch walked back over to Enzo and Liam. They had been watching intently, but neither had intervened or tried to eavesdrop.

"Is she okay?" Liam asked the moment Finch was near.

"Yeah," he replied. "Everything is going to be great."

Liam let out a tense sigh. He was more worried than any of them.

Silence stretched between them. Finch turned his attention to the surroundings. The moonlight glistened on smooth river stones, casting shadows that stretched long and sharp, warping in the moving water. Driftwood was piled along the shore, half-buried in damp sand. The scent of wet earth and cool water hung thick, tinged with the faintest trace of something older, something wilder.

It was a beautiful night. Almost chilly. Finch pulled his jacket tight around his body.

Enzo coughed.

More silence.

"So, you, uh, brought back magical items from Maldonado's estate," Liam awkwardly said.

"Yeah, some weird statue Finch set up in his office, and the *Ashes of the Fourth Sun*." Enzo snorted and crossed his arms. "Weirdest name I've heard for an item. Where are they from? The Andromeda system?"

Liam cleaned the lens of his glasses as he replied, "Well, according to Aztec myth, the world has been destroyed four times and reincarnated. We're on the *fifth sun*, you see. Also, each time the world is destroyed it's by a new and different disaster. The fourth disaster was overwhelming fire that burned everything—so ashes from that sun would be, according to myth, almost too powerful to handle."

"Eh. It can't be that devastating."

"The Aztecs weren't known for being gentle," Liam said with a nervous laugh.

Finch tuned out the conversation, turning his attention to the river. There was a stillness about it that he enjoyed, but the longer he stared, the more concerned he became.

The river was *too* still.

It was frozen.

Not with ice, but in time. The water didn't move. There weren't ripples or splashes or trickles—it was all stiff and motionless, more still than a photograph.

And that was when Finch caught his breath. He whirled on Liam and Enzo, wanting to warn them of what was about to happen. But he was too late.

They were frozen, too. As were the leaves in the trees, and the grass, and the wind—the world had come to a complete standstill.

Finch hadn't activated his magic, but the effect was almost the same. This was just more thorough.

Because it was from Chronos himself.

"Oh, shit," Finch whispered.

Something shifted beneath him. Not the ground—the ground had no will of its own. But something under it.

Then, *fingers*. Five of them.

Not bursting from the dirt, not breaking or shifting the

soil—five fingers just *emerged*. They slid upward like they had always been there, waiting, coming into view from a world beneath this one. They were human-shaped, but wrong.

Each finger was the size of a man, at least five feet long, the thumb thicker than his chest. Pale and colorless, but not white, not even gray—a stark, oil-slick blackness cut with jagged streaks of frozen light.

The fingernails were cracked, splintered, ruined, like they had clawed against stone for centuries and lost. Then they moved. Not smoothly. Not together. Each digit curled and uncurled in sick, disjointed spasms, like a thing awakening limb by limb, discovering itself anew.

Finch's heartbeat pounded in his skull.

The fingers had him surrounded. And he knew, if they kept rising, if they didn't stop at the knuckles, he would be standing in a palm.

"Adair Finch, son of Walter Finch, my last remaining warlock," a disembodied voice said, its origin unknown. **"You stand before me at the crossroads of fate."**

The voice was not spoken aloud. It was not carried by breath or bound by the constraints of sound. It simply *was*, pressing into Finch's mind like the weight of a thousand years.

This was Chronos.

"I—" Finch began, but he was immediately cut off.

"Long have I hidden in the fractures of eternity, beyond the reach of those who sought my ruin. But the hour has come. The pact must be fulfilled. The world turns anew, and with it, a child is to be born. My child, as once Hades, Zeus, Demeter, Hestia, Hera, and Poseidon were born of me. And now, its time approaches."

Finch hesitantly glanced around. Even though Liam, Bree, and Enzo were all nearby, they weren't with him here in this pocket of frozen time. It was just him and Chronos.

"When I granted you my power, we struck a pact," Chronos continued, unmoved by doubt or delay. **"You would safeguard a god of my choosing, protect them in their infancy until they could stand on their own. That moment is now."**

One of the colossal fingers twitched, the movement sending an unsettling shudder through the air. Then it tilted forward, the cracked fingernail splitting open like the surface of an old, dry riverbed.

Something fell from the wound.

It dropped toward Finch in a slow, deliberate descent—a sphere, smooth as polished ivory, its surface gleaming with an otherworldly sheen. A baseball-sized pearl.

Or, more accurately, an *egg*.

Finch barely had time to reach out and catch it. It landed in his hands warm and slick, coated in a thin film of clear, viscous fluid that clung to his fingers like something still half-alive. Chronos gave him no time to question.

"If you refuse, I will take your crown," Chronos said, no shift in his tone even though the threat was clear.

Take the crown was the casual way of saying *decapitation*.

Chronos himself would kill Finch if anything happened to his little baby god.

"Soon, my child will be born, but there are others who wish for its swift death."

"Most people believe you're dead," Finch whispered. "Who wants *this* destroyed?" He held up the pearl. Egg. Whatever it was.

"Other gods who claim dominion over time."

Finch's body tensed. His grip on the pearl tightened. "*Other* time gods?"

"Specifically, *Aeon, God of the Endless Loop, Father of the Zodiac.* He resists my presence, and he will not suffer the birth of my final child."

"I don't think I can fight a time god," Finch said as earnestly as he could.

All gods of time could remember events through a rewind. There was no way Finch was going to "get the drop" on a god and fight him to protect the egg.

"Then do not fight."

Chronos's words had a finality to them, like a decree carved into stone.

He continued. "Aeon will come searching. Keep the child hidden, and there will be no need for battle. But if the egg is shattered before it hatches..."

Finch understood. It would his life, too.

"What kind of god will this egg become?" Finch whispered.

"It will take on aspects of the time it was born in, of the environment it's around, of the things it sees and hears."

Sees and hears? The pearl-egg could *see* and *hear* things? Finch didn't like the sound of that.

He held the pearl close to his chest. "I'll... think of something. I'm a warlock who makes good on pacts."

"There are many paths the future can take. Only in some do you prevail. I hope, for my child's sake, you choose correctly."

CHAPTER
FORTY-TWO

The freakish black-and-white fingers slid back into the ground, disturbing no dirt, grass, or detritus. They moved silently, as though they weren't even part of reality.

Then the river moved. And the wind. And the leaves. One by one, the world came alive as time came rushing back to return everything to its rightful order.

"Aztec lore is some of the craziest shit I've ever heard," Enzo said with a shrug. "Everything I've heard about them is *death and destruction* this, and *world-ending nonsense* that." He flapped his hand like it was a mouth. "Blah, blah, blah."

"Well, I didn't write it," Liam said as he placed his glasses back on his nose. "I'm just reporting what I learned."

Before either of them glanced over, Finch quickly shoved the baseball-sized pearl into his coat and then zipped it up. The object was large, and probably made him look bloated, but he didn't care.

Finch knew he couldn't talk about this. The fewer people who knew about this, the better.

But where was he going to hide it? Was it even possible to hide things from beings who had control of time itself?

Finch wondered.

———

Hours passed. Liam said that was normal. Each witch took her own time absorbing the power of the moon and becoming a new person. Finch wished he had known that before coming out to the river. He would've brought more for entertainment than his phone—which had terrible reception.

"So the full moon doesn't cause you to transform?" Liam asked, giving Enzo the once-over.

"No." Enzo crossed his arms. "Only contagious werewolves are forced into transforming when the moon is full. Something about how *crazy overwhelming* the light is."

"That's good, I suppose."

"I'm getting better at keeping my wolf under control. You don't have to piss your pants whenever I move."

"I-I don't—"

But before Liam could finish his statement, the crunch of leaves drew everyone's attention. Bree came walking out of the thicket, in her witch "uniform," her steps light, but her head held high. She seemed wide awake, even though it was nearly three in the morning.

Bree stepped into the clearing next to everyone, the moonlight clinging to her like a second skin. She appeared different, though Finch couldn't quite put his finger on how. Not physically—she was still small, still twelve, still stubbornly Bree—but something in her posture, her presence, the quiet certainty in her expression had shifted.

"Are you okay, sweetheart?" Liam asked. He stepped closer to her, smiling the whole time. "I wish your mother

—well, what I mean to say is—she would've loved to see this."

Bree lifted a hand toward the sky, fingers stretching, as though she could still feel the weight of the moon's gaze pressing down on her.

"It spoke to me," she murmured.

Finch raised a brow. "The moon?"

Bree nodded, dropping her hand and pressing it against her chest instead. "It... filled me. Like I was empty before, and I didn't even know it." Her voice was small but steady, as if she was still unraveling the thought even as she spoke it aloud. "And Mum was there with me. I... I felt it."

No one spoke for a moment.

Liam cleared his throat. "So... do you, uh, feel different?"

Bree blinked at him, then grinned, and just like that, the moment of reverence was gone.

"I made sure to fill my mind with nothing but my desires," she said, putting her hands on her hips. "And *no*, I didn't think of the Stay Puft Marshmallow Man. I thought about..."

She turned to face Finch.

Then Bree laughed once. "I *really* wanted to be your apprentice, so the moon granted me my wish. My crown core—it functions just like a warlock's. I can make pacts."

Finch didn't know what to say. He kept his jacket closed, his mind half on the giant pearl, and now half on the fact that Bree wanted his mentorship so much, even the moon accommodated her desires.

He was touched.

"You have a warlock core?" Enzo asked. "Seriously?"

"What other magics did the moon give you?" Liam interjected.

Bree exhaled, her gaze drifting back up to the sky. "The

moon said, my eyes would be able to *see* magic, and track even the trickiest of spirits. My heart would wield entropy, the cornerstone of death. And my soul—"

"The *cornerstone of death*?" Liam balked. "W-Why would you ever want that? Was it a desire of yours? Truly?" He was practically shaking when he spoke those last words.

Bree nodded once. "I wanted... the ability to hurt bad guys. To stop them. The moon granted me that."

It seemed as though Liam would continue to demand answers, but Enzo placed his hand on the man's shoulder. He tugged him back, giving Bree some space.

Once things were quiet for a long moment, Bree continued. "My soul core allows me to brew potions."

That was convenient. Not all witches could do that. And brews were special because they granted magical effects without the need to kill something with a spine. The real key was: the brew would go bad after a period of time. Or if the witch died—all her brews would instantly cease being useful.

But brews were highly versatile and useful. A witch with the ability to brew was always welcome in a coven. Admittedly, not usually full moon witches, but still.

"And my loins—the moon said it gave me the power of *mimicry*, but I don't really know what it meant..." Bree scrunched her nose. "It should help protect me."

"You'll figure it out when you're older," Enzo said.

"I'm basically an adult right now." Bree folded her arms over her chest. "I've become a full witch."

Finch snorted, shaking his head. "Welcome to adulthood, kid. It only gets worse from here."

Liam stepped close to his daughter and then wrapped his arms around her in a slow but deliberate hug. "I'm so proud of you. I'm sorry I don't say that enough."

Bree hugged him back. "I love you so much."

Their embrace was heartfelt, but that made Finch feel awkward for watching. He turned away, his thoughts shifting back to the pearl. Enzo also turned away, but his expression was hard, and his gaze distant.

Was he thinking about his own daughter?

Most likely.

"Well, it's getting late," Finch said, glancing at his phone. "We should probably decide if we're rewinding time or not."

Liam and Bree broke apart, both of them with tears in the corner of their eyes.

"I don't want you to rewind time, Adair," Bree said. "I'm happy with my decision. I'm... I'm a full moon witch."

CHAPTER
FORTY-THREE

F inch drove without a destination for a while, the neon glow of Stockton's struggling streetlights blurring past his window. His thoughts churned, his attention barely on the road. It wasn't safe, but he didn't care.

The others had gone home a while ago.

5:12 a.m.

Chronos's gift—no, his *burden*—sat in Finch's pocket, a solid weight against his ribs. Warm still. Too warm. Like something alive, like something waiting. Finch resisted the urge to take it out and check if it had changed, if it had cracked open just a sliver while he wasn't looking. Instead, he tightened his grip on the wheel, willing his thoughts into something orderly.

But that was wishful thinking.

He had promised to protect a god before it was born. He had promised Chronos himself—a being so old he made the concept of time itself feel like a joke. And now there was this pearl-egg, resting against him like a heartbeat, a responsibility he couldn't refuse.

The streetlights grew fewer. The roads emptied. His building stood just as it always did—too tall, too thin, a little slumped, like it had long ago given up pretending to be anything better. The brick was tired, the fire escape creaked when no one was on it, and the fluorescent light above the entrance buzzed like an angry insect.

But it was home. His sad sack apartment building.

He parked, lingering in the car a moment too long.

Then, with a sigh, he got out, entered the building, and then climbed the steps to the second floor. When he reached the hallway, he pulled out his keys, mentally preparing himself to fortify his home into something defensible.

Instead, someone was waiting outside his door.

Finch froze, his heart beating hard. His first instinct was that it was an enemy—perhaps Aeon—but instead, it was a familiar face.

"Oh, Adair! There you are!"

Kull wheeled on her heel to face him.

She was gorgeous in a sort of casual and modern way.

Her hair—a striking, impossibly vivid red—tumbled past her shoulders in a silky cascade of waves. Her skin glowed, her eyes sparkled, and when she smiled, it was with the full force of someone who knew exactly how much attention she could command.

And, because of course she had, Kull had dressed for the part.

She wore a loose hoodie emblazoned with the Fox-Pistol logo—a fox wrapped around a handgun. A pair of headphones were slung around her neck, not attached to anything, no wires. Beneath her hoodie, she wore leggings that shimmered with iridescent threads, catching the dim hallway light like they had been woven from pixels. On her feet? Not shoes. Not even socks. Just a pair of fuzzy house slippers shaped like tiny sleeping foxes.

Somehow, even as a human being, she maintained a little ridiculousness from being a mischief spirit.

Finch exhaled, rubbing a hand over his face. "Kull. What are you doing here?" He shook his head. "Do you even know what time it is?"

Kull grinned, shifting her weight onto one hip. "I knew you'd come home eventually, so I just waited! Oh, and don't worry. I already let myself in and dropped off all my stuff."

"You let yourself in?" Finch groaned as he stomped over to his door and effortlessly threw it open. Kull's mischief magic allowed her to bypass locks—just his luck.

"I thought I'd sneak in and surprise you, but when I got in, you weren't there." Kull shook her head like he was a disappointment. "Were you off having another adventure? I told you to wait until I could join you."

Finch stepped into his apartment. "Don't you have a job or something you need to be doing?"

"Yeah, I'm a *content creator*," Kull said, walking in with him like she partially owned the place. "Did you know people will send you actual money just for being charming on camera? And I can do it whenever I'm feeling inspired. It's that easy. Just vibes and sponsorships."

She spun in a little circle, showing off the pastel-accented headphones slung around her neck before flopping onto his couch like she had always lived there.

Finch shut the door behind him. "You're not filming any of this, are you?" He hated that he even had to ask that question.

"Not right now," Kull said, but then she grinned. "Do you want me to?"

"Never."

Finch looked around, suddenly very aware of the state of his apartment. Half-drunk cups of coffee lining the windowsill like forgotten offerings to some caffeine god. His kitchen piled high with dirty dishes. At least his chairs and couch were free of dirty laundry.

He had been *trying* to maintain his place—to clean up everything in his life now that he had found renewed purpose—but his apartment had been a wreck, and it was going to take a year, at least, to make it beautiful again.

"I have a gift for you." Kull sat up straight, her smile growing. "It took me longer to get than I thought, but here it is." She hopped up and then went to a small lockbox that was propped up on the wall.

Finch hadn't noticed it until then, but it was a safe meant for transporting guns.

"What is that?" he asked.

Kull brought it over to the kitchen counter. Carefully, so as to not break any of the dishes, she pushed everything aside so she could open the lockbox. "You told me you made a pact with one of the fae royalty, right? And that you had to get a gun worthy of a king?"

She snapped open the box.

Inside, nestled in dark velvet, lay two of the most exquisite handguns Finch had ever seen.

Not just impressive. *Masterpieces.*

The first was sleek and predatory, its deep obsidian finish gleaming under his dim kitchen light. Silver filigree traced delicate patterns along the barrel, swirling and shifting like mist caught in moonlight. The grip was polished bone, smooth under his fingers when he picked it up. When he turned it slightly, the silver lines burned, pulsing like a slow heartbeat.

"What the hell is this?" Finch muttered, running a thumb over the engravings.

"It's a magical item," Kull said, positively glowing with

pride. "And *so* fancy, right? Kings like fancy? It doesn't jam. It doesn't misfire. It doesn't even run out of bullets."

Finch frowned. "What kind of magic does that?"

Kull shrugged. "I don't know. I just paid for it." She slapped his shoulder. "There's this black market in LA for people like us, and they had *so many guns* to pick from. I got you two, that way you could pick which one you give to the fae king, and you can keep the other."

"But... why?" Finch turned the handgun over again, admiring its beauty.

"Well, I wanted to be part of this adventure, too. So, this way, I kinda am. I got you the gun that satisfies your pact, right? See? I helped." She gently clapped her hands together. "The man who sold it to me said its name was *Starfall*. Now look at the other one!"

Finch set it down carefully, already feeling a strange connection to the weapon, like it was... watching him back. Then he turned his attention to the second.

It was heavier, sturdier, with a barrel slightly longer than the first. The metal had a burnished copper sheen, darkened at the edges like it had been tempered in fire. Its grip was wrapped in something red and glossy, and Finch had the distinct, unsettling thought that it had once belonged to someone cruel and uncaring.

This one had no delicate engravings. No swirling filigree.

Instead, jagged, vicious etching on the slide, deep enough that Finch could feel it beneath his fingertips.

It smelled like gunpowder and blood and something older than either.

"This one..." Finch hesitated, turning it over.

Kull's grin widened. "It's so angry, right?"

"That's one way to put it."

"This one's from sulfur dwarves," she said, tapping a

nail against the barrel. "The bullets this gun shoots apparently are so agonizing, that even the slightest injury feels like a ring of fire scorching under their skin. Isn't that sick?"

Finch stared at it. "That sounds like a curse."

"Everything powerful is, if you think about it."

"Does it have a name, too?"

"Yes!" Kull spread out her fingers and waved her hands about. "*Agony*." She lowered her arms. "I liked it."

Starfall and Agony seemed a little over the top for gun names, but Finch wasn't complaining. They were better than anything he would've come up with.

Finch picked up both guns, testing their weight, the way they fit in his hands like they had been made for him. He had been expecting something ridiculous—maybe gold-plated nonsense with filigree so thick it couldn't fire properly. He hadn't expected... this.

"Damn," he muttered.

Kull beamed, positively delighted with herself.

"So," she said, "you like these? And I got you one gun for your pact, and one gun for yourself—so you kind of owe me a favor, right?"

Finch placed Starfall back in the box, still staring at Agony, its strange red grip warm under his palm.

"Sure, I owe you a favor," he muttered.

Kull threw back some of her red hair. "Oh, perfect. I was hoping you'd say that."

Finch carefully placed Agony back in the box. "Why do I have a feeling I'm going to regret this?"

She held up both her hands and took a step back. "No, no! It's not too bad. You see... I've been trying to find love."

"Uh-huh."

"So I've been going on lots of dates. Men. Women. Anyone who will say yes—and a lot of people say *yes*—but for some reason, all the dates are... how do I put this... They're absolutely terrible."

This mildly intrigued Finch. Not because he wanted to hear about Kull's dating life, but because it seemed like she shouldn't have any trouble at all. She had tons of money, she had plenty of beauty, and she was extraordinarily kind. What else could anyone want?

Kull awkwardly giggled as she said, "On one date, the man started by telling me that the boob size in Japan was getting bigger because of the hormones we put in milk." She frowned and placed her hands together. "That's a red flag, right? I feel like that's a red flag. It made me feel... uncomfortable. And icky."

"It's a scarlet flag that will blind you if you look at it too long," Finch quipped.

"Right?" Kull sighed. "And then on another date, the lady ordered over a *thousand dollars'* worth of food. All the lobster, all the caviar, and a bottle of wine that was, like, super old. And all she did was eat. She barely spoke to me." She sighed even harder as she continued. "And then *after* the date, she said she'd only go out with me again if we went back to that place. This made me feel icky, too. Like she was using me or something."

"She was," Finch said. "I don't even know her, and she was."

"And then with this *other* guy, he just kept *touching me*, even though I told him to stop, because I wanted to know his personality first, before we know each other physically, and he wouldn't listen. He just treated me like the world's biggest hamburger."

Finch snorted back a laugh.

This was an inside joke. Whenever someone lusted after Kull, they referred to it as "treating her like a hamburger"— something to consume and then move on from.

"What do you want me to do about this?" Finch asked. "You want me to go beat these people up for you or something?"

"No." Kull poked her pointer fingers together. "Actually... I was hoping *you* would take me on a date. Because whenever you do anything, it's always amazing—and I really want to know what an amazing date would be like."

THANK YOU SO MUCH FOR READING!

Please consider leaving a review—any and all feedback is much appreciated!

Adair's Finch's story continues in *Time God Warlock*!

To find out more about Shami Stovall and Adair Finch, take a look at her website:
https://sastovallauthor.com/newsletter/

To help Shami Stovall (and see advanced chapters ahead of time, including Chronos Warlock) take a look at her Patreon:
https://www.patreon.com/shamistovall

ABOUT THE AUTHOR

Shami Stovall is a multi-award-winning author of fantasy and science fiction. Before that, she taught history and criminal law at the college level and loved every second. When she's not reading fascinating articles and books about ancient China or the Byzantine Empire, Stovall can be found playing way too many video games, especially RPGs and tactics simulators.

Shami loves John, reading, video games, and writing about herself in the third person.

If you want to contact her, you can do so at the following locations:

Website: https://sastovallauthor.com
Twitter: @GameOverStation
Facebook: www.facebook.com/SAStovall
Email: s.adelle.s@gmail.com

www.ingramcontent.com/pod-product-compliance
Lightning Source LLC
Chambersburg PA
CBHW020520260626
47156CB00006B/2073